# JORUNDYR'S PATH

# JORUNDYR'S PATH

## WOLF OF THE NORTH BOOK TWO

DUNCAN M. HAMILTON

# ALSO BY DUNCAN M. HAMILTON

## The Wolf of the North Trilogy
The Wolf of the North

## The Society of the Sword Trilogy
The Tattered Banner

The Huntsman's Amulet

The Telastrian Song


The First Blade of Ostia


The Swordsman of Tanosa

The Frontier Lord

# THE NORTHLANDS
# AND RURIPATHIA

The High Places

THE NORTHLANDS

Rasbruck

The Hermitage

Leondorf

Silver
Mines

River Alner

Elzburg

Wetlin

RURIPATHIA

River Rhenner

Rhenning

BRIXEN

Brixensee

The Telastrian Mountains

Northmarch
Castle

Rurip

Baelin

OSTIA

RA
2016

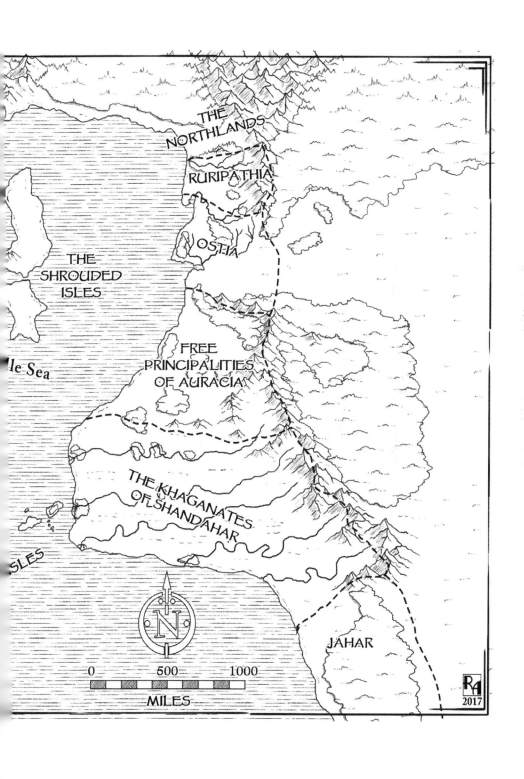

# PART 1

# CHAPTER 1

## THE MAISTERSPAEKER

'SO OUR HERO rides south,' the Maisterspaeker said, 'with nothing but the clothes on his back, the blood of an enemy on his hands, and revenge in his heart. Everything he cared for is lost to him: the love of his life, family, home, and the dreams he has carried since he was a child. What now for Wulfric? How does he overcome these obstacles to become the man you all know as Ulfyr? This evening, we shall find out…'

The Maisterspaeker paused for effect, and cast his gaze around the taproom. It was silent but for the crackling of the great fire. The crowd had grown from the previous night. He suspected that people from outlying farms and neighbouring villages had made the journey to hear him. It was flattering, but he tried not to let it go to his head. Every eye was on him. The story was all that was important. No matter how many he told, he was certain the feeling of satisfaction it gave him would never diminish. There was so much yet to reveal: the history of the mysterious Fount Stone, the adventure that lay ahead of Wulfric, Rodulf's ravenous quest for power, and more. He took one last look around the audience, but Wulfric had not yet arrived. He saw no reason to delay further, so he cleared his throat, and began.

❧

## WULFRIC

Wulfric gripped the reins tightly as Leondorf receded into the distance and his horse thundered along beneath him. He kicked his heels hard into the horse's flanks, regretting that it wasn't Greyfell. As with all impetuous acts, the aftermath hadn't occurred to him until after it had arrived. He was on a horse galloping away from everything he knew before he had time to consider what had happened. Rage had taken over the moment Belgar had confirmed that Donato and Rodulf were behind Adalhaid's murder. After that, everything was a blur.

He struggled to remember, and glanced down at his hands—the blood covering them was a reminder of the violence. He cast a glance over his shoulder, but there was no sign of pursuit. It would take the soldiers time to realise what had happened and respond. By then, Wulfric would be far beyond their reach.

The temptation to turn back to kill Rodulf gripped him, but he couldn't go home. Not yet. He was a marked man. An outlaw. To some, a murderer. He would be arrested as soon as he got back and, having killed soldiers, would most likely be executed on the spot. He knew his actions were justified, but who would believe him? Belgar was dead and could no longer confirm the story.

He felt a pang of guilt at having killed the soldiers—they were only doing their jobs. However, they would have killed him, given the chance, and stopped him from taking the Blood Debt Donato owed him. The Law of the North was clear on Blood Debts, but Wulfric knew only too well that the old laws would count for little in a town that was now part of Ruripathia in all but name.

Rodulf still drew breath, still owed his Blood Debt—and the thought made Wulfric's insides twist with anger. It meant that Adalhaid was not avenged; her Blood Debt still went unpaid and he could not rest so long as that was the case. Jorundyr would rightly frown on him for failing in his duty to the one he loved and was sworn to protect. It was more than that, though. Rodulf had caused her pain and suffering, and that tore at Wulfric's soul like nothing else.

As much as Donato and Rodulf had scurried to satisfy the ambassador's every request, the Ruripathian was the one who had incited matters. Whatever his reasons, he was the cause for her being sent south. Her Blood Debt lay at his door also, and it was Wulfric's duty to settle it. The ambassador first, then Rodulf. It did little to diminish his desire to cut the life from Rodulf, but that day would come too.

The air filled with the scent of pine as the forest closed in around the narrow road. He slowed his horse and made himself comfortable in the saddle. Elzburg was a long ride.

✽

## RODULF

There was blood splattered all over the Great Hall, along with the growing stink of dead men. Rodulf had encountered both before, and they did little to stir him. The southern soldiers chattered away behind him, but Rodulf blocked it out as he stared at his father's bloated body. He had felt no great affection for the man in life, and no sadness now that he was dead. If anything, he felt excited by the opportunity it represented. He had never been under any illusion that his father had seen him as anything other than a tool for social advancement. First, his warrior's apprenticeship, then representing him in the south to improve their business. In recent years, Rodulf had grown to reciprocate that feeling. There had been much to learn from his father, but it was always his desire to take charge himself.

Donato's death was inconvenient, however. His father's grand plan, so close to fruition—the elevation to nobility for him and his heirs—remained incomplete. His death made achieving that aim tenuous at best. There were others who would now seek it for themselves, and Rodulf knew he had to proceed carefully. He felt the first pang of loss with the responsibility of having to make that decision alone.

'Where is he?' Rodulf asked of the garrison sergeant.

'One of the men said they saw him riding south like draugar were chasing him.'

'Have you sent anyone after him?'

'No.' The sergeant shuffled awkwardly.

'Why not?' Rodulf could feel his anger rise. He didn't care about avenging his father—that was warrior behaviour—but letting Wulfric get away unscathed was a slight to his reputation, and that was not something he could stand for if he was to achieve all he planned to. Above all, he had the perfect justification to extract from Wulfric the price of an eye.

'No one ordered it. Until the new ambassador arrives—'

'The captain couldn't have ordered it?'

The sergeant shrugged. 'It's getting dark. The roads are dangerous at night.'

'Dangerous at night?' Rodulf said. 'You're soldiers. Act like it. I'm ordering it now. Get after him.' With his father dead, the order of things would be disrupted. He needed a fast display of authority and strength.

'On what authority?' the sergeant said. 'There's a way to do these things—'

'On mine. As acting mayor. Until this mess can be resolved at the very least. If the new ambassador has a problem with it, he can take it up with me when he arrives. Until then, send your men out to hunt that bastard down and bring him back. I don't care if he's alive or dead.'

The sergeant hesitated for a moment, a look of fear in his eye. They were all terrified of Wulfric—they had been ever since the tavern brawl—and Rodulf thought them pathetic for it. All he could see when he looked at Wulfric was the fat little coward he had been for most of his life. He glared at the sergeant until he nodded and hurried away. Rodulf realised he was clutching the strange stone in his pocket, something he found himself doing increasingly, particularly when he was vexed. It seemed to fit so perfectly, as though its curves and contours had been shaped to his hand, with the angular etchings a comforting sensation on his skin.

✻

## WULFRIC

Wulfric drew a deep breath when the walls of Elzburg first came into view. They reminded him of the High Places, but were a barrier of red brick rather than grey rock. The city's conical slate-capped towers were its peaks— they were taller than anything Wulfric had ever seen built by a man. They were imposing and terrifying. How did they remain standing? How could any man live encircled by such a behemoth? Simply looking at them made Wulfric feel as though he was being suffocated. After the long, uninterrupted ride from Leondorf, he wondered if he was simply imagining it.

As he grew closer, it became clear that his tired mind was not playing tricks on him. The road led him toward a gaping maw in the wall, a great gate flanked by two towers. People passed in and out while soldiers watched with lazy eyes. Wulfric wondered if word from Leondorf could have reached them faster than he did, but he thought it unlikely.

He watched the people and noticed the odd looks they gave him. He realised how scruffy he appeared by comparison. Even in his finest clothes he would have attracted attention, and what he was wearing was far from his best. He would stand out like a sore thumb if he tried to enter the city.

Wulfric checked himself over. He wasn't particularly dirty, but his clothes were rough and his hands were still crusted with dried blood. It had felt like a mark of honour as he had ridden south, but now it could be his undoing. Even the most inattentive gatekeeper would stop anyone looking as he did.

There was water pooled in the ditch at the side of the road, so he dismounted and washed the blood away as best he could, ignoring the curious stares of passers-by. It wasn't perfect, but it would have to do. Once he was in the city, surrounded by so many people, he could disappear.

As clean as he was going to get, he rode forward to the gate. He was still several paces away when one of the soldiers stepped forward and held up his hand. Wulfric forced himself to remain calm and not reach for his sabre.

'Can't bring that horse into the city,' the soldier said. 'Sword neither. Not unless you're a nobleman or a banneret.'

The other soldiers sniggered at the mention of the title; the title Captain Endres had, the one that meant you'd gone to a school for warriors. He wondered what it was about him that said he wasn't one. Surely he looked as much a warrior as any man alive?

'What am I supposed to do with them?' Wulfric said.

'Go to the east gate. Leave the horse at the stables, the sword at the Watch Post. You'll be given a token and can get both back when you leave the city.' He gave Wulfric an appraising look. 'Northlander?'

Wulfric neither confirmed nor denied.

The soldier nodded. 'Lots of Northlanders passing through these days. Suppose you'll all be Ruripathians before much longer. Best move along now; you're blocking the gate.'

Wulfric nodded. He headed east, skirting around the base of the enormous red walls. The exchange had been far more civil than he'd expected and Wulfric felt more relaxed when he arrived at the other gate.

There was even more activity at the east gate, and a cluster of buildings lined the road outside. One had a sign with a horseshoe on it. Wulfric called there first. He left his horse and got directions to the watch post, which was in one of the towers flanking this gate.

The watchman there gave Wulfric a curious look. He passed his sword across the counter, which took the watchman's attention. It wasn't anything special, but it was well crafted and inscribed with old runes—various warriors' prayers calling for Jorundyr's blessing. He knew it was likely that the watchman had never seen anything like it before.

The watchman regarded it greedily, and carefully looked it over as he carried it into a back room. He returned and handed Wulfric a token. Wulfric realised he might not see the sword again. Even if the watchman did not steal it and claim it had gone missing, Wulfric expected to be leaving the city in haste. He took the token and left the watch post. He stared at the dark, cavernous passage under the city wall, and imagined all that brick and stone collapsing down on top of him. It was a marvel that it all stayed up. He hurried through with his heart racing, and nothing more than a dagger on his belt to settle his Blood Debt.

WULFRIC

Wulfric's first reaction to Elzburg was a mixture of confusion and panic. The street before him was lined with buildings that stretched up for as many as five storeys. Taller than any house he had seen before, they loomed over the street and with each step Wulfric was convinced that they would collapse on top of him. They were mismatched—some of brick, some of white plaster, some with gables—and each a different height, giving the skyline an appearance like a mouth full of broken teeth. The city was crowded with more people than Wulfric had ever seen in one place before.

Wulfric stared up at the buildings as he walked, his heart in his throat. As though they were not already big enough, a number of even taller towers reached skyward, capped by finely pointed green roofs, a curious contrast to the red or slate tiles on most of the buildings. He had seen few buildings with tiled roofs in his life. In Leondorf, only the Great Hall and the church had warranted the expense of tiles. Everything here spoke of a wealth that was almost unimaginable.

A thought struck him as he walked deeper into Elzburg. How was he ever going to find the ambassador? The city was massive. There were so many people. He had never thought it could be so big.

## Wulfric

Wulfric wandered the streets for a short while before finding what was unmistakably a tavern. Having completely given up on the idea of being able to find the ambassador by himself, he went inside. It was the middle of the day and the taproom was quiet, but there was a man standing behind the bar.

'I need to deliver a message,' Wulfric said. 'Can you tell me where I'd find the Markgraf's officials? An ambassador.'

'Chancellery, most likely,' the barman said. 'It's on the main square.'

Wulfric's expression must have spoken volumes. The barman leaned forward and pointed. 'Continue up the street until you reach the junction, turn right, and that will bring you to the square. You'll know it when you see it.'

Wulfric nodded in thanks and went back outside. The directions proved easy to follow and the Chancellery was not hard to spot, a grand grey stone building that dominated the square.

If this was where those in the Markgraf's administration came to work and receive their instructions, it stood to reason that Ambassador Urschel, or whatever his title now was, would have to pass by. It was a slim hope though, which could mean Wulfric having to hang around watching for a very long time—time he might not have. Once Urschel learned what had happened in Leondorf, Wulfric expected he would be nigh on impossible to get to. He thought about asking after Urschel specifically, but feared that might draw unwanted attention.

The task seemed so impossible that for a moment, Wulfric considered abandoning his plan. The thought shamed him. At least if he failed in the task, the gods might consider the Blood Debt paid, and permit Adalhaid to join him in their halls. To give up was unthinkable. One thought of how afraid she must have been, how much she had wanted to live, and how much he missed her drove the hesitation from his mind. Each second that Urschel continued to draw breath was an insult to Adalhaid, and to him.

Wulfric watched from the edge for a few minutes to get a feel for the place. The square was bubbling with activity. There were countless market stalls and even more people, some dressed in fine, brightly coloured clothes and some in rags. Ne'er-do-wells moved about the crowd, trying to stay away from the suspicious gazes of the watchmen, looking for their next victim. Beggars ambled about, all but ignored. Wulfric had to admit his appearance was not far removed from theirs, and it seemed the best way to blend in.

He found a quiet corner—not the best spot for a beggar—sat down, held out his hands for alms, and started to watch the Chancellery. It wasn't a perfect plan—it wasn't even particularly good—but it was all he had.

※

## Wulfric

As the day faded into evening, Wulfric struggled to stay warm. Traders were packing up their market stalls and the crowds had abated. Wulfric had all but given up on his plan as folly when he saw a familiar figure emerge from the Chancellery. He blinked twice to clear his eyes and took another hard look.

Failing light or not, it was Ambassador Urschel. Wulfric got to his feet as quickly as his stiff limbs would allow and followed. He watched Urschel walk across the square, pompous, self-important. It kindled a flame of anger within him that made him forget how cold, stiff, and hungry he was. The desire to walk across the square and cut Urschel down there and then was almost overwhelming, but a rash action was bound to end in failure. He would follow Urschel to his home, and cut the bastard's throat where no one could see it happen. Then he would run for dear life.

# CHAPTER 2

## RODULF

RODULF SAT AT the council table in silence. He couldn't help but stare at the spot where his father had been killed. There was still a faint stain on the floorboards, which someone had tried to scrub and sand clean. It distracted him from the uncertainty of what was going to happen next. He had walked into the Great Hall as though he belonged there, and as yet, no one had questioned his presence, but he knew as well as everyone else he had no right to be there. That a confrontation had not already happened meant things were going better than he had hoped for.

With his father's death, the order of things in Leondorf had been disrupted yet again, and Rodulf had to make sure he was in a position to benefit from it. None of the men sitting in the Great Hall would have dreamed of being there a few years previously. Given a taste of power, they all wanted more. Under the old ways, none of them would have been allowed to set foot inside, let alone speak. There was not a single warrior among them now. The couple who still lived spent their days lounging around outside their houses, drinking and doing little of use. A pathetic end to an ancient tradition.

Rodulf's father had seized the initiative and made the council his own. His death meant the rewards for all that hard work could go to any man sitting at that table. Rodulf intended it for himself, but he would have to fight for it. Someone would be ennobled, and given Leondorf and its territory in vassalage to the Markgraf of Elzmark. The planning had been carried out by Donato in secret, but they all knew what was coming, and wanted it for themselves.

The new ambassador had arrived that morning, and the others fell over one another as they tried to ingratiate themselves. They were lined up outside his residence to lavish gifts upon him within moments of his arrival. They all knew Donato's death was the opportunity they had been waiting for. Rodulf needed to make it clear that it was nothing of the sort.

The real power in Leondorf resided with the ambassador, and that would continue to be the case until the territory was formally annexed and handed over to its new lord. Rodulf had a brief window of opportunity to prove his worth to the ambassador, and show the others up as incompetents. He was his father's son, and he'd make sure they all knew it before the day was out. He only hoped the new ambassador did not have his eye on the territory for himself. It seemed unlikely—Leondorf was still far too untamed for the southern nobility and gentry.

The dozen men in the room were discussing future administrative arrangements as they awaited the ambassador's presence, but Rodulf was paying the barest attention. No one agreed on anything, each trying to show that his opinion was the most important. There was nothing to be gained by involving himself before the ambassador arrived, so he remained silent. The old ambassador, Urschel, had not taken much interest in the day-to-day running of things. His only concern was keeping watch of the ledger sheets and calculating his percentage of the wealth flowing south. Rodulf hoped the new man would be the same. It would make his life easier. He would show the new ambassador that he could protect that stream of wealth, help it grow, and he would paint the others as useless scoundrels who would see it wither and die.

Their prattling voices intruded on his thoughts until he could stand it no longer, and he deviated from his plan. If he allowed alliances to be formed, his opposition might become insurmountable. 'I'll be taking on my father's responsibilities as mayor,' Rodulf said, interrupting Andhun, a fur merchant who draped himself in the products of his trade and appeared to be moving ahead of the others in terms of influence.

Andhun glared at him. Since the arrival of all the southern luxuries, Andhun had grown corpulent, making his eyes narrow and beady. His fur-trimmed clothing was hot, his face red and sweaty. Rodulf glared at him. They all wanted the job—likely Andhun most of all—but they were all too spineless to say it out loud. They would posture and manoeuvre, trying to build enough support to advance unopposed, but that was not the way Rodulf intended to do things. The years he had spent training as a warrior had taught Rodulf one thing well: Men take what they want; sheep wait for someone else to give it to them. For the first time in his life, Rodulf understood the contempt in which the warriors had always held the merchant classes.

'I, uh, we, uh, I mean to say, we'll have to take a vote on it,' Andhun said. His voice lacked the certainty it had held only a moment before.

'I see no need for a vote,' Rodulf said, maintaining his glare, his fingers wrapped tightly on the Stone. He couldn't remember reaching for it, but the comfort it brought in times of stress was great. 'You all know your jobs, and I know my father's. I've been assisting him with every detail since we entered into our alliance with Elzburg. For a seamless transition, I'm the obvious choice.'

'There's a proper way to do things,' Oswyn, another of the front-runners for his father's job, said. Where Andhun had grown fat on the spoils of trade with the south, Oswyn had worked himself to skin and bone to take advantage of it. His greed was limited to gold and silver. 'A way we all agreed upon when we first formed this council.'

'There's a slow and ineffective way to do things,' Rodulf said, 'and there's a way to ensure things continue to run smoothly. The new ambassador will be here shortly, and I doubt he will be impressed by the disorganised rabble you currently are. Do you want him to take what little power we have for himself?'

'I think I speak for us all when I say the procedures we have established are effective and efficient,' Andhun said. The tone of his voice showed he had not missed Rodulf's insult. 'To change them now—'

'Is not in any way necessary,' Rodulf said. 'Things can continue exactly as they are, but with me taking my father's place. No disturbance. No interruption. Business as usual.' He gripped the Stone even tighter. He could see the veins pulse in Andhun's temples. He glanced back at Oswyn, who was flushed. They looked as though someone was squeezing their heads in a vice.

There was a commotion at the door which distracted everyone from the impasse. A tall athletic man dressed in expensive southern clothes walked in, flanked by two soldiers. His mode of dress would have marked him out once, but no longer. Every man at the table was dressed similarly. The rough-spun cloth of the Northlands was no longer commonplace in the Great Hall.

'I am Ambassador dal Ruedin, Minister Plenipotentiary of the Most Honourable Markgraf of Elzmark. I have my patents under his seal here for your inspection.'

He swept through the room and sat in the chair Rodulf's father had once occupied, his soldiers standing behind either shoulder. Rodulf felt his stomach twist. This man was clearly cut from a different cloth to Urschel. Could he intend to have a more involved role in the rule of Leondorf? Rodulf did his best not to jump to unwanted conclusions.

'Names and roles, please,' dal Ruedin said when he had finally settled in the chair.

'Andhun,' Andhun said, cutting in before anyone else had the chance to speak. 'Fur merchant and elected man of Leondorf. We've been—'

'Names and roles will suffice for now,' dal Ruedin said. There was a hard edge to his voice.

Andhun shut his mouth, but failed to mask the anger on his face. Rodulf stifled a smile. Andhun had already antagonised the new ambassador—and in doing so, taught Rodulf an important lesson. Dal Ruedin was not a man to cross, but that only meant he had to be handled differently. Rodulf remained silent.

'Oswyn. Elected man.'

There was a sense of urgency to Oswyn's voice, as though he had also spotted Andhun's mistake and wanted to capitalise on the opportunity. Rodulf was content to bide his time.

'Oswan. Elected man,' said the next man at the table.

'Oswan?' the ambassador said. He frowned. '*Oswyn* and *Oswan?*'

Both men nodded.

'No, that won't do at all. Far too confusing.' Dal Ruedin gave them both an appraising look. He pointed at Oswyn. 'You. Get out. You're no longer part of this council.'

Oswyn's eyes widened and his jaw dropped. Rodulf hid a smile behind his hand as the colour drained from Oswyn's face. From front-runner to replace Rodulf's father to merchant once more.

'You can't,' Oswyn said. 'The people of Leondorf have—'

'I can and I have. If you're not out of here by the time my soldiers get to your seat, you'll be beaten and dragged from this hall.'

Oswyn hesitated for a moment, but as soon as the soldiers started to move he jumped from his chair, knocking it over, and ran from the Great Hall as quickly as he could.

'Next,' dal Ruedin said.

The remaining councilmen listed off their names until it came to Rodulf's turn.

'He's not actually an elected member of the council,' Andhun said, before Rodulf had a chance to speak.

Dal Ruedin snapped his gaze onto him. 'Was it your turn to speak?'

'I... No,' Andhun said. 'I thought you might want to know.'

Dal Ruedin's withering glare was far more effective than any words, and Andhun shrank back into his seat, his fleshy jowls pressing out around his flushed face. Dal Ruedin turned his gaze back to Rodulf.

'Rodulf Donatoson. My father was mayor before he was murdered.'

'Yes. I understand some soldiers were killed also. Finding the culprit will be a priority once I have put everything in order here. Now, tell me why you are here, if you are, as fatty there says, not a member of this council.'

'I assisted my father in all of his responsibilities. I know how to carry out his duties better than any other man here.' Rodulf could see impatience creep over dal Ruedin's face. 'I can keep the silver flowing south without interruption. I can provide fast and effective decision making. I can make sure things get done, and get done right.' He spoke with far more confidence than he felt. He could feel the etchings on the Stone dig into his palm, but the sensation was pleasing.

Rodulf looked at the ambassador, willing the answer from him. A muscle in the ambassador's face twitched once, and then again. He opened his mouth, closed it, then opened it again.

'For the time being,' the ambassador said, 'I think Rodulf assuming his late father's responsibilities is for the best. Os... whichever one he was.' He gestured to the empty seat. 'His place is vacant. I'm appointing Rodulf to it. He's shown initiative at the very least, and none of the rest of you have impressed me at all.'

Once again, Rodulf suppressed a smile. He looked at Andhun expecting some protest, but the fat man was smart enough to know it was time to keep his mouth shut. Rodulf relaxed his grip on the Stone. The first victory was his. A week or two of efficient leadership, and pouring as much money into the ambassador's coffers as he could, and his position would be solidified. Then he could raise the issue of ennoblement. If he played his cards right, he would be Baron Rodulf dal Leondorf by Midwinter's Day.

'As I'm sure you are all aware, the process to annex the territory of Leondorf into the Principality of Ruripathia—and more specifically, into the Markgrafate of Elzmark—is well underway,' dal Ruedin said. 'I am here to see that it is completed smoothly, and appoint the most capable of you gentlemen to its rule. At that point I can return home and leave you savages to your wilderness.'

Rodulf had to stifle a sigh of relief. With the ambassador removed from the equation, only Andhun remained. He was taken aback by how openly contemptuous the new ambassador was, but the more he hated the Northlands the quicker he would want to be finished with his task. And that could only work in Rodulf's favour.

# CHAPTER 3

WULFRIC

WULFRIC WALKED PAST Urschel's house with as much nonchalance as he could muster. It was part of a long terrace of redbrick houses. The street was wide and cobbled, and the buildings were more ornately decorated than any he had seen so far. He peered into the windows as he passed, but saw nothing of note. There was no reason for Urschel to expect trouble; he was in the heart of his city and was entitled to feel perfectly safe.

Wulfric knocked on the door, and took a deep breath. He heard a latch being pulled and the door opened silently. A neatly dressed man stood on the other side of the threshold. His eyes widened when he saw Wulfric, but he subdued the expression as quickly as it had appeared and replaced it with something closer to practised indifference.

'Can I help you, sir?'

Wulfric punched him in the face and shoved him back into the house as he walked inside. The doorman fell back. He remained unmoving on the floor. Wulfric looked around and wondered where Urschel might be. He walked farther into the house as quietly as he could, peering into each room as he went. Wulfric found his quarry sitting at a desk in his study on the ground floor at the back of the house.

'Ambassador Urschel,' Wulfric said.

He looked up from his desk and furrowed his brow. There wasn't the faintest hint of surprise on his face. Wulfric glanced around, feeling naked without his sword, but there was no sign of a trap.

'Young Wulfric, isn't it?' Urschel said.

Wulfric was concerned by how comfortable Urschel was. Wulfric's appearance should have caused him some sort of visible reaction. Perhaps he was just completely clueless as to the reason for Wulfric's being there.

'You're not surprised to see me,' Wulfric said.

'Nothing surprises me anymore,' Urschel said.

'I killed Donato. I'm here to kill you now.'

'Might I ask why?'

Wulfric gave him his most glowering look. He knew why; there was no need to say a thing.

Urschel smiled, which unsettled Wulfric.

'You seem to have forgotten your sword,' Urschel said.

'Don't need one.' Wulfric took a step forward.

'I think you'll wish you had one all the same.' Urschel picked up a small bell from his desk and rang it.

The door behind Wulfric slammed open, and two soldiers entered the study. Two more emerged from a cupboard beside Urschel's desk.

'I'll bet you'd like a sword around about now,' Urschel said. 'You'll find these men to be a different calibre to those you beat at the inn in Leondorf.' He smiled with satisfaction.

Wulfric said nothing; he had no idea what the word 'calibre' meant. He focussed all his attention on the men surrounding him.

'I got word from Donato's son yesterday. He said you were most likely on your way here looking for me, having already killed his father.'

'You know why I'm here then,' Wulfric said.

'I do. Things are going perfectly to plan right now, and I can't have you causing a scene and spoiling it.' He switched his gaze to one of the soldiers. 'Take him outside and kill him. The rug is expensive. I don't want you causing a mess in here.'

A soldier nodded and made to grab Wulfric. Wulfric sprang at him. He was the leader, and killing him first would make the others think twice. His sudden move was unexpected, and the soldier didn't have time to react before Wulfric's fist thundered into the side of his head. He dropped to the ground like a sack of rocks and Wulfric reached for the soldier's sword.

'Kill him! Now!' Urschel screamed.

Wulfric pulled the sword free as the three remaining soldiers charged him.

'Anton! Get to the guardhouse and bring more men!' Urschel shouted.

Wulfric didn't know who Anton was, or where the guardhouse was, but it meant he needed to be quick. He parried a high blow and kicked the man who made it between the legs. Wulfric cut down the next and reversed his movement to slash through the midsection of the third. He could feel rage well within him, the sign that Jorundyr's Gift was not far away. He didn't want it, though. It dulled his senses, and he wanted them to be keen and sharp when he took Urschel's life.

The long, slender sword felt clumsy in his hand, making him wish he had his curved sabre with him. Nonetheless, a sword was a sword, and it was the hand wielding it that mattered most. His speed and brutal strength overcame the greater technical skill of his opponents. They seemed surprised when he followed a thrust with a fist, elbow, or knee.

It was all over in a few blinks of the eye. He finished off the last soldier with no more ceremony than killing a speared boar. Urschel was edging around the side of the office toward the door, his hands raised defensively.

'It wasn't my idea,' Urschel said. 'It was the Markgraf. He wanted her brought here. None of it would have happened otherwise. Why would I want to bring her here? How would it serve me? It was all his idea. And Donato's. He said you'd have to be out of the way. The plan was his. He's the one who wanted you dead. There's no need to kill me. We can work something out. It was Donato and the Markgraf. I was only a go-between. I can be a very powerful friend to you.'

Wulfric knew he couldn't dally, but the Gift was taking its hold and clouding his senses. It felt as though he was watching the scene from afar, and couldn't directly influence what was going on. He took a deep breath to still himself. He wanted the memory of this to be clear.

'Adalhaid died because of you,' Wulfric said, 'and it's to pay her Blood Debt that you die.'

Urschel's eyes went wide, the terror of a coward about to meet his end who knows there is no place for him in Jorundyr's Host—or the equivalent for whatever southern god he worshipped, Wulfric thought.

'Wait. No,' Urschel screamed, his hands raised. 'You're making a mistake. Sh—'

Wulfric took Urschel's head from his shoulders in one clean strike. It hit the floor with a dull thud well before the body toppled over to join it.

He looked at his grim work with little satisfaction. He suddenly felt weary, as though all the stress of the past days had finally caught up with him. He was not finished, however. The Debt was not yet settled. Urschel's words had confirmed his suspicion that the Markgraf shared the blame. One more man involved, one more man to kill.

Wulfric had to get away before any more soldiers arrived. He wanted more than anything to go straight to the palace to kill the Markgraf, but the alarm would be raised soon, and the risk was too great. He would fail, and Adalhaid's Blood Debt would go unpaid. They would spend eternity searching for one another in Jorundyr's Hall, but would never again meet. Getting to a man like the Markgraf needed proper planning and preparation. He'd disappear, come back when things had settled down.

He searched the bodies for any coins that might aid his flight. There were a few, but not enough to make much difference. He dropped the sword, knowing it would attract too much attention, and wiped any blood he could see from his hands and clothes. After that, he left the house in as casual a fashion as he could muster.

❈

## WULFRIC

As Wulfric walked from the house toward the city gate, his mind raced with all the possible pitfalls he might face as he escaped. The message Urschel had received meant the authorities would soon know his name and where he came from. There had not been time to look for it, but it made little difference. To them, one Northlander was much the same as another. They would not know he intended to return to kill the Markgraf, which was the important thing, but when he did come back it would have to be with a different name.

In a week or two, perhaps a month, the commotion caused by the ambassador's death would have died down, and he could return to finish the job. The delay was an irritation, but dying foolishly before he had completed his task would be far worse.

Wulfric looked over his shoulder every so often, wondering if he would see a charging pack of soldiers coming for him. Out of the corner of his eye, he spotted a slender, red-haired woman walking away from him. For the briefest moment, his heart leapt, as it always had when he saw Adalhaid.

The sight of the woman felt so familiar that for an instant he thought it was her. The happiness it brought was intoxicating, but it was gone in the blink of an eye. Adalhaid was dead.

He could not stop himself from watching her a moment longer, wishing again for that first flash of happiness the sight of her had brought. Wulfric felt as though his heart was being torn asunder. The woman was carrying several parcels, and she dropped some. His instinct was to go and help her, but he knew he had to leave.

He took one final look at the woman gathering her dropped parcels and allowed himself the brief fantasy that it was Adalhaid, that she was happy and that they could be together. It brought only sorrow. He swore to Jorundyr and Adalhaid he would return, swore that he would take the Markgraf's life, and then Rodulf's. He hoped that somewhere, wherever she was, Adalhaid would hear his oath.

※

## Adalhaid

Adalhaid muttered a curse under her breath. She knelt and set her other packages on the ground to pick up the dropped objects. She grabbed the first, a small knitted bear, and brushed it with her hand to clean off the dust. *At least it's not muddy*, she thought. Clutching it under her arm, she reached for the second, a cloth doll. It had cost twice what the bear had, but she couldn't return to the palace with a gift for Petr and not for Aenlin.

The doll had not fared so well as the bear, its light cloth showing the dirt more. She sighed, but she'd be able to clean it. As she stared at it, the hair stood up on the back of her neck. She looked around, expecting someone to be standing nearby, watching, but the street behind was empty.

※

## Wulfric

Wulfric wanted the city walls to be far behind him before the alarm was raised, but running would only draw attention to himself. He had no idea how the city and its guards would react to the killing of a nobleman, and he did not want to be there to find out.

He walked as quickly as he thought prudent and wondered if it was worth the risk of trying to get his horse and sword back. Once outside the city walls they would be useful, but the delay might lead to his capture.

There was no sign of alarm at the gate when it came into view. Soldiers stood around not showing much interest in anything as people passed through. Wulfric slowed down and tried to blend in with the crowd. In an anxious moment, he wondered if he had managed to clean off all the blood. Killing was a messy thing, and doing it five times was messier still.

He held his breath as he walked beneath the guards' stares. One step at a time. Wulfric could feel the hairs on the back of his neck stick up. He was sure every eye was on him, and everyone there knew exactly what had happened. He passed into the dark shadow under the wall, then out into sunlight on the other side before he drew breath again.

He continued walking and forced himself not to look back, but could not help a longing glance at the stable building. There was a queue outside. It would take too long to get his horse back and saddle it. The first mile was the most important. When Urschel was discovered, they would surely come looking for him. Five deaths would warrant a concerted hunt for the killer. If the messenger Urschel had called to was in any way competent, he would be back at the house with help by now, and the alarm would be making its way to the city gate.

# CHAPTER 4

RODULF

RODULF PLACED THE Stone on the table in the hall of his house, and stared at it. The jumble of symbols etched across its surface were still unintelligible to him, but his mind raced with speculation about their meaning and what the Stone actually did. He was convinced now that it did *something*. He couldn't shake off the feeling of wellbeing he had when he held it, nor could he ignore the fact that every opposition he had encountered since possessing it had fallen before him.

Rodulf was under no illusions about his powers of persuasion. They were good—overwhelming when accompanied by violence—but they had never worked with such ease. Priest magic came from tricks and herbs and poultices. If he was being honest with himself, Rodulf didn't even believe in the gods. Perhaps they had existed, influenced the world once, but they had long since departed and left mankind to its own devices.

When he stared at the Stone, that belief was shaken to its foundation. He leaned forward until his nose was almost touching it. It was old. The edges of the etchings were rounded, not crisp. They were like those covering the standing stone in the warriors' glade, which could be read only by a few. What events and turns of fate had led to it coming into the possession of the man he had taken it from? Perhaps it was the will of the gods? Perhaps they had chosen to favour him at last? Whatever else it did, whatever else it was, it seemed people did what he said when he had it. That was a powerful tool that he would be a fool to ignore.

❁

## ADALHAID

'Adalhaid! Look!'

Aenlin ran toward her. She had stitched two pieces of cloth together to make a dress for the doll Adalhaid had bought her. The stitches were wide and out of line, but her young face beamed with pride.

'Very good, Aenlin. Well done.'

The young girl's smile grew even wider. 'I'm going to make britches for Petr's bear now.' She ran back to her small sewing box.

Adalhaid watched the little blonde girl—still just shy of her eighth birthday—as she worked on her twin brother's gift, the tip of her tongue sticking out as she concentrated on threading the dull needle she was allowed to use. Adalhaid wondered what her own children might have looked like, had she and Wulfric been married. The thought brought a lump to her throat. She shook the grief from her head. There was nothing to be gained by thinking on a life she could never have, no matter how much she had wanted it. Her life was in Elzburg now.

❁

## AETHELMAN

Aethelman sat in a rocking chair on the kirk's porch, a heavy bearskin over his lap keeping his old joints warm. He watched people go to and fro. A few had a salutation for him, but most passed by without so much as a glance. There was a time when he'd known them all, and everyone acknowledged him, but that was past, seemingly never to return.

It seemed that every day brought another wagonload of southerners looking to make their fortunes in the Northlands, whether by prospecting, trapping, or trading. With them came the physicians and the preachers and the shopkeepers who were required to satisfy all demand for those needs. The few who could call Leondorf the place of their birth had also started to turn to these new arrivals for their spiritual and physical well-being. Aethelman was not needed there any longer. It made him realise what a terrible thing it was to grow old.

As he watched the villagers—*townsfolk* was more appropriate now— his thoughts turned to the great men who had once called it home. Giants in shining plate armour with helmets decorated like fierce beasts, they had epitomised the ferocious Northlander warriors so feared in the south. Belgar the Bold, Wolfram the Strong Arm, Angest the Beleks' Bane—all dead, all supping with Jorundyr in his Great Hall beyond the High Places. His reminiscences were shrouded with melancholy, and he knew it was foolish to pine for what had been, but would never be again.

Now that the floodgates had broken, and southern influence had rushed north into the once impenetrable forests, Aethelman wondered how far it would reach. Were the days of the old gods as numbered as his own? His thoughts drifted to the Stone. It represented the only remaining part of his life that felt incomplete. He comforted himself with the possibility that it had been destroyed in the fire that had consumed the old kirk, but in his gut, he knew that to be unlikely. Someone had found it, taken it. That it was almost impossible they would know what to do with it gave him little comfort. Perhaps they had thrown it away? No. That was too much to hope for. There was something about the Stone, something that ensured whoever took it kept it safe, coveted it even if they never knew what it was, or what it could do.

If he was being honest with himself, Aethelman realised that even he knew little about what it could do, and he was among those with the greatest knowledge regarding Fount Stones. He furrowed his brow as his duty became clear. It was unlikely he would ever encounter another Fount Stone, with his remaining life to be measured in years rather than decades. Few men encountered even one, but perhaps the day would come again when someone did. Perhaps his Stone, if he could ever really have called it his. Like as not the day would come when a young priest would find a Stone, just as Aethelman had done all those years ago. Aethelman would be damned if anyone else had to bear the burden of not knowing what to do with it. He'd spend his remaining days seeking out anything he could find about them.

At the time, it had been centuries since anyone had encountered a Fount Stone, and no one could remember why newly ordained priests were required to spend the first year of their vocations searching the land for them. That in itself was a mystery to which Aethelman wanted an answer. What they were to do if they actually found one was an even greater mystery. So shrouded were they in legend and secrecy, much had been forgotten.

That led Aethelman to the question of where he should begin. The

Hermitage, the lonely monastery in the lower reaches of the High Places where young men and women went to train in the priesthood seemed like the best place to start his search, but Aethelman was not overly hopeful of what might be found there. Their itinerant nature did not lend itself to detailed written records. The skills and knowledge of priesthood was handed down by instruction and discussion. They were told the stories of the old gods, of the solemn duties they had given to the priesthood. They were shown how to heal and minister to their congregations. Then, on the day of ordination, they were commanded to fulfil their sacred duty and scour the land for Fount Stones for a year and a day. It was long past time someone went beyond simple obedience, and searched for understanding. Aethelman leaned back in his seat, almost oblivious to the people passing by whether they acknowledged him or not. He had a purpose once more.

❊

## Wulfric

It was getting dark and Wulfric saw no sign of any pursuit. His stomach rumbled—he was starting to feel safe enough to begin thinking about his next meal rather than escape. He had not eaten or slept properly in days, which was beginning to take its toll.

When he heard noise ahead, he retreated to the undergrowth to hide until it passed. The noise—it was voices—wasn't getting closer. Wulfric moved forward quietly, remaining in cover. The voices grew louder. There were several, all male, all agitated. When the source came into view, Wulfric was glad he had opted for a cautious approach.

Three men faced a fourth, older man, who stood by a horse.

'Come and take it then,' the older man said. His hair was short and grey, and he had one of the most impressive moustaches Wulfric had ever seen, thick and carefully styled into points at the end. 'I'll be sending you home to your mother in pieces if you do, though.'

Wulfric grinned. The man was not as elderly as Belgar had been, but he appeared to be well beyond the age where he could back up threats like that. Despite his age, he looked an active type and held himself well, like an old warrior or soldier. However, like many men active in their youth but less so in later years, the rot had set in and his waistline was larger than it should have been. Wulfric reckoned the three men with their backs to him were younger and well accustomed to their work. It didn't look good, and Wulfric felt a sense of injustice at the scene.

'We don't want to kill you, old man, but we're taking what we want, and you can die trying to stop us if you choose.'

The expression on the older man's face said there was no way he was handing over anything that was his.

'I've given you ample opportunity to turn and run,' the older man said. 'Test me and it will end badly for you all.'

The bandits burst into laughter.

'It's going to end badly all right,' the first bandit said.

Wulfric admired the older man's courage in the face of odds he could not hope to defeat. He reached down and scrabbled around in the dusk until he found a fist-sized rock. He crouched, and prepared to explode from the bushes.

The first bandit rushed forward and Wulfric burst from the undergrowth. He needed only a couple of steps to cover the distance between them, about the same as they needed to get to the old man. They were all carrying wide-bladed short swords, while the older man had a longer-bladed weapon strapped to his waist, which he had yet to draw.

The old man's eyes flicked to Wulfric briefly. In one smooth move, he drew his sword and whipped its tip across the first bandit's body. He screeched in pain as the old man stepped forward and cut across the second and then, as Wulfric was drawing close, thrust his sword into the chest of the third, his sword-hand high, with his other held out behind him for balance. He pulled his sword clear and stepped back, taking his guard again, his eyes locked on Wulfric.

Wulfric was left feeling ridiculous, his rock held high above him to strike at the now dead bandits. All three of them had hit the ground at the same moment, and the synchronism was not lost on Wulfric; the entire moment of violence had been perfectly executed. The old man was a master, and his warnings were nothing more than an act of undeserved kindness. Wulfric sheepishly lowered his rock and relaxed.

'Friend or foe?' the older man asked.

'Friend, I think,' Wulfric said. 'Heard what was happening from down the road. When I saw your trouble, I thought I'd lend a hand.'

'Unnecessary, as you can see,' the older man said, cleaning the blade of his sword on a piece of cloth, 'but gratefully received nonetheless. You're a Northlander, by the sound of you?'

Wulfric was reluctant to answer, but there was little point in lying about the obvious. 'I am.'

'A pleasure to meet you.' The older man sheathed his sword and extended his hand to Wulfric. 'Otto dal Rhenning is my name, Graf of Rhenning as was, banneret-errant as is.'

'Wulfric Wolframson,' he said. He reached out and took the older man's hand, and received a firm handshake in return.

'What brings you to these southern parts?'

There was nothing in dal Rhenning's demeanour that gave Wulfric cause for suspicion. He was ahead of Wulfric on the road, so there was no way he could know anything of what had happened in Elzburg.

'Looking for work. Heard there might be some out this way.'

Dal Rhenning looked him up and down, a suspicious expression on his face. 'Anywhere in particular?'

Wulfric shrugged.

'You're travelling light, I see. A little too light, don't you think?'

Wulfric shuffled his feet awkwardly. 'I… wasn't as careful in the city as I should have been. My things were stolen.'

Dal Rhenning nodded at the explanation. 'Cities can be hostile to those not familiar with them. Always try to avoid 'em myself.' He turned his back on Wulfric and went to inspect one of his horse's hoofs. 'Bastards must have thrown some caltrops on the road. Horse went lame and it's too much of a coincid— ah yes, here we are.'

The horse whickered and shifted suddenly. Dal Rhenning turned back to Wulfric and held up a small piece of metal with four short spikes projecting out of it. He looked at it with distaste. 'Should have seen that coming, really. Still, all's well that ends well. Better walk the beast for a time though. I'm headed to Wetlin, on the coast. Small harbour there. Might be some work on the docks.'

Wulfric nodded, as though he knew of it and was headed there too.

'We can walk together, then,' dal Rhenning said as he started off. 'There's nothing between here and Wetlin, and I don't fancy stopping here for the night. There are bears and wolves in the woods hereabouts.'

# CHAPTER 5

WULFRIC

'I'VE HEARD MANY tales of Northland warriors heading off on adventures and getting themselves into scrapes in parts foreign,' dal Rhenning said, as they set off. 'Jorundyr's Path, they call it, don't they?'

Wulfric was amazed that a southerner had heard of it, but dal Rhenning was full of surprises. 'They do.'

'Looking for something like that yourself?'

It was a pleasant night, dry and not too cold. Wulfric had intended pressing on without pause, and the old man made for good company. There was something about him that reminded Wulfric of Belgar and Aethelman. Wulfric had not had a friendly conversation in even a longer time than he had eaten a hot meal, and welcomed it.

'More adventure, fewer scrapes,' Wulfric said. 'Want to see a bit of the world before... before...'

'Before you get too old like me?' dal Rhenning said with a belly laugh. 'I'll have you know there's plenty of adventure left in an old fart like me.'

Wulfric smiled, hoping he hadn't caused offence, but the old man had a cavalier air about him and didn't strike Wulfric as the type to be easily insulted.

'I've always been fascinated by the old Northlander sagas,' dal Rhenning said. 'Many of them relate to places that are now part of Ruripathia, y'know.'

'I'd heard that,' Wulfric said. 'Our village priest said Ruripathia was much like the Northlands in the old days.'

'True,' dal Rhenning said. 'Not so different even now, though. Bigger cities to be sure, but the language is similar enough that we can talk with no difficulty. Our gods have different names, but they are largely the same. History may have separated our lands, but much remains in common.'

Wulfric raised his eyebrows. Most southerners he had met seemed to think all Northlanders were savages.

'Tell me about Jorundyr's Path,' dal Rhenning said. 'I've heard less than half who set off ever make it back.'

Wulfric smiled, happy to talk about something so important to him, and pleased by dal Rhenning's interest. 'It's not that bad usually. But plenty die. Something in the High Places drains the life out of you. Tears your body apart from the inside. I watched my friend drown in his own blood. There was nothing I could do for him. Then there're the belek. They're common in the High Places. I killed my first on the way back from my pilgrimage.'

Dal Rhenning stopped and turned to face Wulfric. 'Your first? You've killed more than one?'

Wulfric nodded. 'I killed a second last season. You don't have the option of running away when it comes to belek. You kill it, or it kills you.' The memory of the ferocious and intelligent beasts sent a shiver down Wulfric's spine.

'I killed one myself, when I was a young man,' dal Rhenning said. 'Only one I've ever seen, and I'd not care to see another. There are many in the Northlands?'

'Not as many as I think there once were. They didn't come near my village during my lifetime, but there are plenty of stories about it happening before I was born. They attack the herds a few times a year, the cattle mainly. They usually stay away from the horses.'

'And your village? Where are you from?'

Wulfric hesitated. 'Rasbruck.'

'Can't say I've heard of it, although I know of few enough places north of the marches. I was little more than a lad when I killed my belek. Only nineteen. We have to go looking for them, deep into the forests and up into the Telastrian Mountains. The thought of it still gives me the chills.'

'I heard you hunt them in the south for sport,' Wulfric said.

'Not exactly, but I suppose it's not far off. It's something of a rite of passage. A bit like your pilgrimage really, although few enough actually manage to kill one. Most who go out on a hunt never even see one. I was lucky, not just to encounter one but to be the first in for the kill.'

'I've never thought of meeting a belek to be good luck,' Wulfric said.

Dal Rhenning laughed. 'No. Having had the pleasure, I don't think I would anymore either. Still, it's something of a coup to achieve, and a young man with a belek cloak gets all the attention from the ladies. Much of what came my way in life was because of those few minutes. Ridiculous when you think about it.'

'It's important where I'm from too,' Wulfric said. Tired and cold as he was, he longed for the warmth and comfort of his belek cloak. He felt his stomach rumble. 'How much farther to…'

'To Wetlin? The road is in fair condition. If you're content to continue through the night as I plan to do, we should be there by late morning.'

❊

## ADALHAID

'What do you think of Leondorf being made part of the Elzmark? Part of Ruripathia?' the Markgraf said.

'I think it's been inevitable for some time, my lord,' Adalhaid said with as much enthusiasm as she could muster. She found formal dining at the Markgraf's table to be a stifling affair—she far preferred the casual family dinners when she was present to keep an eye on the children. However, being invited to a formal dinner was a mark of respect and one that was not given often, so she never refused. They were usually small affairs, as was the case that night, with only a dozen currently favoured members of his court invited.

She always felt drained by it, having to have a constant regard for southern dining etiquette, as well as making polite small talk on matters she rarely had any interest in. This, however, was a subject close to her heart.

'But as someone who was born and bred there, are you in favour of it? The Northlanders have been hostile to any advance into the forests for centuries.'

'Northlanders are fiercely independent,' Adalhaid said. 'But for Leondorf, independence was a luxury she could no longer afford.'

'Very true,' the Markgraf said. 'A sad thing, I suppose. Like seeing a magnificent wild beast stripped of its freedom and caged in the menagerie.'

'A fitting analogy, my lord,' one of the dinner guests, a noble from somewhere near the coast, said. 'Particularly when applied to Northlanders.'

The comment drew laughter from around the table, but the Markgraf only smiled in his wry way. There were many odious personalities at his court, but he was not one of them.

Adalhaid flushed with anger, and the guest seemed to notice it.

'Of course, I'd barely have known you are a Northlander,' he said. 'You've adapted to life here so well.'

She forced a smile at what she knew was a clumsy effort at a compliment, even though it made the original insult all the worse. She watched the guests eat and toady up to the Markgraf as though their prosperity depended on it. It occurred to her that it did. The realisation that she was in exactly the same situation made her feel sick. Only a few months before, the world had seemed nothing but an opportunity. She was going to set up a school in Leondorf, and guide future generations to finding their place in the world. Now she was a child-minder, entirely reliant on someone else for her prosperity and future. The thought made her dizzy. How had she allowed herself to drift from her course so completely?

She knew the answer, but it was no excuse. She wondered if Wulfric watched her from Jorundyr's Hall. What must he think, seeing her allow her dreams to fade away like that?

She looked around the table and felt nothing but contempt, for them and for herself. She had to take charge of her life again, to spend it working toward the dreams she had as a child. If she didn't, what was the point in even having a life? A degree and a profession would make her equal to any of them at the table. More so, even. She would have earned every achievement she called her own, while they were merely born to theirs. More importantly, it would mean she had to rely on no one but herself. No one would be able to take her future from her. She stifled her anger, and smiled.

✿

## Rodulf

Rodulf was always suspicious of knocks on his door late at night. His servant opened it but he watched carefully, ready to react if Andhun or Oswyn had finally plucked up the courage to try and have him killed. One of Ambassador dal Ruedin's men stood outside. He handed the servant a note and left.

Rodulf took the note, wasting no time in breaking open the red wax seal. He scanned the contents and smiled. He had succeeded in the second prong of his plan. Being made temporary mayor gave him charge of the day-to-day administration of the town, but his father had long since put processes and staff in place to ensure it all but ran itself. Rodulf needed to prove himself as more than just a competent administrator. He had to show dal Ruedin he could add value to the role, that he could get his hands dirty and deal with the tougher tasks, something no one else on the council could do.

He had requested that the responsibility for the silver convoys be passed to him. The soldiers had taken full control since the last attack, but they did not like the dangerous duty. Casualties were frequent, and it was an unwelcome drain on the ambassador's coffers. The note told Rodulf his request had been acceded to. He had one week to prepare for the next convoy—and the chance to show the ambassador that he was the obvious choice to be made Lord of Leondorf.

❖

## WULFRIC

They arrived in Wetlin late in the morning of the next day as dal Rhenning had estimated. Wulfric had smelled salt in the air long before they reached the town. It was unlike anything else, the tang of the great sea that he had heard spoken of many times. His excitement to see it for himself had grown with each step toward it—water as far as the eye could see.

Dal Rhenning had been a good travelling companion, curious about the ways of the Northlanders and a fount of stories about wars and battles, many of which he had fought in over a long and active life. Now in his later years, he had abdicated his county in favour of his son, to spend his final years seeing the world and adventuring with a band of likeminded warriors.

It was a notion in true keeping with the Northland epics, and Wulfric admired the fact that dal Rhenning still had the spirit to leave behind all the hard-earned comforts of a long life and venture out into the unknown. They parted company at the gates to Wetlin, dal Rhenning going on to meet his brothers in arms, while Wulfric had to work out what he was going to do next. As he was in a port, the idea of taking a ship struck him as a good idea. Seeing the sea for the first time, and realising just how big the world was, had lit a fire of curiosity within him. He wondered if it would be selfish to see a little of it before returning to finish his duty.

Wetlin was a miniature version of Elzburg, like a younger sibling copying the older in everything but size. It was not all that much larger than Leondorf and there was a bustling energy about the place, with steady traffic in and out.

He had no difficulty getting through the town gate, not even attracting an inquiring glance from the soldiers on duty there. Despite the ease, he was wary of being in another town. He didn't like them. Surrounded by walls, he felt like there was a weight on his chest, and he was no sooner inside them than he was counting the moments until he could leave. There was also the concern of news from Elzburg catching up with him. He would take the first departing ship that would have him. It didn't matter where it was going.

He walked through the town and straight down to the docks to see what was there. The sea caught his imagination every time he looked at it, and he was utterly fascinated by the ships tied to Wetlin's quayside—great hulks of wood that pulled gently against their mooring lines. Each looked slightly different. Some were heavy and cumbersome, like a cart horse, while others were sleek and agile like a horse bred for speed. Their masts and rigging stretched skyward, like bare trees in winter.

As impressive as they were, they were put to shame by one great monstrosity of a ship that was at anchor in the bay. Even that distant, it dwarfed the other ships. Smaller boats were ferrying supplies and other goods out, including one filled with horses, which amazed Wulfric. He wondered how many men and trees were needed to build such an enormous vessel.

It had seemed like such a simple idea—find a ship, flee the land. Now that he was faced with it, he had no idea what to do. Standing around like a naive Northlander idiot wasn't going to get him anywhere, so he walked to the nearest ship and called out.

A sailor put down a coil of rope and walked over.

'What do you want?'

'I'm looking for a ship away from here.'

'You and everyone else with an ounce of sense.' He gave Wulfric a look up and down. 'We don't take passengers. Sorry.'

Wulfric felt his heart sink. 'I'll work my way.'

'Any experience on ships?'

Wulfric hesitated too long.

'No. Sorry. Good luck,' the sailor said.

Wulfric walked away wondering how he should change his approach for his next try. Perhaps he should cut his hair and trim his beard so as to fit better with southern fashion. It seemed worth a try, and a rumbling belly reminded him that he had yet to eat. He still had some of the money he'd taken from the ambassador and his men, so he decided to find an inn, some soap, hot water, and a large meal.

# CHAPTER 6

WULFRIC

PORT TOWNS SEEMED to have no shortage of inns. For Wulfric, the most difficult part was choosing which one to try. Novice though he was to city life, he could discount most of them at a glance—too fancy, too run down, too rough. The last thing he needed was trouble. A middle-of-the-road inn, possibly one where ship's officers gathered, would be perfect. As well as having a chance to eat and clean up, it would allow him to listen in and get an idea of ship-speak, so he could avoid seeming so useless the next time he approached a ship.

He wandered about the small town for a time, coming upon an inn called The Giddy Goose. He would have continued past the nondescript facade were it not for the smell that hit him as soon as he was within range. The scent of cooking—bread and bacon, he thought—had him salivating and his stomach rumbling the second he breathed it in. The smell was as strong a recommendation for an inn as could be had, so he went in.

He hadn't eaten anything other than the meagre rations dal Rhenning had shared with him as they walked. As much as he needed a wash and a fast ship, the smell made him feel faint. He had no idea how much things cost, but his coins were silver and he knew that had value. He reckoned there was enough for everything he needed, and a few minutes to fill his belly seemed little to ask for.

He was halfway through a plate of meat and vegetables when a group of soldiers came in. He felt his stomach twist, but did his best to quell any visible reaction. He was furious with himself for giving in to his hunger. He could have eaten in comfort on a ship making best time toward a foreign land, and never need to have worried about southern soldiers again. He thought about getting up and leaving, but his plate was still loaded with food and it would look suspicious.

The soldiers gathered at the bar and started speaking with the innkeeper. Wulfric found that his appetite had deserted him completely but he continued to eat, mechanically shovelling food into his mouth and keeping an eye on the soldiers. Why couldn't he have cleaned himself up first? He might as well have had a sign over his head saying 'Northlander'.

They surveyed the taproom, but didn't dwell on anyone in particular. He hoped they would be gone by the time he finished his food, but they were still there as he mopped the last of the gravy from his plate. It would appear odd continuing to sit there with no food or drink. Standing up and leaving would draw attention, but for all he knew they weren't looking for him.

One of the soldiers cast a glance in Wulfric's direction. Wulfric pushed his plate away and wiped his mouth. There was nothing to do but leave. He stood and made his way toward the door.

'Where you headed, traveller?' a soldier said. He seemed to be the one in charge.

Wulfric ignored the voice and kept going.

'You, with the beard. I said where are you headed?'

Wulfric stopped. 'To get work on a boat,' he said.

'You've the look of a Northlander about you. And the sound of one. Didn't think you folk were a seafaring lot.' The soldier stared at Wulfric, waiting for a response.

'We aren't usually. Just wanted to give it a try. See the world. I hear it's a big place,' Wulfric said, hoping that a mixture of humour and playing up to the dumb Northlander stereotype might get him off the hook.

One of the soldiers sniggered, and it seemed as though it might work.

'Been in town long?' the soldier said.

Wulfric shrugged. 'No.'

'Pay a visit to Elzburg by any chance?'

Wulfric's skin crawled. 'Where?'

'We're looking for a Northlander. You're not far off the description. Come here and let me take a look at you.'

Wulfric considered his options, which seemed few. There were five soldiers, and there could be more outside. They stood between him and the door, meaning his only way out was through them. That was far from ideal, but he wasn't going to go quietly to a Ruripathian dungeon. He wondered if he could bluff his way out of it by appearing to cooperate.

He walked toward the soldiers. The one who had spoken gave Wulfric a close looking over.

'Hands,' he said. 'Let me see your hands.'

Wulfric hesitated before holding them out. He hadn't paid them any attention, and for all he knew there might still be blood on them.

The soldier looked at Wulfric's hands, then turned each one over to look at the palms. 'Filthy bloody Northlander,' he said under his breath.

It was loud enough for Wulfric to hear, but he was too grateful for the fact that his hands bore all the hallmarks of a man who had been living rough to care about the insult.

'I'm not sure,' the soldier said to his men, 'but he's a Northlander, so we should hold him until they arrive from the city. One less Northlander on the streets is never a bad thing.' He turned back to Wulfric and grabbed him by the wrist. 'You're coming with us.'

Wulfric pulled the soldier forward as hard as he could and sent him sprawling across the taproom's floor, knocking chairs and tables out of the way as he went. The others rushed in quickly. Wulfric dropped the first with a punch so hard he could feel his knuckles crack. He grimaced with pain and took little satisfaction in the fact that the man he had hit dropped to the floor without so much as a grunt.

His eyes widened and his heart raced as he was filled with the joy and lust of battle. Another soldier charged at him. Wulfric grabbed him and slammed him against the bar. He snatched a handful of the soldier's hair and smashed his head on the counter. He threw the soldier's limp body to one side as carelessly as if he were a piece of rubbish, then fixed his gaze on the remaining two, willing them on.

The soldiers drew their weapons, any hope of taking Wulfric alive now gone, and advanced. Wulfric welcomed their approach and watched them grow closer, waiting for the right moment to attack. He felt a dull object strike the back of his head and had enough time to wonder who had hit him before darkness closed in.

❉

## Dal Rhenning

'What in hells do you think you're doing?' dal Rhenning said.

Two of the soldiers paused in helping their comrade from the ground, and looked to the man addressing them.

Dal Rhenning stood arms akimbo and fixed the soldiers with his most withering gaze. 'Care to explain yourselves?'

'And why would we care to do that?' the lead soldier, a sergeant, said.

'Because that's my man you've assaulted,' dal Rhenning said, 'and unless you've got good reason, I'll have the lot of you flogged.'

The sergeant cast a glance at his men. 'And who might you be?'

'Graf Otto dal Rhenning, Banneret of the Grey. That man's paymaster.' He pointed at Wulfric's prone form.

'I'm sorry, my lord, but you say he's one of yours? He told us he was looking for work on the boats.'

'Perhaps he didn't care to share his business with you,' dal Rhenning said.

'Even so, my lord, we're looking for a Northlander who fits his description,' the sergeant said, his voice lacking its previous confidence. 'Killed a nobleman and a dozen soldiers in Elzburg.'

'A dozen soldiers? And a nobleman?'

The sergeant nodded.

'And yet five ugly turds like you were able to drop him with only two men injured?'

The sergeant nodded again, but more slowly.

'I signed that man onto my roster a month ago. We haven't been near Elzburg in that time.'

'I suppose we could be mistaken, my lord. The description wasn't—'

'Piss off, the lot of you,' dal Rhenning said, putting as much impatience into his voice as he could muster. 'Best hope you haven't cracked his skull. If you have, you'll all be looking for new employment before the morrow.'

'Apologies, my lord,' the sergeant said, backing away toward the door. 'And good luck on your next adventure. We all very much enjoy the tales of your exploits.' He doffed his hat, then turned and left the inn as quickly as he could, followed by his men, carrying their unconscious colleagues.

'Explain to me why you did that?'

'Where were you, Jagovere?' dal Rhenning said to the blond-haired man who had appeared at his shoulder. 'I thought that might get rough. Could have used a hand.'

'You'd have had it in time. Didn't want to let my pie go cold. The explanation?'

'This young man was prepared to fight by my side on the road to this poxy little town with nothing more than a rock in his hand. One good turn deserves another.'

Jagovere scratched his goatee. 'What are we going to do with him? Leave him there?'

'No. Once those investigators get here I suspect they'll realise they weren't mistaken after all,' dal Rhenning said. 'It would be a wasted effort if we leave him now.'

'A nobleman and a dozen soldiers?' Jagovere said.

Dal Rhenning shrugged. 'I doubt it. Probably just got caught in the nobleman's daughter's bed. You know what those city girls are like for a bit of rough.'

Jagovere's face split with a grin. 'Only too well, but after seeing him fight like that, I wouldn't be so sure.'

Dal Rhenning nodded as he continued to regard Wulfric's prone form.

'That still doesn't answer my question, though,' Jagovere said. 'What will we do with him?'

❧

## AETHELMAN

When he looked at his haversack, Aethelman realised how little he truly needed to live. A warm hearth and a dry roof were the only luxuries he had ever allowed himself. A good pair of boots, a warm cloak, a blanket, some food, and the tools he would need to survive in the wilderness were the only things he was taking with him. He wondered if he would be able to remember his way to the Hermitage—he wondered if he was embarking on a fool's errand. It didn't feel like one, though. Something deep inside told him it was important. For the first time in decades, the weight of having possessed the Fount Stone for so long and not taking any action with it rested lighter on his shoulders. He hoped that this quest, likely the last thing he'd do with his life, would lift that burden completely.

It would not be dawn for some hours yet, but there was no one to say goodbye to, and no reason to tarry any longer. He hefted the haversack onto his shoulder and set off, not sparing a glance for the place that had been his home for so many years but that he now barely recognised.

❋

## ADALHAID

Adalhaid stared at the university from the opposite side of the square. She had been constantly thinking over her revelation at the dinner, and working out her best way forward. She needed to go back to university and complete her education. A higher degree was the only way a woman could lead an independent and prosperous life, and she would be damned if she was ever going to have to rely on someone else for her survival. The city could be a very harsh place if you didn't have any money, and Adalhaid had no intention of experiencing that herself.

She already had her basic teaching diploma, but so did hundreds of others, and the competition for work was fierce. It had been nothing more than good fortune and her uncle's contacts that got her a position at court. She couldn't count on being so lucky a second time. Her Northland background would always stand against her.

She knew it would be difficult, juggling her duties at the palace with a course of study for a full degree, but she would have to rise to the challenge. She couldn't rely on her uncle for support—he had his own family to take care of, and had already been more than generous. Any quality of life she had would be down to her own making. She wrinkled her nose for a moment, her decision made.

# CHAPTER 7

## WULFRIC

WULFRIC OPENED HIS eyes slowly. It was dark, and he had no idea where he was. He was wrapped in heavy, stiff cloth and was rocking gently from side to side. The feeling of confinement made him panic, but he realised there was a split along the top that he could push open. He grabbed the edges and pulled himself up—he was in a hammock.

It was too dark to make anything out, but the world around him seemed to be moving. Moving and groaning. He tried to remember what had happened, but his head was too fuzzy to make sense of anything.

He heard approaching footsteps, and retreated into his cloth cocoon.

'Reckon he'd have woken by now if he was going to.'

'That's your medical opinion, is it?'

'I've seen plenty of cracked heads over the years, and have cracked my fair share. The longer they're out, the more likely they are to stay out.'

'I'm not sure I follow your logic.' The voice was tinged with humour.

The other voice grunted. 'One way or the other, I reckon it's time to stitch his hammock shut and heave him over the side.'

'The Graf said he's to be fed gruel and water every day, so fed he shall be.'

A hand pulled back the hammock's lip. Wulfric shut his eyes and pretended to be unconscious. A strong, calloused hand gripped him by the jaw and forced his mouth open. He could feel a cold steel spoon press against his lips, and warm gruel trickled into his mouth. It was bland, but it made Wulfric realise how hungry he was. He forced himself to remain still, not wanting to reveal the fact that he was awake to the men feeding him.

The memory of the inn and the soldiers flashed into his mind. He struggled to contain the sense of panic that he'd been captured and was awaiting execution. Would they have bothered feeding him if that was what they were intending? More gruel was dribbled into his mouth, and the process continued for several minutes as Wulfric fought the desire to open his eyes. Eventually a rough cloth was wiped across his mouth.

'That's enough for now,' one of the voices said.

There was some shuffling, the creak and clatter of a wooden door closing and Wulfric was alone again. His stomach rumbled uncomfortably, teased as it was by the meagre amount of food. He sat up and swung his legs out of the hammock, carefully reaching down with his foot until it touched the wooden floor.

Satisfied that he had found firm ground, he slipped out of the hammock and stood. His legs wobbled as the firm ground gently pitched to one side. He reached out and touched the wall to steady himself.

Fumbling around in the darkness, he found the door. It was unlocked— further proof, if the moving floor was not enough, that he was not in a prison. There were some lights farther down the narrow corridor on the other side, which gave him enough to see by. The corridor was empty, so he crept out, needing to constantly lean against the wall to keep his balance. Clad only in britches and a loose shirt, his bare feet made hardly a sound on the wooden floorboards beneath him.

He could hear activity above, footfalls and voices, but could make no sense of the confused noise. He continued along the corridor until he reached some steps. He knew if he climbed them he would be spotted by whoever was up there, but his curiosity was too great.

He had to hold onto the steps as he made his way up them—the movement seemed greater now. His legs felt weak, making him wonder how long he had been in the hammock. His head passed through the bright opening at the end, and he was greeted by a deluge of daylight and fresh air. A great expanse of wood ran in every direction, with men busily working all around. No one paid him the slightest notice.

He continued up the final few steps and out onto the next level. He tried to stand, but in the absence of anything to hold onto, he lost his balance as the floor moved beneath him again, and fell to his knees.

'I didn't expect to see you up and about.' A man stood over Wulfric, silhouetted in the sunlight. The voice was the humorous one from the hammock room. 'Here, let me help you.'

A firm pair of hands grabbed him under the shoulders and hoisted him to his feet. The man placed a steadying hand on Wulfric's arm as his legs wobbled.

'Don't worry,' the man said. 'You'll get used to it fast enough.'

Wulfric barely heard him as he looked around, his mouth agape. Beyond an expanse of wood, deep blue water flecked with white stretched in every direction. The sea. He was on a ship in the middle of the sea.

'Where am I?' he said.

'The better part of a week out of Wetlin,' the man said. 'Sailing sou'-sou' west at a fair clip.'

Wulfric continued to look out and around. A ship. It was enormous, the size of a small village, filled with as many people. Three thick masts stretched skyward, with long arms carrying great stretches of billowing canvas. The deck seemed to be moving in every direction at once. Wulfric found it impossible to keep his balance, and was humiliated at having to rely on the blond-haired man to remain upright.

His eyes felt strained after so long in the dark as he tried to take in the man before him. Shorter than Wulfric, he had windblown, shoulder-length hair and a neat beard. Wulfric couldn't recall ever seeing him before.

'Who are you?' Wulfric said.

'Banneret of the Grey Jagovere dal Borlitz, captain of heavy horse in Dal Rhenning's Company, at your service.' He gave a quick bow. 'I understand you are Wulfric Wolframson of the Northlands. I would welcome you aboard, but you've already been here for some time.'

'How did I get here?' Wulfric said, trying to piece together what little he could remember.

'You had an altercation with some soldiers in Wetlin. I assume you can recall that much?'

Wulfric nodded.

'They were about to haul you off to prison when the Graf'— Jagovere pointed to a man standing by the rail of a raised deck to the rear of the ship— 'decided to intervene. And so you wake on board a ship at sea many miles from the coast.'

'The Graf?' Wulfric squinted at the shape on the higher deck, and recognised him for the man he had tried to help on the road to Wetlin.

'Where are we going?'

'Estranza.'

Wulfric stared at him blankly.

Jagovere smiled. 'It's a kingdom on the other side of the Middle Sea. The Company has a contract there.'

Wulfric tried to assimilate everything. He had successfully gotten away from Ruripathia, but it was not on his own terms, and the loss of control made him anxious.

'When can I go back?' Wulfric said, a hint of urgency in his voice.

'More noblemen and soldiers to slay?' Jagovere said, raising an eyebrow.

Wulfric blushed. He wondered why they had helped him if they knew what he had done. 'I have to get back,' he said. 'For reasons that are my own.'

'Well, you won't be getting back any time soon,' Jagovere said. 'We've another week at sea at least. That's not a bad thing for you.' Jagovere paused and fixed Wulfric with an intense stare. 'Whatever your reasons, I would bide my time if I were you. Before we set sail, the Intelligenciers arrived in Wetlin.'

Wulfric furrowed his brow.

'Very dangerous men who spend their lives hunting down and destroying very dangerous things. People included. They were looking for Wulfric Wolframson of the Northlands, for the killing of the Markgraf of Elzburg's cousin, formerly ambassador to some Northland town the name of which escapes me.'

'Leondorf,' Wulfric said.

Jagovere nodded in thanks. 'In any event, I suspect it will be quite some time before Ruripathia is a safe place for you to be.'

'Why didn't you hand me over?' Wulfric said.

'When the Intelligenciers grab someone, they aren't seen again. There's no such thing as a trial, and the Graf is funny about things like that. He reckoned one good turn deserves another, and that you must have had good reason to travel all that way to kill the Markgraf's cousin. Thinks you deserve a chance.'

Wulfric nodded, trying to work out what this meant for his plans. How long would the Intelligenciers look for him? Months? Years?

Dal Rhenning appeared at Jagovere's shoulder.

'Glad to see you up and about,' dal Rhenning said. 'We were getting worried that knock to the head would be the end of you.'

'I'm fine,' Wulfric said. 'Thank you. What happens now?'

Dal Rhenning shrugged. 'Enjoy the voyage. We drill the men twice a day and you're welcome to join in. The sailors run the ship. We're merely passengers.'

'But after? When we get to Esta…'

'Estranza,' Jagovere said.

'Estranza. What happens when we get there?'

'Well,' dal Rhenning said, 'we have a contract to fulfil with the Duke of Torona, and we'll be marching south as soon as we make landfall. You're welcome to join us or you can take a ship back to Ruripathia—or anywhere else of your choosing. You'll need money for that, though, and judging by the way you're standing I don't have much hope of anyone making a sailor of you to pay your way. I presume Jagovere has filled you in on your… situation at home?'

Wulfric nodded. Being taken ever farther from his goal was frustrating, and he could feel anger start to boil in his gut. If he could not go back straightaway with any hope of settling the Blood Debts, how else might he spend the time?

'What's your contract?'

'My company of soldiers is serving in the Duke of Torona's army for the campaigning season,' dal Rhenning said. 'A few months, a bit of fighting, and you'll be able to go wherever you want—home by then, like as not—with a bit of coin in your purse. Looks to me like you've accidentally ended up on Jorundyr's Path after all.'

Wulfric nodded slowly, the idea becoming ever more attractive.

✵

## ADALHAID

Although the Markgraf had always been kind to Adalhaid, being summoned to his office made her uneasy—like when she had been naughty as a child and knew she was about to be punished. He didn't keep her waiting long, and his private secretary brought her in with a genial smile on his face. She couldn't think of any wrongdoing on her part, but had no idea what the summons could be for.

'I understand you've applied to the university,' the Markgraf said. He leaned back in his chair and arched his fingers in front of his face.

The window behind him looked out over the palace gardens, which Adalhaid had always found distracting. Petr and Aenlin were playing out there with children of other noble families. To be the playmate of the future Markgraf or Markgrafin was a highly sought after accolade for any infant. The thought made her smile. The Markgraf had not yet revealed which of the twins was the older, making the speculation and attached gambling something of a sport at court. Some said he was waiting to see which of them he thought most fit for the task. She liked the idea that a woman could rule in the south. Indeed, Ruripathia was ruled by a princess. In the Northlands, it was ever the First Warrior who was in charge, and although he was elected and was forced to retire when he could no longer lead by example, the First Warrior was always a 'he'. She returned her attention to the question at hand.

'I have, my lord.'

'You're a free woman, and the choice is yours to make,' the Markgraf said. 'Indeed, it's to be applauded, to seek to make more of oneself, and I've always been aware of how bright you are. I'm keen that some of that might rub off on Petr and Aenlin. I hope this doesn't mean you're planning on leaving us?'

'No, my lord. I've looked at it carefully and I believe I'll be able to continue with my duties here while I'm studying.'

'I'm glad,' he said. 'Petr and Aenlin would be distraught without you. After their mother's death, I would hate them to lose another person for whom they care so deeply.'

'I care very deeply for them too, my lord. They're wonderful children.'

He smiled wistfully. Adalhaid knew that his wife's death had been equally hard on him.

'As you'll be staying, I'm only too happy to give you this letter of recommendation. I'd give it anyway, but with regret. I expect it will ease the application process significantly.' He smiled at what could only be taken as an understatement and handed her the wax-sealed envelope addressed to the chancellor of the university. 'I've instructed the nannies and other governesses to help in accommodating your new schedule. Don't hesitate to let me know if there are any difficulties.'

※

## WULFRIC

At first the gentle roll of the deck had been an obstacle to test his agility. He knew he would not best it until he regained some strength, so he found out where the galley was, then stumbled, tripped, and tumbled his way there. He ate his fill and more besides, it having been so many days since he had eaten a proper meal. It had sat in his stomach for only a few minutes. As he was returning to the deck, a wave of nausea overcame him.

A sailor passed by and stopped when he caught a glimpse of Wulfric's face. 'If you're gonna chuck, do it over the side. Havin' to clean up your own puke makes it worse, and we ain't doin' it for you.'

Wulfric was in no mood to argue. He made his best speed toward the bulwark surrounding the deck and looked out into the swirling, frothy mess of the confused sea. He felt his head spin. His stomach tightened, his tongue stiffened, and after several long, agonising retches, his stomach was empty again.

Throwing up had the immediate effect of easing his nausea, but it was not long in returning. Quite why any man would choose a life at sea was beyond Wulfric. It was heartening to see that he was not the only one afflicted, as a half dozen other men of the company lined the bulwark, either pitching the contents of their bellies over the side or looking like they wished they would. The sailors, on the other hand, went about their duties as though they had not a care in the world. Surefooted and immune to the sickness, some deigned to laugh or make an encouraging remark as they passed the afflicted. It gave Wulfric hope that the misery would ease, but for the time being, prison and execution in Ruripathia seemed like the more attractive option.

'Can't be much left in there,' said a voice from behind Wulfric.

He had spent so long doubled over the bulwark that his ribs hurt, not to mention his stomach, from all the violent contractions. How it remained inside him after all it had been through was something of a mystery.

'Doubt there is,' Wulfric said, turning and leaning back against the bulwark. Jagovere was standing there, and for a moment Wulfric was struck by how much like a younger version of dal Rhenning he looked.

Jagovere raised an eyebrow when Wulfric turned to face him, and Wulfric belatedly wiped his face. His beard had been a mess beforehand, tangled with dirt and blood, and he knew it made for a disgusting sight with vomit added to the mix. The thought of trying to shave and tidy it up while on board the constantly moving ship was equally unappealing, though. It could wait until he reached wherever they were going.

'It gets easier. A day should have you over the worst of it.'

'It hasn't for them,' Wulfric said, indicating the men lining the bulwark farther down.

Jagovere shrugged. 'Positive thinking,' he said. 'Anyhow, it's time to start earning your keep. The Graf has asked me to speak with you about joining the Company properly. You'll have to sign the treasurer's roll first. You'll get standard pay—ten florins a day—and we'll billet you with my squadron, the heavies—the heavy cavalry. Northlanders have a reputation for being good at that, so I hope you can live up to it. You'll need to see the quartermaster for clothes and mess kit. Armour and weapons can wait until we land. If you're done saying goodbye to your lunch, we can see the treasurer now.'

# CHAPTER 8

RODULF

RODULF ROLLED GENTLY from side to side with the movement of his horse, and scanned the forest for signs of his men. They were southern mercenaries. Not cheap, but his short-term expense would lead to long-term gain. That this was Ambassador dal Ruedin's way of testing him went without saying. He intended to pass it with flying colours. He had split the men into two groups to work their way through the forest on either side of the road, creating a protective screen against ambushers. Attacks were usually no more than a few harassing arrows fired by unknown bowmen, but they had killed a half-dozen soldiers over the past few months, which the southerners did not like.

Rodulf rode with several more men well behind the wagons, far away from any ambush but close enough to know if one was taking place and counter-attack. Attacking the southern soldiers seemed to be the new sport of choice for Northlanders. Leondorf inviting the southerners across the river had made them unpopular with their neighbours, and the silver convoys, skirting Leondorf's northern border, were always an attractive and soft target.

He could have stayed at home and organised the escorts from there, but he thought it important to show he could be a man of action when it was required. None of the other councilmen would last an hour in the saddle, and it was a useful way to separate himself from them. Rodulf was the only one who could lead both inside the Great Hall and out of it, and he wanted to make that fact obvious to dal Ruedin.

As he rode in silence, he continued to scan the forest. Occasionally he caught a glimpse of one of his men, but for the most part he saw nothing. The progress was ponderously slow, limited as it was by the great ox wagons that would haul the silver ore back to Leondorf once they were loaded at the mine.

He wondered how many times dal Ruedin would require him to do this before he was satisfied that, in choosing Rodulf, he would not be destroying his own reputation. Along that narrow forest road, all the advantages lay with the attacker. He could see why the soldiers all hated this duty. Every time they went out with the wagons, they were rolling the dice, and now Rodulf was doing likewise.

❅

## Adalhaid

There were larger universities in Ruripathia, and better ones, but Adalhaid needed to earn a living if she hoped to continue her studies. There were few better jobs available to her than governess to the Markgraf's children, so Elzburg University was where she would go.

The university was not far from the palace and she made her way there while Petr and Aenlin were having their lunch. She had spent a very happy year there, studying for and earning a diploma in the Arts. A degree was a significant step up from that, and the prospect of it made her nervous.

The foyer was a grand hall of marble and quiet. The only sounds were muted whispers and footfalls as students and academics passed through. Students for a lower qualification used more modest buildings at the rear of the campus, so she had only been in the foyer on a handful of occasions. It was imposing. Intimidating. So much stone reaching so high overhead. That such things could be built took her breath away.

She looked around nervously as she tried to remember where to go. She spotted a clerk manning the ancient-looking wooden counter tucked into an alcove, and approached. The humourless attendant looked over her paperwork and directed her to the appropriate professor. They would consider her application and sign off on it or refuse. If the former, she would have to return to the admissions office to be registered. If the latter, she would have to reconsider her future.

Away from the grand halls and lecture theatres, the university was a warren of corridors and passages leading to offices and study rooms where one could easily get lost. She eventually found the appropriate office halfway down a dim corridor, and took a deep breath before knocking.

'Come.'

She turned the handle, angry with herself for feeling so nervous. Having spent so long placing the university atop a pedestal, it was difficult not to question her ability to keep up with what would be expected of her. She clutched her bundle of transcripts and reference letters to her chest, and walked in.

The office was small, but bright compared to the corridor from which she had just come. A tall, narrow sash window filled the room with light. A heavily jowled professor sat hunched over a desk, his threadbare academic gown stretched over shoulders that were now too corpulent for it.

'What can I do for you?' he said. The tone implied that he would rather do nothing at all.

'I was told to speak to you regarding admission for the coming academic year.'

He frowned when he heard her accent. She had been the only Northlander in her diploma course. For all she knew, she might be the only Northlander on the campus. The only one not mucking out the stables or carrying out night-soil buckets, at least.

'For what course?'

'The Arts,' Adalhaid said. 'I already hold a diploma in them from this university. I have my transcripts and letters of reference here.' She proffered them across the desk, and he took them from her with such disregard that she wondered if he would even look at them.

'Name?'

'Adalhaid Steinnsdottir.'

'Adalhaid, daughter of Steinn,' the professor murmured absently as he leafed through her paperwork. He chuckled to himself and shook his head as he looked at each page, before pausing. 'A first class diploma?' He looked at her with a bushy grey eyebrow raised.

She nodded. He frowned, and continued to regard her for a moment before returning to the papers. He stopped again and moved his head closer to one of the pages so that his nose was almost touching it.

'The Markgraf?'

'Yes,' Adalhaid said. 'I have the privilege of being governess to his children.'

'Governess?'

'Yes. Governess,' Adalhaid said, with an edge to her voice.

The professor chewed his lip for a moment before handing the papers back to her. He drew a sheet of paper from a drawer, dipped his pen and began writing, the scratching sound of the copper nib on the coarse page providing a melody to his wheezing breaths. He surveyed what he had written before sprinkling the page with pounce with a flourish that did not befit a man of his size. He handed her the dusty sheet.

'Your admission paper, accepted and signed,' he said. 'Take it to the department clerk in the admissions office. He will give you your lecture and tutorial timetables.'

Adalhaid breathed a sigh of relief. She was under no illusion that anything other than the Markgraf's letter of reference had secured her admission, but she would accept that. Once she was in the door, she would succeed or fail on merit alone. You couldn't hear a Northland accent in a written exam paper.

❁

## RODULF

Rodulf didn't feel much relief on arriving at the mine without incident—he was in the middle of the wilderness, miles from any comfort—but he was curious to see the place that was producing so much silver. It was in the foothills to the northeast of Leondorf, where the hills were starting to become mountains and the trees gave way to crags and rock faces.

A tall palisade had been built in a semicircle, with one such rock face at its back. There were several soldiers visible at the top, all armed with crossbows. The mine was tucked away safely behind it.

Rodulf fought to hide his agitation. They were at their most vulnerable as they waited to be allowed in, and the process was taking far longer than he liked. A challenge was issued, and the correct response given before the gate was opened, and finally the whole procession entered the enclosure.

He looked around with the same expression of disdain the southern noblemen seemed so fond of before dismounting. He needed to practice it, since he would soon be joining their ranks. There were a number of wooden buildings within, and a large, gaping hole in the rock face. The sound of hammering echoed up from deep within and Rodulf felt a shiver run through him at the thought of being stuck down there in the dark for hours at a time.

There was not a moment to be wasted as workmen immediately started to load sacks onto the wagons. Rodulf had thought they would at least be offered a hot meal, but that did not appear to be the case. He walked over to the pile of sacks and opened one. It was full of dull grey chunks of rock. He took one out and studied it. It sparkled in the light, and Rodulf realised that it contained a silver florin's worth of precious metal at least. He looked back at the pile of sacks and was astounded by the wealth that lay there before him—even more so when he considered a similar sized load was brought south every month.

❈

## Aethelman

The walk to the Hermitage was longer and more difficult than Aethelman remembered—but he had been a young man the last time he'd done it, many years before. It was not intended to be difficult to get there, but it was remote and the paths were overgrown.

He stopped to take the complex in when it finally came into view, nestled in a valley with the High Places stretching up behind it. There had been some alteration to the grey stone buildings, parts that he remembered gone, parts that he did not recall. It was a place of constant change.

Aethelman felt a flash of nostalgia as he looked at the monastery. He had stopped in almost the same place all those years before when his father and his own village's priest had accompanied him. Passing through the Hermitage's gates was the last time he had seen either of them. He searched within for any feeling of regret. It was there, but small, and in a distant corner. He had missed his parents, but their sending him to the Hermitage on the priest's recommendation—Aethelman could no longer remember his name—was the best choice for him, and for them. He was one of nine children, and his parents struggled to provide for them all. Aethelman's talents had manifested themselves early on. The priesthood had given him a life of purpose he could never have hoped for had he remained at home, and his departure had taken some of the burden from his family. Was it selfish of him to rarely wonder what lives his siblings had led? The life of a priest was longer than that of a normal man—their connection to the Fount seemed to imbue them with greater vitality—and it saddened him to realise that they would all be long dead. The thought had never occurred to him before.

He continued on, remembering the nerves he had experienced that first time. They had built with each step, and he'd thought he was going to be ill by the time he reached the gate. Life in the Hermitage had been good, however, his fear a waste of energy. He had met Aesa within minutes of arriving, and fallen in love within hours. He had not thought of her for years—not because he had forgotten her, but pushing her from his thoughts made the hole her absence left within him seem smaller. Never gone, however.

For Aethelman, she and the Hermitage were one and the same, and he could keep her from his thoughts no longer. Her laughter would ever echo in its corridors, her scent ever-present in its air. He thought of her smiling face, and felt a warmth and happiness he had not known in decades. He searched within himself for regret once again, and found it easily this time, for it dominated the place deep within his core. What would the monastery be like now without her to illuminate it?

He reached the gates and knocked on the door without any of the hesitation he'd had when a child. A brown-robed acolyte opened the door and stepped back when he saw Aethelman's grey robes. There was little of value at the Hermitage to make robbery or assault worth the stain it would leave on a man's soul. Great tales were told of the Grey Priests' martial prowess, that they did not carry weapons because they did not need them, but it was a misdirection. They did not need weapons because the legend of their prowess was so great. That it was a lie had never been called into question. No one wished to risk death and immediate damnation for attacking a priest. That threat was as great a weapon as any amount of combat skill.

'May Birgyssa guide you,' Aethelman said to the young acolyte.

'May she show you favour,' the boy said. 'We saw you coming up the road. The rector will receive you once you've had time to wash and have something to eat. A room has been prepared for you.'

Aethelman nodded in thanks. He had not been back since leaving on his Search, and it felt strange to be treated with the respect due to a senior member of their order. It did not seem so long ago that he had been the one wearing the brown robes, bowing and scraping to those in grey. He only hoped the young men and women were better cooks than he had been.

The boy led him into a large building that Aethelman remembered well from his days there. It contained all the guest quarters, as well as the refectory. Aethelman could smell cooking, and his stomach rumbled in protest. He was so hungry he couldn't care less if the current acolytes knew the top of a cook pot from its bottom.

The acolyte led him to the room that had been prepared. A large jug of steaming hot water sat by the washbasin on the counter. Aethelman smiled—he had not once seen hot water anywhere other than the kitchen and refectory when he was an acolyte. Training at the Hermitage was intended to prepare the young acolytes for the hardships of life as an itinerant priest.

'Hot food is available in the refectory whenever you are ready,' the acolyte said as he retreated toward the door.

'And then the rector,' Aethelman said, finishing the boy's sentence for him.

The acolyte nodded and closed the door as he left. Aethelman could remember how in awe he had been of the priests who had called in to the Hermitage from time to time. He wondered at the places they had seen, and the things they had experienced on the road. The world had been a great mystery to him then, as it likely was for the young acolyte who had shown him to his room. Now it held few surprises for Aethelman. The Fount Stone was the only mystery that concerned him. It was his quest—the one that would define his life, and probably his last.

# CHAPTER 9

## THE MAISTERSPAEKER

IT OCCURRED TO the Maisterspaeker that he had not thought to look around for Wulfric when he came down to the taproom. He was so caught up in his tale he had all but forgotten about his reason for being there. He was not ashamed to admit he was coming to his favourite part of the story, the part he had witnessed first-hand and helped to shape. The telling of it breathed fresh life into those moments long past and, for a time, could make him forget the years between then and now, forget the ache in his knees and elbows, and the old wounds that reminded themselves to him on a cold day. It made him feel like Jagovere the young soldier again, not the old teller of tales that he was.

He paused for a moment and scanned the crowd. It would be just like Wulfric to remain silent and watch, and only later spend hours picking out anything he felt was inaccurate in the story. The Maisterspaeker couldn't count the number of times he had explained that just as some facts did not warrant inclusion in the story, on occasion, some had to be embellished for dramatic effect. It didn't seem to lie well with Wulfric's Northland notions of honesty, but that didn't stop the Maisterspaeker.

Wulfric was not there. It took a couple of days to make the journey down to the borderlands, and the same for his message to go north. He knew Wulfric would waste no time coming once he received word, but it would still likely be another day or two at the earliest before Wulfric arrived.

The Maisterspaeker realised the audience were patiently waiting for him to continue, so he did.

❁

## WULFRIC

All the Company men ate with their respective units. Wulfric had taken his meals by himself, but now that he was on the paymaster's roll and was assigned to the heavies, he thought it only natural that he would eat with them.

They were not hard to spot. They were all big men, far bigger than the light horsemen who called themselves 'hoosars' and dressed in garishly coloured jackets. Most of them could have passed for Northlanders, which gave Wulfric a sense of comfort when he sat down at their mess table.

'You're the Northlander,' one of the men said. He was as big as Wulfric, but older, with cropped hair and dark stubble of the same length covering his face.

'I am,' Wulfric said.

'What are you doing sitting here?' the big man said, a hint of indignation in his voice.

'Jagovere said I was in the heavies, so here I am.'

The big man's brow furrowed. 'That's Banneret, or Captain, dal Borlitz. The likes of you don't get to call him by his given name.'

Wulfric glared at him. 'The likes of me?'

'Northland vermin,' the big man said, standing.

'Sit down, Enderlain,' another said to the big man. 'He's new. Give him a chance to learn the rules.'

'I'll give him the chance,' Enderlain said. He sat, but continued to stare at Wulfric.

'I'm Walt,' the other man said. 'Welcome to the heavies.'

'Wulfric.'

He got a nod in return, and started to eat. He picked up a chunk of meat, and bit away a mouthful.

'Bloody savage doesn't even know how to use a fork,' Enderlain said.

'Neither did you, when you first joined,' Walt said.

'Of course I did,' Enderlain said. 'Everyone knows Northlanders don't have the first clue about manners. If we're going to have to eat with him, we'll have to put some on him.'

'You going to put them on me?' Wulfric said, closing his fist.

'Enough. Both of you.' Jagovere had come down into the galley and glared at Wulfric and his new friend.

'Sergeant,' he said to Enderlain, 'this is one of your new cavalrymen. His name is Wulfric.' He turned to Wulfric. 'This is Sergeant Enderlain, your squad leader. I won't have fighting in my squadron. Is that clear?'

'Yes, Captain,' Enderlain said.

Jagovere glared at Wulfric. He nodded.

'Good,' Jagovere said. 'That's that dealt with. I'll leave you to it.'

Wulfric and Enderlain sat and resumed eating, but Wulfric could tell from the way Enderlain looked at him out of the corner of his eye that the matter was far from dealt with.

'I'm Sander,' another man said. 'That's Conrat, Walt, and Ewert.'

Wulfric nodded to him. As he sat under Enderlain's withering stare he felt like a young boy again, being introduced to Rodulf and his friends for the first time. He wasn't going to allow himself to be bullied. Wulfric glared back at Enderlain until he returned his attention to his food.

❀

# RODULF

Rodulf felt the tension leave his body for the first time when the road widened and he started to recognise features along its path. They were close enough to Leondorf to make an attack very unlikely. As the stress eased, he was surprised to find it replaced by disappointment. The ambassador would be pleased at the safe arrival of the wagon convoy, but an uneventful trip did little to enhance Rodulf's standing. Any fool could guide the wagons along a well-worn road. For the convoys to be of use, Rodulf needed to be able to show his ability to fight off an attack and safely bring in the cargo of silver.

He could feel the Stone in his pocket. At the very least it seemed to bring him luck, but he couldn't shake the thought, ridiculous though it seemed, that it did more than that. Perhaps it wasn't so far-fetched? Many Northlanders were convinced of the existence of the gods, and that their power dwelled in the realm of men. He had seen Aethelman do things he could not explain, which the old priest had attributed to the power of the gods. Could the Stone be connected to all of that? Could there actually be something to it? Might it have kept him safe on the convoy? It certainly hadn't been much use to its previous owner in that regard. He wondered if Aethelman might be able to give him the answers he sought, but felt panic grip his chest as soon as the thought came to him. The Stone was his secret. Something to be coveted and kept close. No one could know he had it— not even if they might be able to shed some light on it for him.

✤

## ANDHUN

Andhun sat on his porch and watched the ox wagons roll into town, Rodulf and his mercenaries forming the vanguard. He sat atop his horse with all the arrogance and swagger of one of the warrior class. They had done so much to redress that balance, and the sight of Rodulf brought back unwelcome memories. 'Warrior' was a word seldom heard now. The town's young men were training to be soldiers, soldiers who would be subordinate to the council. Or the feudal lord. Andhun would be damned if he'd let the one-eyed bastard take that.

He waved and smiled. It was not the done thing to reveal what he was truly thinking. Oswyn, who sat beside Andhun, did the same. From rival to unlikely friend, it was interesting and frightening how quickly the balance had shifted. Andhun knew he had blundered with the new ambassador, and had to make amends quickly. He could not allow Rodulf to capitalise on the mistake.

Seeing him ride into the village with an intact cargo was disappointing. A dark thought flashed through his mind, but he wasn't yet willing to resort to murder to achieve his aims. Not yet. There were other, tidier ways. Andhun was a wealthy man. He had almost convinced Oswyn to add his resources to ensuring Andhun, and not Rodulf, won the prize of Leondorf.

'Smug bastard, isn't he,' Oswyn said, when Rodulf was far enough away to be out of earshot.

'Always was. I almost regret the Strong Arm's boy is gone. He was the only one who could put Rodulf back in his place.'

'Pah. We're better off without him and his kind. Wulfric was a wild beast. Rodulf is only a viper. Dangerous, but easier to deal with.'

'And the ambassador?'

Oswyn shrugged. 'He thinks we're all ignorant bumpkins. Let him think that. We'll be rid of him just as quick. I'd rather he underestimate us than have our true measure.'

Andhun nodded. He was glad Oswyn's chances had been destroyed. He was shrewd, and would have been a tough adversary. Andhun wasn't sure he could have beaten him and Rodulf both. Now he would make an invaluable ally.

'If Donatoson is made lord, it will be bad for both of us,' Andhun said.

'It will,' Oswyn said.

'Success like that,' Andhun nodded to the heavy wagons wending their way toward the smelter on the other side of the village, 'will have him Baron of Leondorf before we know it. I'm the only one with a chance to beat him to it now.'

Oswyn grimaced, the skin on his face stretching to make him look even more skeletal. 'I reckon so,' he said, after a moment.

'You'll help me, then?'

'I will. But stopping One-Eye won't be reward enough.'

'If I rise, you'll rise with me,' Andhun said. 'High Chancellor, I think they are called in the south. Next most powerful man after the lord.'

'That could work,' Oswyn said.

'Might even be a title in it down the road for you too, if we can grow the territory.' Andhun would promise him the sun if that was what it took. Rodulf was too dangerous to deal with alone, and as rich as Andhun was he needed Oswyn's help.

'That would work even better,' Oswyn said, watching the last of the wagons pass out of sight.

'I think a bribe is the best way forward. I'll need a lot of coin to be sure.'

'A blade would be even better,' Oswyn said. 'I know a fellow in Elzburg. Born killer. I'm told he's killed dozens. Men, women, children. None of it's a problem for him. It'll be cheaper too.'

'A blade will put Rodulf out of the picture,' Andhun said, 'but it won't guarantee me the lordship. They might decide to send up one of their own if they see us falling about trying to kill each other.'

'The southerners hate this place. The silver's the only thing they like.'

'I'm sure they could find someone who would stick it.'

Oswyn nodded. 'Maybe so. A bribe then.'

'I think that's for the best. We can keep the blade as our fall-back.'

❈

## Aethelman

Aethelman had last knocked on the rector's door the evening before he went on his Search. The memory caused his heart to race as it had then. He had never thought himself prone to nostalgia, but since laying eyes on the Hermitage again, it had threatened to overwhelm him a number of times. The hallway outside was dim, lit only by a small lantern farther down the cut-stone wall, lending the moment an ominous feel.

'Enter.'

Aethelman did as he was bidden, feeling every bit the young acolyte, though now he would likely be far older than the rector.

The rector was indeed younger than Aethelman, although he could not be called a young man.

'Welcome, brother. What is your name?'

'Aethelman.'

'I am Rector Benegrim. What brings you back to the Hermitage?'

'I'm seeking out information, Rector.'

'Really?' Benegrim said. 'I expected that you wished to instruct here. I don't think I've encountered anyone returning for any other reason.'

'I'm afraid not. Not now, at least. It's something I would like to do, if the gods see fit to give me the time, but I have something else that I feel I must do first.'

The rector moved forward in his seat.

'The Search has been playing on my mind for a long time.' Aethelman couldn't bring himself to admit that he had found a Fount Stone. He didn't know what he was supposed to do, but knew he should have done more than he had. It was his great failing.

'I have to admit, since completing mine I've barely given it a second thought,' Benegrim said.

Aethelman smiled wryly. 'Each year, newly ordained priests are sent out on their Search to find Fount Stones but they are not, or at least were not in my day, told what to do with them if one is found.'

The rector smiled too, but in a way that made Aethelman feel he was being indulged. 'No one has seen one in living memory. Far longer, in fact.

I expect they are all long destroyed. It's the tradition and hardship of the Search that makes it significant, not the subject of it.'

'I realise that,' Aethelman said, 'but what if one *is* found? What then?'

'Well, I suppose they should bring it back here and the appropriate action could be taken.'

'Which is?'

The rector stared at him with a vacant expression.

'Exactly,' Aethelman said.

The rector smiled again. 'Come now. I hardly think it important. No one is going to find one. If any remain, they are so well hidden they are as good as destroyed. Generation after generation of priests have failed to turn one up. I am content to say our duty in that regard is satisfied.'

'Would you have any objection to me investigating it?'

'Of course not,' the rector said. 'You're a free man; neither I nor any other member of our priesthood may give you an order. You are an experienced priest. However, I would hate to see you waste your last years on a futile quest.'

Aethelman had expected him to say 'fool's errand', and appreciated Benegrim's tact.

'A man of your experience has much of value to share, and the contribution you could make here, helping to educate and prepare a new generation of priests, would be invaluable. I would ask you to think carefully on remaining.'

'I would like that,' Aethelman said, 'but my compulsion for this quest is… overwhelming.'

The rector nodded, his disappointment clear. 'Then by all means pursue it. Perhaps the gods have placed this compulsion in your soul. Who am I to question it? I will offer you what assistance I can, but I fear it will be limited. Have you given any thought to how you will proceed?'

'Yes, a great deal. But it hasn't brought me to a satisfactory plan. The Stones are little more than legend. Knowledge about them is even more… ephemeral. I realise there is not much here, but I hoped you would allow me to explore the more ancient parts of the monastery.'

'You're welcome to,' the rector said. 'I would warn you that some parts have not been visited in centuries, and may be dangerous.'

'I'm willing to take the risk,' Aethelman said.

'Very well. Then I'd recommend a conversation with the lore master. He might not be able to help, but it's a start. Most of the library's books come from the south. So little of our own knowledge and history is ever written down, but perhaps he will know something. Brother Gundaman is his name. Do you remember where the lore master's library is?'

Aethelman smiled. 'Assuming it hasn't been moved, I remember it very well.'

# CHAPTER 10

## ADALHAID

JUGGLING HER DUTIES at the palace, studying, and attending her lectures required careful time management, but Adalhaid coursed with excitement during her first few days of classes. Literature, music, art—all the refined aspects of southern culture were on the curriculum. These were the things the nobility wanted their children taught, and if she was to be more than a glorified child-minder, she would need a firm foundation in all of them. The act of learning came as joy to her, however, and she devoured every word of her lectures and spent every spare minute cloistered in the bowels of the university's library.

She did her best to keep to herself, unwilling to test the effect her Northlander accent would have on her fellow students. For some time, she had tried to cultivate a southern accent, or at least that of someone from the Ruripathian border, where the differences with her own were not so very great. It still felt forced, however, and she feared people would easily see through the deception. Until she had it perfected, every time she opened her mouth all she could think about was how the southerners would look down on her, irrespective of their ranking in class.

One fear she had held walking into the university on the first day proved to be misplaced, however. Her ability to keep up academically was never in question. Although they had only completed a handful of assignments, it brought her enormous satisfaction each time she looked at the grade on her paper, and her position in class, both marked with a '1'.

❋

## WULFRIC

Wulfric tossed and turned in his hammock. Adalhaid was dragged from the carriage. She was confused at first, not fully understanding what was to come. She was smart, she was calm, she was brave. She knew how to behave in a robbery. Coin and possessions are not worth a life. Then she realised they meant for more than that. Rape first, followed by slavery. She knew it before they intended her to. She became afraid for the first time. Wulfric could feel her fear, and it tore at his heart. He was watching, powerless to intervene, for even in his sleep he knew he was not really there.

She looked left and right, searching for a way of escape, but there was none open to her. She was smart. She knew it. Wulfric could hear the thoughts forming in her mind, and wanted to scream for her to stop. To scream 'let them do as they please, it doesn't matter', to promise that he would search her out and find her no matter where they took her, but he couldn't. He wept as he had when he was a small boy.

He watched her grab for the reaver's dagger. The reaver didn't expect it; she was always one step ahead of everyone else. Wulfric could feel the pressure of the point on her skin, hesitant at first, then stronger as her defiance grew, as her resolve to die a brave death with a blade in her hand overcame the fear of what might come after. Wulfric remained still and mute, an observer and nothing more, as his rage, anguish, and desire to intervene tried to tear him inside out.

His eyes opened to darkness, and the unfamiliar sound of creaking wood. He swayed from side to side, and it took him a moment to realise he was on the ship, in his hammock. The dream was too visceral to release him from its clutches even on waking, and he could still feel the pain. He had watched her die in his dreams a dozen times now. He wiped the wetness from his eyes and slipped out of his hammock, knowing he would not sleep again that night.

He stumbled with the roll of the ship as he walked to the companionway steps, bumping against the solid form of a body in a hammock.

'Watch where you're going, arsewipe.'

Wulfric recognised the voice. Enderlain.

'Fuck yourself,' Wulfric said, the residual anger he felt from his dream still coursing through his veins.

'Fuck myself?'

For a big man, he moved quickly, and in less time than it took to draw a breath, Enderlain was out of his hammock and standing before Wulfric.

'You need to learn your place, boy.'

Wulfric had not shied from a fight in many years, but few were the times he had hungered for one as much as he did in that moment.

'Call me "boy" again, and you'll be picking your teeth out of your arsehole.'

'You must be tired of living, *boy*, that's all I can say.'

'If you two arseholes keep mouthing off, neither one of you'll have to worry about living much longer.' A third voice from the darkness.

'Your hammocks or a long swim.' A fourth voice. 'Your choice.'

Wulfric looked around, his eyes having adjusted to the gloom. He could see the shapes of a number of men watching them from their hammocks. More than enough to make good on the threat.

'Another time, then,' Wulfric said.

'Look forward to it.'

❋

# AETHELMAN

Aethelman had acquired an everlasting light—called magelamps in the south—on his travels. They were magical in nature, but with the extermination of mages in the south there was no one left alive who knew how to make them. Each one was ancient and irreplaceable. They were sturdy and, if given basic care, seemed to be genuinely everlasting. There were a great many in existence and, although expensive, they were affordable if the need was great enough.

Aethelman's was small, a glass sphere that sat comfortably in the palm of his hand, but even at that size it would fetch a high price in the south. He valued it too highly to consider selling, however. It was the only thing he possessed worth passing on after his death, and he often wondered to whom he should leave it. They would likely find good use for it at the Hermitage, but it had been with him so long he preferred to think of it with someone whose life had been of importance to him. So many of them were already dead, it made his heart ache.

The lore master had been a waste of time. She knew nothing more about the Stones than Aethelman had been told when he was an acolyte. She had never even ventured beyond the currently occupied parts of the Hermitage. It struck Aethelman as odd that the person most steeped in the priesthood's ancient secrets and lore didn't have the curiosity to venture into the monastery's forgotten corners in search of knowledge. It was such a waste.

And so Aethelman walked a corridor that had likely not felt the feet of a human in centuries, with nothing but the small, radiant globe in the palm of his hand. It cast a bubble of light around him, and painted the cold stone walls with warmth. His footsteps echoed into the pitch darkness ahead of him, and his task suddenly felt overwhelming. What hope could a foolish old man have of discovering secrets that had been forgotten centuries before? Then again, what else was there for a foolish old man to do with his remaining years? He smiled and pressed on, listening as each footfall bounced between the walls and on to oblivion.

Before the Hermitage was built, there was a cavern on the site. It possibly remained somewhere below, or beyond, in the mountain. Aethelman wondered if he might find it, and if he did, what it might contain. It had been a place of refuge for a persecuted people, millennia ago. In the days before the Empire, ancient magisters had roamed the world, giving spiritual guidance and healing. They had practised magic in much the same way as the Grey Priests, seeing it as the influence of the gods expressed in the world of man. When the Empire grew, and along with it their sorcerers and priests, they sought to push out what had been there before them.

The ancient magisters fled their oppressors until they were too spent to run any longer. They took shelter in that great cavern and waited for the end, but it never came. The Imperial Mages—men and women who saw magic as a science, something to be studied, understood, and controlled—made it their mission to eradicate those who viewed it as something entirely different. Some people could clearly not bear the fact that others saw the world differently to the way they did. While the magisters waited in the cavern for the Imperials to come, they created tools to defend themselves. The Stones were one of those creations.

It was the ferocity of the warriors of the Northland tribes that stopped the Empire. Their armies reached the northern forests and could go no farther. Any that tried were never seen again. The Empire halted after several attempts, satisfied that they had swallowed up enough of the world. The Northmen could keep their forests and their old ways.

Grateful to the men and women who had saved them, the refugee magisters set about using their powers to care for the sick. The gods of the north were the same as the old, persecuted gods of the south, so they fit in perfectly. In a short time they became what was now known as the Grey Priests. They ventured forth among the people, tending to both body and soul. The cavern became a church, and then a monastery, and then the Hermitage, each new iteration built atop the old.

In all they did, they never forgot about the terrible measures they'd gone to in order to survive. The Fount Stones, weapons born of that desperation, had been let out into the world—given to those who had been daring enough to take the fight to the Empire. In an effort to undo this mistake, they made it a requirement for any person wishing to join their order to search the land for a year and a day before they could truly call themselves a Grey Priest.

It was possible the cavern didn't even exist, or if it had it might long since have been filled in. As with much of the rest of the Grey Priests' lore, this story was handed down orally. What was once a small, insignificant cave could easily have become a great cavern in the retelling. Apocryphal or not, Aethelman thought the story held at least a seed of truth. It made the cavern the obvious place to begin, although after such a long time, he doubted anything of worth would remain. As the cavern grew into a monastery, it seemed likely that anything of value would have been relocated. It didn't mean the end, however. There were plenty of old rooms and corridors that had remained shut up for centuries.

The light from his globe reached his first obstacle. The hallway before him was bricked up. Aethelman walked forward and traced along the seams in the masonry with his fingertips. Was the passage blocked to keep something in, or merely to seal an unused and derelict part of the monastery?

Aethelman was tempted to try and go through. His magic had always been strong at the Hermitage, stronger than it ever was anywhere else, but that might have merely been a boon of youth. Was smashing through a heavy stone wall beyond him now?

He placed his hand flat against the stone and took a deep breath, then hesitated. The Hermitage was a labyrinth of known and forgotten passages. He could seek a way around. He might regret wasting his energy in opening up the wall. Such effort took far longer to recover from than it once had. He smiled at the idea of opting instead for a path of lesser resistance.

# CHAPTER 11

ANDHUN

ANDHUN KNOCKED ON the ambassador's door. He looked about nervously, but was confident that Rodulf wouldn't be up and about so early. He and Oswyn had watched Rodulf stumble back to his house with a whore and a bottle when the tavern closed. He reckoned it gave them the morning to conduct their business, but the fact that Rodulf was sleeping off a debauch did not mean he didn't have spies lurking about the place. It was difficult not to be paranoid when plotting against someone as vicious as Rodulf.

Andhun jumped when the door opened. He took a breath and was greeted by a sour-faced servant who stared at him with disdain, but said nothing.

'I'd like to see the ambassador,' Andhun said, irritated at having to break the impasse with a man who was clearly beneath him.

'Do you have an appointment?'

'No. I'm a member of the council, and I need to talk with him urgently.'

'I'm afraid you'll need an appointment. The ambassador is a very busy man, and it's rather early.'

Andhun bit his lip with exasperation mingled with fear. He had already been standing at the doorstep, in full view of anyone who cared to look, for far too long. 'We're all busy men. You'll let me in to see him or I'll have the hide whipped off your back, you jumped up sout—'

'Show him in, Ruger.' The ambassador's voice came from the back of the house.

The servant smiled, his demeanour unaffected by Andhun's outburst. 'This way.'

He led Andhun through to the back of the house. It was decorated in the southern style, and showed far more refinement than Andhun's. He took note of several features he thought would improve his own home, although if everything went to plan he would be relocating to his newly built castle in the near future.

The ambassador was sitting at a large wooden desk. He watched as Andhun walked into the room. The servant disappeared silently.

'What's so urgent you've had to disturb me in my home?'

'There are some matters that I need to discuss with you in private,' Andhun said.

'My choice of who will be awarded the barony, perhaps?' dal Ruedin said in a fashion that left no doubt as to it being rhetorical.

'In short, yes,' Andhun said. He always felt more comfortable with a little small talk before cutting to the core of an issue.

'It's not looking good for you,' dal Ruedin said. 'A wild province like this needs a firm hand. A hard man comfortable with violence and action. You don't strike me as either. Men who are skilled with coin are useful, don't get me wrong, but in service. Not leadership.'

'I assure you, when it's called for I can be capable of a great deal.'

'I'm sure you can,' dal Ruedin said.

Andhun shifted on his feet, but it didn't elicit an offer to sit. 'Perhaps I can make the decision easier on you?'

'You want to escort the next silver convoy?' Dal Ruedin actually smiled.

Andhun laughed, comforted by the fact that they were finally getting down to business, something he considered himself highly skilled at. 'No, nothing like that. I had something altogether different in mind. Gold, in fact.' He and Oswyn had put together a sum few men would be able to turn a blind eye to, and certainly not a man who had to work for his living, like dal Ruedin.

'You mean to bribe me?' Dal Ruedin said.

'Everything has its price,' Andhun said. 'How much does a barony cost? I'm sure you're eager to leave this place, and get back home. I can help that happen all the sooner.'

'I left home when I was four years old,' dal Ruedin said. 'Fencing schools, the Academy at Brixen, the war against the Ostians. I haven't had a home for more than a few months at a time. As for family? I'll take a campaign tent and a willing whore over either.'

'That still doesn't answer my question,' Andhun said, the sickening feeling that the deal was slipping away from him forming in his stomach. 'Your price?'

'Fat people disgust me, Andhun,' dal Ruedin said. 'I didn't think I could find you any more disgusting, but here I am, surprised. Trying to bribe one of the Markgraf's officials? I don't even have to convene a trial for that. You there, Ruger?'

'I am, my lord,' came the reply from outside.

'Have the sergeant of the watch called to take Andhun to the village square.' He turned his gaze back to Andhun. 'Twelve lashes is my price.'

'Lashes? You can't—'

'I can. I have. I suggest you get out before you make it worse for yourself. Irritate me again and twelve lashes will seem like a sweet mercy.'

✳

## WULFRIC

'In pairs,' Enderlain shouted.

All the men formed up into pairs. Everyone avoided Wulfric's gaze and stayed well clear, leaving him standing on his own, just like his first day of training in the glade at Leondorf. At first he thought they were afraid of him, but he quickly realised it was something very different.

'You're with me,' Enderlain said.

Wulfric raised his eyebrows.

'Last man standing gets an extra ration of ale,' Enderlain said. 'I don't want anyone getting sent to the infirmary, so as soon as you're knocked down, you're beat.' He turned his gaze back to Wulfric. 'Except for us, that is.'

Standing next to him in full daylight, Wulfric realised how big he was, both a fraction taller and considerably wider. It wasn't something he was used to, even in the Northlands.

'Let's see what you're made of, Northlander.'

✳

## Jagovere

Jagovere made his way toward the upper deck at the rear of the ship to join the Graf. By rights he should have been taking part in the training, but with the Estranzan coast drawing ever nearer, he was under pressure to complete a huge amount of paperwork to ensure their logistical requirements were met when they got ashore.

'Skiving off, Captain?' dal Rhenning said, when Jagovere reached the top of the steps leading to the upper deck.

'I wish. Too much to arrange before we make landfall.'

'How's the Northlander fitting in?'

'About as well as I would expect,' Jagovere said. 'Which is to say, not at all.'

'Give him time,' dal Rhenning said.

'I don't know why we're bothering. Saving him from the headsman's block more than repaid his attempt to help you on the road.'

'There's a good, brave heart in the lad, but right now it's full of emotion that will lead him to nothing but trouble—and, like as not, straight to the headsman we saved him from. You benefitted from someone giving you a chance, as I recall.'

'Pay a visit to the Northlands twenty-odd years ago?' Jagovere regretted saying it as soon as the words left his mouth.

Dal Rhenning's face darkened. 'No. He's not one of mine.' He paused a moment before continuing. 'I did right by your mother, and you. I could have as easily turned my back. There are plenty who would have.'

'I'm sorry,' Jagovere said.

'It's all right. Situations like ours are never easy. I only wish I'd found out about you earlier.'

'All's well that ends well.'

'That boy has seen tragedy. I can see it in his eyes. I'll help him if I can,' dal Rhenning said, 'but even my patience is limited. If he can't settle in with the others, we'll cut him loose.'

They fell silent as they watched the men start their exercises, their eyes on Wulfric and Enderlain. Wulfric was almost as tall as Enderlain—the biggest man in the Company—who had the advantage of experience and the lean muscular bulk that came from years of soldiering.

They circled each other for a moment, and Jagovere felt a pang of regret that he had not chosen to join in. He had no enthusiasm for the pile of paper waiting for him in his cabin. Enderlain made a probing jab, but Wulfric easily moved out of its way. Jagovere had seen Enderlain fight many times, both in training and when the stakes were far higher. When he chose his moment, Jagovere knew the fight would be over quickly.

Enderlain pounced forward but, with a burst of speed that surprised Jagovere, Wulfric was out of the way. Enderlain appeared to be equally surprised. Wulfric snapped a fist out at Enderlain so fast it was little more than a blur, but the cracking sound it caused could be heard from the upper deck. Enderlain roared and raised his hands to his face, which was splashed with blood from what Jagovere assumed was a broken nose.

The young Northlander casually circled around Enderlain, then swept his legs out from under him with a kick. He paused to survey his handiwork for a moment, then reached down and grabbed Enderlain by the scruff, his fist ready to deal more punishment. He hesitated, however, and turned to cast a glance toward the upper deck. Even from the quarter deck, Jagovere could see the fire in Wulfric's eyes, and the manic smile on his face. It sent a chill through him.

'Enough,' Jagovere shouted.

Wulfric held his pose for a moment, giving Jagovere time to think steel might be called for, but he dropped Enderlain to the deck and stood straight, a look of satisfaction on his face.

'Gods alive,' dal Rhenning said, 'he's quick. I've not seen Enderlain dealt with like that before.'

'Neither have I,' Jagovere said. 'He won't be pleased about it.' Trouble in his squadron was the last thing Jagovere needed.

'Enderlain's a big boy. I'm sure he's had his nose bloodied before, and if he hasn't it's not before time. He'll know to be more careful in future.'

'I hope so,' Jagovere said. 'Did you see the expression on the Northlander's face?'

'The joy of battle is strong in him, I won't deny that,' dal Rhenning said.

'*Joy of battle* is a delicate way of putting it, don't you think?'

Dal Rhenning grunted. 'We have time to settle Wulfric down. I'll have a talk with him.'

'The perils of a charitable heart,' Jagovere said.

Dal Rhenning laughed. 'It wouldn't be my first error of judgement.'

✸

# Wulfric

Men stood when dal Rhenning stepped onto the mess deck. He waved at them to sit and made his way along the mess groups until he found the one he was looking for. Wulfric had watched the Graf's progress through the mess as he ate and saw the deference the men showed him, even when he had ordered them to ignore him.

'Wulfric,' he said.

It came as a surprise that it was him the Graf wanted to speak with. Since Wulfric had woken, dal Rhenning had only spoken to him once, becoming a distant figure of authority.

Wulfric put down his spoon and stood. 'Graf.'

'I wonder if I might have a word with you. I thought we could take a turn on the main deck.'

He started for the companionway without waiting for an answer. Wulfric hastily shovelled the last two spoonsful of food into his mouth, and followed dal Rhenning up the companionway steps.

They walked in silence until they reached the bulwark, and dal Rhenning took a long look out at the horizon.

'I've never taken to sea travel,' he said. 'I've travelled countless miles over the ocean, but give me a good horse any day.'

'Can't say I've taken to it either,' Wulfric said.

'It's not my habit to pry into affairs that aren't my own, and I won't ask you any questions that you won't want to answer, but I can't help noticing that there's an anger in you, Wulfric. A rage. I've seen it twice now. When those soldiers tried to arrest you in Wetlin, and again when you broke Enderlain's nose.'

Wulfric had no idea how to respond, so he remained silent.

'Your willingness to help a stranger on the road spoke volumes about you also. Were it not for that, I may well have already written you off as too great a liability. You're a young man, and I wonder if you're at a balance point in your life—the point where your actions over the next few months or years will define the man you become. A kind-hearted, brave man who would help a stranger and risk great peril to do so, or a bloodthirsty savage who lives for killing.'

It occurred to Wulfric that dal Rhenning, and everyone else in the Company, made their living by the sword. He opened his mouth to speak, but dal Rhenning cut him off.

'I know what you're thinking. Criticism about violent behaviour from a man who's spent his life soldiering.' He laughed. 'There's a difference, though. Subtle perhaps, but being a professional soldier means setting boundaries. You may fight for a living, may even enjoy the adventure and excitement it brings, but you should never allow yourself to descend to savagery. It's an easy slope to fall down, and many have. There are mercenary companies more famed for rapine and pillage than fighting. You can choose not to be like that. You'll be a better man for it. You'll sleep better at night too, that I can promise you.'

'I'll think on it,' Wulfric said. 'I'll do my best to pick the right course.'

'Good,' dal Rhenning said. 'You've a good heart, and a strong arm, Wulfric. Use them wisely. Become a good man.' He patted Wulfric on the back and started to walk away, then stopped.

'And try not to break any more of my soldiers. I'll need them when we get to Estranza.'

He chuckled and continued on his way, leaving Wulfric to dwell on his words. He considered what dal Rhenning had said, and thought back to the day he and the others had attacked Rasbruck. The soldiers had butchered people, while he and the other warriors had stopped. The thought that he was in danger of becoming like the soldiers horrified and disgusted him. Would he act the same way now? He couldn't deny the anger that had been his constant companion since Adalhaid's death. At first he had welcomed it—Jorundyr's Gift seemed to come to him so much more easily than it had before. But now, if dal Rhenning had noticed it, he feared he was destined to become one of those mindless berserkir who were as much a danger to friend as enemy, as Aethelman had warned him. It did not seem so simple as to merely make a choice. How could he direct himself down the better path?

# CHAPTER 12

AETHELMAN

AETHELMAN HAD ALWAYS known the older parts of the Hermitage were a maze. He had gotten lost on more than one occasion when he was an acolyte, and smiled when he recalled that excuse had been used more than once when he had lost himself on purpose. He had rarely been alone when that had happened.

When he concentrated hard enough, he could hear her laugh, smell her, feel her breath on his skin. Aesa. Coming back to the Hermitage had stirred memories and feelings that had been dormant for decades. He had sacrificed much, and in moments like that, he wondered if it was all worthwhile.

He had ventured far beyond any part of the Hermitage he recognised, and was relieved the passages on the new route were clear. He left a faint trail of magic as he walked, an invisible trail he would be able to follow back out. The stone dampened magic, as it always did, and the deeper into the Hermitage he went, the more isolated he felt, his small tendril representing a tenuous connection to something he could usually feel rushing all around him.

He reached a flight of stairs and went down them, his knees and hips protesting with each one. The air grew colder and damper as he went, and he felt encouraged that he was going in the right direction. That presumed there *was* a right direction. After all the sacrifice and service he had given, the gods would surely not be so cruel as to see him spend his last days on a wild goose chase?

His faithful little globe of light continued to illuminate the way, its warm glow glistening against the damp stone surrounding him. The smooth sheen changed and the reflection became broken, but Aethelman had gone several paces before he realised.

He stopped and looked closely at the wall. It was etched with runes. Aethelman's heart jumped. The Grey Priests favoured speech and memory over writing and paper, but it seemed it had not always been so. Reading and writing were of course studied, but written paper records faded and rotted to nothing. The chore of re-transcribing them was considered too great a drain of time for knowledge that should be in the head of every priest. There was sense in it, but the myth of the Fount Stones was an unfortunate consequence.

Runes were a very different thing, however. They were timeless, but an old practise that had long since fallen out of favour. Aethelman was one of the few priests who could read the more recent runes, which in themselves had developed to a form far removed from their ancestors. The older ones were as much a mystery as the Stones.

He held up his small lamp and traced his fingers along the chiselled runes. His eyes flitted to ones he recognised, seeking out a safe harbour in the unknown script. There were more he could read than not—the runes must have been relatively recent—but the relief led to quick disappointment. It was the story of a priest who had brought succour to a village scourged by a mysterious plague. While interesting, and possibly even of importance, it was not of any use to him.

He shook his head and moved on down the corridor. Were he rector, he would send teams of acolytes down into the bowels of the Hermitage to recover as much knowledge as they could. The priesthood's itinerant ways had cost them as much as they had given, and he was coming to realise a better approach was needed to preserve the wealth of experience each priest gathered over his lifetime. Passing on their lessons by word of mouth was too prone to error. More than that, it was a step backwards from the time when their forebears had spent hours with hammer and chisel.

Every so often he stopped and took another look, but of the Fount Stones there was no mention. There were remedies, adventures, and dedications to various gods, but no legends and no reference to the Search. On Aethelman went, down dark corridors and ancient staircases.

❧

## Andhun

'Be careful, you fool.' Andhun squirmed in pain beneath the ministrations of the physician.

'You'll have to hold still, councilman,' the physician said.

Andhun screeched in pain. His back was covered in angry red gashes left by the flogging. 'It feels like you're rubbing salt into them.'

'There *is* some salt in the poultice. It helps to clean the wound.'

'Isn't there anything else you can do? The old priest here was able to take the pain away just by looking at it. Can't you do anything like that?'

The physician took a step back. 'If you're referring to magic, I can assure you that I will do nothing of the sort. That kind of savagery may be allowed in these parts, but no civilised man would have anything to do with it. My poultices are the product of years of experience and testing, and I can assure you the making of several of them is taught in more than one university.'

Andhun let out a long sigh. 'Get on with it then.'

The image of Rodulf's face as he watched the flogging popped into Andhun's mind. As painful as his day had been, it was nothing compared to the suffering he would experience if Rodulf was made baron. Leaving Leondorf would be the only option open to him, which he did not want to consider. Whatever else one could say about Leondorf, it was his home, and the only place he could ever hope to thrive. In the south he would fade into the crowd. Even if the barony was beyond his reach, he had to ensure that Rodulf did not get it. Oswyn's friend with the blade seemed like the obvious course.

❧

## Wulfric

Wulfric lay in his hammock. There was little else to do when not training, but it was a struggle to keep his thoughts away from things that distressed him. There was a tap on the cloth, startling him.

'Captain dal Borlitz wants to see you.'

The messenger turned and left without another word. Wulfric was starting to feel like a naughty child, and he didn't enjoy the experience. Even those who had been civil to him were giving him a wide berth since he'd broken the sergeant's nose. Jagovere's summons was no doubt to mete out some punishment.

He rolled out of his hammock and headed for Jagovere's cabin. He knocked on the door and entered on command.

'Sit.'

Wulfric was tired of being obstinate. He was tired of everything to do with his situation, so he sat without protest.

'You're going to be a problem for me, aren't you?'

Wulfric shrugged.

'If it were up to me I'd have you pitched over the side, do not doubt me. But I have my orders and I follow them.' Dal Borlitz studied Wulfric for a moment. 'You've impressed everyone with the way you dropped Enderlain, so if that was your intention, congratulations. Impressed doesn't mean accepted, or liked. I don't need men put in the infirmary in training. We are all comrades here, and may have to depend on one another for our lives when we get to the fighting. Together we make something far more than the individual sum of us. Remember that. Besides, we're a commercial company and need every man fit for the field when we make landfall. Until we do, you can take on Enderlain's duties.'

Wulfric opened his mouth to protest, but Jagovere cut him off.

'You've already shown everyone that you can fight. The extra duties will show them you can work as well. If you can do both, they'll respect you, and when they do it won't matter a damn that you're a Northlander.'

❧

## WULFRIC

Wulfric couldn't recall having seen Enderlain scrubbing the deck, but it must have been how he had spent the majority of his day, as it was now what Wulfric spent most of his doing. Quite how two black eyes and a broken nose prevented Enderlain from rubbing a piece of stone back and forth over the deck planks was a mystery. Perhaps his pride had been too badly injured to cope with such a menial task. Perhaps the entire thing was a fiction to allow Jagovere to punish him without actually doling out a direct punishment. His hands were red-raw from the abrasive stone, and his knees and back ached so badly he nearly wished they had flogged him.

The ship's crew largely kept apart from the mercenaries, but Wulfric's task brought him into proximity with them. He watched them go about their business of running the ship, barefoot with hands covered in sticky rigging tar. A young man, a few years younger than Wulfric, was securing a rope to a cleat on the bulwark. His hands were slow and lacking the practised speed the older sailors showed, but he was humming a tune under his breath and had a relaxed smile on his face. Wulfric wondered what had led him to choose a life at sea.

Two other sailors walked over. One of them shoved the novice sailor to the side and inspected his knot. Both the humming and smile disappeared.

'Made a right pig's ear of this, you have,' said one. He was of average height, but strong and sinewy-looking, like most of the crew. 'Is there anything you can do right?'

Wulfric looked over. There were a half dozen identical cleats along the bulwark, each with a rope tied to it. He had seen them tied there by other crewmen over the course of the morning, and they looked no different to the one the young sailor had tied. The only difference was it had taken him longer.

'Well, what you got to say for yourself, squeaker?'

'It looks all right to me, Frans,' the young sailor said.

'"It looks all right to me, Frans",' the older sailor, Frans, said in a high-pitched voice.

Frans shoved the young sailor again, proving to Wulfric beyond a doubt that there was nothing wrong with the knot.

'Piss off, Frans,' the young sailor said. There was fear in his voice rather than indignation.

'Tell me to piss off, squeaker?' Frans said. He stepped forward and grabbed the young sailor in a headlock, then twisted him violently. The young sailor let out a cry.

Wulfric felt a pulse of blood in his forehead, and a momentary light-headedness. He saw Rodulf. He saw himself.

'Let him go,' Wulfric said. The words were out of his mouth before he realised he was speaking.

'Mind your own business, mud-kicker,' Frans said.

Wulfric closed the distance between them and grabbed Frans by the wrist, freeing the young sailor who fell to the ground clutching his throat.

Frans swiped at Wulfric with his free hand, but Wulfric was able to twist him out of the way. Wulfric punched him hard, a loud crack accompanying the impact. Frans dropped like a sack of stones. The other sailor jumped onto Wulfric's back. The young sailor called out a warning, but it came too late.

Wulfric roared and grabbed at his attacker, pulling him from his back and throwing him to the ground. Wulfric grabbed him by the shoulders and head-butted him. He stumbled backwards as Wulfric moved forward to follow up.

'Enough.'

Jagovere's voice, and a word Wulfric was becoming all too familiar with.

❈

## Jagovere

Jagovere kept his gaze locked on Wulfric until he was certain the violence was at an end. Having a man under his command causing trouble with the crew was the last thing he needed, and this incident had gone too far. Satisfied that it was over, he gave Wulfric a nod and turned back to dal Rhenning who stood next to him in their usual spot on the upper deck.

'That's why I want to give him a chance,' dal Rhenning said. 'He stepped in to help that lad without a second thought. His compass points toward the right thing every time, and his own safety comes second.'

'It was the decent thing to do, I agree,' Jagovere said, but there was no enthusiasm in his voice. 'The decent thing isn't always the best thing, though. Violence is his first choice, every time, even when he's doing the right thing.'

Dal Rhenning grunted, as he always did when his opinion was straining under scrutiny.

'Perhaps best get the lads ready for trouble,' dal Rhenning said. 'I suspect we may have issues with the crew.'

# CHAPTER 13

ANDHUN

'WE SHOULD HAVE killed him,' Oswyn said. 'Left the southerner with no one to choose but you. Now you've destroyed your chances, and handed the barony to Rodulf. You've gone and fucked us both.' He stood and paced around the room.

Andhun moved stiffly and carefully in his chair to avoid aggravating his wounded back. In hindsight, there was little with which to argue against Oswyn. However, he still believed resorting to killing was recognising that you had failed in business. It was the last resort, and he felt justified in having kept it as such, twelve lashes and defeat or not.

'He can't be made baron if he's dead,' Andhun said. 'Killing Rodulf is still as much an option now as it was before. With him gone, even if I can't get my hands on the title, we'll be able to control whoever does between us.'

Oswyn took a deep breath and sighed. 'You'd better be right.'

Andhun shrugged. 'If you can think of an alternative, I'm all ears.'

'No, I can't,' Oswyn said. 'I can't because there isn't one. I'll send word to Ruripathia to bring my man up. He's quick, so we should be done with it all in a few days.'

'The barony might still be awarded to me, you know,' Andhun said.

'Might it?'

Andhun smiled. 'If not Rodulf, then who is there other than me?'

'Me for starters. Even I have more favour with the ambassador than you do now.'

Andhun narrowed his eyes and watched Oswyn as he paced around the room. It had been a careless comment, motivated of frustration, but Andhun knew only too well that truer words had rarely been spoken. Oswyn thought he had a chance of being made baron once more, and in allowing that to come to pass, Andhun knew he had made his most serious blunder. It occurred to him that Oswyn's knife man might offer two-for-one discounts. If so, he needed to make very sure he wasn't the bonus victim. From enemy to ally to enemy. How quickly politics moved. He sighed and felt himself pining for the old days, when such things were left to the men born to it and all he had to do was worry about his business.

❄

# OSWYN

Oswyn took a deep breath as soon as he stepped outside of Andhun's house. Andhun's clumsy attempt at a bribe had at first seemed like a disaster. Oswyn had planned to go straight home and load all his important belongings onto a wagon and head for anywhere but there. If he remained after Rodulf was made baron he was a dead man, and that was all there was to it.

Now, however, he saw opportunity. The one great philosophy he had come to from his years of trade was that only fools whined about circumstance. Men of success always searched out the opportunity, even when all appeared to be going against them. Andhun had ruined his chances, but there was nothing to connect Oswyn with that. The southerner might be harsh, but he was no fool. When it came to it, he would not discriminate against the most competent choice for having a similar-sounding name to another man in the village. Oswyn knew that had all been about stamping his authority on Leondorf, and he had merely been the unfortunate victim.

Andhun might not be in the running for the barony any longer, but he could make things difficult for Oswyn if he realised their brief and uneasy alliance was at an end. As he walked back to his house on the other side of the village, Oswyn wondered if he would get a discount on a second assassination.

❄

# RODULF

Rodulf stroked the young woman's thigh, but his mind was elsewhere. Andhun and Oswyn had been living in each other's pockets since Oswyn had been kicked off the council, and Rodulf knew that could only mean one thing. They were up to something, and past experience had taught him that whatever they did would be to his detriment. Andhun's clumsy attempt to bribe his way to the top had failed spectacularly. There were few options left to him other than to strike directly at Rodulf.

Both Andhun and Oswyn knew well that Rodulf's first act as baron would be to string them up to a gibbet and watch them dance. Fleeing wouldn't do them any good. He would hire the best sellswords to hunt them down and drag them back to him.

The barony had to come first, however, and that was causing him a headache. The girl on his lap purred with content. They had both smoked some seeds he had bought from a southern trader—dream seed, it was called. He hadn't much liked it, and after only one inhale had given the girl the pipe. She wasn't much to look at—likely the only reason she was in Leondorf at all was because she couldn't make a living in the south. Once he was baron, he wouldn't have to lower his standards to the likes of her any longer. Women wouldn't notice his eyepatch then, nor wonder at what grotesque sight lay behind it.

The thought brought Wulfric to the fore. Word had arrived that he had murdered Ambassador Urschel then disappeared, despite Rodulf's warning. Rodulf could only hope Wulfric was rotting in a ditch somewhere, but it did little to satisfy his desire to have watched the bastard die at his own hand. It was a distant problem and not worth bothering himself over. He looked at the pipe, long since finished and lying on the girl's lap, and cursed it for clouding his thoughts. A budding headache added to his discomfort. Quite how the southerners had developed such a taste for the drug was beyond him.

The most recent silver convoy had also returned unscathed, and as happy as Rodulf was that the flow of silver continued, it was clearly not enough for dal Ruedin. How could he show he was able to protect it if no one bothered to attack? Andhun's blunder should have seen Rodulf's promotion announced, but it had not. What more did he need to do? A plan began to form in his drug-addled mind. Dal Ruedin was a military man. What would he appreciate more than a military victory?

A dozen reavers would be enough. He had twice that many sellswords with him when escorting the convoy, so they would be easily able to deal with the attack. There would be enough corpses on both sides to make it look like a proper fight. He would tell the reavers it was a scam, that they would split the stolen loot afterward. Their greed would blind them to the ploy, and Rodulf would have a victory to show dal Ruedin that he was the man to lead Leondorf.

Rodulf smiled, but could feel his headache grow worse. He instinctively reached for the Stone, knowing it would bring him comfort. He idly wondered why it would not make dal Ruedin give him the barony as he closed his eyes and drifted toward sleep. Even its powers had limits, it seemed.

❁

## WULFRIC

Word of the incident between Wulfric and the sailors spread through the ship like wildfire. An uneasy atmosphere developed, but there was no retaliation and Wulfric was beginning to relax, when he found himself alone and facing down a dozen sailors on the foredeck after using the head.

'This is the one, lads,' Frans said.

The others stood behind him but didn't seem as thirsty for retribution as Frans.

'Are we gonna let one of these mud-kickers push us around?' Frans said.

There were some subdued responses.

Frans looked around angrily. 'Well?' He pointed to a purple bruise that was fading to brown and yellow on the side of his face. 'It'll be you next.'

There were some more murmurs of support, enough to embolden Frans. He stepped forward and prodded Wulfric in the chest.

'That'd be a mistake,' said a deep, rumbling voice that sounded more like a growl than speech.

Wulfric looked around to see Enderlain standing at his shoulder, having just emerged from the other head. He looked more comical than menacing—his nose still swollen and his black eyes fading to yellow like

Frans's face—but both he and Wulfric were nearly twice the size of the largest sailor before them, and would make any sensible man think twice.

'Maybe you had it coming, Frans,' one of the sailors said. 'I know what you're like, and I'm not getting my head cracked for you. Not today, leastways.' He turned and walked away, and was followed by more, until Frans stood with only three other men.

Wulfric could see the confidence drain from Frans's face. There was a flicker of anger in his eyes, but the rage was impotent. The impasse lasted a moment longer before Frans turned and left, followed by his few remaining supporters. Wulfric looked at Enderlain, who glowered at him. He smiled uncertainly.

'Doesn't mean we're friends, arsehole,' Enderlain said, before walking away.

✳

## ADALHAID

Lectures were held in a semi-circular amphitheatre, with rows of benches and desks rising up toward the back of the room. A single staircase ran down the centre leading to the doors at the side. At the end of class, it became a mash of students eager to get to their next class or into the fresh air, or anywhere but class. Adalhaid usually waited until the press of bodies had subsided before making her escape.

There was a cry that cut above the din of the exiting students, and the ensuing silence was filled by a series of thuds that could only be the sound of someone falling down the stairs. Adalhaid winced in sympathy. She craned her neck to see what had happened. The crowd parted at the bottom of the stairs, revealing a young woman writhing on the ground, her face contorted in pain.

Before she knew what she was doing, Adalhaid was pressing her way through the gawking students to get to the injured woman. Along with a number of visible bumps and scrapes, the young woman clutched her wrist. Blood flowed from between her fingers.

'Fetch a physician,' someone shouted.

Adalhaid ignored the commotion and knelt beside the injured student. 'Let me see,' she said.

She had to prise bloodied fingers from the young woman's wrist, and swallowed hard at the sight of a jagged end of bone protruding from the torn flesh. A student to her left let out a gasp at the sight and crumpled to the ground. Adalhaid took a handkerchief from her satchel and wrapped it around the young woman's wrist. It was not nearly enough for the amount of blood flowing, but it was all she had. She pressed hard on the makeshift bandage while holding the injured limb as high as she could, remembering the lessons Aethelman had taught her.

The young woman was clearly in such pain that Adalhaid wished she could do something more to ease the suffering.

'What's your name?' Adalhaid asked, hoping to distract herself as much as the young woman.

'Wilhelmina,' she said between gasps.

Her face was growing ever paler, and Adalhaid's concern over her blood loss increased.

'That's quite a mouthful,' Adalhaid said. 'Is that what everyone calls you?'

'No. Mina,' she said with a disproportionate amount of effort. 'Apart from my father. He calls me Willy. Old git.' She managed a strained laugh.

'What else are you studying, Mina?' Adalhaid said.

'Whatever takes my fancy,' she said. 'The Arts, for now. Then, who knows?'

It seemed to Adalhaid that the bleeding had lessened, and some of the colour had returned to Mina's face.

'Make way, make way,' an authoritative voice called. The crowd parted and a tall, slender man of unusually dark complexion stepped forward. Almost every Ruripathian, and Northlander for that matter, had hair running from mid-brown to so blond it was almost white, with a fair proportion of red—like hers—mixed in. This man's hair was jet black, and his jaw was covered with several days' worth of stubble. To call him handsome was an understatement, and Adalhaid realised the eyes of every woman in the lecture theatre—hers included—were locked on him.

He knelt by Adalhaid and placed his bag on the floor. 'Who's the patient?' he said. 'Him or her?'

'Both,' Adalhaid said, 'although her need is far more pressing. He just fainted at the sight of blood.'

He nodded, took Mina's wrist from Adalhaid and carefully unwrapped the handkerchief. He gave it a close look and frowned.

'There's not much between them,' he said. 'A nasty cut, and I'd say a bad sprain, but nothing a little rest won't fix. Not as serious as I was led to believe, although that is quite a lot of blood.' He frowned for a moment, then turned his gaze to the other casualty. 'I'd better take a look at our friend here with the cast-iron constitution.'

He turned to treat the young man, leaving Adalhaid in a state of confusion. She took Mina's wrist once again and gave it a second look. There was no sign of a break at all, let alone a jagged piece of bone sticking through her skin. Had she imagined it? The wound was little more than a deep cut, but it had stopped bleeding and looked nowhere near as serious as it had moments before. Adalhaid stared at it in confusion.

'That's odd,' Mina said. 'I'd have sworn it was far worse before. Must have been the shock of the fall. It's barely anything. I feel like a bit of a ninny now.'

There was a groan to the left as the physician revived the other student with pungent salts, while the crowd began to file away as they realised there was no more excitement to be had.

'I'm going to take you both to the infirmary for a proper check, but I don't foresee any further problems,' the physician said on standing. He turned to Adalhaid and smiled. 'Thank you for your help. I'm Doctor Jakob Strellis. You are?'

'Adalhaid.' She could feel her face grow hot.

# CHAPTER 14

## RODULF

RODULF'S KNUCKLES WERE white on his reins as they approached the ambush spot. The reavers were the best he could find on short notice, which did not say much for their skill. However, all they had to do was cause a fuss and die. They had been instructed to fire only on the wagons, not the party of men following, but that did not mean an errant arrow or two mightn't find their way to Rodulf. He steeled himself with the thought that his goal was worth dying for.

The first sign it was starting was the thud of an arrow into the side of one of the wagons. It took Rodulf a moment to realise. He bit his tongue and it took the impact of several more before anyone else realised what was happening. None of them had been expecting it.

None of Rodulf's men knew about his plan. The fewer who did, the smaller the mess to clean up. A wagon driver was hit by an arrow. He stood and toppled from his wagon as he cried out in pain. Rodulf nearly laughed at how theatrical it seemed. His bodyguard made to attack, but he held out a restraining hand.

'Not until we can see them,' Rodulf said. As soon as the reavers broke cover, he intended to charge them. They would not expect it and should be easy pickings. It would also give them no chance to reveal that they knew him.

Another wagon driver cried out in pain, the second life paid for Rodulf's barony.

'We're here to protect them,' one of Rodulf's bodyguards said.

Rodulf cast him a filthy look. 'We're here to protect the silver. We can't do that if we get ourselves killed by an unseen force. Wait until I say so.'

The mercenary did as he was told, but a man with a conscience was of no use to Rodulf. If the mercenary survived the encounter, he would be seeking new employment when they got back to Leondorf.

The reavers broke from the tree line, shouting and whooping, fully in expectation that the guards would break and run, as Rodulf had promised. They finished off the wagon drivers before Rodulf blew a small hunting horn to signal the other men he had concealed in the forest. They burst forward, roaring as they charged. Rodulf signalled for his bodyguard to join them.

'No mercy,' he shouted, then spurred his horse to follow.

The reavers were taken completely by surprise, and cutting them down was like running a scythe through ripe wheat. The reavers were thieves peppered with a handful of mercenaries, whereas his sellswords were among the best that could be had. One or two were overpowered and cut down, but for the most part it was little more than a slaughter.

The final few reavers tried to run, but they didn't get far. His men circled around the wagons looking for any more threats, but the fighting was done. Rodulf made a show of riding up and down along the wagons to inspect them. Peppered with arrows and splattered with blood, they couldn't have looked any better if Rodulf had contrived the entire scene. He had to stop himself from letting out a sigh of relief.

'Take their heads, then get the wagons moving again,' Rodulf ordered. 'We're vulnerable so long as we're stopped.'

The men set about their grisly task, and Rodulf smiled. If this didn't impress the ambassador, nothing would.

✾

## ADALHAID

'Excuse me, miss!'

It took a second shout before Adalhaid realised she was the one being called. The physician who had come to the lecture theatre was walking toward her.

'You're the girl who helped the student who fell? Adalhaid, wasn't it?' the physician said.

'I am. Is she all right?'

'She is. It was a nasty fright for her, and she'll be a bit sore for a few days, but that's it.'

'I'm very pleased to hear that,' Adalhaid said.

'I was impressed with the way you handled things before I got there,' he said. 'Not everyone keeps their head in situations like that.'

'That's very kind of you,' Adalhaid said, concentrating on not blushing. She noticed the looks passing female students were giving her.

'I apologise,' he said. 'I didn't fully introduce myself earlier. I'm a lecturer in the School of Medicine, and a physician, of course.'

Adalhaid didn't know what to say, so she smiled.

'What you did for that girl, and the way you reacted, impressed me. I was wondering if you'd ever given thought to studying medicine?'

Adalhaid felt her heart drop. She hadn't known what she was expecting from the conversation, but it hadn't been that.

'I… Well, no, not really,' she said.

'I hope you don't mind, but your professor told me your grades. They're more than high enough to allow you to transfer to the School of Medicine, if that interests you. From what I've seen, I feel it would be a terrible waste not to put your natural talents to use. The transfer can be easily done.'

Adalhaid thought back to the incident in the lecture theatre, and couldn't deny the flush of excitement it had given her. She considered the time she had spent helping Aethelman tend to his patients, a time that was the happiest in her life. Finally, she remembered Wulfric, and was overcome with sadness.

'I'll think about it,' she said, and she walked away.

❧

## RODULF

Rodulf was almost as nervous riding back into Leondorf as he had been heading out to the ambush site. He had to sell the attack to the ambassador or his plausibility would be ruined, perhaps irrevocably. People stopped what they were doing and watched when they spotted the arrows and the bloodstains. Rodulf tried to adopt as triumphant a pose as he could.

They reached the village square, and Rodulf stopped outside the ambassador's house to make his report. The wagons, and his men, continued on toward the smelter. They left the sack of heads with Rodulf.

He dismounted and knocked on the ambassador's door, waiting for Ruger to answer.

Ruger opened the door and regarded Rodulf's blood-spattered and entirely contrived appearance. He looked at the blood-soaked sack, which Rodulf opened to display the heads, but showed it no more disgust than he had Rodulf.

'Silver all accounted for?' Ruger said.

'We were attacked,' Rodulf said.

'Really? Who'd have known.'

'I'd like to speak with the ambassador.'

'Silver all accounted for?' Ruger said again.

'Yes,' Rodulf said. 'The ambassador?'

'You're not coming in covered in that filth. Have a wash. I'll pass on the message. The ambassador will send word when he's ready to see you. Take your sack with you.' Ruger shut the door.

Rodulf's stomach twisted with anger, but he swallowed it, galling though it was to take disrespect from a servant. The time would come when no man would be able to speak to him like that and get away with it, but it had not yet arrived. Soon, though. The thought helped ease his rage, and he cast a look at the bloodied sack. He had no idea what to do with it, nor had he any desire to take it home. It was taking a risk, but Ruger's disdain had angered him so much that Rodulf left it where it was and went home.

He spotted Andhun and Oswyn on Andhun's porch, their beady eyes on him. Usually they merely irritated him, but today their gaze caused his gut to twist with anxiety. They were up to something. He clutched tighter on the Stone in his pocket, but it did nothing to salve his unease. If anything, it grew worse. He pulled his cloak up around him and hastened his pace home.

❀

WULFRIC

Both soldiers and crew breathed a sigh of relief when land was spotted and the captain, after taking his sightings, declared they were only a few hours north of their destination—a port called Aldova on the coast of Estranza.

Tension on board had remained high, but the situation had not descended into violence. While the sailors rallied around one of their own, and would have fought against Wulfric if it came to it, they didn't seem to be willing to initiate a retaliatory strike.

Wulfric was not comfortable with being in someone's debt. Were it not for Enderlain's intervention, Wulfric knew he would have been beaten senseless. Alone, he would have made it difficult for them, and more than one sailor would have spent the remainder of the voyage with the ship's physician, but he would have lost. With Enderlain at his side, the sailors had known the price for restoring Frans's pride was too high.

Enderlain stood by the bulwark, staring toward the coast with an expression of hungry anticipation. He gave Wulfric only a cursory glance as he approached, before returning his gaze to the shore.

'Never been fond of ships,' Enderlain said.

'First time on one,' Wulfric said. 'Can't say I'm looking forward to my second. There's something I wanted to say before we get ashore. I wanted to thank you for standing with me against the sailors.'

'It was nothing. Couldn't have them knocking the snot out of one of ours. Makes us all look bad.'

'Still, I appreciate it. I owe you.'

'You'll have plenty of chances to settle the debt.' He continued to stare out to the foreign land on the horizon.

Wulfric knew such conversations were always difficult among warriors, and that this one was over. He left Enderlain in peace and watched the land slowly fill up the horizon with a feeling of growing excitement at the discovery of a foreign land and the prospect of new adventures.

# CHAPTER 15

RODULF

EACH CRACKLE OF the fire made Rodulf jump. He didn't know what was causing his unusual mood, but he didn't like it one bit. Perhaps it was the fact that the ambassador had still not shown any reaction to his fighting off the silver bandits. Perhaps it was the comedown from the excitement of the ambush. Perhaps it was fear of his ruse being discovered. If anyone found out the truth of it, Rodulf knew he would be tried for a dozen murders and hanged.

'My lord.'

Rodulf jumped, but he recognised the voice—the Humberland accent belonged to one of Rodulf's mercenaries, a banneret called Grenville. He had shown himself to be the most useful of the bunch and Rodulf had recently appointed him captain of his personal guard.

'It's not "my lord" yet,' Rodulf said.

'Habit,' Grenville said.

Rodulf wondered what had brought Grenville across the Middle Sea, far from his home in Humberland and anything that southerners considered civilisation.

'Anything to report?' Rodulf said.

'Not a thing.'

Rodulf rubbed under his eyepatch. 'Perhaps I'm imagining it.'

'Perhaps,' Grenville said. 'There's a lot at stake right now. Best to be careful.'

Rodulf nodded absently. Giving in to paranoia was the last thing he wanted. 'Keep a watch through the night. As soon as the ambassador makes his announcement, I can deal with Andhun and Oswyn. Until then, my hands are tied.'

He heard Grenville move away, and looked down at his hand. The Stone was firmly clenched between his fingers, yet he had no memory of taking it from its pouch.

❊

# RODULF

Rodulf woke with a jolt. The fire was low, little more than embers, but he couldn't be sure of how long he had been asleep. Something had woken him. He sat up and looked around. He had left his sword by his chair, and felt a momentary panic until his hand found it.

Any remnants of sleep were blown from his head by a hand covering his mouth and pulling his head back against the chair. He struggled, but the hold was strong and he was in a weak position—all he could do was flail his arms and legs impotently. He felt the cold touch of steel to his throat. His eyes widened and his heart raced but he remained deathly still, as if to do so would cause the blade to leave him be. He wondered how his guards allowed this to happen, as the blade started to bite into his flesh.

The grip relaxed, and Rodulf felt the blade fall away from his neck. There was a pained, hissing gasp from behind him, and he jumped to his feet. A man dressed in black slumped over the back of Rodulf's armchair. Grenville stood behind him, sword in hand.

'Grenville?' he said. 'What in hells?'

'My lord.' The characteristic accent. 'Someone's tried to assassinate you.'

Rodulf laughed in exasperation. 'I can bloody well see that. How did he get to me? I told you something like this would happen.'

'He's dead. You're alive. Sometimes you have to lure the mouse into the trap. I've done my job, my lord.'

Rodulf had to agree that he had, terrifying awakening or not.

'What's going on? What happened?' Rodulf said.

'I spotted him a couple of hours ago, mooching around in the dark,' Grenville said. 'He's good. Took all that time working his way up to the house. Patient. The other chaps missed him completely. I didn't. He killed Jakop out by the oak tree in the yard. He's not much of a loss, to be honest.'

Rodulf stood, arms akimbo, and chewed on his lip. This was Andhun's move. There was no other explanation. It sent a shiver through Rodulf to know how close Andhun had come—he could still feel the cold touch of the steel on his throat.

'He told you Andhun and Oswyn paid him to kill me,' Rodulf said.

'He didn't say anything,' Grenville said.

Rodulf fixed him with a withering stare.

'Now that you mention it…' Grenville said.

'Have the body brought to the Great Hall and the men ready in five minutes.'

❅

## RODULF

Rodulf's small force of mercenaries was gathered outside his house. Rodulf looked them over, but could not remember what Jakop, the sellsword who had been killed, looked like. He would have to arrange a replacement the next morning, but he had more than enough for what he needed to do.

'You, you, and you,' he said, pointing to the men in question. 'Drag Oswyn from his house, and bring him to the Great Hall. Hold him outside until I call you in. So long as you don't kill him, I don't care how much force you use. The rest of you, with me.'

It was late—early perhaps; Rodulf had no idea—and there was no one on the streets. A crowd of witnesses would have been better, but in a few moments there would be such a great commotion, he would have as large a crowd as he could want.

It didn't take long to reach Andhun's house. Rodulf knew him for the fat coward that he was, so he was the one to start with. Oswyn had steel in him and would be harder to break, but he knew as well as Rodulf what Andhun was made of, and that could be used against him.

Rodulf smiled with satisfaction as he pounded on Andhun's door. A servant opened it, but Rodulf and his men pushed past him and into the house. Andhun was coming out of a room in his bedclothes, a sight that pushed Rodulf's enjoyment of the experience near to reverie.

'What are you doing in my house?' Andhun said. 'And at this hour?'

'I'm here to arrest you, you fat pig,' Rodulf said. 'Take him. Bring him to the Great Hall.'

He watched as his man seized Andhun and bound his hands.

'You can't do this,' Andhun said.

'And yet here we are,' Rodulf said. He waited for his men to bundle Andhun out and toward the Great Hall before following them.

❊

## RODULF

The assassin's body was draped across the council table in the Great Hall when they arrived. Rodulf watched Andhun's eyes widen and the colour drain from his face when he saw it. Considering a man had attempted to kill him only a short time before, Rodulf was having a surprisingly enjoyable night.

'What is this?' Andhun said. 'Who is this man?'

'You don't know him?' Rodulf said, allowing Andhun enough time to start shaking his jowly head. 'Because he knows you. Said you paid him four hundred crowns to kill me.'

Andhun shook his head with more vigour. Rodulf knew it wasn't Andhun; he didn't have the nerve to arrange an assassination. Oswyn would have taken care of the details. Rodulf walked around the table and sat down.

'I have his confession,' Rodulf said, gesturing to the corpse. 'He named both you and Oswyn as his employers. Admit to what you did, and this will go easier on you. I'm tired, and if you insist on keeping me from my bed it will make me very angry.' He gestured to one of his men, who laid a cloth bundle on the table and opened it. Contained within were a number of metal tools, whose purpose was obvious.

'You can't,' Andhun said. 'You wouldn't. It had nothing to do with me.'

'Who did it have something to do with?' Rodulf said. He had the Stone firmly gripped in his hand. 'If it was someone else and you tell me, it will mean exile for you rather than death.'

Andhun shook his head furiously. He squeezed his eyes shut, and tears streamed down his face. 'Oswyn,' he said in a gasp. 'It was Oswyn.'

Rodulf smiled and turned to Grenville. 'Be so good as to bring Oswyn in.'

Grenville nodded and left the hall, returning a moment later with a bound and gagged Oswyn. Oswyn's eyes flicked from the corpse on the table to the weeping Andhun, and finally to Rodulf.

'Remove his gag,' Rodulf said.

'What's the meaning of this?' Oswyn said as soon as his mouth was free. 'You've crossed the line this time, you one-eyed shit.'

'It's you who's crossed the line, Oswyn. Trying to murder a council member? After all that's already happened, there's not a man in the Northlands who would take umbrage with me killing you here and now.'

'Thought we lived by southern rules now,' Oswyn said.

'We'll be living by my rules soon enough. I thought I'd give them a trial run now. The sentence for trying to kill your liege lord is hanging.'

'Looks to me like your only evidence is rotting on the table,' Oswyn said.

Andhun started to whimper at the side of the room.

'Andhun has stated the plan to have me assassinated was yours. As a councilman, his word is beyond doubt.'

'You stupid, fat fucker,' Oswyn said. 'I should have sent him to your house first.'

'And by inculpating Oswyn, you, Andhun, have demonstrated your complicity, which is also a crime punishable by death.'

'Wha—wha— But you said exile if I—'

'I don't recall saying anything about exile,' Rodulf said. 'Did anyone else hear me say anything about exile?'

No one said a thing.

'Didn't think so. Take them outside and hang them from the roof beam, Grenville,' Rodulf said. 'Make it quick. I don't want to be interrupted.'

❈

## Adalhaid

Adalhaid stood at the doorway to the School of Medicine, staring at the letters carved into the limestone lintel over the ancient double doors. She had lain awake all night thinking about it, and there was no doubt in her mind that this was what she wanted. Her only concern was uncertainty if her decision was motivated by finally realising her vocation, or by the handsome dark-haired physician. The thought filled her with guilt. Might Wulfric be watching from Jorundyr's Hall? What would he think of her?

He would want her to follow her dreams. She held her transfer request in her hand, and strode forward resolutely. Dreams aside, the life of a physician could offer her everything she sought—security, independence, and status—more so than simply being an academic.

She opened the doors, and was almost overwhelmed by the smell of chemicals. She suspected she would grow so accustomed to it that soon she wouldn't even notice it.

❋

## WULFRIC

Unloading the ship had required a full day of back-breaking work. The harbourmaster, and later the town's mayor, had been horrified to see the arrival of a full company of soldiers. Assurances that the town wasn't going to be pillaged did little to quell their unease, but with letters of safe passage from the duke, there was nothing they could do but offer hospitality. The mayor had acquiesced to the Company setting up camp on the quayside until preparations to march on to the duchy's capital at Torona could be made.

The squads sat around their campfires, using sacks of provisions and crates as makeshift furniture.

'Why is the Graf doing all this?' Wulfric said as he swirled the last of his coffee, a drink he was rapidly developing a fondness for.

'Doing what?' Enderlain said.

'Leading the Company. Adventuring. Where I'm from, this is something only young men do.'

Enderlain shrugged. 'Ask Conrat. He's from Rhenning. He's been with the Company from the start.'

Everyone gathered around the fire looked over at Conrat.

'When his wife died, he decided he'd had enough of running his lands. He handed everything over to his oldest boy—his oldest legitimate boy—and started the Company. Just before the Ostian war.'

There were several murmurs at the mention of the Ostian war, something Wulfric had never heard of before.

'Ostian war?'

'Long story,' Conrat said. 'The old prince declared war with Ostia. Lots of rumours why, secret deals and such, but can't say I know much about that. Things went well to start with—we were within sight of Ostenheim before the retreat—then the Usurper took power in the south, and commanded his armies himself. Gave us a hiding. In a few weeks, there were Ostian soldiers camped outside Brixen's walls and the royal family were on a ship heading across the Middle Sea into exile. With everything lost, what was left of the Graf's regiment followed not long after, along with most others who'd fought the Usurper and didn't want to live in an occupied country. We picked up a few strays along the way, like Enderlain there. Had to earn our keep, so we did some soldiering in Humberland, served Her Highness for a time at her court-in-exile in Venter. That was something, I'll tell you. You should see the Ventish women.' He made a gesture with his hands that the others laughed at.

Wulfric gathered the meaning, and joined in. 'Who's the Usurper?' he said.

'Who *was*,' Enderlain said. 'The Duke of Ostia, as was. His own people killed him a few years back.'

'Anyhow,' Conrat said, 'after that, the new duke withdrew his armies and Her Highness came home to rule, what with her father having passed. After the restoration, we all realised we liked the life of a travelling company, the Graf included. Ruripathian sellswords had made a good name for themselves abroad during the exile, so work wasn't hard to come by. Now we're only ever at home between contracts.'

'And Captain dal Borlitz?' Wulfric said. 'Is he…'

There were nods and murmurs from around the campfire, but no one said anything, which Wulfric took as a hint to shut his mouth. They finished their coffee in silence as Wulfric marvelled at the new experiences all around him, from the warm air to the unusual smells. Only a few weeks before, he had never even heard of Estranza. Now he was sitting there, so far from home he could barely imagine it. He stared across the sea in the direction of home, and wondered what his mother was doing, what Aethelman was doing, and if he would ever see either of them again.

# Chapter 16

## Rodulf

THE SUN HAD risen and both men had long since ceased twitching when the ambassador arrived. The bodies continued to swing gently from side to side in the breeze, something Rodulf found incredibly relaxing after an intense day and night.

'Explain this,' Ambassador dal Ruedin said.

'Among the other injuries these men have done me, Andhun and Oswyn tried to have me killed last night. This settles the Blood Debt.'

The ambassador looked at the swinging bodies. 'This is not how things are done.'

'It is in the Northlands. We're still in the Northlands, aren't we?'

'Bloody savages,' the ambassador said under his breath. 'Yes,' he said in his normal voice, 'I suppose we are.'

He turned and headed back toward his house. When he had gone a few paces, he stopped. 'Well done with the silver wagons yesterday, by the by.'

Rodulf smiled, and returned his gaze to the swinging bodies. He would go home and sleep for an hour or two, and later in the day he would seize everything that had belonged to the two dead men hanging before him.

※

## Aethelman

The damp seemed to seep into Aethelman's tired joints, causing them to stiffen and ache. The air was cold and his breath clouded in the light of his small lamp. It had been an age since he had seen any source of natural light, and it was impossible to tell how long he had been walking. The only thing he felt certain of was that he was in the mountain behind the Hermitage. If the cavern existed, it could not be far.

Tired though he was, only hunger would force him to turn around. He had taken some light rations with him, balancing the burden of a heavy satchel against his estimated need. Having come so far, he was determined to continue until he could confirm or discount the cavern's existence.

Another dozen paces, and the little bubble of light created by the reflections from the damp ceiling, floor, and walls disappeared. He stopped and looked around, but in every direction, there was only absolute darkness.

'Hello,' he called out, the 'oh' echoing into the abyss. He felt a flush of giddy excitement. This was it. He wondered how long it had been since the last person had stood here. It was humbling to be somewhere so ancient, where all that he had dedicated his life to had begun.

Aethelman backtracked to where the corridor opened out into the great black void. There was an architrave to mark the passing, and on closer inspection it looked as though doors had once been suspended from it. There were inscriptions too, but the runes were a complete mystery to Aethelman. He scanned them in frustration, hopeful that one at least might give him a clue as to what was being said. For all he knew, the message might have read, 'Danger. Death to all who enter'.

He walked back into the void, his eyes fixed to the ground as he sought to keep his footing. A well-worn path showed him the way, pressed into the rock by the passage of countless feet over countless years. Aethelman followed it, moving ever farther into the darkness. With nothing but his small magelamp to guide him, his mind started to swim. There was nothing to focus on whenever he looked beyond its meagre glow, and his balance faltered. He grew dizzy and stumbled, falling to his hands and knees. He heard the *tink, tink, tink,* of his precious little lamp as it bounced away from his grasp.

He watched its receding light, hopeful that it would stop and be easily recovered. A loud 'pop' extinguished both that hope and the only light in that great, dark abyss.

Aethelman sat and clutched his knees to his chest. He was cold, so very cold. He had never been afraid of the dark before, but he had never before experienced a darkness like this. Despite the great space all around him, it felt like it was pressing in on him. For the first time he could remember, he felt fear.

✾

## RODULF

The bodies still hung from the roof beam outside the Great Hall when the council next sat. The corpses rotated slowly as the breeze twisted the ropes, presenting an obstacle to be avoided by all who entered.

Rodulf smiled as he watched the others make their way in, all at pains to dodge the rotting flesh of men with whom they had professed friendship. Rodulf wanted to be the last man to enter, with one exception, but feared he had overplayed his hand when the ambassador strode purposefully from his house toward the Great Hall, giving Rodulf no chance of getting there before him. It wouldn't be prudent to be seen running, so he would have to wait.

The ambassador showed none of the squeamishness of the others, pushing one of the bodies aside and going into the Great Hall. As soon as he had done so, Rodulf hurried after him.

Andhun's seat was conspicuously empty, its vacancy seeming to create an air of tension in the room. They all knew Rodulf would have no compunction in killing any one, or all of them. They also knew that with Andhun and Oswyn dead, there was no one in Leondorf to challenge him for the barony. All they could do was pray that Ambassador dal Ruedin would overlook Rodulf and appoint one of his countrymen. Rodulf had to suppress a smile at the thought.

'Over the past few days, it's become increasingly apparent to me that there is no point in my delaying the appointment of the new baron of Leondorf,' Ambassador dal Ruedin said. 'There is only one man realistically in the reckoning, and I am satisfied that he is capable of carrying out the tasks the Markgraf requires.'

Rodulf fixed his eye on the ambassador, willing the words from him. The engravings on the Stone pressed into his hand in his pocket.

The ambassador's eye twitched twice. 'Rodulf Donatoson, you are to travel to Elzburg forthwith to swear your oath of fealty to the Markgraf of Elzmark, and be invested as Baron of Leondorf.'

Rodulf felt a weight lift from him, and could see it visibly drop on the other men sitting around the table. He forced himself not to smile.

'When you return, my assignment here will be complete, and I will leave,' dal Ruedin said. 'I would say it has been a pleasure, but that could not be further from the truth. That is all.' He stood and left the Great Hall without another word.

Rodulf stretched back in his chair and allowed himself to smile. The others watched him furtively. 'That was not all,' he said. 'That, my friends, was merely the beginning.'

# CHAPTER 17

AETHELMAN

AETHELMAN KNEW HE was going to die where he was sitting. It was clear to him now that the gods did not want him to complete his quest, that they desired the knowledge he sought to remain forgotten. The darkness seemed to swirl before his eyes, but he knew it was simply his brain trying to make sense of the nothingness all around him. When he heard the laugh, he knew it was his ears trying to do the same. His imagination was trying to fill the void, and it would drive him mad before long.

He heard the laugh a second time, and wondered if it already had. He recognised the laugh. It resurrected memories and stirred dormant feelings. If madness was to bring his mind back to that place, he realised he had not the strength or the desire to fight it. He stood and turned to face where it had come from. He heard it again, and took his first hesitant step toward it.

✽

WULFRIC

They gave Wulfric a horse, clothes, some old, ill-fitting armour, and a sword. The Ruripathians favoured two types, a sabre similar to those Northlanders used, and a long, straight-bladed rapier with an elaborate hilt. Even the rough munitions-grade swords were things of beauty to Wulfric's eyes, but he had no experience of using one, so stuck to what he knew. He longed for Greyfell, his own armour, his own sword, but they were all lost to him. Probably forever. The horse he rode was a solid beast, but it paled in comparison to Greyfell. He wondered what had become of him.

He looked over to the others in his squadron, taking the central spot in the marching column. They all looked like good fighting men, with Enderlain riding at their head. Coloured banners fluttered in the air from lance tips. Some were in the Company's colours, while others bore the sigil of their owners, and Wulfric finally understood the term 'banneret'. Those who bore the title could carry their own banner into battle, and it struck Wulfric as a fine thing to be able to do. Perhaps the opportunity to become one would present itself, although he remembered mention of an academy and schooling, which wasn't so appealing.

Jagovere rode alone to the side, a small writing desk set up on his saddle. Every so often he would scribble something down, seemingly lost in his own world. The Company had a scribe and a treasurer to look after paperwork, making Wulfric curious about what he was writing.

The land of Estranza was as different to home as he could imagine. The terrain was flat, stretching out as far as the eye could see, and arid, liberally scattered with squat, scrubby vegetation. The sea had long since receded into the background and Wulfric felt it disorienting not to have the mountains visible in the distance to help guide his journey.

Jagovere looked up and noticed that Wulfric was watching him.

'It's an account of our adventures,' he said. 'Recorded for posterity.'

'Can't you just remember them?' Wulfric said.

'To preserve a story as it really happened, it needs to be written down,' Jagovere said. 'With a little embellishment, of course. Then it can be retold in the way its author intended.'

'The Company's stories are worth retelling?' Wulfric said, only realising after he had said it the offence it might cause.

'Whether they are or are not makes little difference,' Jagovere said, showing no sign of irritation. 'The Graf was a very popular man with his people. When he decided to abdicate his county in favour of his son for a life of adventure, he promised them he would send back news of his exploits. The Graf asked me to take on that responsibility. It's not a chore. I enjoy it.'

'Everyone there can read?' Wulfric said.

Jagovere laughed. 'Not even close. Spaekers read to people, in taverns and inns. The most famous stories are also recounted at the courts of great lords. I'm told they've spread well beyond the borders of Rhenning. It seems people are starved for a little adventure.' They continued in silence for a moment before Jagovere spoke again.

'I've always been interested in the Northlander epics. I expect you know a great many?'

'I've heard most of them told at one time or another,' Wulfric said.

'I should like to hear them,' Jagovere said. 'And write them down. The style is similar to what I'm trying to achieve in my own little epics.'

'I suppose I can remember most of them,' Wulfric said, not sure if it was something he had any interest in getting into.

'It strikes me as an excellent way to pass the time on a long journey,' Jagovere said. He fixed Wulfric with an expectant stare.

Wulfric could see no way out of it, and knew he had to make some effort to improve relations with the members of the Company if his next few weeks were not to be an utter misery.

He cleared his throat, and started with the first tale that came into his head.

❧

## RODULF

Rodulf spent the journey south thinking on all the things he was going to do when he got back to Leondorf. His own house would not do at all now that he was a nobleman. He briefly considered taking over the ambassador's house when he left the village, but decided against it. He wanted to build his own place, something that put his mark on Leondorf.

It would need to be a manor house of some sort. Something that spoke to his authority and power. However, it couldn't be entirely given over to luxury. Once Leondorf became a province of Ruripathia, it would be seen as fair game for every Northlander raider, and she was bordered by hostile territory on three sides. The house would need to be fortified. A castle might have been more appropriate, but they were old-fashioned, and he didn't want his southern peers to think him an out-of-date country hick. Whoever designed the house would have to be clever about it, mixing the appearance of modernity and wealth with the reality of defence.

He wondered how much autonomy he would have when he was baron.

He remembered how the Markgraf had to go to his own overlord, the Princess of Ruripathia, for permission to absorb Leondorf into the principality under his control. Would Rodulf have to go begging for permission every time he wanted to do something? It could make life difficult for him, especially with the ambitious plans that were forming in his head. With a remote location on the fringe of Ruripathia, so long as he kept the silver flowing south, he hoped he would be able to get away with quite a bit. The question was, how much? Now that he had achieved his barony, what else was there for the taking? There was nothing but opportunity ahead of him, and he intended to take full advantage.

It occurred to him that he had all but forgotten about Wulfric. There had been so much to occupy him in securing his future during the days following his father's murder that he hadn't been able to give him much more than a cursory thought. In a sense, Wulfric had done him a favour. Were it not for his actions, Rodulf knew he would still be nothing more than his father's errand boy. He would never forgive the loss of his eye, but he would not allow that to blind him to what was important. Revenge would be satisfying, delicious even, but he had big dreams and there would be little time for diversions. Should the chance to even the score present itself, he would jump on it, but he would not waste his life chasing it. Notions such as Blood Debts were for backward savages like the old warrior classes, like Wulfric, not for modern, progressive men like him.

The thought that he might be a target for Wulfric's misplaced thirst for revenge made his stomach twist. He quelled it with the knowledge that in a few days he would be a lord, and his power would grow with each passing moment. He would be untouchable, and if Wulfric chose to sacrifice himself in that endeavour Rodulf was quite happy to let him do so.

※

## AETHELMAN

Aethelman heard the laughter so clearly it seemed as if Aesa was only a few steps in front of him. He knew it could not be her, but he had given up questioning his sanity and was satisfied that it was not a figment of his imagination. There was something else at work in that great dark cavern.

At first it had frightened him, but that feeling had passed quickly. If whatever was making the sounds had wanted him dead, it would have happened. He was being led somewhere, and his natural curiosity meant that he followed. What did he have to lose? He focussed on the sound and forced himself to ignore the oppressive weight of the darkness surrounding him.

After a time, he thought he could see a blue glow in the distance, but he dismissed it as a trick of his eyes. He blinked once, then again, but it remained. He had never been in such utter darkness for so long. He tried to ignore it, but realised it was directly on the path the laughter was leading him, and that the light was growing stronger.

❦

## RODULF

'We'll need to send someone to court to let them know I'm here,' Rodulf said when he had walked through Elzburg's gates, and horses and weapons had been deposited at their respective places. As soon as he was a lord, he would be able to ride through the city as he pleased, with a sword at his waist. It was not lost on him that Grenville, a banneret, was allowed to carry his.

Grenville nodded.

'And I'll need a tailor sent over to measure me for my investiture robes,' Rodulf said. 'Find someone good. I want to make the right impression.'

Grenville continued to walk alongside him, so Rodulf cleared his throat.

Grenville looked back at him. 'Now?'

'Now,' Rodulf said.

Grenville nodded and broke away from Rodulf and the remainder of his bodyguards, who continued on to the inn he was staying at. A nauseated feeling formed in his gut. He was more nervous than he was willing to show. His father had spoken often of how poisonous the intrigues at southern courts could be, and Rodulf had seen first-hand how quickly people turned on one another when he'd been apprenticed to southern merchants. Those he encountered at the Markgraf's court would seek to take advantage of him at every juncture, and the thought that he might not even be able to recognise when it was happening concerned him. Until he had established himself, he had to view everyone as an enemy. It excited him as much as terrified him, however. There would be a hierarchy of noblemen at the

Markgraf's court, and Rodulf intended to be at the top of it in as short an order as possible.

❀

## AETHELMAN

The light grew ever stronger, until Aethelman had to accept that it was as real as anything else he had encountered. A final laugh told him this was his destination, and he could not help but feel disappointment. Instead of finding Aesa waiting for him at the end of the path, there was nothing but a large rock. It was a ridiculous notion that she might be there, but in that strange, dark place, anything seemed possible.

A blue glow rippled across the rock's surface. It was faint and glimmered in and out of view, which went to explain why he had believed he was imagining it for so long. Aethelman instantly knew what it was, although he could not explain why. It was like Jorundyr's Rock, though that was something he had never seen. It was a Gods' Stone, made from the same material as the Fount Stone he had found; here was a place where the boundary between the world of man and the world of gods broke down, where the energy from that mystical place flowed into the world. How it had come to be forgotten was a mystery. They were few and far between, but the connection with the gods they had once provided had long since been broken. Even Jorundyr's Stone was dead, or so he had thought until Wulfric had told him he had seen it glow blue, just like the one Aethelman was looking at.

The warrior apprentices had to touch Jorundyr's Rock to become full warriors. It was said to strike down the unworthy, although Aethelman had never heard of that happening. If the rock in the High Places belonged to Jorundyr, he wondered who claimed this one. Birgyssa, perhaps? Audun? He was tempted to touch the rock before him; he had never been more tempted in his life. What would happen if he did? There were hundreds of questions flying through his mind, but they were all pushed into the background by his desire to touch the rock and see what happened.

There was another laugh, all around him this time, which put him entirely at ease. Almost with a mind of its own, his hand moved toward the rock. His heart raced as he was mesmerised by the beautiful blue glow dancing across the surface of the rock. The glow coalesced and enveloped his hand with a speed that surprised him. He made to pull his hand away, but realised it had not done him any harm.

There was no temperature to it. Other than a slight tingling, he would not have even noticed it. The glow lasted a moment longer and then it was gone, leaving Aethelman in darkness. The sense of curiosity that had invigorated him fled, and he felt the darkness close in around him again. He took a deep breath, knowing that unless the laughter were to guide him back out, he would be fated to remain there until he died. Why had the laughter led him there in the first place, if only to leave him to die?

He closed his eyes and rubbed them hard to give them some relief from the great, swirling darkness. He opened them again, and everywhere his eyes fell, he saw runes, runes glowing as though they were filled with flame. He took another sharp intake of breath, and with little care for his footing, started toward those closest.

# CHAPTER 18

AETHELMAN

'SHRINE OF AUDUN the Wise' were the first words Aethelman read, answering his question. While that was the god's proper title, it had not been used in that form for centuries. The runes went on to tell several of the stories of Audun's deeds when he still walked the world of men, some that continued to be recounted by the Grey Priests, others long since forgotten. Aethelman had read a number of them, fascinated by how the runes now glowed, before he realised he was able to decipher them. Hours before, when these runes carved into the cavern walls had been cloaked in darkness, he would not have been able to identify a single one of the carvings.

As Jorundyr's gift to man was great prowess in battle, something with which he believed the boy Wulfric had been bestowed, Audun's was knowledge. He was one of the patron gods of the Grey Priests, the other being Birgyssa the Kind, and it amazed Aethelman that his shrine could be forgotten. He looked around, and realised the cavern was not as large as he had first thought. Its walls were completely covered in runes, all glowing. It would take hours, perhaps days, to read it all, but Aethelman doubted there was so great a store of knowledge anywhere else in the Hermitage or its ancient depths.

He moved along the wall slowly, taking in each rune carefully, but the meaning of each one was clear to him. They were as familiar as the back of his own hand. The Fount Stones were of the same age as the runes, and Aethelman felt his excitement rise as he read, hoping that eventually he would come to a mention of them. He felt a pang of regret that he no longer had the one he'd found, for he realised he would now be able to read everything inscribed upon its surface.

Aethelman scanned and disregarded tale after tale of Audun's deeds and grew frustrated. He had covered half the cavern, but there were only stories intended to spread the god's repute. There was nothing that mentioned the Stones. Finally, he reached something more relevant:

> With each day, the power of the shrine diminished. The blue light of Audun's presence grew ever fainter until at times it was no longer visible at all. There was much discussion as to why this should be so, and most opinion was in agreement: We drew too heavily on his beneficence, we sought to exclude all others from his grace, and our greed pushed us from his favour.
>
> Others argued that he would wish our survival as his chosen, and that his grace was there for our use. With the Emperor's mages hunting us like game and their desire to extinguish the light of the gods from this world and to replace them with fictional deities of their own, it was our duty to do what we needed to survive, and ensure that Audun, Birgyssa, Jorundyr, Ghyda, and Agnarr the Father are not forgotten.
>
> That was when we created the Fount Stones here, and in so doing finally extinguished Audun's light in the world of men. For better or for worse, that was our choice, and may he forgive us if we were mistaken. Nothing remains here now, but a memory of what once was. I pray he may restore life to this place, but I know we will be remembered only for our legacy then. We will leave the cavern, and the Rock, in the hope that without our interference, he may look favourably on man once again, and return to this place.

Aethelman looked back to the shadowy form of the rock, silhouetted against the burning runes. It was no more remarkable than any other lump of rock, any trace of the blue glow now gone. It seemed Audun had used up what little strength he had pooled at the rock to give Aethelman the ability to read the ancient runes. This was where the Stones had been created. Perhaps this was also where they could be laid to rest.

He scanned the rest of the wall, but there was no more mention of the Stones. Wherever the answer lay, it was not here. However, with his newfound ability to read the old runes, many more avenues were open to him.

The burning runes led Aethelman back to the cavern's entrance. As soon as he stepped out of it they were extinguished, as though it was only his presence that had kept them alight. He knew where he had to go next. The ruins of the old temple where he had found the Stone were covered in runes that had been meaningless to him at the time. Now they might hold the answers he sought. There was an irony to think his quest might end where it had begun.

*

# Rodulf

Rodulf's heart raced as he walked through the foyer toward the Markgraf's audience hall. He had been kept waiting all morning, hanging around the palace's foyer like an unwelcome salesman. He was dressed in his newly purchased southern clothes, as well as the fur-lined grey cloak of a nobleman. He carried the pearl-rimmed coronet, as it felt ridiculous to wear, and in any event he was not yet a baron. His retainers followed him, wearing uniforms that the tailor had also rushed, which awaited the addition of his coat of arms. It had all cost him a small fortune, but at least they looked the part to his eye. He only hoped they all looked that way to the Markgraf's court.

They followed one of the Markgraf's servants to huge double doors, which opened onto the audience hall. It was not as large as Rodulf had expected, but a number of people were gathered there. They all turned to look when Rodulf walked in, making him feel as uncomfortable as he ever had. He puffed out his chest and forced himself to look straight ahead.

He could hear whispers as he walked by, and didn't fool himself into thinking they were complimentary. He wasn't one of them, and they wanted him to know it. He wasn't going to give them the satisfaction of reacting, but he cast a sideways glance. He would not forget these faces.

His ennoblement was only one small part of the day's official business—and as monumental an achievement as it was for Rodulf, no one else cared. The servant bade Rodulf stop, then hurried forward to confer with one of the Markgraf's officials. The Markgraf cocked his head to listen, but had his eyes fixed on Rodulf. By reputation he was formidable, a strong ruler who was always looking to expand his territories and wealth, as his annexation of Leondorf had demonstrated. Rodulf wanted to make a good first impression. His fortunes were now tied to this man.

'Come forward,' the Markgraf said.

Rodulf did as he was told, his eyes fixed on the Markgraf. He had to appear strong. He tried to gauge the Markgraf as he walked forward. A trim man, his clothes plainer than most in the hall.

'Rodulf Donatoson,' the Markgraf said. 'I welcome you to my court, and accept your entreaty to swear fealty and do homage unto me.'

The official stepped forward and stood next to Rodulf, his mouth close to Rodulf's ear.

'Say that it is your solemn and earnest wish,' the official whispered.

Rodulf did so. The Markgraf nodded in approval.

'Now, kneel and repeat these words,' the official whispered. 'I, Rodulf Donatoson, swear before those gathered that I will in future be faithful and true to Walken, Markgraf of Elzmark, and to those who may follow of his name. I will carry out my responsibilities and obligations to him without deceit, and always in good faith.'

Rodulf did so, enunciating each word as carefully as possible.

The Markgraf nodded in approval again. 'I, Walken, Markgraf of Elzmark, do recognise and accept your oath, so sworn. Be it known to all men that I freely give to Rodulf Donatoson and the heirs of his body the newly created Barony of Leondorf, and acknowledge him as my liege man. Rise, Rodulf, Baron of Leondorf.'

Rodulf stood. All through the swearing, a scribe sat at a small table behind the Markgraf, scribbling furiously on a piece of parchment. He sprinkled it with powder and stood, presenting the document to the Markgraf. He gave it a cursory scan and indicated his acceptance with a wave of his hand. That done, the scribe melted some red wax onto the parchment, into which the Markgraf pressed his ring. The scribe offered the sealed document to Rodulf.

He took it reverently. It marked the culmination of all his and his father's hard work. It also put into the shade the shame and failure of having not been made a warrior. He was so much more than that now. After looking over the scribe's elegant hand and the crest pressed into the wax, Rodulf felt awkward, standing out in front of everyone with no clue what he should do.

'The Markgraf requires you to attend on him at nine bells of the morning, tomorrow,' the official said, leaving Rodulf in no doubt that his investiture ceremony was over, and that he was now in the way.

*

## ADALHAID

There were many moments when Adalhaid wondered if she had made a mistake transferring to the School of Medicine. Most of those were when she was rushing from one lecture or meeting she had arrived at late to another she was going to arrive at late. It was obvious to her why she had never met a medical student before—they were too busy. Added to her duties at the palace, she was stretched as far as she had ever been, and looked forward to her bed each evening with a desire she had not thought possible.

As eager as she was, she stopped dead in her tracks when she spotted Rodulf walking from the audience hall with a small retinue, wearing a baron's gown. Her stomach twisted at the sight. She had always known he would be a strong contender to be awarded the title when Leondorf inevitably fell under the Markgraf's control. She had not had any news from the village since leaving; there was nothing left to connect her to the place now. Her family were gone, and everyone she knew and cared for with them. That Rodulf was wearing the gown gave her the consolation that his poisonous father must be dead. She wondered if it had been natural causes, or if Rodulf had taken matters into his own hands. The latter certainly wouldn't have surprised her. She retreated behind a pillar and waited until he was out of sight. She had no desire for a reunion, and hoped he would be returning home soon.

# PART 2

# CHAPTER 19

## THE MAISTERSPAEKER

THE MAISTERSPAEKER PAUSED when the door to the tavern opened, wondering if Wulfric had finally arrived, but the notion was quickly dispelled. It was flung open with the carelessness of men who had no concern for causing damage, bullies who were used to having their way without any opposition.

They were men of arms, pieces of steel and boiled leather armour visible under their cloaks. They pushed their way through the crowd towards the bar, five of them in all. It was not until they reached it that Jagovere realised only four of them had done the pushing. The fifth walked among them with the relaxed air of a man accustomed to having everything done for him. He turned his head, revealing the patch covering his right eye. It was the man the Maisterspaeker had seen several days previously. The man he believed to be Rodulf.

The Maisterspaeker realised Rodulf was looking directly at him and felt his heart quicken. They had only encountered one another briefly, all those years before, but might he remember? The Maisterspaeker had been Jagovere the warrior then, young, strong, without even a hint of grey in his hair. He was the Maisterspaeker now, old, wrinkled, with no trace of blond in his hair. He wondered what Rodulf was doing visiting an inn that was not on his land. Perhaps he knew his own people would poison him, given half the chance?

Rodulf continued to stare and the Maisterspaeker felt uncomfortable under the gaze of his story's villain. He was bound to have heard the stories before, to know he was considered the greatest dastard in the land. Perhaps he had grown used to it. Perhaps he had distanced himself from it enough to no longer notice, for he wasn't going by the name 'Rodulf' anymore. He called himself Lord Mendorf now. Jagovere smiled as he thought of it. The man before him could not react to the name Rodulf unless he wanted to reveal himself as an imposter—a liar, a traitor, and a murderer. He had done enough in that life to earn himself the death penalty many times over. He would have to swallow whatever insults Jagovere directed at him without reaction. The Maisterspaeker's smile widened as his mind raced to work out where insults could be worsened and infamy embellished. He met Rodulf's stare and continued.

*

## RODULF

Rodulf had mixed feelings as he left the Markgraf's private office the next morning. It was obvious to him that all the Markgraf cared about was the silver, and that boded well for the freedom he would have in pursuing his own ambitions. However, his title and lands felt no more secure now than they had before Ambassador dal Ruedin had named him as baron. It was made abundantly clear that if the silver did not keep coming south in ever-increasing amounts, he would find himself bowing to a different lord in Leondorf.

He had thought the Stone might soften the Markgraf's demeanour, but he hadn't so much as batted an eyelid no matter how hard Rodulf channelled his desire through it. Was he using it incorrectly? Was the Markgraf impervious to it? It was puzzling, and Rodulf knew all the speculation in the world wouldn't bring him closer to the answer. It was a frustration, but one that would have to be dealt with at another time.

One thing was certain: Before he embarked on any of his own plans he needed to make sure he kept the Markgraf happy. What could he want with all that silver? He was already a wealthy man—and in any event, for an aristocrat wealth was measured in land, not coin. It was a mystery, but one Rodulf didn't have the time to solve.

He stood outside the Markgraf's office trying to decide if he could afford to stay in the city and enjoy all it had to offer, or if he should return to Leondorf immediately. He had never truly appreciated the size of the task ahead of him until that moment. The oath of faithful service was taken more seriously than he had expected. Once the ambassador left, all the administrative tasks he and his staff had taken care of would fall to Rodulf. There wasn't long to hire and put in place people who could do that for him. The city was the best place to hire. With that thought he justified another night in the city. Some hiring during the afternoon, then a fine meal and a finer brothel in the evening.

As he moved off with a smile on his face, a man of later middle age with slicked-back grey hair approached him.

'Graf Henselman dal Geerdorf,' the man said, adding a curt nod to the greeting.

'Graf' placed dal Geerdorf one step up the social ladder from Rodulf. Even with his elevation, there was a hierarchy to conform to, and it rankled Rodulf that he was at the bottom of it. After so long dreaming about being ennobled, how quickly his thoughts turned to advancing himself within that order.

'Baron dal Leondorf,' Rodulf said, returning the gesture.

'The man of the hour,' dal Geerdorf said, his smile widening. 'How are you settling in to your new title?'

'It suits me very well,' Rodulf said.

Dal Geerdorf laughed. 'I believe it does. Shall we walk together a while?'

Rodulf nodded, still trying to work out what a man who was his social superior might want.

'The coming days will be busy for you,' dal Geerdorf said. 'There's much to do and few you can ask for advice. We were all born to our titles, lands, and the systems that make them run.'

'I have some ideas of where to start,' Rodulf said.

'I'm sure you do,' dal Geerdorf said. 'I've always found self-made men to be the most useful. It's going to be expensive though.'

Rodulf raised an eyebrow. It seemed the conversation was finally reaching its purpose.

'I realise the Markgraf retains the monopoly on the northern silver, but that leaves a great many very valuable things on the table.'

'It does,' Rodulf said, wanting to force dal Geerdorf to lead the conversation to wherever it was he was going with it.

Dal Geerdorf smiled and nodded. 'You'll quickly come to know of me, and who I am. Many would consider me to be the premier peer of the Mark—after the Markgraf, that is. I have contacts and resources that would be very useful to you in generating the income you'll need to build your barony into a functioning part of the Mark.'

Rodulf nodded. 'I've never been one to turn down offers of friendship.'

Dal Geerdorf's smile widened. 'That's exactly it. There are a great many people in Ruripathia who won't be able to look beyond your northern heritage. A friend like me can help to break down those barriers. There are few who would not wish to be counted among my friends, and that friendship brings with it many useful things, opens many otherwise closed doors.'

Rodulf nodded slowly. Dal Geerdorf likely thought he was considering the offer. He wasn't sure whether to take the words as an act of friendship or a threat. Implicit in everything he said was the fact that doors would be slammed in his face if Rodulf didn't do business with him. Nonetheless, it was a hard sell, and not something Rodulf would have expected from a nobleman, and certainly not from one as senior as dal Geerdorf, whose name he had heard mentioned previously. He was the second powerful man obsessed with money that Rodulf had dealt with in as many hours, and he was again curious. What was driving dal Geerdorf to extend the hand of friendship to a northern arriviste? It was interesting, and Rodulf filed it away in his head for future investigation. Who knew what he might find, or how it might be of use?

*

## AETHELMAN

Aethelman had received some odd looks as he left the Hermitage, all but ignoring any effort at conversation with him. He had not even stopped for a hot meal in the refectory, instead hastily bundling enough food for a few days into his satchel.

Decades had passed since Aethelman had been at the ruin where he and... He couldn't recall the name of the young priest he had carried out his Search with. The years robbed the mind of the most curious things. He could remember so clearly the expression on his friend's face as he fell from the narrow bridge that had led them to the ruin. The fear. The feeling of panic as he had rushed forward in an effort to help him, but to no avail. He had plunged to his death in the churning rapids below. Aethelman hadn't thought about him in decades, yet at the time it had been devastating.

Despite the years, Aethelman's feet seemed to know the way. His mind had kept secure the location for all that time, as though deep down he had always known he would need to return. Even by travelling straight to it, the journey would take him several days. He was not daunted, however—merely impatient.

*

## RODULF

Rodulf's mind raced as he rode back toward Leondorf. He had known the Markgraf's court would be difficult to navigate, but he'd had no idea it would be such a nest of vipers. Like the tribes of the Northlands who vied with one another for supremacy and power, there were factions at the Markgraf's court that did the same. That was only one level of it, though. The Markgraf himself was subordinate to the princess, who lived farther to the south—where the exact same situation existed.

Rodulf wondered if his court in Leondorf would follow the same model, or if it was too small and insignificant for it to matter. He supposed it was inevitable. His decisions could mean ruin or success, even life or death for his subjects, and there would always be those who would seek to curry his favour to ensure their own prosperity. It would be entertaining to watch the little factions spring up, and he began to speculate along which lines alliances would form.

As engaging a thought as it was, he had his own prosperity to think on, and he hoped he had taken the first steps toward ensuring that by aligning himself with dal Geerdorf. Their agreements were couched in the broadest terms and would need to be refined once he had a better handle on things, but he knew he would need to give a little at first. Until he had an administration keeping track of everything, and the barony running like an efficient business, he couldn't waste time driving a hard bargain against a man who, as he had said, could smooth his entry into the social hierarchy.

The first thing he had to do was build a tightly controlled silver process. From ground to smelter, this was already in place, but from that point on the southerners had managed things. Now he would have to do it for himself, and the potential for theft and fraud was great. He wanted every ounce dug out of the ground to reach the Markgraf's coffers. Once the Markgraf took his effectiveness for granted, his attention would fall elsewhere and Rodulf could do as he pleased. That would involve growing his own wealth and territory.

He was surrounded on all sides by land and peoples hostile to Ruripathia, so nobody would shed a tear if he helped himself to whatever he could take. He had hired bookkeepers and lawyers to administer his barony, but the mines would need to be worked as well. To do that he needed men, and he needed to work them long and hard. He could not expect to treat the townsfolk like that and live long.

The obvious answer was slavery. He had stopped by the slave market in Elzburg before departing, but the prices were high and he knew the attrition rate in the mines would be higher still when he upped production. The laws in the south regarding slavery were complicated and tiresome in any event. Far better to take what he needed from the neighbouring lands.

It meant war. Not war as the southerners understood the word, however. War in the Northlands was rarely more than skirmishing and raiding. Putting some warriors to the sword, burning their villages, and driving off their herds and people could hardly be considered war. "Conquest" seemed a more appropriate word. All that remained was to find some men to do the conquering for him and help his elevation from baron to Graf.

# CHAPTER 20

WULFRIC

J AGOVERE HAD BEEN correct on one count, the telling of tales did make the journey pass more quickly. To Wulfric's initial embarrassment, others had noticed him recounting the stories to Jagovere, and had ridden closer so they too could break the tedium. During the course of the ride south to Torona, he had told all the stories he knew, those related to him over and over by his father before their hearth in the evenings when he was a child. All the stories but one.

He had held one back until the end, taking the time to order it in his head. It was his favourite, and the one he wanted most to get right. The tale of Jorundyr and Ulfyr.

'The war had lasted for a decade,' Wulfric said, 'and had brought the deaths of many brave men. The draugar had been all but wiped out, or driven into dark places far from men. One great foe remained, however, one who Jorundyr had to face alone: Fanrac, King of the Draugar. The legends of Fanrac and how he came to be are many. Some say he was brother to Agnarr, Father of the Gods, but that he chose a dark path which twisted him and his disciples into demons. Whatever the truth might be, he was a powerful and fearsome foe, one whom Jorundyr could not be certain of defeating.'

Wulfric cast a self-conscious glance to the side—most of the cavalrymen were listening. He had grown used to it, however, and could hear the scratching noise of Jagovere's pen stop, so he continued.

'After weeks of tracking him, Jorundyr finally met his nemesis in a glade by a waterfall. While many of the draugar were mindless beasts, Fanrac had the cunning of the smartest of men. More than that, for he was a fallen god. He sat on a stone by the waterfall's pool, sharpening the head of an arrow with a small piece of flint.

"'Won't you join me?" Fanrac said. "Your journey has been long and tiring. Rest a moment, before we get to what we must. There is cool water, and fresh food."

"'I would rather sup on my own entrails than break bread with you," Jorundyr said.

'Fanrac smiled at him, his withered face a picture of horror. "Mayhap you will, before the day is out."

"'As you said, my journey has been long and I would rather be about my business, so to hasten my return home."

"'Such confidence," Fanrac said. "Such arrogance. You address a god, and you are but a man." He stood, and in the blink of an eye his bow was in his hand and he had loosed the arrow he had been sharpening.

'It struck Jorundyr in the thigh. He bellowed from a pain like none he had known before. The arrowhead was made from the metal found only in the High Places and it caused a pain so savage Jorundyr feared he had lost the fight before it had started.

'Fanrac stood watching him, a sword now in his hand. He wore an expression of amused curiosity. "I am many things," Fanrac said. "Among them merciful. Join me, and you will live on forever and enjoy such power as you can only dream of."

'Jorundyr roared, and pulled Draugarsbane from its sheath. It too was made from the metal of the High Places, the only thing that can injure a god or a draugr. Despite his wounded leg, he charged Fanrac. Fanrac stepped to the side and parried Jorundyr's first strike.

"'I would have forgiven you the persecution of my children," Fanrac said. "But to strike at a god—I will not let that pass. You will die here today, Jorundyr, in this pretty little glade, by this waterfall. You shall stain its waters red."

'Fanrac struck at Jorundyr with his sword, its tip slicing through Jorundyr's armour as though it was paper. Fanrac continued to smile, enjoying the encounter, relishing the prospect of killing the man whom Agnarr had chosen to wipe his pestilence from the world of men.

'Jorundyr stumbled. Never before had he faced a foe so strong or fast. In that moment, the task that had been laid before him seemed impossible. He was just a man, a farmer from a small village for whom the gods had chosen a greater destiny. He wanted nothing more than the embrace of his loving wife, Cecilia, the warmth of his hearth, the comfort of home. To die alone, so very far away, seemed a terrible thing. He swallowed hard, and refused to allow his courage to falter.

'He struck again, but once more Fanrac swatted his blade away as though it was no more an irritation than a buzzing fly. He cut at Jorundyr again, through armour, and deep into flesh—a strike that Jorundyr knew was mortal.

'"Agnarr should choose his heroes more carefully," Fanrac said. "It will not take me long to undo all you have laboured for in his name." He looked toward the High Places. "This land is mine. Do you hear me, brother? Mine!" He let out a laugh as he turned to finish his bloody task, but the laugh turned to a gasp as Jorundyr plunged his blade through the fallen god's chest. The momentary distraction was all he had needed.

'"He chose well," Jorundyr said, as he twisted the blade and watched the expression on Fanrac's face change to fear. There is no afterlife for the gods, only oblivion.

'Jorundyr held the blade with the last of his strength until he felt Fanrac's dead weight on it. Only then did he pull it free, stumble back, and collapse to the ground. He wanted so much to see his beloved Cecilia one last time, and the thought that he might not planted the seed of fear in his heart for the first time. The memory of her face motivated him to fight on. He tore some cloth from his cloak to staunch the flow of blood. If he could stop it, he had a chance of getting home.

'He was startled from his task by a long, rumbling growl. He looked up to see two belek walk into the glade—Fanrac's familiars, Renic and Ursal. They had been hunting, too far away to aid their master, but close enough to avenge him. Their eyes were like great sapphires fixed on him, their wicked fangs still coated with blood from their hunt, ready for use once more to finish what their master could not.

'Jorundyr looked up to the High Places, his heart mourning for what he knew was to come. "Why must you test me so?" he whispered.

'He forced himself to his feet, and lifted Draugarsbane one last time. He had lived without fear in his heart, and he would not die with it there. He would have to wait until he was with the gods to be reunited with Cecilia, but the knowledge that they would be together once again filled his heart with the courage to persevere.

'Agnarr heard his hero's plea, and felt sorrow that the bravest and greatest of men was to die alone and far from home. Even the gods cannot change what Fate demands, though, and her price for that day's victory was clear. What comfort could he grant a man whose destiny was beyond the control of even a god?

'A great white wolf walked into the glade, and stood by Jorundyr's side. It was as fantastic a beast as Jorundyr had ever seen, so magnificent that he all but forgot about the two belek and the savage wounds that caused him so much pain. Resigned to his fate, Jorundyr chose to enjoy this wonder for one of his few remaining moments.

'The belek moved closer, and the wolf watched each step. They circled, revelling in the anticipation of the kill, emboldened by the additional challenge posed by the new arrival. That was their folly. The wolf pounced, tearing Renic's throat from her body with one snap of his great jaws. Ursal, realising this was no ordinary wolf, jumped back, hissing in outrage that a humble beast would dare kill his mate. Undeterred, the wolf pounced again, smashing into the belek with all his weight. Smaller by half, the wolf almost disappeared from Jorundyr's sight as the two beasts fought in that small glade. Jorundyr watched in amazement, until the struggle finally ended, and the wolf stood victorious over Ursal's dead body, his once-white fur drenched with red. He padded back to Jorundyr, who had once again collapsed to the ground, and sat by him.

'"I thank you for your help, wolf, but I fear it is already too late," Jorundyr said. "I call you Ulfyr—friend—and I am in your debt."

'Jorundyr felt the strength flow from his body, but noticed that his new friend had not escaped unscathed either. The beleks' fangs had rent great wounds across his body, and his life's blood coursed from them. Ulfyr sat and lay his head on Jorundyr's lap as they both awaited what would come.

'And so Jorundyr drew his final breath and departed this world, but he did not leave alone, for Ulfyr went with him. So great was Jorundyr's courage that the gods granted him a place among them. Patron of warriors, god of all men and women who deny fear to their hearts.

'From that day until this, Ulfyr is ever by Jorundyr's side.'

✺

## Adalhaid

'Ms. Steinnsdottir, if you would be so good as to demonstrate the treatment.'

Professor Kengil held up a piece of chalk and waited silently for Adalhaid to make her way down to the blackboard at the front of the lecture theatre. One of the professor's favourite putdowns was the term 'Northlander,' with any one of a number of pejoratives before it. Adalhaid had done her best to keep her head down and remain anonymous, but eventually a question was directed at her, and the professor had instantly recognised her accent. Now, any time there was a difficult answer or demonstration required, the task was directed to Adalhaid. Thus far she had been unable to trip Adalhaid up.

She walked down the stairs to the front of the theatre, going through the treatment's steps as she went. It was part of the required reading given to them at the start of the week, and Adalhaid knew for certain there would be hardly anyone in the class who had gotten that far with it. She had made sure to have it finished the day it was given. A sleepless night and the long day following were far preferable to humiliation by a bigoted professor.

Adalhaid kept her eyes on the blackboard as she took the chalk from Kengil's hand. She walked to the board, and began.

'The treatment begins with administering a mild dream seed sedative,' Adalhaid said. She was about to continue when Kengil interrupted.

'The concentration of the sedative?'

The reading materials hadn't mentioned the concentration; such things were not set in stone, usually left to the preference and experience of the individual chemist mixing the tincture. However, Adalhaid had found the vagueness of the approach frustrating, and had looked it up.

'I believe a mild tincture is usually made of ten to fifteen parts per hundred of crushed dream seed to distilled grain alcohol.'

'I think you'll find it's five to ten,' Kengil said, seemingly disappointed that Adalhaid had managed to put an answer together at all.

Adalhaid chewed on her lip for a moment, but she was speaking before she allowed herself time to consider if it was politic to do so. 'I'm quite sure it's ten to fifteen.'

Kengil's face darkened. 'Perhaps in the Northlands, but in the South we prefer not to turn our patients into seed addicts. Five to ten parts per hundred.'

'Actually, she's correct,' a familiar voice said.

Jakob Strellis was leaning against the doorframe by the entrance to the lecture theatre. Adalhaid wondered how long he had been there.

'Although it might seem like a large quantity for a mild sedative,' he said, 'the grain alcohol denatures the narcotic effect of the seed powder, meaning a little more is needed to get the required effect. If one were to use grape alcohol, however, it would indeed be five to ten, but that's by the by. I'm sorry to interrupt, but I need a word in private, Professor Kengil.'

Kengil's face was ashen with anger, but she remained silent as she walked over to Strellis. He held the door open for her, and flashed Adalhaid a smile that sent her heart racing before closing it.

## RODULF

Rodulf shielded his eye with his hand as he watched the bird soar high in the clear blue sky. She was little more than a black dot. Each time he launched his falcon—one of a dozen that had cost him a small fortune in Elzburg—he was convinced that she would not return. The falconer had laughed the first time Rodulf had expressed his misgivings, but had quickly learned Rodulf was not a man to laugh at if he wished to keep his new and lucrative position as master falconer to Ruripathia's newest baron.

Falconry was one of the noble pursuits Rodulf was trying hastily to master. If he was to blend into the Markgraf's court, all the diversions with which his noblemen filled their time had to appear as second nature to Rodulf.

The falcon sat in the air, her great wings stretched to their limits as she seemed to float motionless in the sky. Rodulf's heart raced and he grinned like a fool as he watched her, not daring to pull his eye from that tiny speck so far above.

She let out a piercing shriek before pulling in her wings and dropping like a stone—'stooping,' the falconer called it. Rodulf's heart accelerated, although he had witnessed this spectacle a number of times before. Each and every time it looked like a death-plunge. The falcon fell so quickly that it defied belief she could arrest her descent before smashing into the ground. She disappeared from view and Rodulf held his breath.

A moment later she appeared again, soaring above the trees with a small object clutched in her talons. Rodulf let out a peal of laughter and clapped his hands, not caring that it was behaviour unbecoming of a baron. Such sights should be greeted with quiet indifference, but Rodulf doubted it would ever fail to excite him so.

'She's a magnificent hunter, ain't she,' Rodulf said, in the clipped style of Ruripathian nobles.

'That she is, my lord,' the falconer said. 'I only train the finest birds.'

'A good hunter, my lord,' Grenville said.

Grenville's years of service to various noblemen had made him adept at all the skills Rodulf so desperately needed to acquire. It made him even more valuable. He was far more than a hired sword to watch his back, and Rodulf had decided to make Grenville his steward.

Rodulf watched the falcon glide through a wide circle as it descended toward them. The object clutched in her talons became clear, a still bundle of fur that had moments before been a marmot or rabbit. The rabbit would make for better eating, but that was of little importance. She swooped in and landed on the ground a few paces from their horses. The falconer jumped down from his horse and ran over to the bird, quickly prising her catch from her talons.

'Leave her be,' Rodulf said. He enjoyed watching her tear into the object of her exertions, but the falconer shook his head and took the small, furry carcass away from her.

'It'll ruin her, my lord,' the falconer said. 'If she learns she can fill her belly from somewhere else, she won't come back to you.'

Rodulf nodded sullenly and raised his gauntleted hand. As always, he held a piece of chicken in it, and the falcon was quick to respond. With one great flap of her wings she was off the ground and onto his wrist. She greedily gobbled down the chicken, to Rodulf's delight, and they continued on. She had another flight left in her that day, and Rodulf's desire for the spectacle was not yet sated.

They came up a rise, and Rodulf reined his horse in. A small village of thatched buildings lay in the valley below. From his vantage point, Rodulf realised how his falcon must feel when she finally spotted her prey while soaring through the sky. Such was the village for Rodulf. Ripe for the taking, and unable to do a thing about it. Falconry alone would not win Rodulf the respect of his peers; it would only stop him from looking like an ignorant fool.

'I'm going to need men, Grenville,' Rodulf said, as he watched the distant villagers go about their day, oblivious to his predatory gaze, no different from the falcon's rabbit. 'You know the sort I mean.'

'I do, my lord. How many?'

'Enough for that place, and more like it.'

# CHAPTER 21

Wulfric

I T TOOK THE Company a full week on the road to reach Torona. Wulfric felt a degree of trepidation when its towers came into view. The walls were a yellowy-beige colour, and the buildings he could see within were white-washed with rust-coloured roofs.

Jagovere rode ahead to the city, while the rest of the Company waited for instructions about where to make camp. Any approaching army was viewed with suspicion verging on hostility, hired or not. Jagovere had told him that disagreements over contractual terms could turn an employed force into an enemy army in an instant. He said they would continue to be viewed with suspicion for as long as they were in Estranza. They wanted men to fight for them, but that didn't mean they would ever trust foreign mercenaries.

Eventually, the order came and they rode to a rocky, arid field away from any of the city's gates. Tents were assigned by squad, so he, Enderlain, and the others set about clearing a section of rocky ground to set up their tent.

'Will we be here long?' Wulfric said.

'Your guess is as good as mine,' Walt said. 'Days, weeks, who knows? Doesn't matter much; we still get paid either way. Better sitting here bored than being used as the vanguard for the duke's campaign south.'

'Getting scared of a fight in your old age?' Gotz said.

Wulfric gave Walt a good look. He didn't look at all past his prime. His hair was starting to grey, something the others gave him a hard time over, which Wulfric found odd. For a warrior, age meant you possessed the skill to have survived countless battles, and to have slain many foes. In the Northlands, it was something deserving respect, not mockery.

'Not scared,' Walt said, 'just experienced enough to know boredom is better than having some fucker tryin' to kill you.'

'If you don't start clearing more stones, this fucker's gonna try to kill you,' Enderlain said.

There was a chuckle from the others, then silence as they applied themselves to getting the ground clear for their tent.

'They could have at least given us some decent ground to camp on,' Walt said.

Wulfric tapped it with the shovel he was using to clear the stones. It was baked hard with little vegetation. He could see more verdant land simply by looking around, and it appeared they had been given a rough piece of wasteland that served no purpose. Even though it was well past noon, Wulfric was feeling the effect of the heat. Cooling breezes blowing across the ship had made the transition as they sailed south less noticeable. It was the same on the coast, but as they marched inland it had grown hotter than Wulfric had ever experienced before. Sitting on horseback, it had been pleasant. The heat felt good on his skin, which was turning a golden brown—far darker than it had ever been in even the hottest summer at Leondorf.

However, now that he was trying to work in the heat it felt oppressive. Sweat dripped from his nose every time he bent over, and his shirt was soaked through. The others seemed better able to deal with it, although he could see it was taking its toll on them too. He wondered if he would ever get used to it, and what it would be like to fight, armoured, under that blazing sun.

❉

AETHELMAN

Aethelman wasn't sure who maintained the bridge, but there had to be someone doing it. Some planks looked newer than others, and there was no fraying on the rope that held it over the grey canyon and churning river below. He had expected it would have long since fallen into the chasm. The waters were just as violent as he remembered—the waters that had swallowed up his friend. It must have been an awful death; the fall, the cold, being smashed against the canyon's sides, the terror of drowning. It would not have been quick, and Aethelman wished he could have done more—but he was not a strong man, never had been. Not in the body, at least. There had been only so long he was able to grasp his friend's scruff before his grip had failed. The look in his eyes as he fell…

Aethelman squeezed his eyes tightly shut and wished that one memory from his head forever. He had spent many hours thinking about his young friend on the long walk to the canyon, but still could not remember his name. The years were not the only thing to blame. He had done his best to forget, and that much he had achieved.

His heart fluttered as he set his foot on the gently swaying rope bridge. It moved under his boot and he saw himself falling through the air like his long-dead friend. He forced himself to put one foot in front of the other, and continue on. He did not take a breath until he reached the other side.

❁

## RODULF

'This is the best you could get?' Rodulf said, looking at the motley group of men gathered before him.

'Aye, on short notice it is,' Grenville said. 'It's campaigning season. Any company worth having is already engaged.'

Rodulf looked at Grenville curiously. He had spent months trying to adopt the hard, clipped tone of the southerners. Grenville, on the other hand, seemed to quickly adopt the northern lilt. Rodulf turned his attention to the gathered assembly, only twenty men, and did his best to hide his distaste. Beggars, cutthroats, and ne'er-do-wells, the lot of them. Not a soldier in sight.

'Grundorf has at least twenty warriors,' Rodulf said. 'They'll cut through this lot like butter.' He looked at the rotten clothing one of them was wearing, a man clearly only recently departed from prison. 'Rancid butter.'

'The warriors won't be expecting it,' Grenville said. 'With my lads backing them up, they should be enough. If half of them get killed it'll cost us less. You less.'

Rodulf smiled, happy to be reminded why he had come to value Grenville's service.

'They'll need some training,' Rodulf said. 'I have to make sure they get the job done. After that, I don't care.'

'I'll make sure they're up to it.'

'Good,' Rodulf said. 'Take care of it.'

He turned and walked away. The motley group behind him might manage to overwhelm an unsuspecting hamlet, but they would be of no use in helping achieve his bigger aims. With a good enough offer, he was sure he could lure a large enough company of mercenaries to his service to carve a swathe through the Northlands. However, that might draw too much attention. He reckoned it was better to ask forgiveness than permission. The Markgraf wouldn't complain when he realised how much more territory he was lord of, but he might try to stop Rodulf from embarking on a campaign of conquest.

His next stop was a large area of cleared land that had until recently been a small wooded area near the village. It was craggy with shallow soil, which would make for the perfect foundations for his manor.

As yet, little had been done. The trees were cut down and the soil cleared back to the bedrock, it was a humble beginning, but with the outline imprinted on the ground, it didn't take a great leap of the imagination to envision high walls, towers, turrets, and flags flapping proudly from the battlements. He paced along the cleared soil, allowing his mind to fill in what would be there. Kennels for hunting hounds, a mews for his falcons, stables, kitchens, guardhouse, gardens. Then there would be his house. The preference, he was reliably informed, was for a statement of wealth and power rather than a purely defensive structure, although he thought it would be foolhardy to opt entirely for style over substance. It would be more of a fortified residence than a residential fortification, as his architect had put it. Most importantly, it would be at the cutting edge of southern fashion. Rodulf wanted something to show everyone he could do style, taste, and sophistication as well as anyone, that Leondorf was not a rural barony of knuckle-dragging savages.

He had chosen a white stone. It had to be brought from the south and would be expensive, but it would be worth it in the end. From the top of the turrets, he would be able to see for miles around. For now it would mean being able to see beyond Leondorf's boundaries, but he would not rest until even the highest vantage point fell too short. Leondorf might have joined Ruripathia as a barony, but he would see it a county, perhaps even a markgrafate.

For now, the old Great Hall served for his audiences, and the former ambassador's residence as his home. The southern architects and builders told him that the manor house would not be finished for five years at least, the defensive walls and outbuildings longer still, which struck Rodulf as ridiculous. More money would speed it up—for southerners, more money seemed to be the solution to every problem—but the manor and the house he had bought in Elzburg, not to mention the multitude of other costs coming out of the woodwork, left him with little to spare.

'A word, my lord.'

Grenville's voice gave Rodulf a start. He had been so absorbed in his dreams of grandeur that he hadn't heard the mercenary approach. 'What is it?'

'Business to attend to in the hall. Urdo the carter reckons Fedra has cut him short on manure.'

'Fedra? He's a herdsman?'

Grenville nodded.

Herdsmen were allowed to keep the manure from the herds they watched over—a perk of the job, as it was easily sold as fertiliser. 'Carters, herdsmen, and manure.' Rodulf sighed. 'Best be to it. Can't allow legal uncertainty to prevail in my demesne.' He started toward the Hall, and Grenville dropped in beside him.

'I need to be back in Elzburg next week,' Rodulf said.

'I'll be ready to go,' Grenville said.

'No. I want you to stay here. Keep an eye on things. "Seneschal", I think they call it in the south.'

Grenville smiled. 'Seneschal Grenville.' He took a deep breath and looked out toward the High Places. 'I like the sound of it.'

'Good,' Rodulf said. 'Do right by me, and there'll be more like that for you here.'

'You know, in the south, a seneschal's a man of influence, wealth. Land.'

Rodulf laughed out loud. 'The new village, and five hundred acres around it. "Seigneur Grenville, Master of Grundorf, Seneschal of Leondorf".'

'Buying things with land you don't own yet, my lord?' Grenville said.

'Think of it as having a vested interest in my new venture.'

'And if it doesn't work out?'

'Then you don't get your five hundred acres. Or your seigneury. I might still keep you as my seneschal, though.'

'Best make sure it works out then,' Grenville said.

❋

## WULFRIC

Jagovere appeared at the entrance to Wulfric's tent.

'Pack your necessaries,' Jagovere said. 'You're coming with me.'

Wulfric started to throw some things into a sack. He was growing used to the concept of taking orders. 'Where are we going?'

'Into the city. We're to stay at the palace.'

'Why me?' Wulfric asked.

'Several reasons. The first, and most important, is because I said so. I'm to stay there as the liaison between the Company and the duke. For much of the time, that will mean doing nothing, which brings me to my second reason. I'm missing details on some of the epics, so it will be a good chance to go through them with you to make sure they're right. Finally, you're a big bastard, and it never hurts to have a big bastard with you when you're going into the unknown. Bring a sword. Enderlain is coming too. Two big bastards. You can never have enough.' He left Wulfric to finish packing his things.

When they arrived at the city walls the gates were open to them. The guards watched them warily, their hands gripping their halberds. Jagovere was a little taller than the guards, despite being the slightest of the three, while Wulfric and Enderlain were head and shoulders over them.

Wulfric's height was not the only thing that made him stand out. His fair skin and sandy hair contrasted against the dark hair and tanned complexions of the locals. The women were undeniably beautiful—dark and mysterious-looking—and he found he was turning his head so frequently that Jagovere had to tell him to keep his eyes ahead. The men were consistently shorter than the Company's average, rarely reaching much over Wulfric's shoulder. He could see immediately why Northlanders and Ruripathians, tall and broad more often than not, were so sought after for fighting.

The streets felt less imposing than Elzburg's, with the white-washed buildings giving them a friendlier, brighter character. They were a bustle of activity as people went about their daily business, and led them gently uphill to the castle, where their arrival was expected. Guards brought them in through cool, high-vaulted hallways, a welcome respite from the heat outside. Even in plain linen britches and shirt, Wulfric was too warm after the walk up to the castle.

The duke's audience hall took Wulfric's breath away. Higher than any of the halls they had passed through, its barrel-vaulted ceiling hung dizzyingly far overhead. Great leaded-glass windows lined either side, filling the hall with golden light—and at the far end, behind a man sitting on a dais, was an even greater window, its panels stained in a multitude of different colours. Wulfric had never seen anything like it, and took a moment to realise it depicted a scene—a man slaying a great serpent-like creature. A dragon. It was the first time Wulfric had seen one depicted, though he had heard them described in stories. It looked far more terrifying than he had imagined, more so even than a belek.

The hall was full of people and the murmur of quiet conversation. Dal Rhenning awaited them there, standing to the side of a group of courtiers, waiting for his turn in front of the duke. Wulfric couldn't tear his gaze from the scarlet dragon on the window.

Jagovere followed Wulfric's gaze and smiled. 'The first Duke of Torona was reputed to have been a great dragon slayer. Something every duke since has been very proud of.'

Wulfric nodded, but did not say anything. His head was filled with snippets from Northland epics. Dragons were said to have once made their homes in the High Places, but none had been seen for centuries. The beast in the window was magnificent. It almost seemed alive. His eyes were locked on it—the scales, the fangs, its great, devious eyes. There were some who believed dragons still lived in remote places—the far east, hidden valleys in the High Places, across the Great Sea—and a shiver of excitement ran over his skin as he wondered what it might be like to fight one.

'How is it?' Jagovere said.

'A vipers' nest,' dal Rhenning said quietly. 'More likely to get stabbed in the back in here than in a back alley on a moonless night.'

'So no different to any other noble court, then,' Jagovere said.

'Not in the least. Almost feels like home. Two distinct factions as best I can tell so far—those who support the duke and those who favour his younger half-brother, the Count of Valeriano—but there are plenty who'll jump between them as best serves their interests. You'll have to tread carefully.'

'I always do.'

A man approached them. 'His Grace will see you now,' he said, gesturing for them to come forward.

They did as they were bade, and Wulfric felt his skin crawl with every eye in the hall on the northern curiosities.

'How long will it take before your men are ready to fight?' the duke said as soon as they reached him.

'We're ready now, Your Grace,' dal Rhenning said. 'The men acclimated on the march here. A good night's sleep and a hot meal will have them ready to go again.'

'My army is camped on the border with Darvaros, but have as yet made no progress beyond that,' the duke said. 'If you live up to your reputation, I am hopeful you will inject some energy into the campaign and see it carried to success before the end of the season.'

The duke was younger than Wulfric would have thought. He was not accustomed to the idea of a man being born to leadership. In the Northlands, it was always the strongest, most cunning warrior, but not until he had many seasons of experience under his cloak.

'I assure you my company's reputation is well deserved, and we will not be found wanting.'

'My half-brother, the Count of Valeriano, Marshall of Torona, commands the army. He will be returning to it at the end of the week. I would suggest you and your company travel with his party. Until then, I grant your men liberty in my city in groups of no more than—' he paused and conferred with the man standing beside him '—of no more than five men. They will be treated no differently to my citizens if they are found to have breached the law.'

'I can vouch for the good behaviour of my men,' dal Rhenning said.

'Very good. As arranged, I will require you to leave some of your men at my court to liaise with my officials until you depart.'

'Of course. My captain and his… lieutenants here will be at your disposal,' dal Rhenning said.

Wulfric raised an eyebrow.

'Looks like we got a promotion,' Enderlain whispered, a broad smile spreading across his face.

'Excellent,' the duke said. 'Apartments will be made ready for them.'

# CHAPTER 22

AETHELMAN

A ETHELMAN DID NOT know what the ruined building had been in the past, but it seemed safe to assume it had been used by the men who established the Grey Priests. There was little of it left, other than the remnants of a few walls and pillars, scattered stones, and a flagstone floor. He tried to imagine what it had looked like when it was complete, but it was difficult. The fragments remaining spoke of a time when the people of the north had greater skill in working stone. He had seen similar remnants across the Northlands, the last vestiges of a civilisation that had been strangled into oblivion by an empire now also long dead.

Moss covered most of the surfaces, and tendrils of ivy grasped every upstanding piece of masonry. The air was filled with the sound of a waterfall, which fed the chasm Aethelman had just crossed. It was a serene place. The perfect place for reflection, or a kirk, or whatever they had called their temples in that long-forgotten time.

He sat on a mossy chunk of stone and surveyed the ruin, trying to pick out anything he remembered from his previous visit so many years before. Then, as now, it had been a picture of lush green and grey, with the mist thrown up by the waterfall drifting in thin clouds across the small plateau surrounded by sheer cliffs. It was easy to sit there and allow his mind to drift to a place of comfort, but Aethelman forced himself to stay focussed.

He and the other priest had been searching for a long time when they had come to that spot, long enough to have tired of their seemingly pointless task. This place had appeared to be a dead end—the termination of a trail they had been following for weeks. Aethelman realised that the Search had been a test of character, that it was supposed to be difficult, isolating, frustrating. It had certainly been all of that and more. He could remember constantly being cold, tired, and hungry. His friend's voice echoed against the sheer mountain walls surrounding the ancient ruin so clearly that it took Aethelman a moment to realise it was merely a memory. His friend had been angry when they had come to the belief that the ruin was another dead end. The frustration had eaten away at his soul, while for Aethelman it had done the opposite: It had given him resolve and the knowledge that his faith was strong enough to see him through hardship and disappointment. That was when he had felt something tug at the fibres of his very being.

At first it was subtle, like the sensation of falling, even though he had been sitting down, not far from where he now sat. It grew more forceful until it felt so strong he thought the contents of his stomach would be pulled from his gut. That was when he had stood and followed the force urging him toward some unknown.

He stood now, and allowed the memory to guide him, across the cracked, centuries-old flags of the kirk's floor to the shambled mass of cut stone, vine, and leaf litter that might once have been an altar. On that previous occasion, he had cleared away what vegetation had been there, but knew what he had found long before he ever laid eyes upon it. It was as though it had spoken to him, told him what it was and where it might be found. It had called him to come and take it. His friend had still been cursing the priesthood, the Search, and every person they had met along this path who had spoken of an ancient ruin overlooking a river gorge at the side of a mountain.

Aethelman had taken the Stone from its resting place in a dark nook, and brought it out into daylight for the first time in generations. The skin of his hands had tingled as he held it. He could remember the sensation of terror and excitement and triumph so clearly a tingle ran up his spine as he dwelled on the memory. The vegetation he had cleared those years previously had long since regrown, but the nook was empty. He almost felt disappointed as he gazed into the dark, empty space. A Stone was not what he was looking for, however. It was the ancient runes carved onto the lintel above.

The ravages of weather would have erased them centuries before were it not for the protective covering of moss and ivy. It only took a few moments to clear several runes well enough to make them legible. Where they had been indecipherable to him before, they were now as familiar as his own name.

'Here lies the object of our salvation and our downfall. Abandoned to a place soon to be forgotten in the hope that it too might be forgotten.'

The words sent a chill down his spine. He had possessed it for so long. How could every detail of something so ominous been forgotten?

Aethelman traced his finger along the runes to double check the meaning, the incongruity making him question his newfound literacy. He read it the same way on the second pass. Salvation *and* downfall? How could that be? He cleared more moss and ivy, hoping there would be more to elaborate on the cryptic inscription, but there was nothing. Frustration weighed on him, which a deep breath did little to dispel. Why did the gods have to make everything so complicated?

❧

## RODULF

Thick black smoke drifted away from the village, much to Rodulf's satisfaction. Death, destruction, conquest. There was something so compelling and intoxicating about it. He felt more alive than he ever had before. Since dangling it as a carrot before Grenville, his newly-appointed seneschal had gone to great pains to instruct their men to leave the village as intact as possible. He cared little for the villagers, as they could easily be replaced, but repairing a devastated village would cost money, money that would have to come from Grenville's purse as seigneur of the territory. Men were men, however, and bloodlust made orders a distant memory. If anything, Rodulf was surprised that the scum they had hired had been so restrained. Nonetheless, a village was a necessity if Grenville hoped to have his demesne worked to a profit, and his temper at the destruction that had unfolded was as entertaining a spectacle as Rodulf had witnessed in some time.

He rode back and forth, beating at the men as he tried to turn them from continued rapine and pillage and put them to work in extinguishing the fires their lust for carnage had ignited. Rodulf made no effort to help. His revenues were undiminished by the small tragedy unfolding before him. All that mattered to him was that a swathe of land had been added to his barony, and a number of slaves to his mines. More wealth would flow to him, and that would bring him respect, but more importantly, greater power.

He laughed at Grenville's frustration, but decided he would help pay for the repairs—Grenville was too useful not to keep happy. There was more territory for the taking, and Rodulf would not be satisfied until he had it. Not all the villages would fall as easily as Grundorf, however, and the vermin running amok in the village below him would not be up to it. Rodulf doubted Grenville would make any arguments in their favour after the mess they had made of his seigneury. Indeed, Rodulf reckoned the majority of their casualties would come from Grenville's sword rather than those of the village's warriors. Still, as Grenville had said, dead men don't need to be paid.

※

## ADALHAID

Adalhaid's blood boiled as she walked away from the School of Medicine's noticeboard. Attending clinics was a vital part of every student's training. After their basic indoctrination, each student was assigned to one of several free clinics in the city, to assist the qualified physicians and learn the practical application of their studies. Once again her name was absent from the list, and she knew exactly why.

Professor Kengil was in charge of assigning the duties. She was also head of the School of Medicine, so there was no one to whom she could complain.

'That's not a happy face,' a voice said. Doctor Strellis.

'Dr. Strellis,' Adalhaid said. 'Good morning. I wanted to thank you for backing me up the other day. It was… good timing.'

'You're very welcome, but it was the least I could do. Professor Kengil was incorrect, and I couldn't allow all those young and inquiring minds to be led astray. I can't help but ask: What's ruined your day?'

'Kengil—pardon me, Professor Kengil—has left me off the list for clinics. Again.'

Strellis frowned. 'She shouldn't do that. Every student is supposed to have a weekly clinic. Perhaps it's just an oversight?'

Adalhaid raised an eyebrow.

'No, perhaps not. Medicine has moved along a lot in the past few years. I probably shouldn't be saying it, but Kengil is still stuck in the dark ages, and she refuses to consider new techniques coming from abroad. It's made her angrier and angrier over the past few years. She's not the easiest person to deal with.' He scratched the stubble on his chin for a moment. 'Look, I run a weekly clinic in the city. You can come along and get your hours there. I can sign off on them for you. If Kengil makes a fuss I'll say I was correcting the oversight. She'll know she's in the wrong.'

'Thank you,' Adalhaid said. 'You're very kind.'

'More than worth it to see that frown replaced by a smile,' Strellis said.

❉

## WULFRIC

Wulfric's apartment was amazing. There was an enormous bed with a feather mattress, covered in blankets that were so soft he didn't want to take his hand from them. A knock on the door took him from his quandary. He opened it to be greeted by Jagovere, with Enderlain standing behind him.

'Good, you've space for roommates,' Jagovere said, as he walked in with his duffel bag slung over his shoulder. Enderlain nodded to Wulfric as he followed Jagovere in.

'Didn't they give you rooms?' Wulfric said.

'Oh, yes. Of course. We'll be staying in here with you, though.'

'Why?' he said, not certain he wanted the answer, but reluctant to give up his newfound luxury and privacy.

'Because everyone knows I'm the Graf's captain, and all the servants saw me take the other room. No one saw me leave it and come here, however.'

Wulfric raised an eyebrow and looked at Enderlain, who shrugged.

'At some point tonight, someone will break into my room and try to kill me,' Jagovere said. 'Not being there will go a long way to ensuring that doesn't happen. If they decide to call here, the three of us will be more than able to handle whatever we're faced with. If not, we deserve an assassin's blade.'

Wulfric cast a glance to where he had left his sword. 'I thought the duke invited us here,' he said.

'He did,' Jagovere said as he dropped his duffel on the polished wooden floor and flopped onto a couch. Enderlain sat on the other and tested it, bouncing up and down with an expression on his face as though he was an expert on couch softness.

'As it's your room, you can take the bed,' Jagovere said. Seeing the confusion on Wulfric's face, he continued. 'Just because the duke invited us here doesn't mean everyone in his court is happy we've arrived.'

'But why kill you?'

'To send a message, which is often the reason for killing someone. Me not being there also sends a message. It tells them we know what their game is, and we can play it just as well as they can.'

# CHAPTER 23

AETHELMAN

ONCE THEY HAD discovered the Stone, everything else was forgotten. That there might have been anything else of value in the ruins had escaped them completely. Aethelman wondered what they might have missed. His friend had become ebullient with joy and excitement once they had realised what they had found. 'We've succeeded where hundreds, thousands of priests before us have failed,' he had said. 'Our names will be carved into the Hermitage's walls, never to be forgotten.'

Aethelman had remained quiet, sitting on a rock and staring at the strange object on his lap. The initial excitement he had felt at discovering such a rare object, and achieving the goal of the Search dissipated quickly. All that remained was concern. What was this strange thing? Why had the Grey Priests searched for them for so long? What danger might its discovery bring into the world? Above all, what was he supposed to do with it? No one, least of all Aethelman, had expected them to find anything. They had not been told what should follow this discovery. Should he destroy it? He had no idea how to attempt that. Should he return it to the Hermitage? Would they not have been told to do that before they left? Was he supposed to safeguard it, to dedicate his life to keeping it from anyone who might use it irresponsibly? Should he put it back under the altar, and forget all about it? He had no idea what it did, or how it might be made to work.

Ritschl had waxed lyrical about what they could do with it—Ritschl. His name was Ritschl. After scouring the recesses of his mind for so long, he had finally remembered it when he wasn't even thinking of it. In the remembering, Ritschl became so much more than a shadowy memory. He took on colour and character.

Aethelman's fear of the Stone had grown with each of Ritschl's exhortations. Nothing he said was in the character of a Grey Priest. There was no humility, no self-sacrifice. Everything he wanted, he wanted for himself. Aethelman knew that Ritschl could not have the Stone. He realised he had seen the change in personality over the previous weeks of the Search. All the tests and discomforts placed on them pushed him farther from the tenets of their faith, while they pulled Aethelman closer. While Ritschl ranted about the futility and stupidity of their task, Aethelman had searched for and found comfort in their dogma. He could see Ritschl once more, pacing back and forward on the moss-covered flag stones, talking animatedly with wild gestures of his hands about the opportunities their discovery had offered. Aethelman had wondered at the significance of him being drawn to the Stone, rather than Ritschl, for they had both been as close to its hiding place.

The look on Ritschl's face as their grips faltered and he fell from the bridge returned, banishing all else from Aethelman's mind. He shut his eyes and turned his head in an effort to escape it. When he opened them, he saw a shadow on the mountain face that he had not noticed before. He stood, and walked toward it.

❧

## WULFRIC

'Which one is your favourite?'

Wulfric wanted to go to sleep, but Jagovere seemed determined to chatter through the night. He thought for a moment.

'I always enjoyed hearing the stories the warriors told when they came back from battle or hunting more than the old epics,' he said.

'I suppose all the epics started out like that,' Jagovere said. 'As tales of hunting or fighting or drinking.'

'Or wenching,' Enderlain said.

'I suppose,' Wulfric said, after a lengthy pause which he hoped would slow the conversation down to a halt.

'Shhhh,' Jagovere said.

Wulfric sat up on his elbows and looked across the gloomy room to where Jagovere lay on the couch. He had been the one prattling on, but Wulfric realised with disappointment that his hushing didn't mean it was time for sleep. He saw the glint of steel in the moonlight as Jagovere drew his sword. Wulfric swung his legs from the bed and placed them on the floor as quietly as he could. He picked up his sword and waited for a signal from Jagovere. Enderlain snored, but Wulfric could see the shine of his open eyes in the moonlight.

Jagovere walked to the wall and pressed his ear to it, a finger held to his lips. Even from where Wulfric stood, he could hear noise in the next room. It was the sound of frustration, and he wondered if it would mean a visit to his room. His skin tingled in anticipation.

More sound, some voices, then silence once more. It seemed unlikely an assassin would come through the door, so he crouched and crept toward the window.

They waited in silence for several more minutes before Jagovere relaxed.

'Hopefully that's the end of that carry-on.'

'Why won't they just come here?'

'Because they know we're ready for them. Trying again would mean a fight they might not win. All the same, I think we should take turns keeping watch tonight.'

❋

## ADALHAID

Adalhaid felt a mix of excitement and terror when she arrived at Strellis's clinic on her first day. She had heard other students talk of their experiences, but they seemed to be limited to boiling metal instruments and changing bedsheets. What greeted her when she went in came as a complete surprise.

A small, shabby waiting room was packed with people, ranging from the very young to the very old. Life in a busy city was hard, and broken limbs were rife, but there were other things that caught Adalhaid's eye—the physical manifestations of subjects that had been discussed in her classes. She looked around with embryonic professional curiosity, until she was called by name.

'Adalhaid?'

A blonde woman, not much older than Adalhaid, stood by a doorway with an inquiring look on her face.

'Yes.'

'Doctor dal Strellis said you'd be coming. I'm Rosamund.' She offered her hand in the hasty fashion of someone with more tasks than time. 'Follow me and I'll get you oriented.'

She led Adalhaid through the door into a corridor and pointed to a small door on the right. 'You can get a clean smock in there at the start of every clinic.' To another on the left. 'Dry supplies are kept in there— bandages, towels, sheets. Next door is medications. That one's kept locked. I have a key, as does Doctor dal Strellis; just ask us if you need anything from it. You have to be a Junior Sophister or higher to get one.'

Adalhaid still had five terms of tuition to go before she was a Junior Sophister. They passed down the hall and through the door at the end which led into a large treatment room. Little effort had been made to smooth out the scars of the transformation.

'You said "Doctor *dal* Strellis",' Adalhaid said. 'I thought it was just "Strellis"?'

'Ah, yes. Jakob has had some… family issues,' Rosamund said. 'His father's a baron, and doesn't approve of his career choice. Noblemen aren't supposed to work for a living. He prefers to be thought of as a physician rather than an aristocrat. He'll be in shortly and will go through what he'll want you to do.'

Adalhaid raised her eyebrows and took a deep breath.

Rosamund laughed. 'Don't worry. For the first few sessions he'll just have you sit in and observe. You'll have plenty of time to find your feet.'

❧

WULFRIC

The crowds were beginning to gather at court when they arrived in the great hall the following morning, the wealthy elite of Torona all vying for the attention of their duke. Colour abounded, with the clothes made of cloth so fine it was almost impossible to see the weave. Wulfric looked around as surreptitiously as he could and wondered which of the men standing there had sent an assassin against them the previous night. Might it have been a woman? He recalled that Ruripathia was ruled by a princess. If they could hold power, it stood to reason they would be as ruthless in taking it.

The beautiful women of the Estranzan court suddenly took on a far more sinister appearance.

'Nice and relaxed,' Jagovere said. 'We want to act like nothing at all happened last night. We know it happened, whoever arranged for it knows; by not reacting at all it will confuse the hells out of them.'

Wulfric nodded and followed Jagovere. He was aware of how scruffy his appearance was by contrast to the others there, and how much it made him stand out. However, Jagovere walked through the hall with the confidence of someone who belonged there, so Wulfric did his best to follow suit, taking comfort in the fact that Enderlain was equally scruffy. Some of the curious glances cast in his direction bordered on hostile as they moved to the front of the hall, but Wulfric ignored them.

They took a place to the left of the dais at the front of the hall. Jagovere acted as if he didn't have a care in the world, but Wulfric could not let the fact that someone in that room had ordered their assassination leave his thoughts. He looked at the count of Valeriano, standing in pride of place to the right of the dais with his entourage. He was the duke's greatest rival, yet had been given the honour of commanding the army, which didn't make sense. He had a shrewd and hostile appearance, his finely pointed greying moustache and beard lending him a harsh look. He didn't seem like a man capable of taking what he wanted by force of arms, though. He looked every inch the plotter. The predatory gleam in his eyes made Wulfric think of Rodulf's father, Donato—hawkish, observing everything, and deciding which morsels he wanted to snap up for himself.

The first man with him was slightly built and bookish looking. He was bald, and initially reminded Wulfric of Aethelman the priest. However, his demeanour was as far from Aethelman's benevolence as could be. Sharp and calculating were the words that came to Wulfric's mind. He would be the advisor, Wulfric thought, while the remaining man was most certainly the fighter.

He caught Wulfric's stare, and regarded him with an expression of curious amusement. He was younger than the others, with dark curly hair and a neat, pointed beard. He looked every inch a fighter. He was broad of shoulder and stood straight, yet was visibly lighter on his feet. He pushed his cloak back from the hilt of his sword, the message clear. Was this the man who had broken into Jagovere's room the night before? Wulfric allowed his gaze to drift across the audience, as though he had not even noticed the swordsman.

A court official emerged from a door at the back of the hall and scanned the gathering. The count locked his gaze on the official, who ignored him completely. Wulfric could see a cloud of anger descend over the count's face. On spotting Jagovere, the official made his way over.

'The duke would like to speak with you in his private chambers.'

'Lead on,' Jagovere said. 'This should be interesting,' he whispered to Wulfric and Enderlain.

❁

## WULFRIC

The official led them to a small, austere stairwell that brought them up and into a private wing at the back of the palace. They popped out of the stairwell into a lushly carpeted hall lined with sculptures and paintings. The official shut the door behind him, which was almost invisible against the wall, erasing any hint of the dark, cobweb-filled servant's passage behind. They continued to follow him down the hall until he brought them into a study lined with bookshelves, and the duke, sitting at a grand desk covered in dark green leather.

'Thank you for coming,' the duke said.

'We are at your convenience, Your Grace,' Jagovere said.

Wulfric bowed his head, not sure of what he should do. As Jagovere's subordinate, silence seemed most appropriate. Enderlain did likewise.

'I understand someone broke into your apartments last night,' the duke said.

'You are remarkably well informed, Your Grace,' Jagovere said. 'Happily I was not there at the time.'

'I can assure you, and Graf dal Rhenning, that it had nothing to do with me.'

'I didn't think for a moment it did, Your Grace.'

'You have suspicions in this regard?'

'I do, Your Grace, but it would be impolitic of me to voice them at this point.'

The duke drummed his fingers on the desk. 'In the absence of evidence, of which I am certain there is none, you are right. I need you to take these papers to Graf dal Rhenning. Once you've done that, return here. My brother, the marshall, wishes to discuss the march south with you.'

'At once, Your Grace.'

'Have a care around my brother,' the duke said. 'He can be... prickly.'

'I will, Your Grace. By your leave?'

The duke pushed a stack of envelopes across his desk. Jagovere took them, saluted and left, with Wulfric and Enderlain following like faithful hunting dogs. They did not utter a word to one another until they were safely shrouded in the noise of the streets outside the palace.

'Do you believe him?' Wulfric said.

'I think I do,' Jagovere said. 'In the grand scheme of things, and with my admittedly limited knowledge of how things work around here, I think the duke needs us more for his stated purpose than the benefit any subterfuge could afford him. Bringing us all the way here and then arranging an assassination to blame on his brother seems overly complex. No, I think the marshall is the most likely candidate at this point. Assuming the absence of any other interested parties...'

# CHAPTER 24

AETHELMAN

ETHELMAN CLEARED AWAY the vegetation from around the shadow. At one point in its existence, it had been nothing more than a fissure in the rock face, but somewhere along the way it had become more than that. Men had arrived, and altered it to fit their needs. A stone archway carved into the rock now framed it, inscribed with a prayer to Audun, the god of wisdom and knowledge. It was rare to see Audun mentioned. There were few who followed his creed now—not since the days of true magic had that god held a large following.

Aethelman took a step back and looked around. From the outline of the ruins, it looked like there had once been a building around the fissure. The works of man faded into the mists of time, but those of the gods remained. He peered into the gloomy opening and remembered all too well the suffocating darkness of the cavern beneath the Hermitage. He was without his little orb of light now, an absence he was feeling keenly, but the gods had stood by him beneath the Hermitage. Perhaps they would again.

He stepped through the threshold and resisted the urge to reach for the pocket he had kept the magic light in for all those years. There were steps. He carefully followed them down into the darkness, wondering what awaited him down there. What had he and Ritschl overlooked all those years ago?

❄

## WULFRIC

When they got back to dal Rhenning's tent—a canvas expanse with a number of flags flying from lances outside—the Graf had already covered his camp table with maps. He paid them little attention as he lounged in a canvas chair with his boots up on the table, contentedly puffing away on a twist of tobacco. It was a habit Wulfric had seen many southern men indulge, but he had yet to try it. It looked like a foul thing, yellowing the fingers and the teeth in many who partook, although dal Rhenning did not yet appear to suffer from either side effect.

'Dispatches from the duke,' Jagovere said, dropping the bundle of letters on the table.

'Did they try anything?' dal Rhenning said.

'They did,' Jagovere said, sitting on a chair and adopting the Graf's pose, minus the twist of tobacco. The resemblance between the two at that moment was startling.

'Glad to see you're still breathing,' dal Rhenning said.

'I appreciate your concern. There wasn't much to it,' Jagovere said. 'They thought we'd be surprised. We weren't. They'll make more of an effort next time.'

'The duke's brother?'

'I think that's the most likely,' Jagovere said. 'He didn't look happy when we turned up at the hall this morning. Then again, perhaps he's always a sour-faced bastard. Still, the split at court couldn't be more obvious if the different sides were waving opposing flags. I don't reckon the duke has the power base to do anything direct to get rid of dal Valeriano. Not yet, anyway. I suspect we fall neatly into the middle, and he hopes our presence'll stir things up enough to give him the opportunity to move.'

Dal Rhenning stroked his moustache and nodded. 'Not the first time I've seen something like that. We'll have to play it canny. And you, Wulfric? How did you enjoy your night of luxury?'

'Well enough,' Wulfric said. 'The bed was too soft.'

Dal Rhenning barked out a laugh, sat up straight and slapped his hand on the table. 'Now there's a man made for campaigning. None of your warm inns, music, and painted ladies.'

Enderlain let out a *humph*.

'There's a place in a man's life for all those things,' Jagovere said. 'It would be a waste of a life not to sample them all.'

'True,' dal Rhenning said. 'But back to business. Dal Valeriano. Is he going to cause us more problems?'

'Most certainly,' Jagovere said. 'Shandahar's the only place I've been as treacherous as this. Seems the king of Estranza's all but forgotten this part of his realm and his nobles are happy to have at one another every chance they get. Torona's as unstable politically as anywhere I've been, though.'

'The king of Estranza's forgotten everything but his seraglio,' dal Rhenning said. 'I'm amazed he's lasted on his throne this long. The only thing that's saved him is that his nobles hate each other more than they do him. That and the fact that the Mirabayans are too busy with the Szavarians in the east. Otherwise they could march south and take whatever they want. Once one of his dukes gathers up enough power for themselves, I suspect the king won't be long for this world. Not our concern, happily. What of Prince Peruman of Kandamar?'

'Not a mention so far. Everyone here is obsessed with what's going on at court. If I didn't already know they're at war, I wouldn't have noticed.'

'The war will decide who holds the Duchy of Torona, as well as the Principality of Kandahar. Whoever holds Torona and Kandahar will be poised to make a move on the throne. The stakes here are high, and will likely determine the fate of the whole country. I'm told the entire west of the Duchy favours dal Valeriano. The duke's mixed blood is something of an affront to them. Dal Valeriano's mother was a good Estranzan girl—a milkmaid by all accounts—not a Darvarosian princess like the duke's. The only thing keeping them in line is the threat posed by a strong and ruthless leader. They don't know whether the new duke is or not. Yet. If he asserts his birthright in the south, it should secure his rule here. If not, dal Valeriano will feed him to the wolves and take the Duchy for himself. That's why we're here. To help make sure the duke wins. It's a sad day when a ruler can only trust mercenaries.'

'Why would the duke make his brother commander of his army, then?' Wulfric said. It only occurred to him after it was out of his mouth that he should probably have remained silent.

Jagovere turned to him. 'There's the genius of it. The duke honours his brother with a prize office. It's hard to grumble when such honours are laid at your feet, but it's also a poisoned chalice. If dal Valeriano successfully prosecutes his brother's claims in the south, the duke can claim the credit. If he fails, the duke can dump all the blame on him and get rid of his strongest rival.'

'Clever,' Enderlain said.

'Indeed it is, and that's why dal Valeriano has the army sitting on the border doing nothing,' Jagovere said. 'He's delaying as long as he can, hoping that something will turn up in his favour. Then we arrive to inject some vigour into the campaign. Not surprising dal Valeriano ain't pleased to see us. Now he has to do something, and if he's smart, he'll know that if he makes the wrong choice the game'll be up.'

'What do you think his next move will be?' dal Rhenning said.

'Who knows,' Jagovere said, going through the letters he had brought, 'but whatever it is, it'll be interesting.' He held one of the letters up. 'He wants to discuss the campaign with you this afternoon.'

## RODULF

'Who have you told about it?' Rodulf said.

'No one,' the peasant said.

Grenville gave the peasant a filthy glare.

'I mean, no one, *my lord*. I came to you straight away. I recognised the ore from my time labouring at the mines.'

Rodulf looked at the pattern in the rock face, but his eye was far from expert.

'What do you think, Grenville?'

'Looks the same as at the mines. Except there's a lot more of it. And that's just on the surface.'

'Indeed there is,' Rodulf said. He looked back to the peasant. 'No one, you say?'

'Not a soul, my lord. Not even my good lady wife.'

'Your good lady wife? An interesting way to put it, eh, Grenville?'

'I'd say she's as filthy a wretch as he is, my lord,' Grenville said.

Rodulf laughed, and the peasant joined in after a moment, his laughter tense.

'I expect you'll be wanting a reward?' Rodulf said.

The peasant didn't react for a moment, but when he saw Rodulf was still smiling he nodded slowly.

'Indeed, one good turn deserves another. Now, what shall I give you?' Rodulf scratched his chin for a moment, then drew his rapier and pierced the peasant through the chest. He gasped when Rodulf twisted and then withdrew the blade, before collapsing to the ground.

Grenville leaned forward to inspect the body. 'Dead. Remind me never to ask for a reward.'

'Freeing him from his miserable life *was* a reward,' Rodulf said. 'Do you think he was telling the truth?'

Grenville shrugged. 'He's not going to be telling anyone else now, leastways.'

'No, that's something, I suppose,' Rodulf said. 'Probably best deal with his lady wife too. Just in case.'

'Would've been easier if you asked him where he lived before you killed him...'

'Leondorf's not that big,' Rodulf said.

'Consider it done, my lord.'

'Better. I don't want word of this getting south. This all stays within the barony. In my coffers.'

'It'll take some organising,' Grenville said. 'We'll have to bring extra smelters in from abroad, otherwise news of the discovery will find its way there sooner rather than later. That will take some time. There are plenty of prisoners from the last village still breathing, so we can put them to work here instead of using them as replacements for the old mine. We'll need more, though. The scum we used on Grundorf won't get the job done. Word has spread to the other villages. They'll be ready for us, and near half of the men we had were killed at Grundorf.'

'Most of them at your hands, as I recall,' Rodulf said.

'They were vermin, and they were burning my village to the ground.'

Rodulf laughed.

'I'll get the men we need on my next trip south. For now I want you to focus on getting this place up and running.'

'My lord,' Grenville said with a nod.

'This could work out very nicely,' Rodulf said, as his mind raced to estimate the wealth contained within the rock. 'Very nicely indeed.' What he'd thought might take a decade to achieve could be realised in a year or two. Perhaps less. Rodulf was not one given to smiling—he felt it made him look like an idiot—but he could not wipe the grin from his face in that moment.

❊

## ADALHAID

Adalhaid did her best not to grimace. The sight of the badly broken leg did not bother her at all—she had seen as much and worse before. It was the pain and anguish on the young girl's face that distressed her. The girl had been struck on the street by a wagon, her young bones shattered by the impact. Her mother had brought her in, both of them wailing in panic, pain, and fear.

Strellis frowned as he examined the damage. Bone had pierced skin and Adalhaid had to constantly hand him cloths to staunch the flow of blood. They had already administered a tincture of dream seed, but the girl's pain was such that it was taking time to affect her. He stood, moved to the door and gestured for Adalhaid to join him.

'The bones have been pulverised,' he said. 'There's no way to mend them and it won't heal. It'll turn bad and kill her. I'm going to have to take the leg off.'

Adalhaid went pale at the thought of the girl losing the limb. Life for the poor was difficult enough, but with only one leg, she was destined for a short life of hardship. Adalhaid had seen cripples begging on the street, being kicked, spat at, starving slowly to an uncared-about death before their bodies were dumped in a paupers' grave outside the city.

'I want you to stay with her until the tincture takes effect and she falls asleep. Give her what comfort you can. I'll get my saw and instruments ready.' With that, he left.

Adalhaid turned and looked at the girl, who was still sobbing gently. They had given her enough dream seed to put a man three times her size into a deep sleep, but her pain was so intense that she was merely in a stupor. The dressing on her leg had become soaked through, so Adalhaid removed it and placed a new one on the wound, gently pressing it down.

It broke her heart to think of the girl going through life on only one leg. She wished there were more she could do for the little girl's suffering. The city's churches made meagre efforts to help the poor and unfortunate, but it was simply paying lip service to their credos. They viewed the decoration of their shrines, churches and cathedrals as being far more important than caring for the gods' most unfortunate children. The Bishop of Elzburg's house in the city was ample proof of that. Taking the girl's leg off was not a kindness; it was a condemnation.

As she looked down at the young girl, Adalhaid felt a wave of light-headedness sweep over her. It struck her as odd—she had never been squeamish before and had helped her mother clean animals for the cooking pot from as early in her life as she could remember. She gripped the treatment table to steady herself, and was almost overcome by a feeling of nausea. She took a deep breath and closed her eyes as she fought down the urge to vomit. It *couldn't* be squeamishness. Perhaps she was coming down with something—she spent a great deal of time in contact with sick people.

The door opened and Strellis came back in. She stood and stepped back from the treatment table. The dizziness and nausea subsided as soon as she did, leaving her feeling well, but confused by the suddenness of it all.

'I can ask Rosamund to assist me, if you don't feel ready for this yet,' he said.

Adalhaid took her hand away from the wound and stood. 'I'll be fine.'

Strellis placed his instruments on the table and stepped forward. He lifted the girl's eyelids with his thumbs, and, satisfied that she was senseless, moved to the fresh dressing on her leg.

'You may need to hold her still,' he said. 'Even with the dream seed, her body may react. I can do the rest myself. When I tell you, I want you to go out and get the heated metal paddle from Rosamund so I can seal the wound. It will be glowing hot, so be careful not to burn yourself on it. Use the heavy gloves. Do you understand?'

'Yes.'

He lifted the dressing and reached for his knife, but his hand stopped in mid-air. 'What? What in hells?'

Adalhaid strained to see over his shoulder.

'Am I going mad?' he said. 'What in hells?'

'What is it?' Adalhaid said.

'Her leg. It's half-healed. I could probably leave it alone and it would be fine in a couple of months.'

Adalhaid said nothing.

'A moment ago it was destroyed. I've not seen much worse after a battle. What happened? What could have happened while I was gone?' His eyes widened. 'That day in the lecture theatre. That woman *was* as badly hurt as they said, wasn't she? What did you do?'

He went pale and took a step back.

Adalhaid felt a flash of panic. She had no idea what had happened. 'I didn't do anything,' she said. 'I just changed the girl's dressing. Nothing more.'

'You had to have done something,' Strellis said, his voice wavering. 'Bones crushed to powder do not suddenly become whole again. I doubt even magic could do it.' His mouth dropped open. 'But it could. Northlander magic.'

Adalhaid felt her insides clench at the mention of magic. The southerners hated it. It was illegal, actively hunted down, and execution was the only penalty. She had never had cause to think about it before, but now? Had she really performed magic on the young girl? She couldn't understand how that might be possible—she had no training, no knowledge of it. Surely she would need both to be able to use it? The wound had been as bad as Strellis had said. She had seen that with her own eyes. Now it was all but healed. The same with the girl in the lecture theatre. At the time, she had dismissed it as the girl over-reacting. Southerners weren't made of the same stuff as Northlanders, so it hadn't seemed out of the ordinary. Now, however, the evidence was staring her in the face.

She remembered the way Aethelman had chosen her from among all the others to help him when he was treating patients, even above those who said they wanted to become healers. She thought of her old dog, Spot, and the day he had started following her. He had been lame, but then he wasn't. She had thought it an act to get sympathy, but now? What had she done? How?

She looked back at Strellis, and felt true fear. He looked terrified of her, his dark, handsome eyes wide. She had seen a woman being dragged from a back street by dark-cloaked agents of the princess. The word 'witch' was whispered, everyone too afraid to utter it aloud. She had no desire to meet the same fate. Not when she didn't even know what she had done, or how she had done it.

'I didn't do anything,' Adalhaid said, her voice filled with fear. 'I just wanted to help her.'

'It never occurred to me that as a Northlander you might...' His voice was stronger now, his confidence returning. 'You know magic's illegal here? It's very serious.'

'I know,' Adalhaid said, still trying to make sense of what had happened. 'I didn't do anything. I only changed her dressing. I'm not a witch.'

'There are people here who claim to be magical healers, but most of them are fraudsters. I've heard stories about people in the east who can do unbelievable things, but I never really believed it. Can the priest healers in the Northlands use magic? I'd never have believed that, either. But now?' He shook his head.

Adalhaid had no idea what to say. The danger was real, and close. She knew Strellis's reaction could mean life or death for her. She considered running from the room, from the city, but she still could not believe what had happened, and what that meant.

'I wish I was mistaken, but I don't make mistakes that big,' Strellis said. 'What else could it be?'

Adalhaid opened her mouth to speak, but closed it again. *What else could it be?*

'What's going to happen to me?' she said a moment later.

'Nothing,' Strellis said, the waver gone from his voice. 'But we can't tell anyone about this, and you can't do it again. Ever. Someone will find out, and the Intelligenciers will come for you. When the Intelligenciers come for you, you are never seen again. Do you understand?'

She thought of the men in the black cloaks, and realised the people who had been watching weren't just afraid of the witch. They were equally afraid of the Intelligenciers.

'Take a week's break from the clinic. You need to work out what you did, how you did it, and how to make sure you don't do it again. I'll tell the mother the injury wasn't as bad as I first thought, and wrap it up in so much bandaging it will take them a week to get it all off. If I tell her the leg will drop off if they touch it before it's ready to be removed, they'll believe me, but if this type of thing happens again, someone will get suspicious. We could both burn for this.'

Adalhaid nodded, the feeling of nausea in her gut refusing to go away.

# CHAPTER 25

AETHELMAN

THE DARKNESS THAT swallowed Aethelman up as he descended into the mountain immediately brought him back to the memory of the Hermitage, and the laughter he had heard. He felt himself hoping he would hear it again, and had not realised the loneliness that had lived for so long in his heart. To hear Aesa's voice would always be a gift indeed.

This descent into the bowels of the mountain proved to be shorter. He had not gone down more than a dozen shallow steps before he reached a plateau, the comfort of being able to see the bright doorway welcome. He waited for a moment in the hope of hearing the laughter, but it did not come. Despite the light coming through the door, it did little to light the main room. He wondered if he might be able to fashion a torch. As soon as he thought of it, the cavern lit, as though by a thousand candles—but these candles were no more than their flame, each one dancing ephemerally in the air above his head. At first, he felt afraid, but they seemed benign and everything suggested it was he who had caused them to be there. *How* was an entirely other question, one that would have to wait.

The first thing that caught his eye was the altar. As the inscriptions on the exterior had indicated, it was dedicated to Audun. Audun was a god without a following. The warriors prayed to Jorundyr, the priests to Birgyssa, farmers to Ghyda, craftsmen to Herolt, merchants and those who sought good fortune to Vikta, and everyone to Agnarr, father of them all. Whoever had favoured Audun had died out long ago. It had struck him as odd that the Hermitage was built over a shrine to Audun, rather than Birgyssa. Might the Grey Priests, or their forebears, have once dedicated themselves to Audun? If so, he was curious as to what had motivated the change to Birgyssa. It made him wonder if the creation of the Stones might have had anything to do with it.

There was something strange about the altar. It didn't look like something intended for use in religious services. This one may have started as an altar, but it had been used for rough work for many years, as evidenced by the etches and scores all over it. In its centre, there was a small, circular hole framed by a disc of metal that was delicately inscribed. It looked like it was Godsteel.

Aethelman leaned forward and squinted to read the small runes.

*The Fount of the Gods.*

The light from the ethereal flames flickering in the air only reached a few handspans down into the hole in the centre, but the hole seemed to go far deeper than that. He walked around the altar and started to explore the rest of the cavern. There was a shelf recessed into the wall with several objects on it. They were immediately familiar, and Aethelman felt his heart race. He went over and reached out, but stopped.

Touching the Stone could, by itself, be enough to seduce a man to its powers. He had been a young man when he had carelessly picked up the Stone with his bare hands, and his will had been strong. He was so much older now, and not so arrogant as to think his resolve was as immutable. These stones were different, however. Even from the distance his hand maintained, he could sense it. There was no power in them.

Satisfied that it was safe, he reached out and picked one up. Like the Stone, it was the size of a large potato and of an irregular shape. It was also made of Godsteel—Telastrian Steel, as they called it in the south. Unlike the Stone, there were no runes etched into its surface. This was the raw material from which the Stones were made. His eyes widened as he realised that this was where they had been made.

Might it also be where they could be unmade?

❈

## ADALHAID

Adalhaid found herself constantly looking over her shoulder in the days following the incident at the clinic. She had no idea how the Intelligenciers tracked their quarries, but her imagination was offering up a great many possibilities. Every time she saw someone dressed in black, she held her breath for a moment. Even in the palace's private apartments while looking after the Markgraf's children, her heart jumped every time the door opened. Fear was a terrible thing, and there was barely a moment when she did not feel it.

As bad as the fear was, her inability to understand what she had done was worse. Everything else found its root there. There was nowhere she could go to learn how to control it, no one to ask. She had no idea where to begin. She wondered if Aethelman was still in Leondorf. He was the only one she could think of who might be able to help, but she didn't know if he was still alive, let alone in the village. He had talked for so long about leaving. Without him, her only option was to wait, observe, and experiment until she had mastery of whatever it was. The thought of rationalising it and applying the experimental processes she had learned in her medical studies gave her some comfort, but it was a terrifying prospect. It felt like walking around juggling knives, hoping you did not cut yourself, with the spectre of the Intelligenciers looming over you all the while.

❧

## WULFRIC

Wulfric's father had played host to the warriors of Leondorf many times. All great war leaders were expected to offer their followers hospitality, so it came as no surprise to Wulfric that the duke did the same. However, nothing could have prepared him for the scale. The feasting hall in Leondorf had seated a hundred or so. The banqueting hall in Torona must have been able to accommodate five times that many. Wulfric wondered how much it must cost to feed so many on a daily basis.

It was clear that there was more to it than merely eating. Only the most important at court were invited to the hall, while others had to take meals in their apartments or elsewhere. There was ceremony to it. Servants buzzed around like bees at a hive; women posed in dresses so elegant they more resembled statues than living people; men of every shape and size postured in their finery, many wearing waist sashes of navy with white dots. Despite wearing his best clothes, once again Wulfric felt like a beggar.

'What are the sashes?' Wulfric said.

Jagovere held up the steel-grey one he wore. 'Ruripathia's colour is grey. Estranza's is the starry field.'

'That's not a colour,' Wulfric said.

Jagovere laughed. 'It's just a name. More like a flag. Certain bannerets, the very best, are awarded their nation's colours. The Graf and I have the Grey. In Ostenheim it's the Blue, in Mirabaya the White, and so on. In Estranza, it's the Starry Field.'

'Why a starry field?'

'When the Empire conquered this land millennia ago, the emperor himself led his army. When he landed on the Estranzan shore, he looked back at his approaching fleet, hundreds of white sails on a deep blue sea, and said it looked like a starry field.' He paused for effect. 'Or so the story goes. The name stuck, and here we are. Far more romantic than grey, blue, or white, don't you think?'

Wulfric shrugged. It seemed pompous to him. He was more concerned with how not to make a fool of himself at dinner. His first encounter with a fork was still fresh in his mind. 'What do we do?' he said.

'We mind our manners, we smile and nod to anyone who acknowledges us, and we keep our mouths shut until we have no alternative but to speak. And we eat,' Jagovere said.

'I hope the food's good,' Enderlain said.

As they took their seats, Wulfric noticed a woman staring at them from across the audience hall. Like most Estranzans, she had jet-black hair and deeply tanned skin. It lent her a smouldering, mysterious air, and Wulfric felt himself puffing out his chest in response as he realised she was looking at him.

'Mysterious, exotic, intoxicating,' Jagovere said. 'The young Northlander hero discovered the greatest danger lay not in facing his enemies, but in the gaze of a southern beauty...'

Wulfric felt his face grow red. Being the subject of a joke was not something he dealt with well. 'Was just looking, is all.'

'Well, at least find out who she is before trying to bed her. The last thing we need is for you to be caught in the sack with one of the duke's mistresses.'

Wulfric tried to be discreet, but continued to watch her out of the corner of his eye. The only other woman to have that much of an impact on him was Adalhaid, and the memory made him feel guilt—that he was thinking of another woman, and that he had not yet settled her Blood Debt.

The slightly built man whom Wulfric had seen in dal Valeriano's entourage joined the woman and whispered in her ear. Wulfric's feelings were immediately replaced by jealousy. The man was well dressed, and had the look of easy wealth many of the courtiers displayed. It said he was a man who knew how to navigate the perils of court, a man who could talk with authority on matters of culture and politics, a man who had far more skills than merely being good at killing people. A man with enough money to turn his will into reality without ever having to get his hands dirty. To him, Wulfric reckoned he must appear an ignorant savage. To her, he must appear a pauper.

'I was wondering,' Wulfric said. 'When we're working on the epics, could you teach me to read and write?'

Jagovere raised an eyebrow. 'Really?'

Wulfric nodded.

'How will it help with swinging a sword?'

Wulfric felt his temper flare. 'It won't.'

Jagovere held his hands up. 'All right, no reason to get cranky. I'll teach you. It would be my pleasure.'

Wulfric looked back to where the Estranzan woman had been sitting, but she was gone. He wondered if he would see her again.

❁

## Wulfric

'Northman.'

Wulfric stopped in his tracks. He had left the banquet table to use the privy, and had spent several minutes wandering around darkened service corridors without any success in finding it. He had not expected to be engaged in conversation in the process. Without Jagovere there to do the talking, he felt a chill of fear worse than if he was preparing to face this man in a fight.

He turned and was presented with not one, but two men. The slightly built man he had seen whisper to the beautiful woman the night before, and the swordsman from the count's entourage. Wulfric wondered what they wanted of him. His eyes instantly fell on the swordsman. He was the immediate threat. He had the look of a killer—dark, intelligent eyes and a cavalier posture that shouted absolute confidence in his environment. He was the type of man you wanted fighting at your side, not against you. Wulfric had seen few enough of his like since arriving in Torona, but Estranzans had a reputation for producing some of the finest swordsmen in the world. He regarded Wulfric with a wry smile, and Wulfric knew that he too was wondering what it would be like for them to fight.

'His Lordship, the Count of Valeriano, wishes to speak with you,' the slight man said.

'I think you've got the wrong fellow,' Wulfric said. 'If you want to talk, my captain's the man you need to talk to.'

'You'd be well advised to do what you're told, Northlander,' the killer said.

'Peace, Diego,' the slight man said.

*Diego*, Wulfric thought, making note of the name. He wondered if they would cross paths again.

'You'll do,' the slight man said. 'For now.' He gestured for Wulfric to follow.

Wulfric hesitated.

'The count would like the conversation to remain private. We mean you no harm.'

Wulfric looked at Diego, ignoring the slight man. He was the only one who interested Wulfric. His clothes were cut for fighting and he had a complex-hilted rapier strapped to his waist. Unlike the others Wulfric had seen, Diego's was undecorated. It seemed Diego knew the difference between a weapon and an ornament. They stared at each other for a moment, then Wulfric nodded.

'Lead on.'

Diego smiled, but his eyes shouted disappointment. The slight man led the way, their bootfalls echoing along the stone-walled corridor. Two women—servants—appeared at the far end, walking toward Wulfric and his escorts.

'And how do you find the weather, sir?' the slight man said loudly, as though the question was part of an ongoing conversation.

Wulfric looked at him out of the corner of his eye. 'Hot.'

'I expect it must be very different from the cool northern climes,' the slight man said. 'I've yearned for many years to visit them. I hear there are seas of ice in the mountains that never melt, even in the height of summer.'

The servants passed by and continued on down the hall. The slight man glanced over his shoulder as he walked, watching them until they disappeared out of sight once again.

'It's true,' Wulfric said. 'There's lots of them in the High Places. Your piss will freeze before it even hits the—'

The slight man was glaring at him with an expression that was a mixture of exasperation and boredom. Wulfric realised what the short exchange had been for, and felt foolish for continuing it beyond its need. He knew he was not a stupid man, but in the south he often felt as though he was. To survive there, you needed to have a mind as keen as the edge of his sword. He had allowed himself to drift into ignorance in the past. In the Northlands, reading, writing, and numbers were not important for a warrior, but in the south, they were everything, no matter who you were.

'Where are we going?' Wulfric said.

'Would you even know where it was if I told you?' the slight man said.

Wulfric shrugged.

'Suffice it to say, it is somewhere the count may speak to you without unwanted ears or eyes nearby.'

Wulfric took another look at him out of the corner of his eye. He was balding, and had cropped what was left of his hair, but his beard and moustache were still dark. There were faint lines at the corners of his eyes, almost unnoticeable, but they added years to him.

Eventually they arrived at their destination: a turn in a stairwell with a large bay window that overlooked one of the palace's many gardens.

The count stood by the open window looking out, and cast only a furtive backward glance at their approach.

'I'll assume you have not the authority to make any decisions,' the count said, still looking out the window, 'so I'll get to the point and you can take the message back to your master. Thirty thousand crowns, and you pack up and head back to your frozen northern homes and your frosty northern women.'

Wulfric thought it amusing that this far south, people treated the Ruripathians as ignorant savages from frozen northern wastes, just as the Ruripathians did the Northlanders. The slight man gestured for Wulfric to return in the direction he had just come. It seemed carrying a message was all that was required of him. For a piece of intrigue, the first Wulfric had been involved in, it came as something of an anti-climax. Diego put his hand on Wulfric's arm to guide him, which Wulfric slapped away.

Diego instantly reached for his sword, and Wulfric had no intention of being left behind. In the blink of an eye, both men faced each other at sword point. Wulfric stood higher on the stairs, which gave him the advantage, but if Diego was aware of it, he showed no sign.

'Diego!' the count said.

Diego's eyes flicked from Wulfric, and a look of resignation descended on his face.

'Let him pass, Diego,' the count said.

Diego delayed a moment, then sheathed his sword and stood to the side. He gestured that the way was clear with a sweep of his arm and a condescending smile. Wulfric walked down until he was standing on the same step as Diego, but towered above him.

'Good boy, Diego,' Wulfric said. 'Do you roll over on command too?'

He held Diego's gaze for a moment, and revelled in the anger burning in his eyes, then smiled and walked down the stairs, chuckling as he went.

# CHAPTER 26

RODULF

RODULF FELT ANXIOUS at the thought of travelling south the next morning, as if the Markgraf would take one look at him and know he was hiding something. It was ridiculous, but faced with a man with so much unchecked power, it was easy to become paranoid. Although he bowed to the princess in Ruripathia, it seemed to Rodulf that her hold on power was tenuous and she had to allow her powerful noblemen a great deal of freedom. Not only had Rodulf conquered a village and its territory, he had no intention of sharing any of the newly discovered silver. He knew he was treading dangerous ground and would have to be careful, but the rewards he sought demanded that risks be taken. Not even the Stone could bring him peace that evening.

He had decided that his new silver would need to be completely self-contained if he was to keep it a secret. Those who worked there would live, and die, there. Word would not leak from that source. Smelting would be done on site, with the silver packaged securely for transit so those carting the crates would have no idea of what was within. Transit to where, though? He sat before the crackling fire in his living room wondering where he could deposit his silver without the Markgraf finding out, growing more agitated with each moment. He would be damned if he would allow anyone else to take what was rightfully his. He needed a way to keep it safe, yet access it where and when he needed it. *Where* was almost always going to be in the south.

Silver was heavy, and needed large carts to carry it. They drew attention from ne'er-do-wells, and that meant they needed escorts, which drew attention from the type who would report unusual activity back to the Markgraf. He could send them by a longer route to avoid the Elzmark entirely, but that increased the danger, and whatever lord ruled that territory would no doubt find out and want his cut.

When the solution came to him, a smile spread across his face. He was still unused to having unfettered power in the new barony. There had always been someone to ask for permission, someone to convince, but now he could do as he pleased—within the confines laid down by the Markgraf. Leondorf required a bank. As well as the convenience it would bring him, it would send a clear message that Leondorf was a town on its way to being a city, with all that one would expect to find there. He added a trip to the bank to his list of tasks in the south, and tried to push away the thought of the Markgraf chopping off his head for defrauding him.

❉

## AETHELMAN

Aethelman worked his way around the edges of the cavern, hoping to find something that had hitherto gone unnoticed. With the bridge maintained, he suspected the plateau and this cavern had probably been looted at some point, although he hoped they had missed something. He had the benefit of magical illumination, a constellation of tiny flames filling the cavern with as much light as if the ceiling were removed and the sun allowed in.

He spotted a section of the rock face that looked different. In more meagre light, it would have been invisible, but now the small, rectangular anomaly was obvious. He traced his finger around its edges. There was a seam, no wider than a hair, but it was there, and ran the whole way around the lighter patch of stone.

Aethelman sighed. He was not made to be an adventurer or a treasure hunter, and he had nothing with which to extract the block. He looked around the floor, hopeful that something useful might remain, but there was nothing. He rested his hand on the stone and wondered. Might whatever magic that had allowed him to create the light help him now? The mystery of everything was starting to grate on his nerves. How could his forebears have been so afraid of magic to have allowed so much knowledge disappear?

He thought deeply, and willed the block to pop out of the wall. Nothing happened. He leaned against it in frustration. There was a click that echoed through the cavern. His heart raced and he looked around, fearing he had set off a booby trap. He saw no danger and breathed a sigh of relief.

Looking back at the differently coloured block, he realised it was protruding from the cavern wall far enough for him to get a hold on it. He gripped it with his fingertips and pulled. It was stiff at first, but gave to his efforts and slid out of the wall. He peered into the hole and could see that it went back farther than the block had filled.

He made to put his hand in, then stopped. What if something unpleasant lay within? A hand-sized mousetrap? He forced his fear to one side and reached in. His arm was in all the way to his shoulder when his hand fell on something: a leather bundle. He took it out and brought it over to the workbench, his hands shaking with excitement. What long-forgotten knowledge was he about to discover? Might it be what he sought? He could certainly see the appeal in being a treasure hunter. The excitement coursing through him made him feel like a boy again.

The leather bundle was a roll covering numerous sheets of parchment, all of which were covered in writing. Writing which he could read. He took a deep breath to steady himself. He wanted to go about this in a systematic way, to make sure he missed nothing. He wondered how parchment could have survived in such good condition for so long—a thousand years at least—but there was magic in that place, and magic could do almost anything.

*Having finally found a way to bind the Lifespring to an object, I have infused a quantity of it into several items. Most allow the energy to dissipate over the course of several hours to a day, but Godsteel seems to hold the energy indefinitely. Indeed, once the bindings have been created, and the steel given its initial charge, it self-perpetuates. It recharges itself, which is a wholly unexpected, but entirely welcome, result. I am now experimenting with the optimum size for the reservoir. If these objects cannot be kept to a size that is easily portable, they will be all but useless. However, for the first time in memory, I feel hope. If I can make these reservoirs work, we will have an advantage over the Imperial Mages that may well allow our survival.*

Aethelman felt his heart race. Could this journal really have been penned by the man who created the Fount Stones? It seemed almost too much to hope for. It struck Aethelman that the author spoke in a positive way about what he was creating, with such hope. These were things Aethelman's order had been created to seek out and destroy, they were such a blight to the world. He turned the page, and continued to read.

> *A piece of Godsteel the size of a large man's fist appears to be the perfect compromise between capacity and portability. I continue my experiments now to discover the capabilities and limitations of my Lifespring Reservoirs—*

Aethelman presumed that when the author said 'the Lifespring,' he was referring to the Fount.

> *—I cannot in good conscience send men and women forth in reliance on these reservoirs without knowing what they can and cannot do. To have someone killed because my invention let them down would be unforgiveable. It is my wish to save the lives of my brethren, not put them in greater danger or create a false sense of security.*

Aethelman's heart raced as he read, not just from the thought that he was close to succeeding in his quest, but at the thrill of learning secrets long forgotten. He cast a glance around the cavern, and wondered what it had looked like when the author had inhabited it. His hand continued to shake as he turned the page.

> *There have been some interesting, and somewhat worrying, discoveries in my experiments. The first is that the reservoir does not return all the Lifespring that has been invested in it. I would speculate that the output is less than half of the input. I am putting my mind to ways of improving this. At this point I feel the answer most likely lies in the method of binding, but there is much to be done before I will have time to address this.*

*The second, and most worrying, fact is that the reservoir seems to be usable by those uninitiated in magical ability. My assistant, Urt, has had no training, and is possessed of a dull mind. He is strong, eager to be of help, and affable, but he bears none of the qualities required to become an initiate. On three occasions now, I have witnessed him carry out minor feats of magic, all related to the tasks I had set him, while carrying one of the reservoirs.*

*The dangers of this are obvious—the thought of those uninitiated in the use of the Lifespring being able to wield it is too terrifying to contemplate. Again, I feel confident that the solution lies in the method of binding. As soon as time permits, I will experiment with variations in the runes used to create the binding.*

The passage made much clear to Aethelman. When this man and his brethren had ceased to exist, the danger of his creation remained. Perhaps one or two of them survived to found the Grey Priests to eradicate the danger they had created?

*I have not updated this journal in some time due to my workload, and a pervasive feeling of being unwell. Work and clear thought has been difficult, but my task is an important one so I persevere. Urt ran away with one of the reservoirs several days ago. There is nothing I can do about it. The only consolation I can take is that it is most likely he will bring about his own demise in trying to use it. I have notified the Brethren to keep a watch out for him, but their time is limited. Word has come of an expedition of Imperial Mages and their servants crossing the river and venturing into the Northern Kingdoms for the first time. Until now, this has been our last sanctuary, chased as we have been from all the places that were our own by those who see the Lifespring as a thing that can be controlled, rather than channelled. A science, rather than the great mystery of our world. I would call them fools if they had not managed to best us on nearly every occasion the Brethren have encountered them in confrontation.*

Aethelman found himself reading more quickly, eager to see where this ancient man's writings ended.

> *I have already mentioned the poor input and output ratios of the reservoirs, and that once bound and charged, they can replenish themselves. They draw unrelentingly on their surroundings until their capacity is filled once again, as though the cold, dead metal is thirsty for the touch of life. I have seen one of my reservoirs brown and kill a patch of grass outside that I had absently left it sitting on. I had almost drained it in my tests, then placed it on the lawn. In only a few moments, the process had begun. I now wonder if my own feelings of lethargy are caused the same way, if the reservoirs are taking from my own minor store of Lifespring. Might the thing I created to save the lives of those who possess them, leach them also? The feeling is worse when I have spent a great deal of time working in the cavern. When I am outside in the fresh air, rather than surrounded by rock, the ailment fades. It leads me to the conclusion that the reservoirs will draw on the ambient Lifespring by preference, and only on more difficult sources, such as my own, when there is no alternative—in much the same way an inexperienced initiate draws from their own at first rather than that surrounding them.*
>
> *It is difficult now to think of the creation of my reservoirs without regret. Due to necessity, I distributed a number of them to my brethren, and they have proved of only limited value. We have won more battles, but the Imperial Magisters are too many. All the reservoirs have done is slow their advance, and in delaying the inevitable, prolong the destruction. They come north of the river in ever greater numbers, and I realise that our time in this world is limited.*

There was only one entry left. How this tale ended seemed inevitable, and there was a sadness in reading the thoughts of a man whose time was coming to an end.

> *A good man seeks to leave the world better than he found it.*

*I have always thought myself a good man. I am a good man, but I have created something that will affect the world for the worse. I cannot depart it without trying to undo what I have done. Although I have destroyed all references to the bindings required to create new reservoirs, many of my creations are out in the world.*

*I have spoken with two of my brethren, who, like me, are of the opinion that our days have passed and all our struggles do is prolong the inevitable. They have agreed to go far into the north to hide, to wait until the Imperial Magisters believe they have accomplished their task and erased us from this world. When that time arrives, they will dedicate themselves to tracking down and destroying each and every reservoir I have created.*

*My recent efforts have been limited to creating the tool for this task. Just as the reservoirs exist because of the runes of binding, I realised they can be destroyed by a rune of undoing. I have tried many ways to apply these new runes. Overwriting what is already there does not work. The power of the magic is enough to fend off any attack of this nature. They cannot be polished smooth to allow fresh inscribing. As greedily as they absorb power, they jealously defend it. How then to do it? The answer came to me as I slept—a blade bearing runes of undoing cleaved the reservoir in two, and destroyed it.*

*It took time. At first I used ordinary blades of steel, and none worked the way they had in the dream. It took a blade of Godsteel to destroy it. With the runes of undoing inscribed on its length, the Godsteel knife cut through the reservoir like it was a warm pat of butter. It released its captive Lifespring back to the world like a welcome breeze on a hot day. It told me that the burden I had placed on the world could be lifted, and in that knowledge, I can go to my rest with some peace in my heart.*

*There is one thing I seem to be unable to do. I can feel each of the reservoirs I created, sense them and where they are, but I am too infirm to leave this sanctuary to aid in seeking them out. I have left my charges with as much information as to their whereabouts as I can, but for whatever reason, they do not seem to be able to sense them. Might it be the physical contact I had with each of them has created a connection between us? I wish I could find a way to allow them to feel them as I do before the gods call me to join them, but try as I might, I cannot.*

That was all the ancient magister had to say, but he had drawn the runes of undoing below his words. Aethelman's heart soared. As he opened his mind to the possibility, he realised he too could sense the Stone he had touched.

He knew where it was.

# CHAPTER 27

RODULF

R ODULF WAS TIRED when he arrived at his inn at Elzburg. He
had been ruminating over what he needed to do for the entire
journey south, and was too impatient to rest. He headed straight
for the market square where the mercenary companies were to be found.
Getting more men to Grenville was the priority. He needed fresh slaves to
work his mine, and for that he needed mercenaries to capture them. The
sooner he had them marching north, the sooner Grenville could act on
their plan. With luck, Grenville would have taken another village by the
time Rodulf got back.

Different market squares provided different offerings, and the one
where mercenaries were to be had was smaller than Rodulf had hoped—
little more than a cloistered courtyard surrounded by tall, crooked buildings
that all but blotted out the sky. A few rough-looking men moved about
with no appearance of purpose, and the curious glances they gave him made
Rodulf regret leaving Grenville behind. He wore a rapier at his side, the
weapon of choice among southern gentlemen, but he had little practice
using it. Northlanders usually fought from horseback, and the sabre was
their preferred blade, the slash being the better strike from the saddle than
the thrust. The sabre had its drawbacks on foot, but when everyone was
penalised in the same fashion it made little difference. Against a rapier,
however, a warrior with a sabre was at a disadvantage. Rodulf was well-
trained with the sabre, but with a rapier he might as well have been wielding
a mop—it was for appearance only. It was something he needed to address.

The path he intended for himself made the fighting of at least one duel almost inevitable. He had no desire to lose everything he had worked for at the wrong end of a rapier because of an aristocrat's injured honour.

'I have a contract I need filled,' Rodulf said as loudly as he could. He attracted little attention. Eventually a man ambled over.

'What's the job?' he said.

He was crippled, and not what Rodulf needed. Perhaps he would have to go to Brixen to find what he needed.

'There'll be fighting, but also plunder involved. That's all I'm saying for now,' Rodulf said. 'Are there no companies here?'

'Not this far north,' the cripple said. 'Things is too quiet up here these days. There's war in the South, so that's where most of them are.'

Rodulf sighed in frustration.

'I'm with the Adventurer Companies' Guild,' the cripple said. 'If you tell me the nature of the work, and how many men you need, I can put the word out and see if we can find you what you need.'

'No soldiering for you anymore?' Rodulf asked, relieved that this was not the only calibre of man available to him.

The cripple frowned. 'What do you think? Took an Ostian pike in the thigh and a bolt in the shoulder. Work for the Guild now. Like I said.'

'Two hundred men. Work for a full season. I pay standard rates, and there'll be plunder for the taking.'

'I'll see what I can do. Where can I call on you?'

'The Brazen Belek Inn, for the time being. Grenville's my name,' Rodulf said. 'How long will it take to find what I need?'

The cripple shrugged. 'How long is a piece of string? Tomorrow if there's someone around. Next month if they have to march from somewhere.'

'Tomorrow would be better than next month. Do it fast and I'm sure we can find something more interesting and rewarding for you to do than sit around here all day.'

The man nodded, and Rodulf walked away. Every day he was delayed was a frustration, and increased the chance that the opportunities which had fallen into his lap would be taken away. If the man didn't have something for him in a day or two, it would be time for a trip to Brixen.

❀

## WULFRIC

'Thirty thousand crowns?' dal Rhenning said.

Jagovere raised his eyebrows and Wulfric nodded.

'Well, he must really want to see the back of us,' dal Rhenning said. 'What could we do with thirty thousand, Jagovere?'

Jagovere shrugged. 'Retire. Happily.'

'This *is* my retirement,' dal Rhenning said. 'And it's a damn sight more fun than managing estates. We have enough coin to pay the men, and a reputation that would make Gandaman and the Hundred green with envy. Tell him to stuff his thirty thousand.'

'With pleasure,' Jagovere said.

'Wait.' Dal Rhenning held up a hand. 'No. A demonstration of fidelity would be better. Give the order to break camp. We march south to the border to join the duke's army, with or without the marshall. Go and tell the duke that we'll await his instructions there while we season the men.'

❈

## AETHELMAN

There were few smiths in the Northlands who could properly work Godsteel. The old smith in Leondorf had been among the best, but he was long dead. So too the smith in Rasbruck. Aethelman wondered if a southern smith might be a better option. The southerners also greatly prized what they called Telastrian Steel, and with the few lumps of it Aethelman had taken from the cavern, he would be able to have several knives forged with the runes of undoing inscribed on their blades. Were he to sell the pieces he had found, it would bring him enough southern coin to live in luxury for the rest of his life. Duty and comfort so rarely went hand in hand.

He had finally found a smith of some repute at a small village in the north called Krendorf. Each step he took toward Krendorf drew him farther from the Stone. The sensation was ever-present now and he could feel the distance grow like a call getting ever quieter.

Godsteel was hard to come by. It was only found in remote spots in the High Places, and the best quality could fetch a higher price than gold. He felt oddly self-conscious with a half dozen lumps of it in his satchel. Even in these troubled times it was unlikely anyone would bother a priest on the road, but it did give him cause to worry. The feeling of possessing great wealth was almost as uncomfortable as the feeling of possessing the Stone.

He stopped on a hill overlooking Krendorf. It was a village much like any other—a clutch of thatched buildings huddled around a small village square. The smithy was easy to spot—there was a tendril of black smoke twisting up through the sky from its wide chimney.

Small villages always viewed new arrivals with a healthy dose of curiosity. Some were suspicious, while others were hungry for news from the rest of the world. His priestly robes meant his welcome would be warmer than most, and he would need to pay a courtesy call on the incumbent before he left.

The air was cold and damp and filled with the acrid tang of woodsmoke mingled with manure. He stopped outside the smithy and watched the man at his work. His hammer fell with the rhythmic certainty of a movement that had been repeated many thousands of times. He was so focussed on his work that it took him a moment to realise he was being watched.

'Greetings, priest,' the smith said, looking over his shoulder as he continued to work. 'The kirk's at the end of the lane.'

'Thank you,' Aethelman said, 'but it's you I'm here to see. I have a commission for you.'

The smith stopped and turned, giving Aethelman his full attention. 'I don't work silver,' he said.

Religious symbols were always crafted from silver. Aethelman had no idea why that was. Another piece of knowledge lost to the passage of time.

'I have something different in mind,' Aethelman said. 'A blade.' He reached into his satchel and took out one of the pieces of Godsteel.

❈

# Rodulf

Rodulf surveyed the house from the street. It was huge, and it looked magnificent. The price was insane, but it seemed the agent would not take a penny less. He had decided he would have it the moment he saw it. The wealth he had cobbled together would be wiped out in one stroke, and he would be entirely reliant on his clandestine silver mines to restore it. That wasn't taking into account the battalion of servants that would be needed to run it. At times, he felt despair that they would not be able to dig the silver out of the ground quickly enough—being an ambitious nobleman was a prohibitively expensive occupation.

'My lord? Will you be taking it?'

'Of course I'm taking it,' Rodulf said. 'Do you mean to say you think I can't afford it?'

The agent blanched. 'No, of course not. I was merely wondering if it pleased you enough to want it.'

Rodulf smiled. Southerner tradesmen would debase themselves in so many ways for coin. It almost made Rodulf agree with the dislike warriors in Leondorf had for merchants.

'Send the paperwork to my lawyers,' Rodulf said as he walked away. 'I have other engagements.'

❀

## ADALHAID

Adalhaid pressed the bandage down over the wound, her heart racing as she did. She concentrated harder than she ever had before, both willing and praying that she did not use magic. She still found the idea almost too fantastic to believe, but Strellis had been right; the little girl's leg had been completely destroyed. Then it wasn't. How else could something like that be explained? She was the only one to intervene; she was the only possible cause.

As she had grown to accept this new reality, shock and fear had given way to a growing feeling of anger. Why would something that could ease the suffering of so many be demonised? She realised she already knew the answer. She had studied enough southern history to know that hundreds of years in the past, sorcerers had become powerful tyrants. The war that pulled them from their pedestal had torn apart the Empire, and magic was swiftly outlawed. It seemed ridiculous to her that everyone still had to suffer for events in the distant past. Surely there was a better way than to impose a blanket ban? Even if there was, she knew she had no way of making it come to pass. That left her frustrated once again. And afraid.

She lifted the bandage again before strapping it down. The wound was still open, and she felt guilty for breathing a sigh of relief. It meant she could restrain whatever power it was she had, though it was a small comfort. Just knowing she had it made her feel like a plague bearer.

'How's our patient doing?' Strellis walked into the treatment room. She could tell he was forcing himself to behave as he had before. His casual confidence seemed strained.

'May I see your patient notes?' he asked.

Adalhaid handed him her notes. The review was part of her training, the keeping of good notes being one of the required skills of a competent physician. Her hand brushed against Strellis's and her skin tingled at the touch. She blushed, and it was obvious he noticed, but his touch lingered. In that moment Wulfric's face popped into her mind, the touch of his stubble against her cheek.

'I have to get back to the palace,' she said.

# CHAPTER 28

WULFRIC

WULFRIC RETURNED TO the palace with Jagovere that
night. When dal Rhenning had decided they would march
south, Wulfric had thought they would break camp and be
on the road that day. There was more to marching an army than giving
the order, though. Road provisions had to be gathered, and guides had to
be arranged. It would take a day or two, but setting the process in motion
was enough to send the signal dal Rhenning desired. They would adhere
fastidiously to the terms of their contract, and would not be bought by
anyone else for its duration.

They walked through the large, airy chambers of the palace toward the
audience hall, where everyone of importance spent their day. While the
duke was present, they all vied for his attention; when he was gone, they
found quiet nooks and alcoves to bargain and plot. Wulfric couldn't see
the appeal in it. In the Northlands, a man owned what he could win and
hold onto by force of arms. In Torona, power was ephemeral. It was an idea
rather than a reality, and it only existed for so long as people believed in
it. It occurred to Wulfric that dal Rhenning, with his company of battle-
hardened men, could walk in and take everything from them. For all their
fine clothes and fancy swords, there was nothing of substance in Torona.
Everything was a facade. The men who had the most were worth the least.
He had not been there long, but already Wulfric hated Torona.

Being in the audience hall was tedious. The only thing that caught
Wulfric's imagination was wondering if the woman would be there. He

thought it unlikely that a woman of sophistication and refinement would be anywhere else. Quite how she might have any interest in him punctured the fantasy, however. He had no land, no wealth. Those were the things southern women wanted.

He spotted the slight man who had brought him to dal Valeriano. Wulfric had asked around and found out his name was Carraterro dal Suera, a powerful nobleman in his own right, who had aligned himself with the duke's half-brother. Diego spotted Wulfric and smiled, doffing his hat in a gesture that was as much threat as salutation. Wulfric felt the tingle that preceded all conflict run across his skin. Would it impress the mysterious woman?

'The exercises?'

It took Wulfric a moment to realise that Jagovere was speaking to him.

'The exercises? They weren't too difficult?'

'I told you I know how to make my letters,' Wulfric said. 'I'm not a complete idiot. I need to improve, not start from the beginning. Give me some of the stories you wrote down. I already know what they say. I can work the rest out.' The woman had walked into the hall, and he suddenly felt the need to prove himself. She wore a dark purple gown that hugged her figure in all the right places.

'Women like that are only ever trouble,' Jagovere said.

'Do you know her?' Wulfric asked.

'No, but I've known plenty like her,' he said. 'She'll have caught the eye of someone with more wealth and power than the likes of us, and he'll do whatever it takes to have her all to himself.'

Wulfric cast Jagovere a glance. The wistful sound in his voice raised questions, but Wulfric's attention was too drawn to the woman in the purple dress to give it much thought. She moved through the crowd with grace that seemed almost ethereal, until she stood next to dal Valeriano. Wulfric saw Diego give her an appraising look, then glance across the hall to Wulfric. His smile widened when he saw where Wulfric was looking. His hand moved to the hilt of his sword. A woman like that would be worth fighting to the death for, Wulfric thought. It would be a story worth writing down.

❧

## AETHELMAN

Aethelman clutched the blades in his hand. They seemed like such insignificant things. They were bare metal, the long blade thinning into a slender tang that could have a handle mounted on it. The smith had wanted to know what the symbols meant, so Aethelman had told him they were prayers to Audun. Few even remembered the name of that god—no one was interested in wisdom or knowledge in the Northlands anymore. They were not necessary to survive the daily trials of life, so Audun was ignored. Aethelman wasn't sure if the smith had believed him, but it didn't matter. He had four long knives of Godsteel, with the runes perfectly inscribed along their lengths. The fifth piece of steel had been payment for the work—a hundred times more than it was worth, but it was the only currency Aethelman had.

He weighed them in his hand as he walked down the path to the Hermitage's gate, and decided to keep two for himself. He needed to be sure he could complete his task, and two would be more than enough for the Hermitage—they had the resources to make more if need be.

He was quickly admitted to the ancient complex, and refused all offers of food and drink. The rector saw him immediately, showing the respect befitting Aethelman's age and seniority.

Aethelman laid the two blades down on the rector's desk and pushed them forward.

The rector picked one up and turned it over in his hands. 'Beautiful craftsmanship,' he said. 'What are they for?'

'Fount Stones,' Aethelman said. 'We've long forgotten what to do with them, but this is how they are destroyed. That is what we are supposed to do. The blade will cleave the Stones in two.'

'Fascinating,' the rector said. 'Godsteel is always so beautiful when it's worked. He traced his finger along the rippling pattern in the steel. 'And the runes? What do they say?'

Aethelman shrugged. It would take too long to explain them. 'It doesn't matter. All that is important is that if more are ever made, the runes should be copied exactly.'

The rector frowned and touched his finger to his lips. He stood and without a word went to a cupboard at the back of his large, rambling office. Aethelman did not doubt there were piles of papers there that had lain untouched for decades, the writings of rectors past. Perhaps he should have started his search there? The rector rummaged in the cupboard for a few minutes, taking out a variety of objects and boxes, unceremoniously dumping them on the ground.

'There it is,' the rector said. 'I knew I'd seen something like this before.' He returned to Aethelman holding a knife in his hand. He passed it over.

Aethelman looked at it, laughing at how the gods played with mortal man. How foolish his efforts must seem! The blade looked as fresh as if it had been forged with Aethelman's new blades, but the bone handle was browned and cracked with age. It was ancient, but it was identical to the knives Aethelman had brought. For an age it had sat in the cupboard, all but forgotten, its purpose actually so. It was rare in Aethelman's life that the path to his destination had been a direct one.

He sighed, and tried not to let the revelation frustrate him. 'Tell everyone,' Aethelman said. 'This is the reason for our existence. At least it once was. We can't allow it to be forgotten again. Every novice must be told. The Search is not futile. The Stones are a blight and they are real. I have seen one. They must be destroyed. It is our sacred duty.'

The rector regarded him with wide eyes. 'Indeed. Indeed. I'll be certain to.'

Aethelman felt a flash of frustration. How could he be certain the rector was taking him seriously?

'I've read much about these Stones, what they were created for, and what they did. It is your duty to ensure our Order fulfils its responsibility.'

'I hardly think I need to be told what my responsibilities as rector are. I understand the importance of what you are saying.'

'Good,' Aethelman said, entirely unconvinced that his words had registered. 'The gods will judge us all on how we have conducted our lives.'

That seemed to hit the desired note.

'Will you sup with us, brother?' the rector said, but Aethelman was already heading for the door.

❖

# Rodulf

No visit to Elzburg would be complete without paying a visit to court. Rodulf had no desire to be condescended to again, but he knew he needed to be seen there as often as possible. Nonetheless, a visit to the bank took precedence.

There was a plethora of banks to choose from in the city, but Rodulf had picked Kuyt and Valk's, for no reason other than he had liked the sound of the name. He sat in the waiting room for longer than he liked, and was certain it was a show of power by the manager. Eventually he was led through to an opulent office occupied by a bespectacled man with far broader shoulders than one would expect of a banker.

'Lord Leondorf,' the banker said. 'Burgess Berengar at your service. I'm sorry for the wait, but you have to understand it's not at all usual for the manager to open an account. I'm not even sure I remember how.'

He smiled, but Rodulf could tell it was false.

'I'm not here to open an account,' Rodulf said. 'I'm here to open a branch.'

Berengar's mouth opened, then closed, and he smiled again.

'There are no banks in Leondorf,' Rodulf said.

'I was given to understand that coin was not of much use in the Northlands.'

Rodulf tried to gauge if the comment was an observation or an underhand insult, but couldn't decide.

'Perhaps in the past, but things change. I'm sure you're aware of the silver mines.'

'I am,' Berengar said. 'We are fortunate enough to count the Markgraf as one of our customers.'

'That's a fraction of the wealth in the Northlands,' Rodulf said. 'Furs, gems, ores. Leondorf will be a hub of trade that opens the Northlands to the world. I'm offering you the chance to be there from the start, and to enjoy the benefits that will bring.'

The bank manager stroked his chin. 'Do you not think you are being a little optimistic?'

Rodulf slid a piece of paper across the desk. 'The taxes generated on last month's trade,' Rodulf said. 'It grows by multiples every month. Coin and bullion is being dragged up and down the road to Leondorf in ever greater amounts, and banditry has risen tenfold. A bank would mean fewer trips needed. Trips that can be properly escorted. Money that can be better protected.'

Berengar read the numbers on Rodulf's piece of paper. 'That is quite surprising. Quite surprising indeed. These figures haven't been... embellished at all, have they?'

Rodulf frowned. 'I'm sure Sherbane's or Austorgas's would be happy to find out for themselves.'

'I'm sure they would,' Berengar said, 'but the setting up of a new branch is no small undertaking.'

'I think these figures show it would be one that is well worthwhile.'

'New markets do tend to favour those who arrive the earliest,' Berengar said, tapping his finger on his desk. 'Leave it with me a day or two. I'll be able to give you an answer then.'

Rodulf nodded. He hadn't expected anything more than this on a first meeting, but he wasn't willing to allow the balance of power to favour the banker.

'Two days. Then I talk to Sherbane's.' He didn't wait for any further pleasantries, and left the office. If Kuyt and Valk's didn't want to make money, that was their business, but he would not allow it to slow his plans. His growing anger was interrupted by a raised voice he recognised.

'You'll simply have to sort it out.' It was Henselman dal Geerdorf, storming out of a different office and from the premises.

The only reason for that reaction in that building was financial difficulty. Rodulf smiled. It was deeply satisfying to him to see that the man might not have everything his own way. All power but no coin, Rodulf suspected—a common thing amongst the nobility, and the former rarely lasted long without the latter. Opportunity appeared in the most unexpected places.

Rodulf turned and walked back into the manager's office without knocking, and sat. Berengar looked at him with an expression of surprise, but said nothing.

'Count dal Geerdorf,' Rodulf said. 'I understand he's in some financial difficulty.'

Berengar frowned. 'I'm afraid that's really not something I'm in a position to discuss. Our clients' details are always kept in the strictest of confidentiality.'

Rodulf nodded. 'And if I were to say I wanted to help the count with his situation?' Rodulf knew he was fishing, but he had seen enough to make the effort worthwhile.

'Help in what way?' Berengar said.

'Something that would be of benefit to all parties involved,' Rodulf said. 'Perhaps I could buy all of his debts from the bank?' With the house purchase, Rodulf barely had a purse of silver to his name. *Reward requires risk*, his father always used to say. He could find the money afterwards. The influence this could give him was invaluable.

'That's something we only consider in the most extreme of circumstances.'

'Would offering you ten percent over the value make it an extreme circumstance?' Rodulf said.

Berengar licked his lips. 'Not as extreme as twenty percent over the value.'

Rodulf leaned back in the chair and smiled. Things were so much simpler in the south. It was avaricious, but it was refreshing.

'Just how extensive are the count's debts?'

'Extensive. Very extensive.'

He was going to need to get his new silver mines up and running very quickly if he hoped to stay afloat. He was starting to regret buying the house. Rodulf reached into his pocket and grasped the Stone. 'I think ten percent is more than fair.' He fixed his gaze on Berengar, and waited for the Stone to do whatever it was it did.

Berengar narrowed his eyes, as though concentrating on some great problem. 'I... I... Yes, ten does seem to be a fair figure.'

Rodulf stifled a sigh of relief. He had come to realise that the Stone did not influence all men, for whatever reason. It was a question he would have to seek the answer to one day. 'If you agree to raw silver, and to take possession of it in Leondorf, then we have a deal.' It occurred to him that the offer might even add weight to the argument in favour of establishing a bank in Leondorf. He released the Stone from his grip, and the banker visibly relaxed.

'That will be acceptable. Will you prefer to pay the two hundred fifty thousand crowns, plus the ten percent premium, by instalment or in one payment?'

Rodulf swallowed hard at the number, but did his best to conceal the fact. He had no idea how long it would take to get that much silver out of the ground—a few weeks at least, if the other mine was anything to go by. That didn't take into account the start-up time though. He would simply have to find a way to make it work.

'However you prefer,' Rodulf said. 'It makes little difference to me. Naturally it will take a few weeks to put together a sum of that size.'

'Naturally,' Berengar said. 'Made all the easier by the presence of a locally situated banking house, I expect.'

Rodulf smiled.

# CHAPTER 29

## THE MAISTERSPAEKER

THE MAISTERSPAEKER CONTINUED his story with the added excitement of not knowing how Rodulf might react to the things he was saying. By the time *The Wolf of the North* was finished and had spread throughout the inns and taverns of the land, Rodulf would be the most hated person in Ruripathia, perhaps farther still. Would he snap and order his men to clear the tavern when he realised how his name was being blackened? Would he order them to kill him?

Rodulf had featured only as an invisible spectre in Ulfyr's epics up until that point, but he was now taking centre stage. He would be a villain of the ages, his name living in infamy long after he had left this world for the next. He could not react if he did not want to draw unwanted attention. Rodulf of Leondorf was still wanted for treason in Ruripathia, and to reveal himself was to invite his execution. However, every man had his limit and few liked the truth when it was brought out into the harsh light of day.

Rodulf looked prosperous, so the men with him were likely bannerets, and wouldn't die easily. If Rodulf ordered them to deal with him, the Maisterspaeker knew he wouldn't stand a chance. The danger was thrilling, though. It was a sensation he had not properly experienced since hanging up his sword. Wulfric would never forgive him if he precipitated a confrontation, and the Maisterspaeker was not so arrogant as to think he would survive the encounter. Rodulf was Wulfric's, anyway. He had waited half his life to be reunited with his one-eyed nemesis, and now that meeting was no more than a matter of hours away.

The Maisterspaeker watched as he spoke, but Rodulf showed barely a flicker of reaction, and none of recognition. He wore a sly smirk, one that said he was master of all around him, and nothing could knock him from his perch, not even a tale so vilifying. The Maisterspaeker was irked that Rodulf seemed so immune to the tale of his misdeeds, but found it deeply satisfying to know that his reckoning would not be long in coming.

❈

## WULFRIC

Wulfric returned to his room to pack up the few belongings he had taken with him to the palace. He had just unlocked and opened the door when he heard a footstep behind him and turned, his hand automatically reaching for the grip of his sword. He expected to see Diego standing down the hall, but it was the woman in the purple dress, and she was far closer than the footstep had indicated.

Wulfric relaxed. 'My lady,' he said, giving a curt nod of his head as Jagovere had shown him. His breath shortened at the sight of her; dark hair and eyes, and full lips. Her gown accentuated her figure, and Wulfric felt a thrill run through him similar to the prospect of battle.

'You like what you see, Northlander?' she said.

Her accent was rich and syrupy, like honey in his ears. He had never encountered a woman like that before, and found himself at a loss as to what to do.

'I… you look very well, my lady,' Wulfric said, trying to remember the brief lessons on court etiquette Jagovere had given him. He hadn't thought she had even noticed him, but here she was.

'I think you like me better than that,' she said, her dark eyes drawing him in. She took a step forward until she was pressed up against him. She stared up at him and he could feel the heat of her breath on his chin, the press of her breasts on his chest. She pushed him back into his room as he felt himself respond to her advance. As soon as the door closed behind them, he could feel something else—the point of a blade pressing under his chin.

'Tell your master nothing waits for him in Darvaros but death.'

The point of the blade had as quick an effect on him as her breasts had when they first pressed against him.

'Go home, Northman,' she said. 'Stay away from things that don't concern you.'

He kept his eyes fixed on hers. 'Why does everyone think I'm a messenger?' He grabbed her hand, and pushed the blade away from his throat. 'I'll go where I please,' he said.

She grabbed his wrist with her free hand and twisted it in such a way that he could not stop himself from releasing his grip. She smiled, and shifted the point of her knife to his crotch. She pressed it against him for a moment.

'Go home,' she said in a throaty whisper, then reached behind her, opened the door, and was gone.

It was the closest he had been to a woman since Adalhaid but the feeling it left him with was very different, and not at all pleasant. Who was she? His immediate reaction was that she was another one of the Count of Valeriano's retainers, but something told him it was more complicated than that. He wondered what Jagovere would make of it all.

## AETHELMAN

Aethelman had thought that his journey would take him back to Leondorf, or at least to somewhere in the Northlands. Part of him believed the Stone had not gone very far from his small kirk, but it seemed he was mistaken. The pull was drawing him south, and it was not long before he found himself crossing the river that marked the boundary between the Northlands and Ruripathia. Whoever had the Stone had taken it South.

## ADALHAID

Adalhaid sat in the lecture theatre, the sound of the lecturer's voice floating in the background. She had been able to think of little other than Jakob Strellis since their last encounter in the clinic. She could still feel the spot on her hand where they had touched. The memory of it quickened her heart and sickened her stomach. She knew Wulfric was gone, and that she could not spend her life wishing that were different. He would not have wanted that, but for some reason she could not shake him off. It felt as though some part of him was still with her, that their connection was not broken. Perhaps he watched her from Jorundyr's Hall, waiting for her to join him. The thought caused a pain in her heart so great she thought it would crush her. It was foolish thinking; Wulfric would want her to be happy, not to live in a state of pain and anguish. Perhaps Jakob was her future, in this world at least.

❄

# RODULF

Rodulf felt a giddy excitement when he arrived at court. The anticipation of his meeting with Henselman, Count of Geerdorf, excited him like the prospect of a night at The Red Carnation, Elzburg's premier brothel. He sat at the side of the hall watching people come and go, waiting for dal Geerdorf. He wondered how dal Geerdorf would take the news that his debts were no longer held by Kuyt and Valk's—not that it mattered. Taking the news badly wouldn't change the fact that Rodulf owned him.

Dal Geerdorf was part of the Markgraf's privy council, and attended court each and every day to carry out his duties. Rodulf hoped to catch him there, and break the news.

While Rodulf's comings and goings at the palace were all but anonymous, dal Geerdorf's were anything but. He arrived to great fuss, a belek cloak draped across his shoulders. Two bannerets walked behind him, haughty in their wide-brimmed hats with hands casually resting on the pommels of their swords. There were others too—private secretaries, notaries, scribes, and servants.

Rodulf had only a single banneret as bodyguard, the one he had brought with him from home. He was amused by the ironies of perception. To an observer, dal Geerdorf would appear the centre of power with his fine clothes, superior demeanour, and large entourage. Rodulf would barely be noticed, yet all the puppet strings were in his hands.

'My lord dal Geerdorf,' Rodulf said, standing. 'I wondered if you might have a moment to talk?'

Dal Geerdorf stopped and glared over, a look of irritation on his face. 'That's the Northlander, isn't it?' he said to the notary, loud enough for Rodulf to hear.

'I believe so, my lord,' the notary said.

Dal Geerdorf grunted. 'Tell him to piss off. Cheeky little prick thinking he can address me like that.'

The notary nodded and made his way over. 'My lord dal Geerdorf is very busy,' he said. 'Is there something I can help you with?'

'My lord,' Rodulf said.

The notary frowned.

'Is there something I can help you with, *my lord*,' Rodulf said. 'I'm a baron of Ruripathia.'

'Of course, I'm sorry, my lord.'

'Think nothing of it,' Rodulf said. He took a sheaf of papers from a leather folder and handed them to the notary. 'I think these may be of interest to Lord dal Geerdorf. They are notarised copies of the originals which I hold in my vault at Kuyt and Valk's.'

The notary took them and started to leaf through. 'How did you get these? These are the mortgage documents for the count's properties.'

'Yes,' Rodulf said, sitting back down and easing into a relaxed smile. 'I thought it distasteful that a man of the count's position had his notes held by tradesmen, so I took the liberty of buying all of his loans.'

The notary blanched. 'They can't do this,' he said.

'On the contrary. I'm told that once repayments are in default the bank is entitled to recover their monies by whatever means they choose.'

'You... you have all of them?' the notary said.

'Every single one,' Rodulf would have smiled wider, if he were not already at his limit. 'Perhaps you should go and have a chat with the Graf. I have an appointment with the chancellor, and I'll need to speak with him before then.'

The notary hurried after dal Geerdorf without another word, leaving Rodulf to bask in the satisfaction of an impending victory. He watched the exchange of words between dal Geerdorf and the notary with the relish of a man about to start into a fine meal. There was a great deal of gesticulating and head shaking, but Rodulf owned him now, and there would be no refusing, no matter how distasteful dal Geerdorf found taking orders from a Northlander. Not if he wanted to keep his houses, his estates, his horses, and his sons in the Academy at Brixen.

Eventually the conversation stopped, and dal Geerdorf walked over, his face all thunder and fury.

'The last time we spoke, I had thought it on friendly terms,' he said. 'We were planning on forming some trade agreements, as I recall.'

'Friendly terms, so long as I did what you wanted,' Rodulf said. Rodulf remained sitting, and maintained his smile. 'Be very clear on one thing, my lord. React to my greeting like that again, and your sons will be swinging picks in the silver mines, and your daughters will be paying off your debts on their backs.'

Dal Geerdorf's face darkened further, and Rodulf wished he had more than one banneret with him.

'After I've had my fill of them,' Rodulf said, not willing to show any fear. The new dynamic of their association had to be established from the start.

'What do you want?' dal Geerdorf said again, but in a more respectful tone.

'I simply want us to be friends, as you said before,' Rodulf said. 'But friendship on my terms, not yours. I want you to open doors that would otherwise remain closed to me. I want you to aid my rise at court, and to demonstrate to all the stuck-up arseholes here that I am as much a part of society as any of them.'

Dal Geerdorf's lips thinned as he forced a smile. 'It would be my pleasure.'

'Excellent,' Rodulf said. 'I'm told you're hosting a ball this evening. I shall see you there.' He stood and walked away.

# CHAPTER 30

WULFRIC

THEY HAD BEEN riding in silence for over an hour before
Enderlain broke the silence. 'I don't expect that's how you saw it
going,' he said. He was doing his best to hold in laughter, but with
only moderate success.

Wulfric glowered at him. 'Who do you think she was working for?' he
said to Jagovere. He pulled down the brim of the wide hat he had bought
in Torona. He had thought them silly, vain-looking things, but under the
strong sunlight he could see their use. Nonetheless, he felt like an idiot
wearing it.

'Well, not you, anyway,' Jagovere said, 'although perhaps that sort of
thing appeals to Northlanders. I've heard you like your women feisty.'

'Not that feisty,' Wulfric said, realising he wasn't going to be able to get
away with it.

Jagovere allowed himself a laugh, and Wulfric smiled, thinking it better
to be laughed with rather than at. They had several days' ride ahead of them,
and he didn't want to be the butt of jokes the whole way. The episode had
made him think of Adalhaid more frequently. Perhaps it was the treatment
he deserved for having allowed his thoughts to drift. Perhaps he was lucky
not to have been gelded. Perhaps he deserved to be. Until he had settled
Adalhaid's Blood Debt, he resolved not to look at another woman.

'It doesn't really matter who she was working for,' Jagovere said. 'If we
view everyone down here as an enemy, we won't go far wrong. Every step of
the way, we have to look out for ourselves. Such is the life of a mercenary.

We can be hired and fired on a whim when it's no longer convenient to have us around, and we can never forget that.'

Wulfric nodded. He was coming to hate the south. At least in the Northlands he had always known who his friends and enemies were.

'Have you finished reading the pages I gave you?'

'I have,' Wulfric said, as he rolled gently in the saddle.

'Any problem words?'

'No, I could manage them all.'

'You've taken to it quicker than I expected,' Jagovere said.

'I had done a little before, I was just never diligent about it. I see the use in it now. More than I did before.'

'An agile mind and an agile blade, is it?'

'Southerners seem to think all Northlanders are ignorant savages. I'm not going to help prove you right.'

Jagovere nodded, but said nothing. They continued in silence for a moment, as Wulfric wrestled with something he had wanted to say for some time.

'I wanted to thank you,' Wulfric said.

Jagovere raised an eyebrow. 'For what?'

'For everything. Saving me from the soldiers in Wetlin, for welcoming me into the Company. For trusting me.'

'It was the Graf's doing, if I'm being honest, not mine.'

'Still,' Wulfric said. He mulled over how to put what he wanted to say next. 'I had good reason to kill those men I killed.'

'Your reasons are your own,' Jagovere said.

'I want you to know I'm no murderer. Those men tried to have me killed, and someone special to me taken away.'

'A woman?'

Wulfric nodded. 'Adalhaid. She was murdered.'

'I'm sorry to hear that.'

'I still have to settle her Blood Debt,' Wulfric said. 'There were more men involved. I can't rest until I do so.'

'I've heard of Northlander Blood Debts,' Jagovere said. 'For what it's worth, I understand.'

'I just wanted you to know,' Wulfric said, before falling silent again.

❀

## ADALHAID

As much as Adalhaid loved the practice of medicine, there were parts of it that she found mind-numbingly tedious. After each clinic, all their tools and implements had to be painstakingly cleaned, not just those that had been used. Jakob had told her the risk of infection was too high to limit oneself to those that had seen use that day. Forgetfulness and cross-contamination were ever-present dangers, so they all had to be cleaned, after every session.

Each instrument was boiled and then carefully scrubbed, and it was the responsibility of a good physician to personally attend to their own tools. She scrubbed each of the steel implements and passed them to Jakob—she wasn't sure exactly when she had moved from calling him Doctor Strellis to Jakob, but it felt perfectly natural now—who dried and put them away.

'You did well today,' he said. 'I was right when I said you have a real talent for this.'

Adalhaid blushed, but kept her gaze fixed on the task at hand.

'And I do so love it when I'm right,' he said.

She laughed and looked up. His steely blue eyes were fixed on her, and he wore the crooked smile he adopted whenever he was teasing someone. She could not help but smile back as she passed him something—she had completely forgotten what it was. This time when their hands touched, she did not pull hers away. Before she knew what was happening he had leaned in and kissed her. She found herself returning his embrace.

Before she closed her eyes, she saw Rosamund standing at the doorway.

❀

## RODULF

'How the winds of change do blow,' Rodulf said, as he walked into the Markgraf's great hall beside his new best friend. He said it as much as a statement of fact as to irritate dal Geerdorf. He knew he needed to be more circumspect in the way he treated dal Geerdorf—even a cowed dog would bite from time to time—but for the moment he was enjoying the experience too much. Owning slaves had always felt empowering to him, but owning one of the most influential men in the Mark was utterly thrilling. For the past few days, he and dal Geerdorf had been near-constant companions.

Rodulf was at his side at each social occasion, his presence announcing to everyone that he was a man of status, not an arriviste with a bought title.

'How long, do you think, before I'll be able to take a place on the privy council?' Rodulf said.

'Don't put your cart before the horse,' dal Geerdorf said. 'I'm not the only man who makes such decisions. It can take years to build the support, influence, and reputation needed.'

'I can be very persuasive,' Rodulf said. 'Just direct me to the appropriate people, and I'm sure I can bring them around to my way of thinking.' He had a firm grip on the Stone, the comfort it brought him being a necessity now rather than a treat. He didn't like to be parted from it for even a moment. However, he did not have the confidence in it he once had—it seemed that not everyone was susceptible to its power. He didn't understand the Stone, nor what it really did, and it was frustrating. That it gave him greater influence over some people was a certainty, but with others it failed. He didn't like uncertainty, or things he couldn't rely on, but how could he discover more about it? How could he learn to use it to its full potential? He felt a pang of regret that he had killed the old priest. Who else might be able to enlighten him?

'Count Unsdorf, might I have the pleasure of introducing you to Baron Leondorf,' dal Geerdorf said.

Unsdorf's moustache twitched as he regarded dal Geerdorf. Rodulf realised he was wondering if it was some kind of joke, and felt anger flush through him like a flash fire. Had they really considered him to be such a pariah? Dal Geerdorf gave no reaction, so Unsdorf clicked his heels together and nodded his head to Rodulf, a gesture Rodulf mirrored.

'Don't do that again,' dal Geerdorf said as they walked away.

'Do what?' Rodulf said.

'Click your heels. Just bow your head. Only bannerets click their heels.'

Southern society was layer of snobbery piled on layer of snobbery, Rodulf thought. 'How much does it cost to become a banneret?'

Dal Geerdorf laughed. 'It costs blood, sweat, tears, and at least four years of your life. You may have bought me, but not everything is for sale. You'll never be a banneret. Everything else can be had for coin, but not that.'

It was only then that Rodulf noticed the banners hanging above the stalls that lined the sides of the hall. Each was made from pale grey cloth, but they were decorated with colourful embroidery, every one different from the other.

'Only the top Academy graduates earn a grey banner and a seat in the hall,' dal Geerdorf said. 'Everyone else, you included, has to stand. The banner has to be earned. The son of a tanner can be seated next to the son of a duke. Here they are equal.'

He said it with a hint of pride in his voice, which confused Rodulf. He could remember only too well what a tanner's shop smelled like, and there was no way he would sit downwind of a tanner's son. Money was what made the south work, but here was something it seemed money could not buy. The hypocrisy was frustrating. He could hire a dozen bannerets, but dal Geerdorf was telling him he could never be one, nor make that stupid salute. It was like the warrior class in the Northlands all over again. Arrogant bastards. He told himself it didn't matter. The privy council was where the power was, and dal Geerdorf was going to get him a seat on it whether he liked it or not. He couldn't let dal Geerdorf feel he had won a small victory. The key to obedience was keeping him perpetually cowed. On this occasion, Rodulf chose the biggest stick in his arsenal.

'Talk down to me again,' Rodulf said, 'and I'll sell your daughters to a Shandahari slaver.'

# CHAPTER 31

## PROFESSOR KENGIL

'ABSOLUTELY DESTROYED, YOU say?' Professor Kengil said. It was unusual to have a clinical assistant call on her, but not nearly so unusual as the information she brought.

'Absolutely,' Rosamund said. 'Dr. Strellis was preparing to amputate her leg. He asked me to stand by in case Adalhaid wasn't ready for such a major operation.'

'Take me through it one more time.'

Rosamund looked nervous as she nodded, but Kengil knew her reputation far preceded her.

'Doctor Strellis went back into the treatment room. When they came out a few minutes later, the girl followed them out.'

'Followed them out?' Kengil said.

'Yes. She walked out with nothing more than a bandage on her leg and a limp.'

'Fascinating,' Kengil said. 'Fascinating. You think Doctor Strellis might be resorting to darker powers?'

Rosamund's eyes widened. 'No! Of course not. I've been working in his clinic for two years now, and I've never seen anything like that. No. It's not Doctor Strellis. It's her. Steinnsdottir. The Northlander.'

'Of course it is,' Kengil said, a smile spreading across her face. 'Thank you for bringing this to my attention.'

✽

## WULFRIC

The duke's army was camped on the Estranzan side of the border with Darvaros. Wulfric had not seen anything like it before. It made a Northlander army look like nothing more than a skirmishing party. There must have been more than ten thousand men there. Ordered rows of white tents stretched across the arid landscape, interspersed with occasional larger, coloured ones.

Even from a distance Wulfric could hear chatter and laughter. It was a jovial atmosphere, rather than one of martial discipline, and Wulfric wasn't sure what to make of it. As they grew closer, Wulfric realised it was more raucous than he had first thought. It sounded like there was no shortage of ale, and Wulfric couldn't see a single sentry on duty. Women in heavy make-up and revealing clothes wandered about, arm-in-arm with soldiers. Wulfric wondered if they even knew where they had left their weapons and armour.

'Not the most encouraging sight,' Jagovere said. 'Looks like these fellows think a war is a holiday from their wives.'

Wulfric shrugged. He realised he had no idea about war in the south. Perhaps this was what it was always like, at least until the killing started. He wondered what kind of a mess of the place he could make with a few hundred Northland horsemen. They could have routed the camp before the Estranzans had even found their swords. It puzzled him why their enemy had not done exactly that.

One of dal Rhenning's adjutants rode down the length of the Company's marching column indicating where they were to make camp. Separated from the main army, it seemed whoever was giving the orders did not plan on making the Company welcome.

※

## ADALHAID

Adalhaid was coming to know nothing but guilt. She felt guilty for how little time she gave Aenlin and Petr, the Markgraf's children, beyond what was required by the terms of her job. They had asked why she was there so infrequently, and it made her feel awful. She felt guilty for not applying herself harder to her studies; but above all, she felt guilty for not being able to think about anything other than Jakob Strellis.

As she hurried through the public part of the palace toward the private apartments, she heard a laugh that made her skin crawl. Standing amongst a group of the Markgraf's nobles was Rodulf. Adalhaid had hoped that once his investiture was done with, he would return north and remain there. The southerners were rarely that welcoming to Northlanders, unless there was something they really wanted. She had hoped that treatment would put Rodulf off, but it seemed the wealth she had heard he was accumulating had earned him some new friends. He was too engrossed in his conversation to notice her, and she continued on her way as quickly as she could. The thought of him being a regular feature at the palace made her nauseated.

# CHAPTER 32

## PROFESSOR KENGIL

ONE THING PROFESSOR Kengil had always admired about Doctor Strellis was his meticulous record keeping. All the clinics fell within her overwatch, as projects of the university. Usually she paid them little attention after appointing the physician in charge. Choose the head wisely, she always thought, and the body will perform as expected. Strellis was one of her more outstanding protégés, not that he seemed to realise how much had gone his way due to her influence, something that grated with her.

It was not difficult tracking down the young girl who had been hit by the wagon. Her name and address was included on her treatment record, so all it took was a little legwork. She lived with her mother in a poor part of the city, where the narrow streets bustled with industry and accidents were common.

Kengil disliked venturing into parts of the city like that, but she disliked Northlanders more. Rosamund's story was too intriguing to let pass. The thought that the jumped-up Northlander was dabbling in dark things was as thrilling as it was concerning for Kengil. She knocked on the door and waited a moment. When it opened, she was greeted by the smell of cooking and poor sanitation. She wrinkled up her nose and forced a smile.

'Good evening,' she said to the woman who opened it. 'My name is Doctor Kengil. I'm here to follow up on the treatment received by a young girl living at this address.'

'That'd be Ellie,' the woman said, flustered. 'Your ladyship,' she added.

Kengil smiled. 'It's simply "Doctor Kengil". May I see Ellie?'

'Of course, Doctor. Come in. Come in.'

She stepped back from the door and allowed Professor Kengil into the small apartment. There were five children present in the main room, all staring at Kengil with wide, curious eyes. They were all young and unkempt, and it was not obvious which one was Ellie.

'I'm here to see Ellie,' Kengil said.

'That's me,' one of the children said.

'My name's Doctor Kengil. I'm here to take a look at your leg. May I?'

The little girl nodded and lifted the hem of her skirt, to reveal a now-filthy bandage. Kengil began her examination.

'We were terrible shocked by the accident,' Ellie's mother said. 'The doctor said that can cause all sorts of strange reactions. We thought it was far worse, but mayhap that's just a mother's concern. After the doctor treated it, it didn't seem that bad at all.'

Kengil nodded absently. The residual mark on the girl's leg beneath the bandage suggested a minor injury. Shock could indeed produce an over-reaction, but that was unlikely in a trained physician. Rosamund was a good and diligent student, and would soon qualify to be an excellent young practitioner. Kengil thought her unlikely to make a mistake. Then there was the fact that she had spoken of Doctor Strellis's preparation to amputate. He knew what he was doing. He wouldn't have made those preparations were he not sure they were needed. Kengil wondered if Rosamund might have some reason to make it all up, or if the Northlander might indeed be a witch of some sort. Kengil was all too aware of the reaction Strellis caused among young women. It seemed almost too much to hope for in getting at the brazen young savage.

Kengil made her excuses and left the apartment. As she walked back toward the university, her mind drifted back to a day in the distant past, when the Northlanders had come across the border to her village, bringing death and destruction. Northlanders never brought anything but misery. At last it seemed she would be able to return the favour.

※

## WULFRIC

'Well, my lovelies,' dal Rhenning shouted. 'Time to earn your pay.' With a wave of his hand, the column moved off.

Wulfric rode next to Enderlain, a sign of the unlikely friendship that had developed between the two. Dal Rhenning had ordered a scouting party in force the morning after they arrived at the border. Jagovere had said the Graf wanted to send a clear signal that he didn't intend the Company to join in with the idlers filling the duke's army.

Few of the Estranzan soldiers paid them any attention as they rode by, but those who did watched them with expressions of resentment. None of them had so much as set foot across the border, and few if any had even seen a Darvarosian soldier. Any soldier with a modicum of self-respect would have been shamed by their inactivity while the new arrivals rode toward the ford in the river, and enemy territory beyond.

Wulfric had been able to cobble together a better-fitting set of armour than he had initially been given when he agreed to join the Company, and he had overseen the smith as he reworked both the armour and Wulfric's sabre until they were as close to tailored to him as he could hope for. Nonetheless, he pined for the weapons and armour he had left behind in Leondorf, and for Greyfell most of all.

They forded the river under the watchful eyes of distant Darvarosian scouts, but there was no sign of any enemy in numbers. It seemed no one knew exactly where the enemy army was. Riding into hostile territory, Wulfric thought he should feel more nervous. However, if anything, he felt relaxed. It took some time for Wulfric to realise what was different. The burden of leadership had rested on his shoulders for so long—the responsibility for the lives of the few other warriors of Leondorf had been his—but now he was simply a warrior and didn't have to worry about anything other than fighting.

Riding out in their armour, it did not take long for the sun to heat the metal to the point where it moved from uncomfortable to painful. Wulfric took to removing a length of white bandage cloth from his pack, wrapping it around his helmet and draping it over his cuirass as he had seen some of the other more experienced members of the Company do. It improved the situation somewhat, but he was counting the moments until he could take the armour off.

The landscape was scorched brown, punctuated with verdant patches of vegetation and odd-looking trees with long slender trunks and a crown of long fronds at the top. Other than some birds overhead, he hadn't seen any animals and wondered what the hunting there was like. It was exposed on the open plain, and Wulfric could see uninterrupted to the horizon.

Dal Rhenning had sent two groups of the light horsemen ahead of them to scout their route. Wulfric could see the dust cloud their movement kicked up in the distance, which meant any Darvarosians in the area could also. It was impossible for them to move about a landscape like that without being seen, however, and Wulfric didn't like the idea that the enemy knew where they were while they had no idea of the Darvarosians' positions.

They moved inland for most of the morning until the land grew hilly and Wulfric spotted a strange stone plateau in the distance that rose from the ground.

'It's called *the Warrens*,' Jagovere said. 'A limestone plateau that's had hundreds of narrow passageways carved into it by centuries of flood waters running off it. They say that if you wander in, you'll never find your way back out.'

Wulfric narrowed his eyes as he looked at Jagovere, wondering if he was being teased. 'Best not wander in, then,' Wulfric said.

Jagovere tossed his head back and laughed, before they all returned to the tedious silence of surveying the foreign and hostile land. Their scouts continued to report no sign of anyone and he was starting to grow bored. It appeared nobody there actually wanted a fight.

By midday the heat was growing oppressive, and Wulfric found himself not wanting a fight either—simply riding in it was draining enough. To fight in it would be miserable. No sooner had the thought entered his head than he realised the scouts were riding back at speed.

'Forty horsemen, my lord,' one of the scouts said to dal Rhenning. 'Watering their mounts at a pool to the east near the rocky plateau.'

'Well, lads,' dal Rhenning said. 'Looks like we'll bloody our blades after all. At the canter now.'

They moved off at a quick pace. Wulfric could see the others loosen the fastenings on their weapons. He did the same and readied his lance, the excitement of impending battle making him forget how hot it was in armour.

They moved through a shallow valley between the hills until they could see their prey. The Darvarosians weren't caught entirely unawares. They had reacted and were almost in battle order by the time the two bodies of men faced off against one another. There was a moment of hesitation while the men regarded their foes, each man staring at the potential bringer of his death.

Wulfric could feel his skin tingle, and realised his knuckles were white on his lance.

'There's at least twice as many of them as there are of us,' dal Rhenning said, 'so the advantage is with us!'

The Company men roared with laughter.

'At them, lads!' dal Rhenning shouted.

Wulfric needed no encouragement. He had spurred on his horse before dal Rhenning had finished shouting his order. He had already picked his target, a man with a thick black moustache and a helmet visor that shrouded his eyes. Wulfric would send him to whatever god he worshipped, and claim the Company's first blood on Darvarosian soil. He wanted them all to know how fearsome he was, friend and foe alike.

Wulfric had closed half the distance between them before the man realised he was the target of Wulfric's lance. He carried a small, round metal shield in addition to a long, curved sabre, and despite the fear that was now in his eyes, he raised his sword and urged his horse on toward Wulfric.

As they drew close, he extended his shield out toward Wulfric's spear. Wulfric leaned forward in his saddle and braced the spear. The metal head smashed against the shield with a deafening clatter. With an explosion of splinters, the lance knocked the shield aside and smashed into the Darvarosian's chest, launching him from his horse.

Wulfric flung the shattered stump to the ground and drew his sabre, just as the rest of the Company caught up. There was a deafening crash as steel, wood, and flesh collided. Wulfric's hand shook as he pressed into the Darvarosian line, slashing left and right at anything in reach. There were men everywhere around him, but their movement seemed to slow as his quickened.

Wulfric's face hurt beneath his helmet from smiling. The joy of battle was almost overwhelming. He waded farther into the press of horsemen. He grabbed a man by the cloth draped over his armour, and pulled him close enough so that Wulfric could smash his helmet into the man's face. He slashed back at another, a perfect cut that took a man's head from his body.

Again he pressed forward, seeking out another foe. He had no idea where his comrades were, but so long as he had enemies before him he was happy.

A Darvarosian warrior with a white horsehair plume extending from the top of his helmet came at Wulfric. The plates of his armour were filigreed with gold and he was clearly a man of status. The desire to kill him was overwhelming, urging Wulfric to throw caution to the wind. It was the first time he had encountered so grand a foe. Wulfric wanted to get to him before anyone else did. He wheeled his horse around and spurred it forward, issuing a roared challenge as he went. The man moved toward him, but as Wulfric raised his sword, he was hit from the side by a second man and knocked from the saddle. He fell to the hard-baked ground with a crunch of metal, but retained enough of his wits to know that while he was on the ground, he was in danger.

He rolled onto his front and jumped to his feet, frantically looking for his sword through the narrow eye-holes in his helmet. The man who had knocked him out of the saddle had not attacked, and Wulfric realised why— he was leaving Wulfric to the man in the plumed helmet. He looked around in time to see him goading his horse to trample Wulfric into the dirt. The beast snorted at him and came forward, lifting his hoofs high and stamping them down. Wulfric could only see the rider's legs, but that was enough.

Rather than shying away from the approaching horse, Wulfric charged forward beneath it, drawing his dagger as he did. Once he passed the horse's ribs, he plunged the blade into its belly and pulled it along as he went. He could feel blood and gore splatter all over him. The horse screamed and bucked, and Wulfric dived out of the way to avoid being crushed when it fell.

Realising his master was in trouble, the warrior who had knocked Wulfric from his horse drew his sword and rode forward. Wulfric parried the first blow with his dagger, but he could do little with the much shorter blade. Horses milled around them in a confused tangle of dust, flesh, and steel as the battle continued. With no good options, and running for safety a thought that turned his stomach, Wulfric hurled himself at his enemy with only his dagger to lead the way.

As he launched himself toward the Darvarosian still on horseback, he felt a tug at his ankle—the man in the plumed helmet. Wulfric's pounce became a stumble. Wulfric grabbed the horseman's leg and tried to pull him from his saddle as he fell. He felt a sabre blade clatter against his helmet and his ears rang with the clang. He gave one final pull and felt the Darvarosian give way and fall. They flailed around on the ground, both vying to gain control. Wulfric was larger and heavier, and used his greater bulk to best advantage.

Behind him, Wulfric could hear the man with the plumed helmet freeing himself from the tangle of his horse. As soon as he did, Wulfric knew he would have a sword in his back. He rolled on top of the Darvarosian, and brought his dagger to bear. Stinging sweat flowed into his eyes, and no amount of blinking would clear them. The Darvarosian dropped his sword and grabbed Wulfric by the wrists. Wulfric angled the tip of the dagger toward the eye slits in the Darvarosian's helmet and drove down with all his weight.

The Darvarosian braced his arms against the ground, and Wulfric drove his forearms through the Darvarosian's grip until he felt it begin to falter. With a roar, he threw every ounce of weight and strength behind the dagger, and the blade screeched against the sides of the helmet's eye slit. The Darvarosian didn't scream; he simply gasped as the blade cut through his eye and into his brain.

Wulfric grabbed the dead Darvarosian's sword and got back to his feet just in time to see the man in the plumed helmet stand clear of his dead horse. He drew his decorated sabre and fixed his gaze on Wulfric. Whatever else happened that day, Wulfric knew that only one of them would live.

# CHAPTER 33

JAGOVERE

JAGOVERE FOUGHT THE way he had been taught to, as part of a unit. It was why he was careful in choosing the men in his squadron, and why he had held misgivings about Wulfric. With Enderlain to his right and Sander to his left, they pushed through the Darvarosian light cavalrymen like a battering ram through a paper wall.

Wulfric had stayed with them for the charge, but as soon as the melee had begun, he had pressed ahead, fighting with all the brutal savagery the Northlanders were famed for. Jagovere had considered going through to support him, but it would have meant putting others at risk and breaking up their own formation. Live or die, Wulfric would have to make his own fate.

Out of the corner of his eye, Jagovere had seen Wulfric going for a man who was obviously the Darvarosian commander, in a plumed helmet and a magnificent suit of armour. As someone with an eye for a good story, it was impossible for Jagovere to put the confrontation out of his mind, even though the distraction might be enough to get him killed. He forced himself to concentrate on his own battle, and when he next looked, both Wulfric and the man in the plumed helmet had fallen from sight. He spent a moment wondering if either still lived, and regretted the possible loss of the potential Wulfric had shown, but that was the way of the fates. On a day like that, Jagovere was certain Wulfric's old gods would welcome him to sup with them.

Hacking and slashing, Jagovere, Enderlain, and Sander pushed forward until they came to a clear spot by a fallen horse. Wulfric and the man in the plumed helmet stood beside it, their eyes fixed on one another, neither moving. Wulfric was a fearsome sight. He was so drenched in blood he looked as though he had rolled around on an abattoir's floor, but he didn't seem to notice.

He paused to draw breath and blinked the sweat from his eyes as he watched. Jagovere noticed that the din of battle had lessened, and realised everyone around them had also stopped to watch the fight that was about to start. They continued to regard one another in still contemplation, like there was some invisible force holding them back. Then, as though the spell was broken, they moved toward each other in the same instant.

Jagovere could tell the Darvarosian was a master from the first swing of his sabre. He moved like a dancer, light on his feet and with a grace that made it look like he was floating. Wulfric, on the other hand, moved heavily—as if every step was intended to crush whatever was beneath it. Jagovere couldn't see a way Wulfric could win against a warrior of such skill. He was holding his breath at the first clash of blades and wondered if he should intervene. Their fight had become something of its own, a duel distant from everything rather than one component of the greater battle. It was entrancing to watch, and the thought of interfering felt wrong, for better or worse. Should it come to it, he was close enough to fend off a killing blow, but something told him that would not be needed, despite initial appearances.

The Darvarosian moved with glittering speed, his sabre and dagger weaving together in a mesmerising blur. Jagovere clenched his teeth in expectation of the inevitable. The only saving grace was that Wulfric was new to the Company—the blow to the Company's morale that his death would cause would be minimal. By comparison Wulfric seemed to move slowly. The Northlanders might be lethal in the saddle, but unlike their Ruripathian cousins they seemed to neglect the practice of fighting on foot. Weight and aggression were great assets on horseback, but against a warrior like the plumed man they weren't worth a damn.

Wulfric's blade came up to meet the Darvarosian's, and the ring of steel chimed out. Jagovere was surprised that Wulfric was able to parry the first strike, but he managed it again and again—and took the initiative, raining down blows, each one flowing from the one that preceded it. It was only then that Jagovere realised that despite the heavy and graceless appearance of Wulfric's movements, they matched the Darvarosian for speed. Faster, even, and getting faster still. While the Darvarosian might have moved like liquid, he didn't have Wulfric's strength or size. His attacks had bounced off Wulfric's immoveable defence, while Wulfric's attacks drove the plumed man back each time.

Wulfric closed the distance after each strike with a lack of grace that made Jagovere wince. Jagovere had been brought up to think of swordsmanship as an art form. Whether with rapier or sabre, each strike was an expression of self as much as it was an attack. There was none of that in what Wulfric did. As Jagovere stood watching in that surreal pool of calm amidst the maelstrom of battle, he realised that what he had initially dismissed as ignorant savagery was something else. There might not have been any art in the way Wulfric fought, but each attack was devastating and intended to do only one thing: Destroy.

The Darvarosian tried to regain the initiative. He rolled out of the way of Wulfric's sabre into the space that had grown around their single combat. No one else even pretended at fighting now; they were all spectators. With his blood-stained armour, Wulfric looked the very personification of death, a gory demon sent from the bowels of hell to destroy the glittering Darvarosian hero.

The Darvarosian completed his roll, finishing perfectly balanced back on his feet. Without turning to face Wulfric, he cut back, quick and precise, in a movement he had obviously practised many times. Wulfric's blade was too far away, and as much as Jagovere's hopes had risen that the Northlander might actually win, it looked like a killing strike. Wulfric caught the blade with his leather-gauntleted left hand, twisted it, and yanked it toward him. The Darvarosian tried to pull it free, but Wulfric's grip on the blade did not falter. Wulfric hauled the Darvarosian close, and punched him in the face twice. The combination of fist and sabre hilt pulped the Darvarosian's unprotected face. He wobbled. Wulfric released the blade, put both hands on his sabre and drove it through the Darvarosian's throat.

There was such silence that Jagovere could hear the gurgling sound the plumed Darvarosian made as he sank to his knees. Wulfric ripped the blade free and kicked his foe over, standing in the growing pool of blood with such comfort that it seemed to Jagovere to be his natural environment. Everyone else continued to stare at this vision of death personified.

'Stop bloody gawking!' Dal Rhenning's voice shattered the silence. 'Finish them!'

The Darvarosians needed no further encouragement. As one, they fled.

❧

## RODULF

As Rodulf walked toward the palace, fresh from handing over another bag of silver to an indebted aristocrat, he was troubled by the unsettling feeling in his gut that he was extending himself far beyond his limits. Dal Geerdorf wasn't the only aristocrat to have debts, and letting the power they offered pass him by was proving too difficult a thing to do. Grenville had reported that the secret silver mines were starting to produce ore, but until he had a bank in Leondorf in which he could hide it and then access it as spendable credit in the south, it was of little consolation. He had a solid line of credit with Kuyt and Valk's, but Rodulf was spending through it at a prodigious rate and very soon he would be as exposed with debts as the noblemen he was buying.

He would have wondered if he was throwing good money after bad, were it not for the reception he got as he walked into the palace. Mere weeks before, a sideways glance of disdain was the best he could expect. Now men stopped in their conversations and turned to greet him, delighted to receive a benevolent nod or wave in return. Either he owned them or they realised how much money could be made in the Northlands, for which they needed his favour. Southern aristocrats might have held similar attitudes to Northlander warriors when it came to money, deeming it a vulgarity beneath their attention, but when pressed they were all hungry for it. Coin was everything.

Rodulf knew how much danger all this placed him in. He might own these men—they might smile at him and kowtow—but they hated him for it. Hated him more than anyone they had ever encountered. If they had so much as a hint of a chance to do him over, they would pounce. Rodulf had to keep a tight grip on them, but he also had to put himself in a position where they could not pull him down. There was only one man who could ensure that. Now that he had pushed himself to the fore of his peers, he could get access to the Markgraf. That was where the true power in the Mark lay, and if he was indispensable to the Markgraf he would be untouchable.

❀

## WULFRIC

The Company rode back into camp with two captured battle standards flying proudly at the head of their column, and Wulfric had taken the armour and weapons of his vanquished foe. Their casualties had been few and they were in high spirits, having fought off a larger force, and more importantly, learned what their enemy were made of.

Wulfric had shown what *he* was made of. Everyone in the Company knew he was not a man to take lightly, if there had still been any doubt. He wondered about the man he had killed, the deeds he had done and the battles he had fought. It was unlikely he would ever find out, but his great skill at arms was enough for Wulfric to know he had vanquished a great man and the thought made him burst with pride. His journey along Jorundyr's Path was well and truly begun.

There was a new addition to the camp that drew Wulfric's attention when they returned, a magnificent tent erected in the Estranzans' camp. However, his rumbling belly soon diverted his thoughts elsewhere.

An Estranzan rode into the Company's camp as they started to dismount.

'Count Valeriano, Marshall of Torona, commands Captain dal Rhenning to attend on him immediately,' he said.

'That's Banneret of the Grey, Graf dal Rhenning, you maggot,' Jagovere said, his blood still clearly up after the battle.

The messenger ignored him. 'Immediately,' he said, then rode back toward the Estranzan camp.

Dal Rhenning stood, arms akimbo, and watched the man ride away, not having said anything at all. It was a curious, complicated thing, politics, Wulfric thought. Had a man, any man, spoken to his father like that, he could expect to be beaten senseless and would be lucky to come away from the experience with his life. Wulfric could see the anger in dal Rhenning's eyes, and the frustration of not being able to do anything about it etched on his brow.

Dal Rhenning snapped his gaze from the departing messenger and fixed it on Wulfric and Jagovere, who were attending to their horses. 'Seeing as you're both here, you might as well come with me.'

Wulfric opened his mouth to speak—he was covered in sweat, dust, and most extensively in dried blood, certainly not the way he thought he should look when called to attend on a nobleman.

Dal Rhenning spotted his hesitation. 'Don't wash. I want our lord and master to know what war looks like.'

They remounted and rode over, making no pretence at hurrying. There could be no doubting where Valeriano was. The new tent Wulfric had seen was garish, and in his opinion typical of a decadent southern aristocrat. When they reached it, they didn't wait to be invited in—dal Rhenning brushed past a sentry and into the tent as though it were his. There were a number of men already there, some sitting around a camp table. Wulfric recognised a few of them from Torona, but others were new to him. They looked at him with nervous eyes, all but Diego, who watched Wulfric with his usual wry smile.

Dal Valeriano sat at the head of the table, but the conversation seemed casual rather than anything relating to the war he was supposed to be prosecuting. Nonetheless, they ignored dal Rhenning. After a moment, dal Rhenning cleared his throat loudly enough to drown out the idle chit-chat at the campaign table.

'My lord Valeriano, if you're too busy, I need to debrief my officers on our engagement with the enemy this morning.'

Wulfric smiled at the way the Graf rubbed their inactivity in the Estranzan count's face.

'Ah yes, Graf dal Rhenning. In future, you are forbidden from carrying out any forays south of the border without my express orders.'

'I needed to gather intelligence. It was simply good fortune that we encountered the enemy in force. In your absence, the command structure was not clear, so I took the action that was in the best interest of the campaign.'

'It is my prerogative alone to decide what is in the best interest of the campaign,' dal Valeriano said.

'Wars are rarely won by sitting on your arse,' dal Rhenning said, his eyes flashing with the anger he had so expertly contained up to that point.

'Get out. Stay in your camp until you get my orders. Defy me and I will consider you to be in breach of contract.'

Dal Rhenning forced a smile and gave a curt bow. 'I shall await orders at your earliest convenience.' He left.

Wulfric and Jagovere followed him, and they walked in silence until they reached the Company's camp.

'He seemed rather upset,' Jagovere said.

'Dal Valeriano's been bone idle for months,' dal Rhenning said, 'and within a day of us arriving here, the duke has his first battle and his first victory. Valeriano looks bad. He knows he looks bad, and he knows he's going to have to do something about that.'

Wulfric felt a headache coming. He couldn't fathom why they would seek to make war so complicated or so frustrating. A victory could never make a man look bad. Even with all the intrigues the southerners seemed to relish, how could destroying his enemy hurt the count's ambitions?

# CHAPTER 34

## RODULF

THERE WAS AN army of administrators working at the palace making sure that taxes were collected, justice was administered, and order was maintained. Other than looking important, Rodulf wasn't entirely sure what the Markgraf himself actually did. When Rodulf got a summons to meet with him in private, it was concerning. Might his efforts to advance himself at court have ruffled too many feathers?

'Lord Leondorf,' the Markgraf said when Rodulf was shown into his private office, 'thank you for coming.'

He gestured to a seat and sat down opposite Rodulf, fixing him with his intelligent grey eyes. Rodulf did his best to sit at ease, but he felt like a boy awaiting chastisement for misbehaviour.

'You've settled into life at court very well,' the Markgraf said.

His eyes said he knew everything, that he was toying with Rodulf. Rodulf slipped his hand into his pocket and felt for the Stone. Even if it didn't work on the Markgraf, it would bring him comfort.

'Your noblemen have been most welcoming, my lord,' Rodulf said.

'Ha,' the Markgraf said. 'I find that very hard to believe. In fact, were it not for your liberal application of silver, I daresay you'd have had every door in the city slammed in your face.'

Rodulf did his best not to react to the mention of silver. Might the Markgraf know about the new mine? He didn't see how it was possible. 'I was never in any doubt that I would have to make concerted efforts to establish myself in Elzburg's society, my lord.'

'Buying the debts of half my noblemen is a concerted effort indeed,' the Markgraf said.

Rodulf could not help but go red at this. He had thought himself smarter than the privileged southerners, and hated to be proven wrong. Here was one, at least, who seemed to have the measure of him.

'It begs the question of where you got all that silver,' the Markgraf said. 'Or it would if I didn't already know the answer.'

Rodulf looked to the door, expecting guards to come in and arrest him, but it remained shut. He gripped the Stone so tightly it hurt his hand, but it did him no good.

'There's no need to look so sheepish, my lord Leondorf. Remaining in power is nearly as hard as gaining it, or so I'm told. There's little going on in the Mark of which I'm unaware. The new Barony of Leondorf included.'

'I... my lord...' Rodulf said.

The Markgraf held up a hand to silence him. 'Most of my noblemen are too spineless to steal from me. They're comfortable. They were born comfortable. Comfort robs a man of ambition, don't you think?'

Rodulf had no idea what to say. 'My lord, I was going to...'

'Of course you weren't,' the Markgraf said, a hint of irritation entering his voice for the first time. 'But that's all right. The silver mines in Leondorf that you *aren't* trying to keep hidden already provide me with more silver every year than all the taxes and customs duties from the rest of the Mark. Your little secret enterprise tells me you have something in you that few of my men possess. Ambition and hunger. I see the value in those things. I see how you might be of use to me.'

'In any way I possibly can be,' Rodulf said.

'Don't turn into a toady,' the Markgraf said. 'I want the avaricious little bastard who is sneaking a fortune in silver that doesn't belong to him, and using it to buy the debts of my noblemen so they'll do what he tells them. I've even heard that you've threatened to sell their children into slavery.' He let out an incredulous chuckle. 'That's the man I have a use for, not a lickspittle. I have plenty of them already. The new mine is yours for the time being. I've no use for you if you're bankrupted and thrown in debtor's prison. Now get out. I'll let you know when I have need of you.'

Rodulf stood and made for the door, knowing that the grip of fear on his heart would not ease until he was on the other side.

'Oh—cheat me again and it will be the headsman for you. Understand?'

'Perfectly, my lord,' Rodulf said.

'Just as you own dal Geerdorf, I own you now.'

Rodulf slipped out the door and closed it behind him. Instead of feeling relief, he felt anger. No one had ever gotten the better of him before. He had come down to Elzburg thinking himself smarter than men who owed everything to fortunate birth rather than ability. Now, it seemed he was proven wrong.

Rodulf had wandered through the city for a time before returning home. He sat in the cold hallway in the chair reserved for uninvited guests. It was a southern trick he had learned; they would remain there in discomfort until he deigned to see them. It suited his purpose now. There were no distractions and the cold air focussed his thoughts. He mulled over what his meeting with the Markgraf meant for him; what it would mean for his plans.

He noticed a red mark on the palm of his hand. Puzzled, he gave it a closer look. When he was a child, he had grabbed the handle of a kettle heating on the fire. The red welt it had left had been agonizing and had taken weeks to heal. The memory of it was burned on his mind, and the mark on his hand reminded him of it. He touched the flesh where it was red. It was sensitive. Not painful, but tender. He tried to remember if he had picked up anything hot, but could not. It occurred to him that the mark was about the same size and shape as the Stone, but the thought drifted as his eyelids grew heavy. His mind was tired, and the act of trying to recollect was draining. Everything was tired, now that he thought of it. It seemed city life could be as taxing as it was pleasurable.

'My lord?'

It was the butler Rodulf had hired only a few days previously.

'What is it?'

'A message arrived from the palace a short time before you returned, my lord. Your presence there is required immediately.'

Rodulf groaned. It seemed that whatever the Markgraf had planned for him, he wouldn't be long in finding out. As he levered himself from the heavy leather seat, he momentarily wondered why the Markgraf could not have filled him in before he had left the palace. He stared at the chair for a moment as the answer came to him. As the chair was Rodulf's way of letting visitors know he controlled their time, this was the Markgraf's. He was an owned man now, and the thought made Rodulf's gut twist with anger.

❋

## WULFRIC

Dal Rhenning wasn't invited to dal Valeriano's council of war—but with Jagovere at his side, and Wulfric and Enderlain at his back, no one made any effort to stop them entering the tent. Wulfric looked around, and was again surprised by the casual nature of the assembly. The tent was filled with officers—the Estranzan noblemen dal Valeriano had favoured with command. Platters of food and bottles of wine were laid out across the campaign table, obscuring the maps beneath. Dal Valeriano looked at dal Rhenning and frowned, but said nothing.

'It's illegal, my lord,' one of dal Valeriano's senior officers said.

Jagovere and the Graf exchanged a glance, and returned their attention to the debate at the campaign table. Dal Valeriano remained silent and brooding, allowing Carraterro dal Suera to do the talking for him. Dal Valeriano's hired sword, Diego, was there too. He stood in the background, glowering menacingly at anyone who met his gaze for too long.

'Sorcery is illegal in Estranza,' dal Suera said, 'as it is in all the nations formerly part of the Empire. However, Darvaros was never in the Empire. Magery, while usually limited to little more than parlour tricks, is legal and practised there.'

'This is the path to ruin,' another officer said, earning him a withering glare from Diego.

'On the contrary,' dal Suera said, 'it is the path to victory. As soon as we cross the border, we are as entitled to employ magic as the Darvarosians, which they will undoubtedly do. We will ensure that our sorcerers are better than theirs.'

This attracted a more positive murmur from the assembly. It had surprised Wulfric how suspicious and fearful the southerners were of magic. He had never seen it do anything more dangerous than heal cuts and mend broken bones, but he had heard tales of the old days when truly incredible feats had been done with it. Wulfric doubted it could be of much use, however. Not anymore. If it could, surely mages would rule the world.

'A magister is necessary to ensure the safety of our troops,' dal Suera said. 'We sought out the best we could find to keep us safe from the Darvarosians, but he assures me he can do far more than that. Magister Toribio is as powerful a magister as any alive.'

Since coming to the South, Wulfric had learned much, and he could not help but notice the way dal Suera was speaking. At no point had he mentioned dal Valeriano's involvement in the plan. Did that mean dal Suera was taking the risk of bearing his master's culpability or that he was the brains behind the operation, the man pulling the strings? It made Wulfric's head hurt, the way the southerners carried on.

'As we speak,' dal Suera said, 'Magister Toribio is working on a spell that will ensure a complete victory when we encounter Prince Peruman's forces.'

'The Pretender,' someone said.

'Indeed,' dal Suera said, with a reluctant tinge to his voice. 'Pretender Peruman, as you say. I didn't mean to imply his usurpation of the duke's rightful title was legitimate. Our scouts indicate his army is less than a day's march to the south. As soon as Magister Toribio is ready, we will move to meet them and claim our victory.'

There was much cheering and the banging of fists on tables. It seemed folly to Wulfric to rely on magic in war rather than strength and skill at arms, but much of what went on in Estranza seemed folly to him. Nonetheless, he was curious to see what magic could really be capable of.

❖

## PROFESSOR KENGIL

There were times when Johanna Kengil would swear she could still smell the burning. She knew it was her imagination, but she was aware of an acrid tang that she would never forget. Northlanders were animals, and it amazed her how others could allow even one to live amongst them. Sheltered behind the city's big walls all their lives, they had never known what it meant to live under threat of a Northlander raid, didn't understand that the word *Northlander* was the most terrifying thing you could hear someone shout. As bad as her presence alone in Elzburg was, if Adalhaid was using magic, something had to be done.

A top physician Kengil might be, but she knew she was no spy. She had no idea how to go about gathering enough evidence to ensure Adalhaid's sorcery was stopped. She stared out her office window, looking down on the courtyard below, scratching an elegantly manicured fingernail along the slight cleft in her chin and wondering.

She could not loiter around Jakob Strellis's clinic without drawing attention, and there was only so much she could glean from his meticulous records. Rosamund was a student physician and no spy either. Kengil could not rely on her happening upon damning evidence by chance, and the miraculously cured child could easily be dismissed with no firm proof of the severity of the initial injury. She needed help.

✸

## RODULF

'What's he doing here?' dal Geerdorf said, when Rodulf walked into the Markgraf's private office.

There were a number of men there already, some he recognised, others he did not. Several were men whose debts he owned.

'He's here at my request,' the Markgraf said.

Dal Geerdorf opened his mouth to say something, but hesitated for a moment before he finally found his tongue. 'Are you sure he can be trusted?'

Rodulf wondered how much the Shandahari slavers would pay for the bastard's daughters. Fair-skinned blondes were very popular in the sunny south.

'I own Baron Leondorf,' the Markgraf said, 'and he owns you, so I'm content for the time being. Now, to business.'

'Silver production has greatly exceeded expectations, which means your plans can be expedited, my lord,' the Markgraf's chancellor said.

Rodulf looked at him warily. He was one of the men in the room that Rodulf had not been able to buy.

'By how much?'

Rodulf tried to look as though he belonged there and understood what was going on, but nothing could be further from the truth. He couldn't even speculate about what they were talking about, nor what the need for secrecy was.

'I estimate that we have approximately seventy-five percent of the funds you will require, my lord,' the chancellor said. 'The target will be exceeded in weeks, rather than months.'

The Markgraf smiled and stroked his greying beard. 'That really does bring us far closer.'

He chuckled, but it sounded nervous to Rodulf, further whetting his curiosity.

'With the Northlands acquisitions, you already control a territory equal to Her Highness. It is my opinion that we are ready to move forward.'

Rodulf's eyes widened as the pieces started to fit together. It seemed he was not the only avariciously ambitious man in the room. The Markgraf planned to rebel.

'Are we all agreed?' the Markgraf said.

'I believe we are, my lord,' a man Rodulf did not know said. 'Or should I say, Your Majesty.'

The Markgraf smiled but held up his hand. 'Let's not put the cart before the horse,' he said. 'I thought I'd have longer to come up with a name for our new kingdom. I'd better put my thinking cap on.'

There was some muted laughter in the room, but it did little to ease the tension that was now obvious to Rodulf. Sedition was a very serious matter. It seemed the Markgraf had grand dreams and the spine to chase them. Rodulf was excited and intrigued. In his more ambitious moments, he nurtured thoughts of doing something similar in the Northlands, but now it seemed the future would be bountiful with opportunity. If the Markgraf was fighting a war against his overlord, he would have few resources left over to deal with one of his noblemen asserting independence. Rodulf might even find himself an ally in the princess if he turned against his rebellious liege lord.

His mind raced with possibilities, but he knew that for the time being he needed to be careful. He was part of a conspiracy, and men in a conspiracy who were suspected of wavering commitment wound up dead. It occurred to him that if he was being made privy to the plans, the Markgraf intended to use him in them. Exactly how remained to be answered, and the question left him with a sick feeling in his stomach.

# CHAPTER 35

WULFRIC

WULFRIC FOUND THE excitement of being part of an army marching to war almost overwhelming. Men shouted, drums beat, and horns sounded. Banners and battle flags flew in their hundreds, painting the field with a thousand colours. Wulfric felt left out not having one, but Jagovere had explained that only the special southern warrior, the banneret, could fly one. It reminded Wulfric of the bastard Endres who had tried to kill him in the forest what seemed like a lifetime ago. He might not be a banneret, but he was determined that by the end of the day his blade would have drawn more blood than any other, banner or not. If the enemy carried them, they would make for nice souvenirs.

Beasts complained, equipment rattled, boots and hoofs struck the earth, and the cloud of dust they kicked up gave the day a hazy surrealism. Wulfric's nose was filled with the smell of sweat, horse dung, and the oil men wiped on their blades. They were the hallmarks of war, a deluge on the senses that was unlike anything else Wulfric had experienced. The water of the river turned a cloudy brown as it was forded and churned up by thousands of men and horses. Wulfric wondered how many of them would make the return crossing.

A large tented palanquin was carried at the centre of the army, containing dal Valeriano's sorcerer. Wulfric had not yet seen him, and wondered what a sorcerer looked like. Would he be dishevelled in scruffy old robes, as Aethelman had been? It seemed he would have to wait until the count's master plan was unveiled before he would find out.

The army gathered on the far bank before continuing its southward journey. Wulfric could feel his excitement ebb away as the march entered its second hour, and then the third. He wondered where the enemy were, and why they were hiding. Were they too cowardly to defend what was theirs? Perhaps his killing of their champion had made them too afraid to fight. The thought was satisfying, but he could hear Belgar's voice in his head telling him to never underestimate an enemy. He looked over to the stone plateau as it drew into view on his right, and wondered if it secured their flank as the Estranzans thought, or if it hid enemy soldiers in their thousands among its countless tight, twisting passageways. The thought sent a shiver down his spine.

In the early afternoon, scouts galloped back toward the army with the haste that could only mean one thing. The order to halt was given and slowly, like a team of surly oxen, the column came to a stop. The sound of the march was replaced with silence, then quiet chatter and shuffling as men speculated about what was to come. Wulfric scanned the horizon, but couldn't see anything.

'What now?' Wulfric said to Jagovere.

'We await orders.'

Wulfric realised he and Enderlain had become something of an unofficial bodyguard to Jagovere, always close by.

'How long will that be?' Wulfric said, looking eagerly at the Darvarosians.

'How long is a piece of rope?' Jagovere said. 'I expect our Estranzan friends will want to give their mage a chance to do whatever it is they expect him to do. Then we can go about the real business of war.'

'You don't believe in magic?' Wulfric thought back to the blue glow surrounding Jorundyr's Rock. He knew magic existed; the only question that remained was how powerful it could be.

'I once saw a fellow who claimed he could conjure lightning,' Jagovere said. 'It turned out he was lighting his farts with a hidden flame. Magister Toribio will need to be very full of hot air if he hopes to impact today's outcome.'

Enderlain chuckled, but Wulfric was no longer quite so convinced. What type of fool would the count have to be to centre his plans on magic if there was nothing to it?

The palanquin was lowered, and gallopers set off from the count's position behind the line. Wulfric watched one as he approached the Company.

'The Marshall of Torona requests that you move your Company to the right flank, take up a defensive position and await further orders.'

'We're a cavalry company,' dal Rhenning said. 'We should be used for attack. Does the marshall understand this?'

The galloper shrugged.

Dal Rhenning sighed in frustration and waved a hand in acknowledgement. 'The Company will advance,' he bellowed.

A dust cloud had formed on the horizon—the approaching enemy. Wulfric squinted to see better, but there was no way to estimate numbers. The Company moved to their assigned position at a canter, then formed up.

'What's he playing at?' Jagovere said, as he surveyed the ground they had been ordered to hold.

'Mercenaries are easier to replace than men who'll have to sow and harvest crops when the war's over,' dal Rhenning said. 'This is where he thinks the fighting will be hardest, and I suspect he's right. Still, that's our job, and we can't hold ground on horseback. We'll dismount and form a pike line with our lances.'

'What will we do with the horses?'

'Take them back behind the line. I don't want to lose half of them to arrows.'

'Are you sure?'

Dal Rhenning glowered at him. 'I don't like being separated from them, but if they're within arrow range they're as good as gone anyway.'

Jagovere nodded and went to relay the order. Wulfric continued to watch the horizon, fascinated and horrified by the thought of so many people preparing to fight in one battle. He wondered if every warrior in the Northlands combined would come close to matching even one of the armies. A black mass developed at the cloud's foot as the Darvarosian army continued its advance and Wulfric felt a tingle of fear dance across his skin. He had never felt so insignificant or small, even when Rodulf and his friends had tormented him. How would Jorundyr see his deeds amongst so many?

A deafening explosion thundered across the plain. Wulfric stumbled backward as the shockwave hit him, blasting his face with sand and grit. The horses reacted faster than the men, pulling free and bolting in a cacophony of whinnies. Wulfric could hear nothing but a high-pitched ringing. He looked around, rubbing the tears and dirt from his eyes. A thick black plume of smoke rose from the centre of the Estranzan line.

Jagovere wiped his eyes and looked toward the plume. 'I'll be damned if the bloody idiot hasn't just blown himself up,' he shouted, although Wulfric could barely hear him over the ringing in his ears. 'I wonder how many of the fools he took out with him?'

Wulfric shrugged, his eyes locked on the Darvarosians. The black mass was rapidly growing larger. They were charging.

❄

## WULFRIC

In the moments following the explosion, the sound of chaos reigned in the Estranzan ranks. Wulfric and the Company were only marginally better, torn between trying to recover their horses, and holding the line.

'Form up! Form up!'

Dal Rhenning's voice was the only sound of order, rising high with the power of a man accustomed to shouting. The men clung to his words, allowing them and the hours of training to lead them from the confusion. Disorder could defeat an army as easily as a superior opponent, and Wulfric felt a wave of relief as order started to return. If the count and his command were killed in the explosion, retreat was their best option, but a disordered retreat could quickly become a rout and slaughter.

The Darvarosians grew ever closer, and Wulfric wondered if dal Rhenning would give the order to withdraw. He could see some order return to the Estranzan ranks, but they looked uncertain. He couldn't see if the count's banners still flew, and wondered who was commanding the main army, if anyone. As though reacting to his thoughts, he saw a group of gallopers set off from the centre of the line, near the site of the explosion.

'The Marshall of Torona requests that you hold your position. He asks me to stress the importance of this command. He wishes to anchor his army against the Warrens.'

'I trust the marshall was unharmed in the explosion,' dal Rhenning said.

'He is well, my lord,' the galloper said. 'He was close to Magister Toribio, but luckily the blast was directed away from him.'

'Lucky indeed,' dal Rhenning said. 'Please remind him that we are a cavalry company, but will do our best to hold his flank.'

The galloper nodded and spurred his horse back toward the centre of the line.

'Do you ever get the feeling you're not being paid enough?' dal Rhenning said, as he took his place in the Company's line of makeshift pike men.

'Every day,' Jagovere said.

All along the line, men kicked with their heels into the ground, using their spurs to dig a pocket to rest the ends of their lances in. Wulfric did likewise, glad of having something to do other than watch their enemy's approach. He didn't have a clue what he was doing. He had never fought in a spear line, nor been part of an army so large. There was so much going on that he could barely hold a thought before something new demanded his attention. The ringing in his ears started to subside, leaving an eerie quiet in its place as he looked around, hoping he had done everything necessary.

It was unnerving watching the battle unfold while waiting for his part in it to begin. The Estranzans remained where they were, while the Darvarosians moved smoothly across the plain as one. Their cavalry charged from the line at the far end of the plain, but there was no response from the Estranzan horse. Either their discipline was superb and they awaited command, or they were too afraid to respond. It was never a good thing for cavalry to receive a charge while they were stationary. Unless they moved soon, the day would not go well for them.

'My lord dal Rhenning,' a galloper shouted as he rode along the line. 'The Marshall of Torona requests that you advance your Company against the enemy's right. Once you have engaged, you are to pin them. You will be supported by Estranzan troops in due course.' The galloper did not wait for a confirmation from dal Rhenning, and charged back in the direction from which he had come.

'Hold position, advance. I'm beginning to think the Marshall of Torona does not have a Plan B,' dal Rhenning said.

'Only beginning?' Jagovere said. 'It's now or never. If we don't withdraw, we won't have the chance.'

'And then what would people say of the Company? It would be the end of us. No, we advance.'

❈

## Wulfric

'Level spears, and prepare to advance,' dal Rhenning shouted.

Some men started to hack the ends off their lances to make them more manageable as spears. The hasty alterations made Wulfric feel as though everything around him was unravelling, but he did likewise. He admired the way the other men were following dal Rhenning's orders without question, but Wulfric had an unsettling feeling growing in his stomach. The men formed into three rows with their makeshift spears pointing forward, then waited for dal Rhenning's word.

Dal Rhenning stepped forward from the line. He looked a heroic figure standing out before them, his bannerman holding his battle flag high above his head, his polished breastplate gleaming in the sunshine. Dal Rhenning waved his hand forward, and they advanced.

Wulfric and Enderlain flanked Jagovere, who, like most of the Company's officers, had left his banner with the baggage when they dismounted. Other than better than average armour and weapons, there was nothing to mark him out as a man of distinction. Wulfric realised that being anonymous was not a bad thing in a line of spearmen, but he didn't want anonymity. His hands shook, and he had to clench his teeth to stop them from chattering. He wanted to get to the fight, but he was more confused than the first day he had sparred in training. Nothing was happening as he expected, and it took all his concentration to keep up.

They moved forward quickly and in loose order. As horsemen, their armour was not particularly suited to fighting on foot, and places that were usually protected by the horse were left exposed to the enemy. It was not how he'd seen his first big southern battle going. He felt as vulnerable as a babe, and thought himself a coward for being glad that he was in the third rank with Jagovere.

He looked to his left, but the rest of the Estranzan line remained where it was. Their cavalry had counter-charged and the two bodies of horsemen swirled around each other, filling the space between the two armies at the far end of the line. It was impossible to tell who was winning.

'Halt,' dal Rhenning shouted.

Jagovere looked over his shoulder and noticed the static Estranzan line. His mouth twisted with disdain.

'The bastard's using us as bait to tempt them in,' Jagovere said. 'Ever fought like this before, Northlander?'

Wulfric shook his head.

'Makes two of us,' Jagovere said with a maniacal laugh. 'First time I've started a battle on foot. Curious to see what all the fuss's about.'

'It's overrated,' Walt said from the rank in front of them.

Dal Rhenning moved back through the crowd with his standard bearer and trumpeter, to where he could command the Company. 'Close ranks,' he shouted. 'Now, you lazy whoresons!'

They shuffled together until Wulfric could feel Jagovere and Enderlain pressing on either side. He couldn't see anything beyond the mass of bodies in front of him, so the first he knew of the enemy's charge was the roar they gave as they drew close. A pike passed clear through the tight spaces between the men before him, and grazed past Wulfric's head. His heart leaped and he felt a flash of panicked claustrophobia. He wouldn't have been able to dodge out of the way if it had been coming for him.

He could hear dal Rhenning's voice urging them forward, but it seemed distant now, drowned by shouts, cries, smashes, and crunches. The men remained massed, pushing forward like a wall of flesh with a deadly barbed tip. It was anathema to everything Wulfric understood about fighting. Men screamed as they were impaled on the pikes, but their bodies were held upright by the press of men around them. To Wulfric, it seemed like an inexorable march to death, an insane way to fight a battle. He wanted nothing more than to get out into some space, draw his sword and fight the way he knew.

Every so often, a pike would pass close to Wulfric, and he gave thanks to Jorundyr that they did not hit. Each one caused his heart to race with the knowledge that there was nothing he could do about them. He kept stabbing forward with his spear in the hope of doing to the Darvarosians what they were trying to do to him, but he couldn't see much beyond the men in front of him. It was exhausting but mindless, and Wulfric could feel his frustration and anxiety rise.

He heard the trumpet sound the withdrawal, the first indication he had of how the battle was going for them. He had thought they were holding their own, not having seen many casualties, but they were not an infantry company and were vulnerable to a better drilled enemy. Wulfric could feel himself being pushed backward by the front ranks as they moved back one step at a time. He stumbled and struggled to remain on his feet as he tried to stay with them.

'What's going on?' Wulfric shouted. It was enraging to think his first full-scale battle might end after such an anti-climactic introduction. Where was the glory in fighting like that?

'No idea,' Jagovere shouted back, 'but if the Graf wants us to move back, he must have good reason. So move your arse!'

He didn't seem to be any happier than Wulfric about things, but there was nothing either of them could do about it. They had to place their faith in dal Rhenning having a clearer picture of what was happening than they did. He hated trusting his life to someone else, but there was no way around it if he wanted to survive his first encounter with a completely alien way of fighting.

There were over ten thousand men on the plain that day, but as far as Wulfric was concerned there might have been only a hundred—those closely packed around him. There was no sense of scale, only his small pocket of struggle. As they continued to move backward, confusion swallowed him.

'Form square!'

Even above the crunching, grunting and screaming, Wulfric heard dal Rhenning's voice. It was accompanied by the constant drone of the trumpet, but Wulfric hadn't had time to learn all the signals so it was just another meaningless sound to add to the din of war.

'That's not good,' Jagovere said, pausing in his relentless spear-jabbing to wipe the sweat from his eyes.

'Why not?' Wulfric said, feeling the tip of his spear connect with flesh instead of steel.

'It means they've gotten behind us.'

'What do I do?' Wulfric said. Nothing made sense to him.

'Stay where you are,' Jagovere said. 'We're engaged. The rear ranks will form the square behind us.'

'Then what?'

'Keep fighting and hope your gods are smiling on you.'

# CHAPTER 36

RODULF

RODULF'S ADMISSION TO the lofty ranks of the Markgraf's council leap-frogged him over dozens of lower noblemen, and earned him an apartment in the palace. All the senior nobility were extended that courtesy, among others, and were required to stay there when attending court. Rodulf was under no illusion: The reason was so that the Markgraf could keep a close eye on everyone powerful enough to cause him trouble, and thus he had no choice but to accept the offer gracefully. It was a frustration, however, considering how much he had spent on a townhouse that he would not be living in. The fact that the other nobles also kept houses in the city was of little consolation. It was simply another indication of how much hold the Markgraf had over them all.

He walked into his new apartment and looked around. It was luxurious, and at least his stay there would be comfortable, but he couldn't help but view the tapestry-covered walls and elegant furnishings as being a prison.

'I hope it's to your liking,' a voice said.

Rodulf jumped, and looked around.

The Markgraf sat in an armchair by the door. 'I apologise if I startled you, but I wanted to have a quick chat in private. There's something I want you to do for me.'

Rodulf forced himself not to react to the thought of being the Markgraf's errand boy. 'It would be my pleasure, my lord.'

'Now that you're privy to my plans, you're going to help me bring them about.'

It was what Rodulf had been afraid of. The best way to tie men to a conspiracy was to ensure they were so involved that their only hope for survival was to see it through.

'I can't keep throwing silver away buying myself support,' the Markgraf said. 'As I'm sure you found when buying up all those loans, money runs out far more quickly than you'd like. The money is needed for other things, so the more noblemen I can bring over to my way of thinking for free, the better.'

'Do I have any choice?'

'I made you,' the Markgraf said, with steel in his voice. 'I own you and I can break you. With nothing more than a word. Your title, your wealth, and your lands would not exist without me saying they do.'

'That's a no, then,' Rodulf said.

'You see, Rodulf, that's what I'm growing to like about you. You don't suck up to me. With another overlord, that might be like committing suicide. I, on the other hand, appreciate the candour. My other nobles were born to their land, titles, and wealth, and in many cases their families have held them for as long as mine have held ours. If I were to step in and dispossess them without an extremely good reason—even *with* an extremely good reason—the other nobles would start to wonder if the same might happen to them. Then they would look to each other for mutual support, and before I knew it, I'd be looking at a rebellion. You, however? I could have you stripped naked and flogged through the streets, and no one would bat an eyelid. Remember that and we'll get along famously.'

Rodulf nodded, doing his best to mask his true feelings and appear at least a little cowed.

'There's another reason,' the Markgraf said. 'Things will need to be done, and my nobles have neither the aptitude nor the stomach for it. A hired man can be rehired by someone else. For an endeavour such as this, I need men who owe everything to me and aren't afraid of a little spilled blood—and right now, you're the only one I have.'

'The job?' Rodulf said.

'When I break with the princess, there will be fighting. I want to make sure the nobles in the Mark either remain loyal, or will not bring their men to Her Royal Highness. I have most of the important ones on my side, but a few remain whose loyalty I cannot be certain of. Bribed, blackmailed, or dead. Whatever it takes, although I would prefer the latter two as they are cheaper. Graf Schwalstein is the first such man. He's a proud fellow and he'll look on you as vermin, so there's no point in negotiating. Killing him won't do much good as his son is equally intractable. Blackmail's the way to deal with him.'

'What have you got on him?' Rodulf said, realising that failure would mean the end of his dreams, most likely on the headsman's block.

'Absolutely nothing,' the Markgraf said, smiling. 'But everyone's done something naughty, haven't they?'

※

## ADALHAID

As the days passed, Adalhaid felt the fear of the Intelligenciers knocking on her door at any moment recede. The passage of time told her that Jakob had not betrayed her, and the girl's family had obviously not suspected anything out of the ordinary. She went to lectures, she studied, she worked in the clinic, she looked after the Markgraf's children. Nothing had changed, and there were no black-robed men waiting for her around every corner. The fear that did not go away, though, was the one of it all happening again, and that she would not be so lucky a second time.

If this skill was in her, the danger of it surfacing was ever-present. To prevent that, she had to know how to control it. Ignoring it was not an option. What had started as a project to ensure she never did it again had grown into something more. The time she spent sitting in the library between classes, clinic, and looking after the children, was now spent wondering what she could do if she fully reined her talent in. A small touch of magic could stop a wound from turning bad, could stop blood loss that might otherwise cause death, could take pain from insufferable to bearable; there were so many moments in the practice of medicine where the smallest pressure on the scales of fate could create a different result. Small touches of magic that would go unnoticed, that could easily be dismissed as luck.

The thought was thrilling, but she knew her thoughts were leading her down a dangerous road. Where would she draw the line? When would she decide not to save someone, if she knew it was within her power? The thought made her ill. As a physician, you did your best for a patient. Sometimes that was not enough, but you always tried your hardest. Having the power—and burden—to decide was not something she could easily reconcile herself with. Someday the temptation might prove too great, and she might do something that would denounce her as a sorceress.

The only consolation was that she was getting ahead of herself. She might never learn to control her gift with the precision to use it without damning herself. She might have to accept that it was something that could never be allowed out into the light of day. It could just as easily be a case of it being on or off, as it being an instrument that could be wielded incrementally. First, she had to learn to keep it turned off. Once that was done she could worry about everything else.

❧

## AETHELMAN

At times, Aethelman felt like an old scent hound as he made his way south. The Stone was like a meal cooking on a distant stove. He could taste it on the air, and with each step in the right direction, the flavour grew stronger. It was strange, but he had given up trying to make sense of it. The ways of the gods and their magics was not for the understanding of mortal men, and he had to content himself with the knowledge that it was allowing him to achieve his quest.

The journey was taking longer than he would have liked, and a sense of urgency gripped him like a cold hand clenching his heart. He was an old man, however, and killing himself to get to wherever it was he was going quickly was of no use to anyone. He had to accept that there was a limited distance his tired old body could cover each day, and even less if he hoped to reach his destination in a condition to complete his task. It sickened him to think what the Stone might be used for in the time it took him to get to it, but there was nothing that could be done. It was impossible to live a life as long as his without regrets, and he had done his best to reconcile himself to that fact. He was doing all he could at that time, which was all he could ask of himself. What was in the past was in the past.

❧

## Wulfric

Their predicament was entirely lost on Wulfric until he saw his first glimpse of daylight in front of him. It meant their line was starting to break apart, and their casualties were heavy. Even he knew that once the line was broken, they were lost. He hated how alien this type of warfare was to him.

'Fill the holes!' Jagovere shouted.

Before he knew it, Wulfric was being squeezed forward into one of the gaps left by a fallen comrade. He heard dal Rhenning call a halt to their movement and the trumpet change its note. There was a wall of spearmen before them, and one nearly skewered Wulfric as he slotted into place. All the advantage was with them as they advanced and the Company retreated. There were elbows and arms and spears and swords everywhere. He held his place and shuffled slowly backward, trying to stay in contact with the men to either side. He thrust his lance every so often, but it was half-hearted at best. He was more concerned with making sure he wasn't left behind, or spitted on a Darvarosian spear. Terror pressed on him like a physical presence trying to force its way in. He did his best to keep it out, but the confusion was so overwhelming he couldn't focus his thoughts. How could men make war like that? It was nothing but madness.

# CHAPTER 37

WULFRIC

ON THE VERGE of succumbing to a panic he had never experienced before, Wulfric reverted to what he knew. He dropped his spear and pulled his sabre free of its scabbard, the space beside him no longer occupied. He looked left and right, and felt fear well in him at the sight of how few of them there were left. He roared a battle cry and willed Jorundyr's Gift to take him in its embrace. He left the dwindling line and rushed at the wall of Darvarosians opposite him. He hacked mindlessly at anything that moved in front of him. Men were tangled between the spear shafts, some pinned where they stood. They seemed completely unprepared for this change in tactic. There was no art or skill to it, and he would have been as well off with the axe he had used to chop wood when he was a boy.

The noise was deafening, but Wulfric did his best to block it out. The terrifying confusion felt less oppressive when he thought of nothing more than swinging his sword. A man fell before him, but he was replaced by another before he had hit the ground. This man tried to drop his spear and draw a short sword, but Wulfric cut him down before he had the chance. They were pressed so tightly the Darvarosians couldn't even defend themselves, nor get out of the way. Finally, it felt like he was taking control back. Everywhere he struck, his blade connected with mortal flesh. He felt a chill, as though a cold wind blew over him, but his energy seemed boundless.

It continued like that for what seemed like hours, but he realised was only moments. He hacked and cut and hacked and cut. He had no idea how many men he had killed. Sweat and blood stung his eyes, but he felt like he could go on forever, as though the spirits of those he slew sustained him to continue his brutal work.

He felt a tug on his shoulder and was pulled back from the line. He turned in a rage, ready to strike down whoever had dared to interrupt him. Sanity returned with the subtlety of a hammer blow. The Company, once of several hundred men, now only had a few dozen survivors. Jagovere stood before him, urging him back. Wulfric stilled himself, and allowed the sound of Jagovere's voice to reach him.

'Come on, you madman, we're retreating into the Warrens. The Estranzans have run. They didn't even put up a fight.'

'I've found a defile we can use. This way!' dal Rhenning shouted.

The Darvarosians hesitated as their foe melted away before them. They were likely wondering if they were being led into a trap, or if they really had won the battle that easily. Their doubts wouldn't last long, and Wulfric knew they needed to make the most of it if they hoped to survive.

There were no more than two dozen of them left now. Wulfric searched out familiar faces, seeing Walt's, and the unmistakable shape of Enderlain ahead of him. The passageway was so narrow that Wulfric's shoulders brushed against both sides in places. As they rushed along the narrow path, Wulfric wondered where it would lead. Its confines would negate the enemy's greater numbers, but Wulfric could not forget what Jagovere had told him. Few who entered the Warrens made it out alive.

The trail was labyrinthine, turning left and right until he had no idea which direction they were going in. He raged at the cowardice and perfidy of the Estranzans. Had it been dal Valeriano's plan all along to sacrifice the Company so he could get away?

The path widened. Wulfric wondered if it meant their way out, but without horses, the Darvarosians would chase them down and cut them to pieces. Their only real hope was to lose their pursuers in the Warrens—finding their way back out was a worry for another time. He felt a moment's desperation at what they were doing. Did they flee one death to embrace another? Would he not prefer to die on a sword rather than of thirst wandering around the Warrens under the blazing Darvarosian sun? He wondered if Jorundyr was watching over this foreign land, if he would notice one of his own preparing to make the journey to his hall. He rounded the corner and saw dal Rhenning and those with him standing still. The defile opened into a large grotto, surrounded on all sides by sheer limestone cliffs. They were trapped.

Dal Rhenning was red-faced and gasping for breath. Between the heat and exertion, and perhaps what they now all knew awaited them, dal Rhenning was showing his age for the first time. All the vitality had left him.

'This is where we face them, lads,' he said, turning to look back the way they had come.

There were even fewer of them now, some men having been too tired to keep ahead of the Darvarosians on their desperate flight through the defile. It made little difference. Wulfric knew this was where they would die.

Dal Rhenning joined Wulfric, Jagovere, Enderlain and the dozen others who remained. He placed a hand on Jagovere's shoulder.

'I'm sorry,' he said.

'Don't be,' Jagovere said. 'We're soldiers. We all knew it might come to this someday.'

'Not for this,' dal Rhenning said. 'For not being a better father.'

Jagovere remained silent for a moment. 'You weren't so bad, all things considered,' he said, as the Darvarosians rounded the corner.

There was a moment's pause while the Darvarosians regarded the remaining Company men. Did they expect them to surrender? Wulfric felt time around him slow. If he was about to die, he would take many men with him to serve him in Jorundyr's Hall.

With a roar, the Darvarosians charged forward. They came through the entrance to the grotto in twos and threes, the most the narrow passage would permit. Dal Rhenning threw himself forward and matched their roar. The rest needed no further encouragement. They were warriors all, and not one of them wanted to wait for death to come to them.

The savagery of their counterattack shocked the Darvarosians. The first few men to enter the grotto were cut down in the blink of an eye, which caused the next group to hesitate. Wulfric and the others showed no such uncertainty. They pressed forward to the grotto's mouth.

They continued their gory work. Wulfric's hand was glued to the handle of his sword by sticky, drying blood. Each man who stood before him was cut down. He felt as though he were scything wheat. It was even easier than it had been at the spear line. Tiredness and pain seemed unknown to him, and for a moment he thought he could kill enough of the enemy to scare off the rest.

The Darvarosian soldiers had to haul their dead comrades out of the way to maintain their attack, so choked with the fallen was the entrance to the grotto. Their ferocious defence had not come without cost, though. Wulfric saw faces he recognised being pulled from the path. His nose was filled with the metallic tang of blood. There could not be many of them left now, and he knew he could not win on his own. He prayed to Jorundyr to help him die bravely.

Through the haze of his battle lust, Wulfric could see that the ordinary Darvarosian soldiers were giving way to a different calibre of man. Where he had been cutting one down with each stroke of his sabre, he was now being parried and having to defend himself. The men coming through wore fine armour, the mesh of their mail links between the armoured plates tight and perfectly formed. One of them stepped over the bodies of his lesser comrades and presented himself to Wulfric. His helmet had a mask styled in the fashion of a snarling face. Wulfric smiled. Finally, he had fought his way to men worth killing.

Dal Rhenning's flag fluttered past Wulfric's face. He cast a glance to his right, and saw that dal Rhenning had stopped fighting. He leaned on the flag pole he held in his left hand, his sword limp in his right. He dropped to his knees, blood spilling from the gaps in his armour, then tumbled to the ground, the flag falling on top of him.

Jagovere cried out and rushed over to his fallen father. He grabbed dal Rhenning beneath his armpits and hauled him back away from the fighting. Enderlain roared like a bear and hurled himself forward at the Darvarosians. He towered over the enemy, and they cowered from his ferocious attack. In a mighty slash, he cleaved the head from one Darvarosian and the blade continued toward the next man. Unable to do anything to stop it in time, the Darvarosian shrank back from the inevitable. As Enderlain's thick-bladed battlefield rapier connected with the man's helmet, the blade shattered. Enderlain and the Darvarosian stared at one another for a moment, dumbfounded, but the Darvarosian was still armed, while Enderlain now held only the elaborate hilt of his sword.

Wulfric kicked the man with the snarling helmet in the stomach and slammed his sabre down hard on the man's shoulder over and over until he fell to his knees. He pulled the helmet from the man's head and stabbed him in the face, kicking the body clear of his blade when its job was done. Enderlain dropped back and Wulfric realised he was the only man left at the front. He retreated back to join Jagovere. Enderlain had salvaged another sword from one of the fallen, and together, the last half dozen men of dal Rhenning's Company prepared to make their stand.

The Darvarosians hesitated again, waiting to see what their remaining foes had planned. Everyone knew that an animal cornered was at its most dangerous.

'He's dead,' Jagovere said. 'The Graf's gone.'

'What do we do, Captain?' Enderlain said.

All the men were looking to Jagovere for orders. He remained silent, staring at dal Rhenning's lifeless eyes.

'Captain?' Sander said, desperation creeping into his voice.

The Graf was the beating heart and soul of the Company. The men had loved him and Wulfric could see defeat in their faces for the first time. Still Jagovere was silent.

They would be cut down like lambs if they didn't do something. Wulfric snatched up dal Rhenning's banner and stood, facing the Darvarosians who had slowly made their way into the grotto. He was still holding the snarling helmet. It was fine work, he thought, allowing his mind to drift for one last moment. He had been a fish out of water in the battle, but now, with the enemy coming through the narrow defile in twos and threes, he was on familiar ground. He had been a useless spear-holder in the line. Now he could be death personified.

'We kill as many of them as we can,' Wulfric said, his voice rising, 'and we will feast with Jorundyr before the sun sets.'

Wulfric took a pace forward from the cluster around dal Rhenning's fallen body. 'I am Wulfric Wolframson,' he shouted, spittle flying from his mouth. 'I am First Warrior of Leondorf. I have slain two belek. I killed the man who owned this helmet, and many others. Dozens of your comrades have fallen to my sword today. I am Jorundyr's Chosen, and every man who stands before me today will die!' If Jorundyr did not hear that, Wulfric did not know what more to do.

A Darvarosian stepped forward and pulled his helmet off. It was similar to the one Wulfric held, but he realised that it had a different face. The man's skin was darkly tanned, and his short black beard was as neatly trimmed as Wulfric had ever seen. His armour was magnificent, even more so than the man whose helmet he had taken.

'If you want *my* helmet,' he said, his voice so heavily accented Wulfric could barely understand him, 'come and take it.'

Wulfric's teeth chattered as he dived forward. There was no skill or thought behind his attack. It was all rage, rage at the way the Estranzans had betrayed them, rage at the way the old man who had saved him from arrest and execution in Ruripathia had been killed, rage that his friend's father was dead. If he was going to die and be reunited with Adalhaid, he wanted to empty all that rage out before he got to Jorundyr's Hall.

The force of his attack drove the Darvarosian back toward his comrades, but he easily blocked Wulfric's manic slash. He was a big man, almost as tall and broad as Wulfric, and he was able to shove Wulfric back a few paces. He launched an attack of his own. His sabre was far longer and broader than any the others had been using, and he held it with both hands. He swung it again, a wide, savage cut. Wulfric rolled out of the way rather than block it with his own blade, afraid it would shatter as Enderlain's had.

When he came to his feet, he launched himself at the Darvarosian. He struck him in the midsection with his shoulder, and drove him back again. As soon as Wulfric had regained his balance, he attacked with his sabre. The Darvarosian was able to parry every one of Wulfric's strikes. He was strong and fast, but Wulfric had been chosen by a god, and would not allow himself to be beaten by an ordinary man. He saw a gap and hammered his sabre down. It hit the Darvarosian on the shoulder. He roared, and dropped to one knee as he shrank from the pain. Not wasting a moment, Wulfric smashed the hilt into the Darvarosian's face again and again. They were both on the ground, Wulfric over his foe. He had lost his sword in the tumble and pulled his dagger from his belt, driving it into the Darvarosian's eye.

'Enough!' someone shouted.

Wulfric looked up, gasping. A man had stepped forward from the soldiers, even more splendidly armoured than his companions. His plate cuirass was of blackened steel with gold filigree. Wulfric wanted nothing more at that moment than to fight and kill him.

'Brave men of Ruripathia,' he said, 'you have fought with courage and done all that can be expected by the requirements of honour. Your commander and his army have fled the field, and you alone continue to fight. There is no need for you to die today in the name of a man who has shown himself not worthy of your lives. Surrender now and you will be afforded all battle honours. Give me your parole and you will be my guests until this war ends. You may keep your armour, weapons, and banners.'

'Fuck yourself,' Wulfric said. He was about to leap for him, when he felt a hand on his shoulder.

'We don't have to die today, Wulfric,' Jagovere said.

'It's as good a day as any other,' Wulfric said.

'How will you avenge Adalhaid if you're dead?' Jagovere said. 'How will I avenge my father, and all our comrades who died today because of that bastard Valeriano?'

There was an edge to his voice that told Wulfric he wasn't surrendering, merely thinking ahead. Wulfric felt a pang of regret that such clarity was lost to him at moments like that. He looked up at the man who had made them the offer and down at the man on the ground, a pool of blood forming around his head. He could feel a measure of control return. The desire to slaughter all before him was no longer so strong. He took a deep breath and stood, feeling utterly spent as he did. How had he felt so energised only a moment before? He nodded to Jagovere, and turned to the Darvarosian.

'There is no shame in accepting my offer,' the Darvarosian said. 'The only shame would be in wasting the lives of more brave men.'

Wulfric thought of Adalhaid. Of her Blood Debt. He threw down his sword.

PART 3

# CHAPTER 38

## THE MAISTERSPAEKER

THE MAISTERSPAEKER WATCHED Rodulf out of the corner of his eye as he allowed his audience a comfort break. Rodulf and his men moved away from the bar, and cleared people from a table by the fire. The villagers clearly knew who he was, even though the cluster of buildings were not on his land. He might have prospered, all things considered, but his manor was a far cry from the wealth and power he had been amassing when the Maisterspaeker had first met him all those years ago. The villagers got out of his way quickly, and regarded him warily. Clearly old habits died hard.

His men lounged in their chairs, drinking ale and joking amongst themselves, paying only the barest of attention to the Maisterspaeker's story. Only Rodulf—Lord Mendorf—listened, and he did so surreptitiously, pretending to be part of the conversation with his men. Every so often, the Maisterspaeker could see a stifled response to something he said, and likewise had to stifle a smile each time. It took considerable restraint not to walk across the taproom and plunge a dagger into Rodulf's neck. It was no more than he deserved. Every breath he had taken in all those years was more than he deserved. The Maisterspaeker tried to quench his growing anger. Rodulf's life was Wulfric's, and there was not much longer to wait.

The Maisterspaeker realised that in a way, he owed Rodulf a debt. It was difficult to find such a perfectly created villain, but a man like Rodulf made Jagovere's job so much easier. With that in mind, the tension in his shoulders and chest eased. The taproom had filled once more, and anyone not yet finished in the privy had taken too long. He took a long swallow of ale, and brought the audience back to Darvaros.

❋

WULFRIC

'Did you really kill two belek?' Jagovere said.

Wulfric looked over at him. They had spent several hours riding south with their Darvarosian captors, and the countryside had grown more verdant. It was a warm and pleasant land, but Wulfric could not forget that he was a captive, no matter what anyone called it. *Parole* sounded far too like *prisoner* for his liking.

Wulfric nodded.

'Like Ulfyr, Jorundyr's wolf,' Jagovere said, laughing.

'They weren't at the same time,' Wulfric said, not in the mood to be made fun of. He had fought with every fibre of his being, yet they had still lost. So many men had died. He hadn't known many of them, but their faces had become familiar in the time he was with the Company, and their absence felt jarring. Apart from him, only Jagovere and Enderlain, Sander, Conrat, and Walt had survived.

'Cheer up, Ulfyr,' Enderlain said. 'We're still alive. We live to fight another day.'

'Don't call me that,' Wulfric said, his humour not improving.

'No problem,' Enderlain said, 'Ulfyr.'

'The first rule of nicknames,' Jagovere said, his voice full of forced cheer, 'is to never let anyone know you don't like it. There's no better way to make it stick.'

The joke lacked the energy of his usual wit. Dal Rhenning's death weighed heavily on him, and reminded Wulfric of the day he had found his father's body on the road to Rasbruck.

'I killed many men today,' Wulfric said, glowering at Enderlain. 'A few more won't make much of a difference.'

'Lighten up,' Enderlain said. 'Be grateful you're alive. We all have more to do in this world, and now we get the chance to do it. Every day is a gift from the gods.'

'If they ever let us go,' Wulfric said, nodding to their Darvarosian escort.

'Feeding and housing prisoners costs money,' Jagovere said. 'They won't want to keep us any longer than necessary.'

'How long do you reckon that'll be?' Enderlain said, with childlike curiosity. 'My mother's elderly. I'd like to see her again before she passes.'

Wulfric and Jagovere looked at him. It was hard to imagine a man like Enderlain having a mother.

'Who knows?' Jagovere said. 'The way dal Valeriano fights, I can't imagine there's long to run in this war. It might already be over. They'll let us go then. Maybe they'll hire us, or anyone who wants to stay here.'

Wulfric looked around at the other survivors, six including himself. They all wore sullen expressions. The thought of a life in that foreign land didn't seem to be tempting any of them.

'Do you?' Wulfric said.

Jagovere sighed. 'It might be a paradise: good wine, delicious food, beautiful women. Can we say the same awaits us in Ruripathia? Cold winters, stale ale. Admittedly there are plenty of beautiful women.' He fell silent for a moment, then spoke again. 'The only thing I know for certain is that I'm going to kill that bastard dal Valeriano if it's the last thing I do.'

❖

## Rodulf

Rodulf looked about with disdain as he hopped down the steps of his carriage. The manor house before him bore all the hallmarks of benign neglect. In its youth, it would have been grand, the beating heart of a vibrant estate, but now it spoke of a lord and owner who no longer cared. Weeds grew from the seams between the courtyard cobbles, while moss and mildew assaulted the stone facade of the house. Just looking at it was depressing.

He had travelled through the night, sleeping only fitfully along the way, and was hopeful he could be back in his own bed before nightfall. It was a grey, drizzly morning, and his clothes, the very latest southern fashions, were expensive. He had no intention of letting them get ruined. With luck, Lord Schwalstein wouldn't take up too much of his time. The appearance of the manor house concerned him, however. Would a man who took so little pride in his house succumb to blackmail?

The only relief in seeing things the way they were was knowing that a man who lived in a place like that was unlikely to maintain a retinue of bannerets. It made Rodulf's job easier, and safer. Had Schwalstein possessed such an entourage, Rodulf would have needed to be far subtler in his approach.

The lord's steward hurried out as soon as word reached him that the Markgraf's emissary had arrived. Rodulf was ushered through the house—which bore all the same signs of neglect as the exterior—to where Lord Schwalstein sat drinking tea.

'These papers are for you, my lord,' Rodulf said, holding them out. If he was going to do the job, he reckoned he might as well make an effort. It might stand him in good stead later. He stood in as impressive a pose as he could manage; he had seen the bravos at court adopt similar stances.

Schwalstein regarded him a moment. Rodulf was dressed entirely in black silk, with silver thread embroidery. He was not ashamed to admit he had taken the Intelligenciers as an example, but added his own twist. Mysterious, menacing, but affluent was the picture he wanted to present. The Markgraf's emissary, a nobleman in his own right, a man to be reckoned with. As much as he hated it, he realised his eyepatch made his appearance even more perfect.

'Might I offer you some tea?' Schwalstein said, putting the papers on the table without looking at them.

'That would be very gracious of you, my lord. It would be very welcome.'

Schwalstein, a corpulent man well beyond the age when most had died, grunted and filled a second cup with a shaky hand. Rodulf sat and took the cup when it was offered to him.

'Do much of this sort of thing?' the lord said as he reviewed the papers.

'It's something of a new enterprise for me.' He took a sip and regarded his social superior with an excess of confidence. He enjoyed being oblique.

'Dangerous business.'

'I suppose,' Rodulf said truthfully. You never knew how a man would react to blackmail.

'For you and the Markgraf both,' Schwalstein said. 'So what is it then? The carrot or the stick?'

Rodulf smiled. 'The stick.'

'I'm old, and have little to lose. Make your threats, then scurry back to your master.'

'Liutpold,' Rodulf said.

Schwalstein's face dropped. 'What of him?'

'He's not in a very good way.'

'Of course he isn't. He's dead.'

Rodulf shook his head and smiled. 'On the contrary. He lives.' He gave Schwalstein a moment to digest the revelation. 'After a fashion.'

'Prove it,' Schwalstein said, his face a conflicting mix of hope and disbelief.

Rodulf gestured to the papers. 'He's written you a note. On a news sheet from last week, to prove it's recent.'

Schwalstein shuffled through the papers until he found the one Rodulf referred to. His face went grey as he read it.

'The war was hard on him,' Schwalstein said.

'Wars are hard on everyone,' Rodulf said. 'The dream seed addiction after it has been far harder, though.'

'I thought he'd smoked himself to death by now,' Schwalstein said. 'I haven't heard from him in six years.'

'He sells his arse to pay for seed. To say he's a mess understates things in the extreme.'

Schwalstein flushed with humiliation, and Rodulf worried he had overdone things.

'What am I to do?' Schwalstein said. 'I tried to help him, but there's no money left and problems like his need money to fix.'

'The Markgraf has money,' Rodulf said. 'And he's generous to his friends. Particularly friends he owes favours. He'd very much like to be your friend, and he'd very much like you to do him a favour.'

'What is it?'

'First, what he'll do for you. Liutpold will be taken in to a shelter in Elzburg that cares for people with problems such as his. I'm told the Order of Mendicant Sisters have had great successes in treating their cases. The Markgraf will pay for the treatment to end his dependence on the seed, and see that he returns to you. You'll have an heir again, and the Schwalstein name will not disappear into the mist of history.'

Schwalstein nodded, solidly on the hook.

'In return,' Rodulf said, 'there are three bridges on your property spanning the Rhenner River. The Markgraf would very much like you to pull them down. Two fords also. He'd like you to foul them with caltrops.'

Schwalstein smiled, and his eyes widened. 'I see. I see.' He sank back into his chair and licked his corpulent lips as he thought. 'I do this, and you'll get my son back to me?'

'Home, healthy, and ready to continue the family line.'

'You tell the Markgraf I'll tear down the bridges and make the fords impassable.' He gave Rodulf a knowing smile. 'You tell him that the prissy little bitch in Brixen won't be able to get her troops over the river in my demesne.'

'I'll be sure to convey your message precisely, my lord. Thank you for the tea.'

❉

## JAKOB

Jakob found his monthly meetings with Professor Kengil tiresome, but she was the university's clinical director and they were a part of the job if he wanted to run his own clinic. His greatest resentment stemmed from not even being able to remember the last time Kengil had set foot in a clinic, let alone treated a patient. She was one of the physicians who saw the practise of medicine as an academic subject rather than a practical vocation. It rankled with him that such people could reach positions of prominence, but there was nothing he could do about it so he had to play along.

'Good afternoon, Jakob,' Kengil said.

He nodded in response and sat down.

'How's the clinic going?' she said.

'Same as always. Busy. Not enough resources.'

She smiled. 'It was the same in my day.'

He wondered when that was, and if it might indeed have been only one day.

'Some things never change,' she said. 'We must do as much good as we can with the limited resources we have. It's the vocation and burden of our profession.'

Strellis couldn't help but feel uncomfortable when she smiled. Although older than him by a number of years, she was an attractive woman who had something of a reputation and an eye for her younger colleagues. It made him feel like he was being watched by a beast of prey lining up its next kill each time she looked at him.

'Indeed,' he said. 'Is there anything else? Like the other resources, my time is sadly all too limited.'

'Nothing in particular,' Kengil said, frowning as she thought. 'Oh. The new girl. Steinsdottir. How's she getting on?'

Jakob could feel his face flush slightly. 'Fine,' he said. 'Just fine.'

'You haven't had any problems with her?'

He wondered where she was going with this. He was not an examining lecturer, merely a clinical supervisor, so there was nothing prohibiting him from having a relationship with a student. Even so, they had only shared a momentary kiss. It was nothing he could be censured over.

'None at all,' he said. 'Quite the contrary.'

'She's behaving in a… civilised fashion? You know what these Northlanders can be like.'

Jakob tried not to react. She was fishing, but it had nothing to do with him getting too close to Adalhaid. His stomach twisted. Her questions were so vague, he suspected she didn't have anything to go on—but when it came to magic, rumours could be enough. He knew Kengil didn't like Adalhaid. Perhaps she was simply hoping to stumble on something she could hold over Adalhaid. Nonetheless, there was danger here.

'Perfectly civilised,' Jakob said. 'Far more so than some of our countrymen whom I've taught.'

Kengil's face momentarily betrayed what looked like disappointment. 'Excellent. Let me know if there are any issues. I won't take up any more of your time.'

# CHAPTER 39

## RODULF

RODULF SAT IN the carriage as it rattled its way back to Elzburg. He held the Stone in his hand, but still wore his glove. The experience was akin to chewing food, then spitting it out rather than swallowing—something about it felt incomplete. He had realised that the red mark on his hand, a mild burn as best he could tell, had been caused by the Stone. He had no basis for this belief, but it was the only explanation he could come up with. He felt frustration well up within him at how little he knew about it. Had he put misplaced faith in it? Perhaps it was nothing more than his cunning and power of persuasion that had led him to achieve all he had, and only some underlying insecurity caused him to credit an odd-looking lump of metal ore rather than his own ability. Had he not just convinced a peer of the realm to commit treason with nothing more than a little blackmail? He knew there was more to it than that. The power it exuded was unmistakeable.

He had done his best to leave it untouched in his pocket since realising it had caused the burn, great though the temptation was. Like a beautiful woman's breast, there was something about the object that begged to be caressed. It called to him. He needed to know more about it. To understand what it did to others and, more importantly, what it did to him. Where would he start? And how would he find the time? It was not something he could entrust to someone else. If it did have the power he suspected, even Grenville might be tempted from his service in order to take it.

Dangerous days lay ahead, and if he was to navigate them safely he had to gather every advantage he could. If the Stone did do something, even if only give him additional confidence, he would need it. The question of cost was now never far from his thoughts. What price would it exact from him?

❊

## WULFRIC

Wulfric could see why the Duke of Torona had wanted Kandamar. Even from his first, distant glimpse, it looked like paradise. It was a city of white stone surrounded by lush green vegetation.

'Like the look of your new home?' a Darvarosian said.

Wulfric shrugged.

'Cause any trouble while you're here, and you're a dead man,' he said.

Wulfric glared at him. 'Are you planning to do it?'

The man looked away, and Wulfric smiled. They feared him, and fear was something any great warrior should inspire in his enemy.

Another group of horsemen appeared on the horizon behind them, also moving toward the city. It took an hour to reach them, at which point the leaders of both groups conferred for a time before continuing together. The new horsemen were dressed for travel, in light robes, rather than for battle, and Wulfric wondered where they had come from. Perhaps they were simply travellers caught up in the outbreak of war, or curious nobles who had gone to watch the battle. One of them stared at Wulfric, and though the face was obscured by a swath of cloth wrapped around the head, there was something familiar about the eyes. She removed the cloth and gave Wulfric a cold smile before covering her face again. It was the beautiful woman from the palace. Her lip was swollen and split, surrounded by a dark purple bruise.

He wondered briefly how it had happened, then tapped Jagovere on the arm. 'It's her.'

Jagovere looked over. 'Who?'

'The woman from the palace.'

'The one with the knife?'

Wulfric nodded.

'You're sure?'

'She's taken a beating, but it's definitely her.'

'So, dal Valeriano and the Darvarosians were working together,' Jagovere said.

Wulfric screwed up his face at the perfidy of it all as he realised the meaning of the connection. 'Do you think he meant to lose the battle all along?'

Jagovere shrugged. 'Who knows? I don't see how he'd gain from it. I think it most likely he hoped there would never be a battle. I expect that's why the duke's army was treating the campaign like a vacation when we got here.'

Wulfric nodded, having wondered the same thing himself when they had arrived.

'Whatever deal he had with the Darvarosians probably called for no hostility while dal Valeriano tried to politic his way into power,' Jagovere said. 'When we crossed the border and had that skirmish, I expect we smashed their deal to pieces, and our new friend discovered the hard way that her former ally was now her enemy. Doesn't matter either way. This war won't last much longer. Either dal Valeriano's plan—whatever it was— has worked and he's overthrown his brother, or it hasn't, in which case he hasn't got much longer to live. I can only hope I'm able to get to him before someone else does.'

❁

## RODULF

Rodulf followed his nose back to the palace kitchen. He had just returned from another one of the Markgraf's missions, and was starving.

'You're not supposed to be back here, my lord,' a cook said.

He looked over at the cook who had spoken and smiled. She was a young woman, not much more than twenty. In a fifty-crown silk dress, she would have put every woman at court to shame. Even in linen and an apron covered in flour and splatters of various colours, she stood out like a rose among weeds.

'Come now,' he said. 'I'm just back from a long journey on his lordship's behalf. I missed dinner. I'm not doing any harm, am I?' He looked at her in a way that said it wasn't only food that he hungered for.

'I suppose not,' she said. 'I can give you some bread and broth. That should tide you over.'

'That sounds perfect,' he said. He nodded to the array of fruit pastries out on the worktop to cool. 'Is there any chance of one of those too?'

'Oh no, my lord. The pastry chef would kill me.'

She looked genuinely concerned.

'Ah, but I'm the Markgraf's emissary, back from a dangerous mission. I don't think anyone's going to stop me from taking one, do you?'

She thought for a moment. 'No, my lord.'

He walked over and picked one up. The smell alone was enough to send his taste buds into a frenzy. He walked back toward the girl. It was always handy to have friends in low places.

'I'll tell you what,' he said, splitting the pastry in two. 'You can have this half if you promise not to tell on me. Agreed?'

She laughed, then looked around to be sure no one was watching. She smiled and nodded. He handed her the piece, and looking into her eyes, smiled back. On this occasion, it didn't look like the pastry was the dessert.

❁

## WULFRIC

Their escort led them through the streets of Kandamar until they reached a large walled compound in the centre of the city. They were led inside the walls, and then away from the largest building, toward a complex of smaller barrack houses and stables.

Wulfric frowned when he saw where they were being taken.

'What were you expecting? The palace?' Jagovere said, as they were shown into a bunk house in the palace barracks.

Wulfric shrugged. 'That man said we'd be his guests. That's where we stayed in Torona.'

'That man,' Jagovere said, 'is Prince Peruman of Kandamar. As polite as he was, don't forget that we're his prisoners. If we want to get out of here alive, we should behave ourselves.' They dismounted, and their horses were taken from them.

'You'll remain in here at all times. Meals will be brought to you, and an escort will be required whenever you wish to go outside. Do you understand?'

Jagovere nodded, and they all went inside. Enderlain and the others ignored the conversation and moved into the room, and laid claim to their beds.

Wulfric sat on a free bed and looked around. 'What do we do now?'

❈

## RODULF

Rodulf was starting to become familiar with the inside of the Markgraf's private office. After each errand he ran, the Markgraf called him in and interrogated him on every detail. Although he always conveyed a sense of calm control, Rodulf could tell it was an act. The strain of what he was planning told on him like it did everyone else. The risks were great, but so too was the reward.

'Tell me,' the Markgraf said. 'How did it go?'

'There were no problems, my lord,' Rodulf said. 'Her Highness seems to have little support. In this part of the country, at any rate.'

'They know what I have planned?'

Rodulf shrugged. 'They all suspect. I've heard talk from other parts of the country too. You're not the first lord to see that power is there for the taking. Few think Princess Alys is strong enough to rebuild the Principality alone, as she seems insistent on doing. Once she's refused their offers of marriage, their thoughts turn to rebellion.'

'Perhaps I should have offered first,' the Markgraf said with a forced chuckle.

Rodulf shrugged. 'Then you'd have depended on her goodwill for the rest of your days. Better to take the power than rely on someone else for it.' He stopped himself, worried that he had been too forthright with his thoughts.

The Markgraf gave him a penetrating look, then relaxed. 'Good. Well done. Everything is on track. I'll have another errand for you in a day or two.'

'I'm capable of far more than running errands,' Rodulf said. He was seeing much of the inside of the private office, but not so much of the council chamber. Rodulf did not want to remain an errand boy on the periphery. If the Markgraf was to become a king, there was no reason Leondorf could not become a duchy. 'I can be far more useful to you.'

'You're filling the need I have right now perfectly,' the Markgraf said with an edge to his voice. 'This phase will be done with soon enough. Once it is, there'll be more for you. Don't worry. I won't forget you when the rewards are being handed out. Keep up the good work, and you'll get yours.'

Rodulf nodded, but he was not convinced. He had no intention of sharing all the risk only to receive a small portion of the reward.

There was a commotion at the door, and the Markgraf's steward burst in.

'You must come at once, my lord,' the steward said. 'There's been a terrible accident. Petr's fallen from his horse. He's badly hurt.'

'Call for my physicians,' the Markgraf said as he stood.

He was out the door before Rodulf had reacted.

# CHAPTER 40

## WULFRIC

THE PRIVY WAS a short walk across a back courtyard from the barrack block Wulfric and the others were being hosted in. Even for those few paces, a Darvarosian guard watched him. The privy, three walls and a roof, with a hole in the ground leading to a ditch on the other side, didn't allow for much in the way of privacy, even less so when there was a pair of suspicious eyes burning a hole in his back. He finished, did up his britches, and gave the guard a salute as he returned to the barrack block. Wulfric could remember when the fair had come to Leondorf when he was a child. One year a man had brought a small bear in a cage. He had trained it to do tricks for morsels of food. Wulfric had been fascinated at the time, but he now understood how the bear must have felt.

They were never watched quite so closely as when they trained. True to his word, the prince had allowed them to keep their weapons and there was little to do other than practice in the courtyard outside the barracks. Each day, a large crowd gathered to watch. Wulfric did not know whether to be flattered or intimidated. He was unsure if reputation of their ferocious last stand had spread, or if, like the caged bear, they were simply a curiosity to be ogled and laughed about.

At first, Wulfric had thought it folly for the prince to allow a group of armed and dangerous enemies into his city and palace, but as well as the gathered crowd, crossbowmen lining the compound walls watched their every move. The prince watched from time to time, surrounded by advisors who seemed to be making notes. Wulfric was certain he saw the woman too, always lingering in the shade and swathed in fine cloth that seemed to allow her to blend into the shadows.

Wulfric took the chance to learn how to use the long rapier favoured by Jagovere and the others. Jagovere was an excellent teacher, being one of the elite band who could call themselves a banneret, and the only one remaining of those who had survived the battle. Wulfric took to it quickly, and enjoyed the extra reach it gave, not to mention the pleasure of acquiring the new skills that went with it. After a few days, he had adopted the subtle differences in technique to the weapons he was more accustomed to, and was able to hold his own against Jagovere and even score touches against him in their practice duels. Jagovere told him it was a sport in Ruripathia, and the other countries around the Middle Sea.

When they were not training, Jagovere scribbled in his notebooks, and Wulfric practised his reading. The others lounged in the sun, their fair skin starting to take on a golden complexion.

They spent the morning of the fourth day in sword practice, then relaxed for the afternoon. Wulfric studied the elaborately curved hilt of the rapier he had been using. Northland weapons were usually viewed as little more than tools. Quality and reliability were prized, but usually only the sabre was decorated. The Ruripathians took more pride in their weapons, seeing them as fashion accessories, not just as tools of battle. The hilt was beautiful with its flowing curves, but functional in the added protection they gave the hand. He resolved to have one made for himself when he returned. It would help him fit in better in the south, to move without attracting so much notice.

'What are you going to do with all your scribblings?' Wulfric said.

'What *am* I doing, you mean,' Jagovere said. 'There's a fellow sending them back to Ruripathia for me.'

'From here?'

Jagovere nodded. 'Only cost a few silver shillings. I want everyone at home to know how bravely the Graf died.'

'He was popular in his city?' Wulfric said.

'He was loved,' Jagovere said. 'What do you think of "Dal Rhenning's Last Stand", as a title?'

Wulfric shrugged. 'It's as good as any other.' He continued to study the rapier. 'Am I in it?' he said, after a moment.

'Of course,' Jagovere said, smiling. 'It wouldn't be complete without mention of Ulfyr the Fearless.'

Wulfric frowned. 'I told you not to call me that.'

'And I told you protesting was the surest way to make it stick.'

'You're going to go after dal Valeriano when they let us go?' Wulfric said.

'I am. He betrayed us. Worse than that, even, I'm pretty sure he intentionally sent us to our deaths. After his idiot mage blew himself up, he knew he was beaten, but he sent us forward anyway, then ran. I'm going to cut his balls off, feed them to him, and let him bleed to death.'

Wulfric raised his eyebrows, having never heard Jagovere speak with such vitriol before.

'How are you going to do it?' he said.

'No idea, but so long as the end result is what I want, who cares?' He paused for a moment, and the hatred on his face softened. 'Whatever it is, I'm sure it will make for a great story.'

'You won't be able to do it alone,' Wulfric said.

'He was my father. One way or the other, I'll do it.'

'I owe him too. I'd have been arrested and executed in Ruripathia if he hadn't helped me,' Wulfric said. 'I'll come with you.'

Jagovere looked over to him, genuine gratitude in his eyes. 'Thank you,' he said. 'We'll make a tale that will rival any of the great epics.'

## ADALHAID

Adalhaid could tell that something was wrong as soon as she got back to the palace from the university. The change in mood was instantly recognisable. It was as though a great dark cloud hung over the palace. Where chatter, laughter, and braggadocio usually reigned supreme, there was only silence. Adalhaid spotted one of the scullery maids she was friendly with and made her way over.

'Has something happened?' Adalhaid said. Her eyes widened when she saw the maid's red, puffy face.

'It's young Master Petr,' she said. 'He fell from his horse. His neck broke. He's dead, Adalhaid.'

The news hit Adalhaid like a brick to the face. She had promised to take him to the park that afternoon. There was a pond there that he liked to float paper boats on. Aenlin, his twin sister, would watch and feed the ducks. The two were never far apart. Adalhaid had no idea what to say or do.

'Aenlin?' she said after a moment. 'Is she all right?'

'She's fine,' the maid said, 'but she's inconsolable. His lordship's physician had to give her something to sleep.'

❊

## WULFRIC

'Northlander.'

Wulfric recognised the voice instantly. Its honeyed tone was etched into his memory. He turned to see the woman standing in the shadows. Even knowing she was there, she was difficult to see. *Some sort of southern magic?* he wondered. The bruising and swelling around her mouth had started to fade, but it was clear she had taken quite a beating.

'What do you want?' he said. He didn't like the effect she had on him, and he didn't like the way it made him let his guard drop. Even now, knowing what he knew, he still wanted her.

'You and your friend are going to kill dal Valeriano?' she said.

He wasn't armed, and was not as confident as he would have liked that he could kill her without a weapon. He could remember all too well their last encounter, and how easily she had made him release his grip on her hand.

'I've no idea what you're talking about,' he said.

She laughed, a sound that caused his breath to quicken. 'You wear your lies as obviously as your arrogance,' she said. She remained in the shadow, and made no threatening move. 'You're going to kill dal Valeriano. I'm going to help you.'

'What use would we have of a woman?' he said.

She moved quickly; she was standing next to him in the blink of his eye, and he felt the all-too-familiar sensation of a dagger tip pressing against his crotch.

'I can go places and do things a big ignorant Northlander cannot,' she said. 'I can hear things and see things that people do not want seen or heard. Do not act like you have a choice.' She smiled, revealing perfect white teeth behind her deep red lips. 'Ulfyr.'

He opened his mouth to speak, but could feel the pressure on the dagger increase, so he shut it.

'I can be your friend or your enemy,' she said. 'If you intend to kill dal Valeriano, you want me as a friend.'

'I thought dal Valeriano was your friend.'

Her eyes flashed with anger. 'His goals matched Prince Peruman's. For a time. That was all.'

'And now you want to kill him?'

Her glower said he wasn't going to get an answer. He shrugged. 'This assumes we're ever going to get out of here.'

'You'll be released soon. Tomorrow, perhaps. Dal Valeriano has overthrown the Duke of Torona. Killed him and his family. Peace is being negotiated. The war is all but over. He has no claims south of the border.'

'What's your name?' Wulfric said.

'Varada,' she said, in a way that made it clear that was all the information she was giving him.

※

## ADALHAID

Petr's death had left Adalhaid in a stunned daze. It was hard to imagine that all the life had been snuffed out of the energetic little boy. She wondered if she had been there when the accident had happened, whether she would have been able to help. If the strange talent she possessed might have saved him. It was a tragedy that impacted everyone in the palace. In a place that revolved around superficiality, greed, and ambition, Petr and his twin sister had been a breath of fresh air.

She realised her being there would have made little difference. Indeed, she was thankful she had not been. She still had no idea how to control her magical talent—and even had she been able to, healing injuries such as those Petr had sustained would have revealed what she could do. She would have had to stand idly by, or condemn herself to death. It was a hideous choice to have to make. She might not ever be able to use it to its full potential, but she knew she had to try to tap into it, at least a little. To squander her talent was an insult to the gods, who were the source of all things magical, and was too selfish a choice for her to live with. She thought of Wulfric. He had never allowed fear to hold him back, and she resolved not to either. She would not be careless with her life, but she would not let this talent go to waste, even if it only meant she could offer the smallest of aid to those who were suffering. She might not have been able to help Petr, but there were others she would. She had been playing around with it in her spare time, but she couldn't tell if she'd made any progress. She knew she would eventually have to try it out on a real patient.

A boy was ushered into her treatment room with a cut on his arm. It was small and only needed to be cleaned and stitched, but it was the type of thing that could cause the blood to go bad, and ultimately kill. So small a thing, yet still potentially fatal. At times the world seemed far crueller than it needed to be.

She took his arm and smiled. 'It might be best if you look away,' she said.

The boy did as he was told and she rubbed some alcohol on the wound to mask any sensation that might follow. The boy hissed in discomfort.

'Keep looking away,' she said. 'I'm going to clean it and bandage it. Won't take long.'

She studied the wound, a cut the length of her thumb, and committed its shape and the angry red colour to memory. As she stared at it, she was taken by sudden temptation. A little test couldn't hurt, could it? She took a deep breath, and concentrated on a desire to heal the injury. She could feel her finger grow cold, then her hand and finally her forearm. She barely noticed. She was fixated on the wound as it went from red to pink. She knew it was time to stop, but the temptation was so strong that she couldn't. The closest word to describing the sensation she felt was *joy*. She continued to watch in fascination as the flesh knitted before her eyes.

She pulled her hand away and gasped. She took a step back to balance herself, and a wave of light-headedness passed over her. Nausea followed, to the point she thought she might be sick, but it faded quickly. The boy looked at her with a curious expression on his face. She put her hand over the healed wound so he could not see it, and wished she had not allowed herself to get carried away. She took a moment to settle. She lifted her hand and looked. She had done far more than she intended, and worry twisted in her gut. She hadn't been able to stop herself, and she didn't know why. Curiosity? Lack of control? She would need to work that out as soon as she could. She reached for her needle and thread, and a bandage, hoping to hide her work in conventional treatment for as long as possible.

As she stitched, she cursed her rashness. She had allowed her grief over Petr to dictate her actions before she was fully ready. However, she had learned more about it—the temptation, and the pull to continue past the point her head was telling her to stop—and that was important too. Sometimes an unintended or unwanted result was as important as the alternative. It was progress, and she took satisfaction from that.

# CHAPTER 41

AETHELMAN

I T HAD BEEN many years since Aethelman had visited a city. He had travelled south in his early days as a priest, the only time in his life when he had questioned his vocation. When *they* had questioned their vocations. The memory tugged on the fibres of his heart.

The city had been a dangerous place for two young people to run to, but it was the only option for priests who had renounced their vows. Every god-fearing man, woman, and child in the Northlands would have turned their backs on them, so they ran south, where no one cared for the old gods. It had seemed so romantic. So terrifying.

Grey Priests had only a small ability with magic, some more than others, but it was more than enough to make them pariahs in the south. Aethelman and Aesa had known this, and had sworn to one another they would be careful, that they would keep it secret and live ordinary lives like any other young couple. In those first days, it had seemed like the southern witch hunters were everywhere. He had lived in a constant state of fear and paranoia. Aesa had told him to relax, that there was no chance of them being found out so long as they were careful. She had been cleverer than him, braver. He was terrified that he would be the one to make the mistake, that he would be the one to put the love of his life in peril. In the end that hadn't been the case, though.

Sorrow formed like a heavy lump in his stomach as he stared at the city walls. He could hear her laugh, smell her hair, feel her touch, but they were all long gone. Long dead.

He thought of the laughter that had guided him through the cavern beneath the Hermitage, and closed his eyes as he did his best to remember the sound perfectly. How he missed it. Tears had welled in his eyes by the time he opened them. He wondered how different his life might have been, had she lived. Her kind heart was what had killed her. A child crushed by a runaway barrel had broken Aesa's resolve to keep her power in the shade, and in saving the child's life she had forfeited her own.

The witch hunters had been beating at their door the next morning. Intelligenciers, the southerners called them; a grand name for a grubby job. From arrest to pyre took only the blink of an eye. It had been luck that Aethelman had not been there when they called, otherwise he would likely have joined her on the pyre—she had always gone out to fetch bread from the baker every morning, but for some reason he had offered to do it that day to give her a few extra minutes in bed. He often wondered at the small, thoughtless choices made in life and how they could change it utterly.

He had stood in the crowd that day, hoping he could ease her suffering. It had been futile. His own suffering had been so great that he could do little for her. He had not been man enough to be there for her at her worst moment. All he could do was fixate on his grief at losing her, and so while she had died in agony in the flames, he had wept. A long life had done little to dull the pain of the memory, now that he had allowed it back out of the dusty recesses of his mind. Anger was something he rarely felt, but it flowed through his veins in that moment so strongly it shamed him.

He had run back to the Northlands, the Stone still in the bottom of his satchel, convinced that all that had happened was a punishment for them forsaking their vows. He had dedicated his life to his vocation after that, the few brief months of madness with Aesa seeming like a dream. The memory of her would never leave him, however. He hoped and prayed that the gods had forgiven her, that they had forgiven him, and that she awaited him in the next life.

As hesitant as he was, Aethelman wiped the tears from his face and pressed on to the city. Elzburg. Each step confirmed that this was where the Stone now was. As much as he disliked them, southern cities were impressive places. The high walls and tall towers reminded him the great things men were capable of, and it pained him that they were a monument to violence. He approached the gate, and wondered if the guards knew what to look for—if they could spot a user of magic on sight. They ignored him, though, and he passed through the great gate to whatever fate awaited him.

❧

## Professor Kengil

As much as she might have liked to, Professor Kengil could not spend all her time watching Adalhaid, waiting for her to do something beyond belief. She wanted to believe Rosamund's story, and see Adalhaid dragged away by the Intelligenciers, but she was beginning to have doubts. Rosamund was a pretty enough girl, but Adalhaid had a fresh-faced beauty that was rare. Jakob Strellis was an exceptionally handsome man, and a very talented physician. She had no doubt that one day he would take over from her. She could not dismiss the possibility that what Rosamund had said came entirely out of jealousy. She had not seen anything conclusive in the child who had allegedly received the magical treatment.

For a moment, she was tempted to set aside her vendetta. Adalhaid would not even have been alive when Northlanders had killed Professor Kengil's parents and burned their village to the ground. It was likely even a different tribe, or whatever it was they called themselves. It was petty to hold a grudge against an entire people over the actions of a few, no matter how much injury they had caused, and a small voice inside told her that she should be above such things. That aside, there was something about the girl that Kengil simply did not like. Whether it was her consistently high performance, or the air of perfection and virtue she seemed to emanate, the thought of her succeeding made Kengil rage.

There was a larger issue at stake, though, one that she could not set aside. Sorcery was illegal. It was her responsibility to make sure every physician who qualified under her watch abided by the training and good practices of the profession. To have a graduate of the university use witchcraft was anathema. It would ruin the university's reputation—but more importantly, it would endanger patients. No, she had a responsibility and she would satisfy it. She moved to the side a pile of letters from colleagues regarding an interesting case, and returned to audit the records from Strellis's clinic.

She scanned page after page. It was a busy clinic, and on any day, Strellis, Rosamund, and Adalhaid saw over a hundred patients. She couldn't limit herself just to Adalhaid's work. It was possible Strellis might be covering for her, and putting some of her patients under his name.

The magelamp on her desk coming to life was the first indication of how long she had been at her task. The little glass globe automatically—magically, she thought without missing the irony—illuminated when it grew dark outside. A vortex of energy swirled inside its thick glass enclosure, as it had every moment of the centuries since its creation by sorcerers long dead. They were expensive, as no more had been made since the wars that tore the Old Empire apart, but a great many had survived, lighting the streets, and the homes and offices of the wealthy. They had fascinated her since childhood. She could afford her own now, and every room of her home had one. Each had its own individual character, perhaps an imprint of the person who had created it all those years before. This one had been owned by the professor of medicine ever since the holder of the post was a sorcerer. It was as beautiful as it was useful, and for the briefest of moments it made her wonder if magic was indeed as bad as everyone said. If the destroyed leg of a child could be saved by magic, when conventional medicine would see it cut off with knife and saw, might there not be an argument to support it?

She shook the thought from her head, recalling one or two 'mages' who had held themselves out as healers. The mess they had made was beyond even Kengil's considerable skill to put right. It was a vile thing, and had to be stopped. Medicine was a science, not a reason to dabble in matters that should be left alone.

Her thoughts drifted back to the interesting case she had been corresponding with the other physicians about. What they had thought was a simple infection of the lungs was proving to be far more, and something that neither she nor any of her colleagues had seen before. She had treated the man, and thought her work done until she followed up on it, and discovered he was as bad as ever. It was not unusual for an initial treatment to fail, however, and a second to succeed…

She looked back to Adalhaid's records. Every follow up recorded showed that each of her treatments had been successful. No wounds had gone bad. Not a single one. That was statistically impossible. No matter how diligent the treatment, either through carelessness on the part of the patient, or simply bad luck, infection set in, and occasionally the patient even died. But not with Adalhaid. Everyone she treated healed in accordance with the best-case scenario. It was impossible. Was this it? Was this the proof Kengil needed that she was using more than medical techniques to heal her patients?

Kengil's heart raced with the excitement of thinking she may have snared her prey, but was it enough? Perhaps she had simply been careful, and lucky. She was diligent and damn near perfect in everything else she did. Might it not be the case with this also? She had not treated enough patients yet for the numbers to fully tell a story. Might there be a way to force harder evidence?

She looked back to the correspondence. At first Kengil had thought the man's illness would pass with a treatment of steaming lemon water. It hadn't. His affliction came and went, but it bore all the hallmarks of the colds hundreds of people went to their doctors with every winter. It was only after a number of treatments that she realised he was also passing tiny amounts of blood in his urine, an amount only detectable under a microscope. It was a last resort test—the university only had one microscope and time with it was a limited resource. A detailed inspection showed that his disease had reached his kidneys, and they were all but destroyed. The poor man did not have long to live and, concerned that she had failed, she had consulted with a number of experienced colleagues. Their opinions were the same. They all felt, as she, that it was an isolated disease none of them had ever seen before. It was tragic, but there was no more that could be done.

If she sent this man to Adalhaid, and she chose to cure his obvious, lesser symptoms with magic, might they also repair the irreparable damage elsewhere? None of the prescribed approaches for the illness that would seem most obvious to an inexperienced physician would have the slightest effect on it. If he was cured, there would be only one possible explanation.

※

## WULFRIC

When Wulfric returned to the bunkhouse, everyone was there. There was Jagovere, Enderlain—who had taken to training with a great sword since his rapier had broken in the grotto—Sander, Walt, and Conrat. That was it. They were all that remained of nearly four hundred fighting men, and it was still difficult to take in the fact that all the others were dead. They were discussing Jagovere's plan for when they were released.

'So we're agreed then,' Jagovere said.

'You know we're with you,' Walt said. 'Every man here owes everything he has to the Graf.'

They all nodded in agreement.

'The woman,' Wulfric said. 'She knows.'

They all looked up at him.

'What woman?' Walt said.

'The one who was in Torona,' Jagovere said, his face going grey. 'She's a spy or an assassin, or both, and who knows what else? It's not good news.'

'Perhaps it is,' Wulfric said. 'She wants to help us.'

'Help us?' Jagovere said. 'Why?'

'I didn't ask,' Wulfric said.

'Why not?' Enderlain said, as he ran a whetstone along the edge of his newly adopted sword.

'I didn't think to.'

'Didn't think to?' Jagovere said. 'She could ruin everything.'

'She had a knife to my balls,' Wulfric said.

'Again?' Enderlain said.

Everyone remained silent for a moment, looked at each other, then roared with laughter.

'Ulfyr the Nutless doesn't have quite the right ring to it, does it,' Sander said, adding fuel to the laughter.

Wulfric was about to say something about the nickname, but remembered Jagovere's words and remained silent.

Jagovere stroked his beard for a moment and thought. 'What do you think, Wulfric?'

'She had a lot of anger in her,' he said. 'I believed her. She had been beaten the day we got here. I saw her face. Maybe dal Valeriano did it.'

'Perhaps,' Jagovere said.

'She said she could either be our friend or our enemy,' Wulfric said. 'I've seen the way she can move. I'd rather she was our friend.'

'That makes sense, but she's not one of us. We can let her tag along, but we can't trust her,' Conrat said.

'Do we have a choice?' Jagovere said.

Wulfric shook his head.

'And then we were seven,' Jagovere said, knitting his fingers behind his head and lying back on his bunk.

# CHAPTER 42

WULFRIC

A DARVAROSIAN CAPTAIN CAME into the bunkhouse before the sun had risen.

'Wake up,' he shouted. 'Wake up. You're free to go. Get up and get out.'

They were ushered out of the bunk house, where the few possessions they had been captured with were dumped on the ground.

'Take your things and go,' the captain said.

'Where?' Conrat said.

The captain shrugged. 'That's your business, and no concern of mine.'

'What he means is *how?*' Jagovere said. 'We'll need horses and provisions to get north.'

'No concern of mine either. If you're not gone by dawn, you'll all be put to the sword. Do us both a favour.' The captain left.

'That's bloody perfect,' Walt said. 'How in hells are we going to get north without water and horses? We'll be dead before we get halfway.'

Wulfric looked to the pile of weapons and damaged armour, then up to the walls of the compound, which were patrolled by twice as many bowmen as usual. If they tried to steal what they needed, they wouldn't last long. He wondered if they might have been better off fighting to the end in the grotto.

They gathered up their things and wandered out of the barracks, looking around uncertainly. None of them had any money, so there was no question of them buying anything. Wulfric saw Varada standing across the street in the shade of an arcade. She beckoned for him to follow her, and walked down an alley between two squat white buildings where they would not be seen from the street.

'When you leave the city, walk east for an hour. You'll find a small watering hole there. I'll be waiting for you with horses and supplies.'

Wulfric frowned. 'Why not give them to us here?'

'Because you're supposed to die on the journey north,' she said. 'Dal Valeriano made it a condition of the peace that no Northern mercenaries would be allowed to live. The prince offered you terms that made you his guests when you surrendered, so he cannot kill you. If you were to die when no longer in his care? Well, that's an entirely different matter.'

'How do you know all this?' Wulfric said.

She raised an eyebrow, and for a moment Wulfric thought she was going to smile. It didn't happen, however, leaving him with an odd sense of disappointment.

'Why are you doing this? Why are you helping us?'

'Because I can't get to dal Valeriano on my own, and I want him dead. Our goals align.'

Wulfric nodded. The implication was clear. So long as they wanted the same thing, they were friends, but for no longer. 'Is the prince going to send men after us?'

'Not that I know of,' she said. 'He expects you all to die of thirst on the plain. Without help, that's exactly what I would expect for you. One hour east. I'll be waiting.'

❉

## AETHELMAN

Dangerous though it was, the city was a fascinating place. For a man interested in learning, as Aethelman was, the city was a microcosm of all the strange wonders the world had to offer. Elzburg was small, but an important centre of trade between the Northlands and everywhere else. It was the gateway for furs, gems, amber, ores, and now, silver. Southerners wanted those things, but didn't want to have to cross the river that marked the boundary between the Northlands and Ruripathia. People of all shapes and colours walked the streets, many of them even farther from home than Aethelman was.

He felt some of the thrill that he had when he had first arrived at that great city in the south, Ostenheim, the crossroads of the world. He had been young and in love, and anything had seemed possible. Everything had appeared so vibrant, so new, so fascinating, yet there was also a harsh brutality just beneath the surface. There were slaves beaten into submission, carrying burdens for their masters that would leave them bent and broken before their time. There were cutthroats who would kill you for a penny, and thieves who would steal everything and leave you destitute. There were people so wealthy that the plight of those poor souls beneath them went as unnoticed as the toil of ants. It had seemed so huge, and Aethelman knew that Elzburg was but a fraction of its size. Nonetheless, after so many years in Leondorf it was a daunting prospect.

A man shoved Aethelman to the side of the street, for no reason other than their paths had come close to meeting. Aethelman stumbled and fell against a wall, his wits momentarily shaken from his head. Someone kicked him as they walked past. Another spat.

'Filthy beggar,' someone said.

'Clear off before I call the watch,' said another.

Aethelman struggled to his feet and gathered his wits as he did. He knew he looked scruffy, but if this was the way he was to be treated in the city, his search would be difficult indeed. He had thought his appearance would allow him to be anonymous, but it seemed to mark him out as a figure for hate. He would need to adopt a different approach.

## ADALHAID

Adalhaid could hear the fluid in the man's lungs as soon as she walked into the treatment room. He was middle-aged but looked sickly, as though he had been unwell for some time.

'Good morning,' she said. 'What's troubling you?'

'I feel poorly, and I'm having trouble breathing, Doctor,' he said.

He looked about himself uneasily. Adalhaid had quickly come to realise that few people relished a visit to the physician.

'I'm only an apprentice physician,' Adalhaid said. 'Miss Steinsdottir is fine. How long have you been like this?'

'A while. A cousin of mine said I should come and see you. Said you sorted him out in no time.'

'That was kind of him. I'm going to examine you now,' she said.

She pressed her ear to his chest, but it merely served to confirm the obvious. While his ailment may have started as a cold, it was more serious now. His skin was cold and clammy, and it was likely he was starting to have fevers. Left untreated, he could end up drowning in the fluid in his lungs. However, it still appeared to only be a cold and was within the realm of what she was permitted to treat. Were it much worse, she would have had to pass him over to Doctor Strellis.

She had little faith in the prescribed remedy. Inhaling steam from lemon-scented water seemed like a con to her, and she thought it likely anyone who did improve did so in spite of it, rather than because of it. Still, it was what the texts told her to do.

She took a beaker of boiling water from the crucible and poured in several drops from a vial. 'This is essence of lemon, the standard treatment, and some extra medicinal herbs I've added to the mix myself. I find it to be far more effective.'

In truth, they were little more than the spiciest herbs she could find at the market. She wanted to add something that would make her essence smell markedly different from any other, but that was all it did. She draped a cloth over the man's head and held the steaming beaker underneath, placing her hand on his back as she did.

'Please breathe deeply and slowly,' she said.

She had been practising her talent ever since the boy with the cut on his arm. She had found a sick cat hanging around outside the door to the palace kitchens, and had taken it back to her room to treat. The cat was now healthy and ruler of the kitchen courtyard, where its renewed vitality gave it the edge on its competitors. The experience of treating the small creature was different to the boy. The feelings and sensations it had placed on Adalhaid were far less pronounced, something she put down to the difference in size and amount of magical energy needed. Nonetheless, it had allowed her to separate out all the impacts it had on her, mind and body, and she felt better prepared to deal with them now. It was time to give it a second try.

She focussed on pushing a wave of healing energy through him. She still had little clue of what was actually happening, but this approach seemed to make it work. She counted to five, then forced herself to stop, although the desire to continue was so powerful it was almost overwhelming. She was expecting it, though, and had the strength of will to break off. She took a breath and waited for the dizziness and nausea. It came, but as little more than an echo, and at no time was it enough to overcome her. She smiled.

'Hopefully your breathing will come a little easier now,' she said. 'I'll give you a bottle of it to take with you. Repeat what we've just done at least three times a day until you're feeling better.'

The man nodded eagerly, an expression of surprise on his face. 'It already feels better, miss.'

She could hear as much for herself, and ushered him to the door, beyond which her next half dozen patients would already be waiting.

❄

## AETHELMAN

As a Grey Priest, Aethelman had never needed to worry about personal requirements. He received food and shelter wherever he went, and there was little more that he needed. Being faced with a need for money was an entirely new experience for him. He had no idea where to begin.

He walked with care, moving from the shadows to the verges until he reached a market square, not wishing to be on the receiving end of a citizen's hostility. His body was not as hardy as it had once been, and a bad fall could be enough to bring his quest to an end. It occurred to him that he could sell one of the blades. A Telastrian blade would fetch a hefty price, but he didn't like the idea of having only one. It could be lost, it could be stolen, it might not work. He felt happier having a backup.

The square was filled with stalls, traders, customers, thieves, beggars, and watchmen. He saw other beggars receive the same treatment he had experienced, but took little solace in knowing it had not been reserved for him alone. There was a man running a game with three cups and a pea on a stall to the side of the square. Aethelman had seen the type before. The better ones could move their hands quickly enough not to need to cheat, but this one did. Aethelman watched him swindle three men in a row. He walked up to the stall.

The man looked up to Aethelman. 'Piss off, scum,' he said.

Aethelman laid a silver coin, the only one he possessed, down on the stall. The man looked at it, then up at Aethelman, and shrugged. He turned over the three cups and moved the dried pea to the centre of the stall.

'Find the pea and double your money,' the man said. He covered the pea with the cup and started to move them, slowly at first, but with ever increasing speed. He continued for long enough to remove the pea, but Aethelman didn't bother trying to follow. He felt little guilt for cheating a cheat. When he stopped, Aethelman tapped one of the cups at random. He was well aware of the danger of using magic in the south, but it was such a small thing, he didn't foresee a problem.

The man's eyes widened when he lifted the cup to find a pea sitting there. He looked up at Aethelman, frowning, but there were people watching and it wouldn't do to dispute what was clearly a winner.

'Divine Fortune is with you, friend,' the man said, as he laid a second silver coin on Aethelman's initial stake. 'What do you say, double or nothing?'

He had a glint in his eye that said he was not expecting to make the same mistake twice, and clearly didn't realise he had not made a mistake the first time.

'Why not?' Aethelman said.

The process repeated, and again Aethelman won. The man licked his lips and looked around, but there were even more people watching now, leaving him with no choice but to pay up if he hoped to ever do business there again. He placed two coins on the previous two. Aethelman could see from the man's expression that it was time to leave, so he picked up the coins and walked away. It was far from a fortune, but it was a start.

❋

## Wulfric

The journey to the waterhole was very much as Wulfric remembered the ride south. The sun was hot, and the plain was dry. More conditioned to northern climes, Wulfric reckoned the first of them would have been struggling by the end of the day had they set out on their own, and that none of them would have made it back to Torona at all, let alone in a fit state to go after dal Valeriano.

After what they estimated to be the better part of an hour, a cluster of trees broke the tedium of the otherwise flat plain. The others had taken some convincing to head east, rather than striking out north, but ever since the fight in the grotto, the one Jagovere had christened 'Dal Rhenning's Last Stand', they seemed to listen to what he said. Any sense of rank and discipline seemed to have faded away, with everything being discussed before a decision was taken. Wulfric recalled the way Jagovere had reacted to dal Rhenning's death—that moment when a decision could be the difference between life and death, and he had been unable to make one.

Wulfric could tell it played on his mind, that it had knocked what had seemed an unshakeable confidence into a state of constant uncertainty. It made Wulfric uncomfortable. Decisions should be made by one man. A captain. A First Warrior. Debates took time, and warriors rarely had time when the decisions were the important ones. Sooner or later, Jagovere would have to step up and replace his father, or somebody else would.

He spotted Varada sitting amongst the trees, waiting for them at the watering hole with horses for them all as well as several others that were laden with supplies and what looked like trade goods.

'You made good time,' she said. 'I can't be certain there won't be men coming after you, so I suggest we cross open country for the next few hours, then re-join the road. I've already laid a false trail from the city. Once back on the road, we hide in plain sight.' She gestured to the spare horses. 'A merchant and her escort.'

Jagovere walked up to Varada. 'Banneret of the Grey Jagovere dal Borlitz, at your service.' He aped the gesture of doffing a non-existent hat, but it failed to raise the smile he seemed to be aiming for. 'I understand you'll be joining us.'

She nodded. 'Yes, I am. If any of you stinking bastards lays a hand on me, I'll cut it off and kill you after you've suffered for a few days.'

Enderlain barked out a laugh, but she cast him such a filthy look he cut it short. The episode made Wulfric smile, but he was not so foolish as to allow it to draw attention to him. He had felt cold steel in his nether regions too many times by now.

'Well, now that we've established the ground rules,' Jagovere said, 'welcome to the Co…' His voice drifted off.

Wulfric supposed they weren't dal Rhenning's Company any longer. He had no idea what they were. A band of angry men seeking revenge. Wulfric could barely remember a time when he had not been that way.

'The Wolves?' Varada said.

'Excuse me?' Jagovere said.

He blushed slightly, and Wulfric realised he knew what she meant.

'The Wolves,' Varada said. 'Isn't that what you've been calling yourselves in your stories? The Wolves of the North?'

'I'm not sure I follow,' Jagovere said. 'How do you know that?'

She raised an eyebrow. 'Don't worry. They got where they were being sent. They just passed by me first.'

She let him cogitate on it for a moment, and Wulfric wondered what mention Jagovere might have made of her from their time at the palace in Torona.

'We should go,' she said. 'If you're being followed, we're inviting trouble by remaining here.'

# CHAPTER 43

AETHELMAN

IT WAS LATE evening by the time Aethelman had done his rounds of the city's games of chance, and felt his purse had swelled enough to see him through to his goal. He expected that every proprietor of a card, dice, or cup table would know about him by morning, but it didn't matter. He had enough, and had only taken coin from the dishonest ones—who, it had transpired, were the majority. As he read through the price list at a coffee house, he realised he had more than enough. Far more. Having lived so long in the Northlands with no need for anything beyond what was provided, he had no concept of the value of money. A crown, a florin, a shilling, a penny—they all sounded much the same to him, and he couldn't tell which one was which. When he compared the prices to what he had in his purse, he realised his day's gambling had brought in more than a skilled craftsman would make in a year. He had lived a long life, without a hint of luxury. Surely the gods would not judge him too harshly should he have a small sample so late in life?

He asked around for an inn from passers-by, and one name cropped up frequently, accompanied by attempts at wit that suggested it was the best in the city, but a place someone such as he could not dream of paying for. He felt an inappropriate amount of satisfaction as he stood before it, comfortable in the knowledge that he could indeed afford it. Its name, *the White Horse*, was painted in gilt on a black board over the door. He had spent an hour looking for *the Pale Pony*, until someone had taken pity on him and told him the proper name. With the confidence of a man who doesn't give a damn what anyone thinks of him, he walked into the inn and presented himself at the reception desk.

'I've had a long journey, and a moderate degree of misfortune,' he said, aping the abrupt way of speaking favoured by southern nobility.

'I'm sorry to hear that... my lord,' the receptionist said, hesitating before deciding to err on the side of caution. 'How may I be of assistance?'

'I'll need a room, a bath, and a hot meal for starters,' Aethelman said, starting to enjoy the ruse, his voice growing louder as he settled into the persona. He realised he hadn't come up with a name yet. 'A barber also, and then a tailor. A good one.'

'I'll attend to it directly,' the receptionist said. 'Might I have your name, for the register?'

'Certainly. Gustav dal... Aetheldorf.'

'Very good, Lord Aetheldorf. I'll have the boy take you to your room.'

❉

## WULFRIC

'How long will it take?' Wulfric said as they rode north.

'At this pace, we'll cross the border tomorrow,' Varada said. 'We should get to Torona early the following afternoon. There's an inn near the border where we can get a decent meal and stay tonight. I've had my fill of sleeping on the ground lately.'

They continued to ride in silence before she spoke again.

'Was he really like that?'

'Who?' Wulfric said.

'The Graf. Dal Rhenning. Was he really the man the stories say?'

'I suppose,' Wulfric said. 'I didn't know him all that well. Not for very long, at least, but the men loved him.' He didn't know what else to say. 'Most of them fought to the death for him.'

'He saved your life?'

'He did,' Wulfric said. 'Jagovere writes too much.'

Finally, Varada smiled. 'He's a spy's dream. Too much truth in his tales. He writes well though. I enjoyed his stories.'

Wulfric wondered what else Jagovere had said in his stories, whether he had revealed Wulfric's thoughts when he had first seen her in Torona. He wished he had read them more carefully. For the most part he had skipped ahead to the battle scenes, which he agreed were very well written.

'Jagovere knew him better than anyone. You should ask him,' Wulfric said, hoping to be helpful, but she seemed to take it as rudeness and spurred her horse away.

Everyone breathed a sigh of relief when the inn Varada had spoken of came into view. They had maintained a punishing pace to get themselves out of Darvaros, and the prospect of a hot meal and a proper bed was welcome to them all. They had not seen any sign of pursuit since leaving Kandamar, and Wulfric was eager to get a good rest. Who knew when the opportunity would present itself again in the days to come?

❧

## Rodulf

The Markgraf looked utterly drained of life when Rodulf went into his office. He had been told the Markgraf had taken his son's death hard, and had barely been seen outside of the private apartments in the days since it happened, but he looked not far from dead himself.

'I'm terribly sorry for your loss,' Rodulf said, in as caring and considerate way as he could manage. 'If there's anything at all I can do...'

'That's very kind of you,' the Markgraf said. There was as little energy in his voice as there was vitality in his face. 'I need to send you away on another mission. My...' He paused, as though he had forgotten what he was going to say. 'My steward has the details of the lords you're to visit. You're to leave at once.'

'Very good, my lord,' Rodulf said, then had a thought. He had noticed that the stronger a man's character, the less influence he seemed to have over them when gripping the Stone. The Markgraf didn't seem to be in any way affected by it, but now, distracted and tired as he appeared, Rodulf wondered. He slipped his hand into his pocket and took hold of it.

'I wonder, my lord, if I might put off departure until tomorrow morning?' He concentrated hard, thinking of the pleasure of a late morning in bed with the kitchen girl, and a good breakfast before setting off.

The Markgraf frowned, but his face showed strain. Rodulf realised the Markgraf was holding his breath. He let it out with a sigh after a moment.

'No,' the Markgraf said. 'No, that won't do at all. You must set off immediately. Time is becoming an increasingly important factor.'

Rodulf nodded his obeisance and left. It was the only time he had ever seen the Markgraf react to the Stone, and for a moment he thought it might work. It filled Rodulf's mind with possibilities. If the Markgraf's resolve weakened further, perhaps the Stone would work its magic on him. The thought of what he could achieve if he gained control over the Markgraf was intoxicating. It was only the burning sting of the palm of his hand that moderated the feeling.

❈

## AETHELMAN

There was something to southern luxury, Aethelman could not deny that, and for the briefest of moments he felt a pang of regret that he had ignored it for the greater part of his life. After his session with the barber, his skin felt smoother and softer than it had when he was twenty years old. The tailor had made him a suit of clothes that were soft, comfortable, and fit perfectly. A wonder, considering they had only taken a few hours to make up. When you were willing to pay whatever it took, it was amazing what could be achieved. His funds were not unlimited, but he was happy to spend everything he had to achieve his ends. He had no rainy day to save for.

He allowed himself a moment's vanity as he stood before the mirror in his room at the inn, and marvelled how a close shave and fine suit of clothes could make an ugly old priest look like a man of distinction. He laughed at himself, but knew there was little time to waste. His coin would last only a few more days and he had much to do.

With that in mind, he headed out into the city to continue his search. The streets were far more welcoming to a well-dressed gentleman. Aethelman allowed the Stone's presence to guide him along the twisting streets that buzzed with activity. It was not long before he found himself standing before the palace, and staring at a ghost.

# CHAPTER 44

ADALHAID

ADALHAID WALKED FROM the palace on her way to the university, torn between excitement and guilt. Two hours of lectures, and then the rest of the morning was to be spent in the clinic with Jakob. The prospect of seeing him always brightened her day, and she could no longer deny the feelings she was developing for him.

She had only gone a few paces when she felt eyes on her. She looked across the square in front of the palace and spotted a distinguished-looking old man staring at her. Her first reaction was to ignore the unwelcome gaze of a dirty old lecher—there were many of them in the palace and her Northlander complexion perfectly fit with the Ruripathians' idea of aesthetics. They thought a title and money automatically conferred irresistible charm and impossibly good looks, and took at least thirty years off their age. However, there was something familiar about this one.

She gave him a second look, but from that distance, she could find nothing more than a passing familiarity. He waved, and she stopped. Ordinarily she would ignore it and continue, but there was something about him that urged her to investigate. He had a bewildered look on his face, such that she wondered if he needed medical attention. She took a handful of steps toward him, and realised it was Aethelman. The realisation was followed by a wave of relief. There were so many questions he could answer for her.

'Aethelman?' she said. He looked at her oddly, and it made her wonder if it was a stranger who merely appeared similar. She had never seen the old priest in such fine clothing.

'Adalhaid?' he said. 'Is it really you?'

'Of course it is,' Adalhaid said. 'Why wouldn't it be? What brings you to Elzburg?'

'But Adalhaid,' he said, making her wonder if he had lost his wits, 'I thought you were dead.'

'What do you mean?' she said.

'We were told you were killed on the road south, after you left Leondorf.'

'No, I wasn't, obviously. Why would anyone say such a thing?'

Aethelman's eyes widened. 'So Wulfric wouldn't follow you.'

Adalhaid smiled. 'What do you mean? Wulfric? Wulfric's…' The smile faded from her face.

'Wulfric's alive and well,' Aethelman said. 'At least I think so. I haven't seen him in months. He killed Donato when he heard you were dead. But you won't have heard any of this, will you?'

Adalhaid shook her head. 'I've heard nothing. I've seen Rodulf around the palace, but I've avoided him. I thought I'd not heard anything from Leondorf because all my friends were dead, but they thought I was dead? Wulfric thought I was dead?' She felt her head swim.

Aethelman nodded his head, and related the story of how Donato and the ambassador had conspired to have Adalhaid return to the south, and how Donato had taken the chance to finally get his revenge on Wulfric for taking Rodulf's eye and his dream of being a warrior.

'He blamed Donato for your—for thinking you were dead.'

'And the ambassador,' Adalhaid said, her voice drifting as her mind put the pieces together. 'Ambassador Urschel was murdered by a Northlander not long after he returned to the city. I remember the day. I remember thinking I saw Wulfric on the street, but thought it ridiculous. It was him, wasn't it?' A wave of despair welled up and threatened to swallow her.

'He must have come straight here after fleeing Leondorf. He killed some soldiers as well. He was a wanted man, last I heard.'

'Where is he now?'

Aethelman shook his head. 'I've no idea. The last I saw of him, he was galloping out of the village like a legion of draugar were chasing him.'

'How am I going to find him?'

Aethelman shrugged. 'I don't know. He could be anywhere. If he still lives. Did they catch anyone for killing the ambassador?'

'I don't know,' Adalhaid said. 'There was a fuss at the time, but it all died down very quickly. I didn't pay much attention. I never liked the ambassador. Aethelman, how am I going to find him?'

'He has no reason to come back. Adalhaid, he thinks you're dead. He may well be too, by now.'

Somewhere across the city, a bell rang out. Adalhaid could not focus her thoughts. It was too much for her to take in. The bell imposed itself, and reminded her she had somewhere to be.

'I have to go,' she said absently. 'We can talk later. This evening. Where will you be?'

'I'm at the White Horse,' Aethelman said. 'I'm staying under the name "Gustav dal Aetheldorf". Call on me there.'

She walked away, so dazed she did not even say goodbye.

❈

## ADALHAID

Time passed in a blur for Adalhaid. She couldn't recall anything specific since meeting Aethelman in the square. The thought that Wulfric still lived tore her apart inside. She had lasted only minutes at the clinic before having to make her excuses and leave. She had not been able to look Jakob in the eye.

*Wulfric is alive.* She kept repeating it to herself, but it seemed too much to believe. Too much to hope for. Through the turmoil, she realised it made little difference. He thought she was dead, and he had disappeared. It was a big world, and she could easily spend the rest of her life searching for him without ever getting close. Accepting that seemed like taking the easy way out, though. If Wulfric thought for a second that she was alive, she knew he would search for her until his dying breath.

Where would she even start? It would mean throwing away everything she had worked for. She swung violently between deciding to pack her bag there and then, and putting the foolish notion of ever being able to find him from her head. Would a life spent in search of her great love be a waste if she never found him? It sounded like one of the old tragic epics, and the thought made her laugh. It had never occurred to her that her life might become one of them, and it was as ridiculous a notion as it was painful to consider.

She had been so caught up in her thoughts, she had all but forgotten about Aethelman. There might be more he could tell her about Wulfric, but that was not all. Now that he was there, she felt like she would not be able to continue if he did not explain her strange healing talent. He might even be able to teach her how to use it.

She took her cloak and headed toward the White Horse. It surprised her that he was staying there; it was usually the choice of wealthy merchants visiting the city. However, his clothes had been equally surprising. She had never seen him wear anything other than his old grey priestly robes. She wrapped herself up in her cloak and set off.

'Adalhaid!'

She froze mid-step at the voice. It was Jakob.

'Adalhaid, are you all right?'

'Yes, Jakob, I'm fine,' she said. 'I'm sorry for running out on the clinic.'

'That doesn't matter,' he said. 'I just wanted to be sure you're all right. I'd have come to check on you sooner, but you know how the clinic can be. I thought we could take a walk in the park tonight.' He reached out to take her hand.

Adalhaid pulled hers back. He looked surprised.

'I'm sorry, Jakob. Something has come up, something from my past. I have to deal with it, and I can't do this,' she gestured to his hand, 'until I do.'

She walked away feeling more in turmoil than ever, leaving him standing nonplussed on the street.

❈

## ADALHAID

Adalhaid could see why the White Horse was popular with wealthy men. It was luxurious and heavily populated with servants, and reminded her of the Markgraf's private apartments in the palace. She announced herself at the reception and went into the lounge to wait for Aethelman. The conversation had made her uncomfortable: The receptionist had politely been trying to work out whether he should send her straight up to Aethelman's room, as he clearly did with the majority of ladies calling to the inn, or into the lounge. She shrugged off the indignation as she sat there, but could not help make sideways glances at the other women present and wonder if they were there for business purposes.

Aethelman appeared, looking a little sheepish and uncomfortable in his assumed persona.

'The clothes suit you,' Adalhaid said. 'It's long past time you treated yourself.'

'Thank you,' Aethelman said, sitting down, 'but as with all my madness, there is a reason behind it. I've followed something here, and I wanted to be able to move around the city without complication. Looking prosperous is the easiest way to do that.'

'What is it?'

'It's a very long story, and I've been looking for it for some time. Suffice it to say, I've found it. I think our old friend, Rodulf, has it.'

'Rodulf?'

'Indeed. It's a strange thing, and I won't try to explain it. I can tell when the object is near. I saw him today, not long after I met you, and I could practically feel it. I'm not quite sure how he got it, but he has it and I need to get it back from him.'

'How?'

'Ha,' Aethelman said. 'That's the big question. I'd hoped I might find it in a hole in the ground, but instead that one-eyed rat has it. I don't think he knows what it's capable of, and I have to get it from him before he finds out. But enough about my problems. How are you? What I told you in the square must have come as a great shock.'

'That's an understatement,' Adalhaid said, 'and I have to admit I still don't know what to do. I was just starting to come to terms with everything and move on with my life.' She smiled. 'I'm training to be a physician. It's hard, but I really love it.'

'I'm sorry for dumping all that on you,' Aethelman said. 'I wish I hadn't said anything, but I was so surprised to see you that it tumbled out of me.'

'It's hard to believe everyone thinks I'm dead,' Adalhaid said, laughing sadly.

'There weren't very many people left to fool,' Aethelman said. 'There are so few people in Leondorf now who were born there.'

'What should I do, Aethelman?' Adalhaid said.

'I have no idea where Wulfric is,' Aethelman said. 'He wasn't killed when you thought he was, but after that, who knows what happened to him? What I do know is that Wulfric would want you to be happy, and that a life spent searching for him with no guarantee you will ever find him will not bring you happiness. Hold on to what you have here. Find happiness. If the gods do not intend for you to be together, it won't happen, no matter how hard you try.'

'Is that what you think? That the gods don't want us to be together?'

Aethelman frowned. 'I don't know. But he would want you to be happy. Are you happy here? Happy training to be a physician?'

She nodded.

'It's a decision only you can make, Adalhaid, but if you can find a good, happy life here…'

She nodded. The thought of searching for Wulfric had seemed like madness, but rejecting the idea had made her feel like she was letting him down, that she didn't love him enough. To hear someone else say it eased the pain it caused her.

'Perhaps one day he'll find his way back to me,' she said.

'I hope so,' Aethelman said.

Adalhaid took a deep breath to clear her mind. 'There's something else I want to ask you about,' she said. 'I think I'm a witch.'

# CHAPTER 45

## RODULF

AS LUCK WOULD have it, all the lords Rodulf had to visit were based close to Elzburg and each of them involved bribes, so he was back in the palace the following evening. He had been able to think of little other than his last interview with the Markgraf. If he could make the Markgraf do what he said, the possibilities were limitless. He could allow the Markgraf to take all the risks, and if successful, Rodulf could reap all the benefit. Perhaps he could even have the Markgraf appoint him his heir. It was an outrageous thought, but with the Stone, he didn't think it beyond the bounds of possibility. All he had to do was work out how to extend its influence over him, and see how far he could push it.

It continued to fill his mind, with only the briefest of interruptions that evening when in bed with the kitchen girl. She was becoming a familiar feature, but was too far beneath him to be good for anything more than a tumble. He couldn't allow her to distract him from the bigger fish. As he lay there, he thought through the social conventions to which he would have to adhere. They could be made to work for him, if he was clever about it. His mind had returned to the Markgraf and the Stone when she jumped out of bed.

'I have to go,' she said, pulling a shift over her head. 'I have to prepare broth for the Lady Aenlin. She's been very unwell since her brother died. There're three physicians looking after her now. They must be very worried. Poor little mite.'

'Poor indeed,' he said absently. A thought occurred to him. 'You do that every day?'

'Five times a day,' she said, as she leaned over the bed to kiss him again. 'It's all they have me doing now. I'm the only one who knows how she likes it.'

'Good for you,' he said, a plan beginning to take shape in his head. 'Come back when you're done. I'm not finished with you yet.'

She giggled as she walked to the door.

'And bring one of those fruit pastries,' he said, but his thoughts were firmly fixed on the way he was going to take complete control of the Markgraf. He wondered where he could get his hands on some poison.

❈

## ADALHAID

'A witch?' Aethelman said.

'I can do things,' Adalhaid said. 'I can heal people. Mend cuts, knit bones. I don't know how, but I can do it.'

Aethelman laughed. 'That doesn't make you a witch, but we had better keep our voices down nonetheless. The south is a dangerous place to have this sort of gift.'

Adalhaid's eyes widened. She hoped she hadn't already spoken too loudly. She looked around, but the lounge had emptied out and there was no one near.

'The things you can do can be learned—but some people are born with the ability, as you seem to be. No one knows why. They are among the skills the Grey Priests learn in their training. I'm ashamed to admit it's been some time since I've given it a thought, but I've long suspected you had that ability. I'd all but forgotten about it; so much has happened to distract me from it. There were other reasons I chose to turn a blind eye. Had I fully investigated it, I would have been obligated to send you to the Hermitage for training, but I always knew you would hate that so I let it go. Often the skill fades with time if it's not practised. I thought it might be the same with you. It appears I'm wrong.'

'What is it? How does it work?'

'What is the sun? How does it move through the sky? If anyone really knew for sure, it would all be so much easier.' He sighed and sank back into the armchair. For a moment, the only sound was the crackling of the fire.

'It's the product of the energy of the gods, a gift for some and a burden for others. Both, at times. The energy is everywhere. Stronger in places, weaker in others. It's called the Fount most commonly, but there are other, older names too. Some people can draw on it, intentionally or otherwise. It affects them all in different ways, drawing out innate talents and abilities, and amplifying them to the point where they become magical. To be able to do it without training is a gift from the gods. Your ability will be far, far stronger than that of someone who has been trained to it.'

'A gift?' Adalhaid said.

'Or a curse, depending on what it is,' Aethelman said with a cheeky grin. 'I think I'd call yours a gift, though. In this land, it's not so straightforward. There are men here who would burn you for it, no matter how benevolent it is.'

'I've seen them,' she said. 'Intelligenciers, they're called.'

Aethelman's face darkened. 'You need to be careful. You cannot use it here.' His voice became feverish, manic almost. 'You have to promise me you won't use it.'

Adalhaid nodded. 'I'll be careful,' she said. 'How does it work? I need to know how it works if I'm to keep it under control.'

Aethelman, seemingly placated, nodded. 'In essence, it's a product of desire. When a person is able to draw on the Fount, it will sometimes give effect to what they want. People tend to have a talent in one particular area. It can be anything, and it can take many different forms. Wulfric, for instance—' Aethelman stopped himself.

Adalhaid's eyes widened.

'That's not important,' he said. 'For you it seems to be healing. Desire is the key. When you really want something, your gift will draw on the Fount and give effect to that desire.'

'Slow down,' Adalhaid said. 'The Fount? How do I find it?'

'It's everywhere, surrounding us, inside us. It's not infinite, though. It can be exhausted, but only in very extreme circumstances, and that is not something the likes of us usually need worry about. Only those who can draw on it in the most powerful way need to be concerned about causing themselves injury, and it has been centuries since many people like that existed. Few enough have any ability at all. You'll get cold and tired like you've never known, before the gift will put you in danger. Stop if you feel these coming on, and you should be fine. Dizziness and nausea are common too, especially when you first start using it.'

'You said Wulfric has this too?'

'After a fashion. Your gift is healing. His is different. Jorundyr gave Wulfric his gift on his pilgrimage. Wulfric's gift is killing.'

Adalhaid blanched. 'Killing?'

'His gift makes him stronger, faster. It dulls fatigue and pain. It is something I had heard of, but have never seen. It's somewhat of a poisoned chalice. They are far from invincible. Warriors always seek out fame, and killing one of Jorundyr's Chosen always ensures that.' Aethelman frowned. 'I'm sorry. You probably didn't want to hear that.'

Adalhaid smiled. 'No. Not really. But there's nothing to be gained by dwelling on it.'

'For me it's always been harder to use than not to use,' Aethelman said. 'It requires focus and a strong desire. Eliminate one of those and you won't draw on the Fount. At least, you won't achieve anything with it.'

'How can I not desire to heal my patient?' Adalhaid said, her voice growing frustrated.

'*Strong desire*,' Aethelman said. 'You can desire it, just not so much as to draw on the Fount. Learning how much is too much is the trick though. That's what your challenge will be, if you hope to make a life in the South. You'll have to learn how to shut it out, to turn your back on it. Otherwise one day you'll make a mistake and will be found out.'

Adalhaid took a deep breath. Wulfric, Jakob, a talent that could get her burned at the stake—there were moments she thought it would overwhelm her. When she was a child, Wulfric's company had been her safe harbour when she needed one. She was a ship adrift in a storm now. If she was to remain afloat it would be all down to her. She let out a short laugh. She had never even been on a boat.

'I can do that,' she said.

'You'll have to. It will take time, and you'll have to be extra careful until you do,' Aethelman said. 'At the Hermitage we spent years learning how to, then years learning how to temper it to our needs. From the sound of it, your power is already greater than many achieve in a lifetime of practice.'

'Can you help me?'

'Of course, Adalhaid. Of course I will.'

❀

## Wulfric

Wulfric had not experienced a regime change before, and had expected Torona to be in ruins, with the charred remains of buildings paying testimony to the events that had unfolded. Were it not for Varada assuring them that dal Valeriano had seized power, killed his half-brother and a great many of his supporters, and ended the war because the old duke's territorial claims had died with him, Wulfric would not have known anything had happened. The city looked no different to when they had left. Wulfric couldn't imagine a man allowing power to be taken from him without a fight the devastation of which would be plain for all to see.

They decided to remain some distance from the city while Jagovere and Varada went ahead to scout. They made a small camp out of sight of Torona and away from the roads. That done, Wulfric sat on the ground leaning against his saddle, throwing small pebbles at a larger one. The others tried to doze in the sunlight for the few hours until Jagovere returned.

'We've had a bit of luck,' Jagovere said as he gave Enderlain a kick to wake him. 'Dal Valeriano is travelling through the duchy to ensure the support of his nobles.'

Enderlain rolled over, but remained asleep.

'Where is he now?' Wulfric said.

'No idea,' Jagovere said, 'but we know where he's going, and most importantly, he's not holed up in the city surrounded by walls and soldiers, which is good news for us.'

'Best we get going then,' Wulfric said, standing stiffly from the spot he had occupied for the previous hours.

'No time to pop into the city for some fun first?' Walt said, to a number of disapproving glares. 'No, didn't think so.'

❀

## Aethelman

Aethelman opened his eyes and smiled. The number of mornings he had awoken in such comfort were few indeed, but it was something he could happily grow used to. He took a deep breath and stretched, then widened his eyes in panic. He couldn't feel the Stone's draw.

For so long now, Aethelman had headed toward Elzburg with the absolute confidence it was where he would find the Stone. He could feel it, drawing him ever closer. He had thought it would only be a matter of days before he discovered its precise location. Compared to finding such a small object in the great expanse of the world, recovering it once he had located it had barely seemed like an issue.

He lay on his soft feather mattress and concentrated. Once he had learned what to look for, even when he had been in the Northlands he could feel it call to him. For the past days its song had been like a drumbeat in his head, but now there was only silence. His heart raced as he considered the possibilities. Had he been on the wrong path all along? Might his belief that he was being pulled toward it have been nothing more than a symptom of an old man losing his wits?

He took a deep breath and tried to calm himself. It could be sealed in something that lessened or cut off its call, or it could have moved. He focussed his thoughts and searched out its sound. He could hear nothing but the sound of his heart beating, but gradually it was joined by another regular pulse. The Stone was distant now, but he took comfort in the fact that he could still hear it. He had become used to its almost deafening presence when it was so near, he had grown desensitised to its more distant call.

It told him much, however. Whoever had it kept it with them, which meant they might be using it. He could only hope they would not have learned how to use it to its full potential. The question that remained was whether it would come back to the city, or if he would have to continue his chase. He pulled the blanket up to his chin and thought for a moment. If it was the chase, it could surely wait until after a late breakfast.

❀

## AETHELMAN

Bacon, sausages, eggs, potato hash, tomatoes, fresh coffee, toast, and at least a dozen choices of jam, several from fruits of which he had never even heard: Aethelman could easily see why most of the merchants patronising the White Horse were of a portly disposition. His own wire-thin frame would quickly pad out if he remained there, and he could certainly see the attraction of that lifestyle. He dismissed the momentary guilt of his excesses—he had lived an ascetic life up to that point, and surely not even the gods would begrudge a man a little comfort in his twilight years.

Duty was never far removed from his mind, however, and part of it was now dedicated to listening out for the pulsing song of the Stone. As dangerous an object as it was, it raised so many fascinating questions that remained unanswered, and might always. He had grown better at sensing the Stone the longer he had been aware of its presence. His skill was so precise now that he could feel it move, even over small distances. At first, he had been encouraged by the development, thinking it would make his job easier. That was followed by concern. It meant that Rodulf was using it, to some degree at least. He had felt it move out of the city, then back again. Its pulse waxed and waned, but it always returned to Elzburg, always to the palace.

❧

## ADALHAID

'Adalhaid.'

She stopped on the spot, unable to pretend she hadn't heard Jakob calling her. Things had been so awkward between them that an encounter was easier avoided. The last thing she wanted was to be cruel to him, but she still didn't know which way to turn. She couldn't deny she was attracted to him, but her feelings for Wulfric were still strong, and the chance that he was alive made her more confused than she had ever been.

'Good morning,' she said. She smiled, but it was forced, and Jakob's face was stern.

'Do you remember what we spoke about? After the girl with the injured leg?' he said.

'Yes, of course.'

His face was very serious, and Adalhaid grew concerned.

'You took my advice to heart, didn't you?'

She nodded. 'Why? What's wrong?'

'Nothing,' Strellis said. 'I just wanted to make sure. You can't be too careful.'

'Don't worry,' Adalhaid said. 'I'm not a fool. I know the dangers.'

His expression eased and he smiled, but said nothing more before disappearing into the treatment room, leaving Adalhaid with her thoughts.

She had not lied when she said she knew the dangers. The consequences of being caught terrified her. But how could she go through her life knowing she had turned her back on a gift that could ease the suffering of so many? It was the ultimate submission to selfishness and cowardice. She would not be ruled by either.

# CHAPTER 46

ADALHAID

THE MOOD IN the palace in the days following Petr's death was bleak. She hadn't even seen the Markgraf, who had kept to his rooms, and had not had the opportunity to offer her condolences. She spent more of her time at the university or the clinic for no other reason than to be away from the stark mourning atmosphere. She hurried in and out, not interested in having to deal with any of the sycophants who would try to console with her, in the hope that word of their concern would get back to the Markgraf. She was nearing her own rooms when she was intercepted by a valet.

'The Markgraf would like to see you,' he said, before leading her toward the Markgraf's private office behind his audience hall.

He sat behind his desk in a darkened office. Cloths had been draped over the magelamps and she could not clearly see his face.

'Thank you for coming, Adalhaid,' he said.

'I'm so, so sorry, my lord. I wanted to come sooner, but I knew you needed time to yourself.'

'It's a difficult thing to bear. First his mother, now him. But Aenlin still lives, and she is all I have. Petr is gone—' he choked back a sob '—and there is nothing we can do about that. Aenlin is my life, and all that I do is for her. She and Petr were inseparable and the coming days and weeks are going to be very hard on her. She adores you. I doubt she could have loved her mother more, and I have a request to make of you.'

'I'll help however I can, my lord.'

'I know we've done our best to leave you as much time to pursue your studies as we can, but for the next few weeks I'd ask you to put them on hold and be here for Aenlin whenever she needs you. I wanted to ask you first before I did anything, but I will speak to your professors to make sure it isn't a problem.'

She knew there was no choice to make. The wound of loss was still open on her heart. Anything she could do to ease the suffering of another, she would do.

'It would be my privilege,' she said.

## PROFESSOR KENGIL

'You're certain you didn't mention my name?' Kengil said. She probed the man's kidney area with her fingers.

'No, Doctor, I didn't,' he said.

'And you didn't say anything at all about your condition?'

'No, Doctor. Only that I'd been poorly for a while. I let her work out the rest for herself, just like you told me.'

'Good,' Kengil said.

'Am I cured?' the man asked.

Kengil stepped back and looked him over. His breathing was better. Almost normal. All the inflammation of his kidneys had subsided and his colour looked far better.

'I'll have to study another urine sample under the microscope to be sure,' Kengil said, 'but it looks as though your symptoms are going away.'

The man beamed a smile. 'That's the best news I've ever had, Doctor. Thank you. She was just as good as you promised she would be.'

*She's better than good*, Kengil thought. If the urine sample showed no trace of blood, she would have the proof she needed to take to the Intelligenciers.

## AETHELMAN

Aethelman knew his task was a dangerous one, and the temptation to seek Adalhaid's help was strong. An ally in a hostile land was always a welcome thing, but he could not put her at risk unless it was absolutely necessary. That time might come, but first he wanted to exhaust all other options.

Noble courts were open affairs. So long as you looked like you belonged there, almost everyone would assume you did. Any free man was at liberty to come to the palace in order to seek audience with his overlord, but some would draw more attention from the palace guards than others. Dressed as he was, Aethelman had no difficulty walking into the palace, announcing himself as Gustav dal Aetheldorf to a guard who paid him little attention. It continued to amaze Aethelman what could be achieved with nothing more than a good suit and a dash of attitude.

The palace was where the Stone continually drew him. It moved about, but it always returned to the palace. His fear that it was being used was tempered by the fact that if someone unleashed its full power, everyone in the city would know about it.

He wandered about the public areas of the palace for the better part of the morning, trying to home in on the pull that tugged on the very fibre of his being, but at so close a proximity, it was difficult. At times, it felt as though the Stone was everywhere. Just as he was about to give up for the morning, he spotted the man he was looking for. He was tall and slender, dressed in fine black clothes, and walked with the swagger of a professional swordsman. Aethelman could feel the Stone move with him. The eyepatch was still there, and Aethelman found it shamefully satisfying that Rodulf hadn't been able to regrow his eye with help from the Stone. He wondered briefly how Rodulf had come to possess it and when, but it didn't matter. He had it, and Aethelman had to get it back.

# CHAPTER 47

WULFRIC

THEY HEADED WEST, along the road Varada assured them would bring them to dal Valeriano. Wulfric had given up being suspicious of her. There was nothing about her conduct that said she was leading them into a trap, and she had already let numerous opportunities to kill them all pass her by. They travelled through farmland and wilderness, arriving at a small village early on the second day of their journey. The place was starting to come to life, and they were greeted with curious stares. They had maintained their disguise as being travelling merchants, but the reality was that warriors always stood out—particularly when, with the exception of Walt, they were all fair of complexion.

'Why are they ignoring us?' Wulfric said.

At first he thought it nothing more than the normal reaction of people unaccustomed to seeing strangers, but the village was on a main road west so the locals should have viewed their arrival as an opportunity to make money. When they stopped in a small square surrounded by beige cut-stone buildings, no one approached them.

'Who knows? Who cares? Anyone see anything resembling a tavern?' Conrat said. 'I'm parched.'

Enderlain mumbled something obscene in agreement.

'No,' Wulfric said. 'Something's not right.' A chill ran over his skin, reminding him of the sensation he had felt when he encountered the belek.

'Seems to have got quiet all of a sudden,' Enderlain said.

'Perhaps we should keep going,' Jagovere said. 'Doesn't look like they take kindly to visitors here.'

'I think it's too late for that,' Wulfric said.

A group of horsemen had appeared at the far end of the square. He looked back to see a similar-sized group appear at the end they had come in through.

'I can't help but think these fellows were waiting for us,' Jagovere said.

'How could they have known?' Wulfric said.

'Perhaps someone spotted me in Torona,' Jagovere said.

'Why not deal with you there and then?' Wulfric said.

'Who knows?' Varada said. 'We can discuss it later.'

'If there is a later,' Enderlain said with a light-hearted and fatalistic laugh.

Two of the men at the far end of the square rode forward, but stopped a safe distance from them.

'I am Alfonse, Sherriff of Torona. In the name of Duke Almar dal Valeriano y Torona, I order you to throw down your weapons.'

Wulfric rode forward, pleased to see them urge their horses back a few paces to keep their distance. 'Or what?' he said.

'Or we will use force to take you into custody.' The man spoke with a confidence that his body language failed to back up.

Wulfric looked back to the others, but they remained silent. They all knew that to allow themselves be taken into custody was as good as cutting their own throats.

Wulfric turned back to the horseman. 'Please do.'

The constable looked confused. 'Please do what?'

'Use force,' Wulfric said, drawing his sabre and spurring his horse forward.

The constable's face was a picture of panic for a moment, until he gathered his wits and ordered his men to attack. The small square filled with the noise of men shouting and horses galloping on the sun-baked ground. He had barely drawn his sword by the time Wulfric reached him. It seemed he expected Wulfric to stop and fight, but Wulfric kept going toward the men behind him, slashing as he passed. He felt the blade slide across hard leather, then grip and cut through into soft flesh. He pulled it free with a splatter of blood, and roared at the men before him. They hesitated at seeing their commander cut down, but were smart enough to realise Wulfric was too close to turn and flee from him.

They formed a wall of flesh and steel, knee touching knee. Wulfric could see they expected him to swerve off to the side. He drove his horse toward the centre. He could feel its hesitation, but it obeyed his commands. He drew his dagger, guiding the horse with his knees, and fixed his gaze on the man in the centre. He looked confident, but as Wulfric grew ever closer the confidence leaked away. He pulled his horse hard to the side at the last moment. Wulfric plunged through the gap, lashing out with his dagger to the left and his sabre to the right. Wulfric felt the blades connect, and heard two screams. Then he was past them.

Wulfric wheeled around quickly, and got his first look at how things had unfolded behind him. Enderlain had followed him and dispatched the man who had ridden forward with the constable, and was finishing off the third of the men who Wulfric had ridden through. There were six others at the far side of the square. The others had engaged them, but Varada had hung back. Wulfric wondered why as he turned his horse and rode back into the square to help his comrades. Did she expect them to shoulder the burden of danger and deliver her safely to kill dal Valeriano?

It was three against four by the time Wulfric got there, although Sander had dropped back with a cut to his sword arm. The Estranzans, having seen the fate of their constable and comrades, took advantage of Sander's withdrawal and turned to run. Jagovere hacked one of them down, the final three men making it to the square's exit before Wulfric and Enderlain cut them off and pounced. They died easily, as men fleeing their attackers always did.

Wulfric and Enderlain returned to the square, where the others were already checking the dead men and their horses for anything that might be of value.

'I don't suppose you kept one of them alive,' Jagovere said.

Wulfric looked at Enderlain, and they both shrugged.

'So much for finding out how they knew where we were,' Jagovere said. 'Still, nothing we can do about it now.'

'It makes no difference,' Walt said, his gaze firmly fixed on Varada. 'The answer's obvious. That bitch didn't so much as lift a finger to help.'

'If you had needed my help to deal with some constables, then you clearly aren't the right men for the task ahead,' she said, completely unfazed by the accusation being levelled at her.

'She's worked for Valeriano before,' Walt continued. 'What's to say she isn't still taking his coin?'

'She could have betrayed us at Torona,' Wulfric said, 'where a fight would have been far harder. Or not bothered to help us at all.'

'Who's to say the Darvarosian didn't pay her to lead us into a trap?' Conrat said. He rarely said anything, and only when he thought it important.

With the weight of opinion turning against her, Varada backed her horse away.

'I could have left you to die on the plain,' she said. 'I could have poisoned your water. I could have cut your throats while you slept. I could have paid a dozen men to slaughter you on any number of occasions. If I had wanted you dead, you would be dead. Be very sure of that. I have killed men smarter, stronger, and braver than any of you. I wouldn't have arranged for a handful of badly armed constables to try and arrest you. What type of fool do you take me for?'

Conrat blushed, and said nothing further, but Walt continued to glower at her.

'It's more likely we were spotted in Torona,' Jagovere said. 'They could have been tracking us ever since. With a bit of luck, that will be the last of it before we get to dal Valeriano.' He looked around and nodded at a sign swinging gently in the breeze. 'How about we have that drink now?'

❊

## WALT

'I'm taking a piss,' Walt said. He left the others at the tavern table without another word and walked stiffly toward the back in search of a privy. He was greeted by the stench of stale urine when he walked outside, but he ignored it and breathed deeply to still his nerves, which had been on the point of breaking ever since they had gotten through the attack. That the finger of blame had not been pointed at him yet felt like a miracle. Surely his guilt must have been as obvious on his face as his nose. The question was what to do now. Break and run? Act like nothing had happened? Were the constables the only men sent after them? If they were, then perhaps he might be able to get away with having warned dal Valeriano.

The word *treachery* sprung to mind when he thought of it, but he refused to accept it. He had to look out for himself. No one else would. The Company was gone, and at his age he was unlikely to get taken on by another. He cursed as he tried to work out what to do next. With nothing springing to mind, he took several more breaths and gave his eyes a moment to adjust from the tavern's gloom, then looked around for the privy ditch. His absence would be noted if he took too long.

The door opened and closed behind him. Walt spun around and reached for his sword.

'Easy, friend,' the man who had come out said. 'Just looking to take a piss.'

Walt relaxed, but the man paused and looked at him with an expression of recognition that was theatrical, and obviously contrived.

'Walt?' he said.

'What of it?' Walt said, his hand drifting back toward the handle of his dagger.

'The duke sends his regards.' The man doffed his hat. He held his hands up defensively as soon as he saw Walt make to draw his weapon.

'The duke would like to thank you for your warning and make you an offer.'

'He made a right mess of things,' Walt said. 'I expect he hoped I'd end up dead too, so he wouldn't have to pay up. Well, I will be dead if them inside find out I sent that message, so you better be here to pay up.'

The man shrugged. 'We didn't think anything worthwhile would come from it, but it was worth a try. The duke will make good his debt to you, but will need some more help.'

'He'll have to pay for it.' Walt relaxed again, and let go of his dagger, but continued to regard the man suspiciously.

'Of course.'

'What's the offer?' he said. 'You already know where we are.'

'It's where we *want* you to be that's the issue right now. Ten miles or so up the road, you'll come to a fork. Make sure you and your friends take the right turn, and follow the road toward Belroso heading north. It's the fastest route toward the duke, so you should have little difficulty making a case for it. Even the Darvarosian whore will agree with you.'

'How much?' Walt said.

The man pulled a purse from his belt. 'One hundred crowns now, another hundred after.'

It was enough to buy him a small patch of land, or put a down payment on something a little more substantial. Walt licked his lips, but tempting as it was, there was a glaring question.

'After what?' he said.

The man raised an eyebrow and smiled. He took a strip of red cloth from his pocket and handed it to Walt.

'Wear this somewhere about your person. Somewhere visible, so you can be recognised. You won't be harmed, but you'd be well advised to stay out of the way.'

Walt hesitated for a moment, then took it.

'Can I inform the duke you agree to the arrangement?' the man said.

'One-fifty now. The same after.'

The man smiled, and took a smaller pouch from his pocket. He tossed it over and Walt caught it.

'Tell His Grace he has a deal.'

# CHAPTER 48

WULFRIC

'YOU'RE LOOKING PARTICULARLY dashing today, Walt,' Jagovere said. 'Red is very definitely your colour.'

Walt tugged at the red sash wrapped around his waist, the ends of which were draped over his thigh. 'Sword belt's chafing,' he said.

'Heat, sweat, middle age spread,' Jagovere said. 'It all plays its part.'

'Piss off,' Walt said.

'Lighten up,' Jagovere said as he stopped his horse. 'Which way now?' He gestured to the fork in the road before them.

Walt opened his mouth.

'The northern road will get us to dal Valeriano faster,' Varada said. 'I've passed through this area before.'

Walt closed his mouth and thought for a moment. 'Anything that puts the bastard in his grave sooner sounds like the right choice to me.'

'Where does the southern road go?' Wulfric said. 'Other than south,' he added, before Jagovere could state the obvious.

'It passes through a couple of villages, then joins back with this one,' Varada said. 'The road is far longer.'

'If there's anyone waiting for us, the northern road is the obvious choice,' Wulfric said. 'We should take the southern.'

'We've no reason to believe he knows we're coming,' Walt said. 'No reason for there to be anyone waiting for us.' He involuntarily glanced at the red cloth tied around his waist. 'Jagovere said it's most likely the constables followed us from Torona. Why make life harder than it needs to be?'

Wulfric looked to Jagovere, who shrugged.

'He's right,' Jagovere said. 'The constables must have followed us from Torona. There's no other way. They know the land better so they could have gotten ahead of us easily enough. I want to get home as much as any of you. Right now I can't think of a good reason not to take the northern road. Anyone disagree?'

No one said anything, so Jagovere looked back to Wulfric, his eyebrows raised.

'The northern road it is,' Wulfric said.

❧

## ADALHAID

Adalhaid sat on the chair by Aenlin's bed, watching her sleep. It had come mercifully, without any assistance from the Markgraf's physician, but it did little to ease Adalhaid's worry. The physician sat on the other side of the bed, maintaining a vigil even more strict than her own. Between him and a colleague, not a minute of Aenlin's day went unwatched. They worried Adalhaid, though. They were the type of old-fashioned physician Jakob often complained about—entrenched in practices that should have long since been abandoned. However, as a student physician it was not her place to comment on men who had nearly a century's experience between them.

Since Petr's death, Aenlin had not left her bed, doing nothing during her waking hours other than sobbing beneath her bedsheets. She had to be force-fed, and even then, only gruel. That morning the physicians had noticed she was feverish. Adalhaid was hopeful that all the sleeping draughts they had given her were the cause, and that it would pass after a night of natural sleep.

She had thought of adding her own talent to the mix, but under the watch of two such senior physicians the risk was too great. Their techniques might be outdated, but with such an important patient they would notice any unexplained changes. She was content to observe for the time being. There was no true illness, only the trauma of losing someone so important he felt like part of her. It was difficult, but Adalhaid of all people knew surviving it was possible. Children were resilient, and she was confident Aenlin would improve with a little more time. If her condition worsened, she could try and steal a moment alone with the child and give her recovery a magical nudge in the right direction. Until then, she would wait.

❊

## Aethelman

After a couple of days of bumbling about the palace, the guards had come to recognise Aethelman on sight, and one or two of the less surly ones even acknowledged him as he passed. As this familiarity developed, he started to stray farther into areas of the palace where he was not necessarily permitted to be.

The way the Stone moved around meant that Rodulf kept it on his person, which left only two ways to take it from him: when he was asleep, or when he was not paying attention. Aethelman didn't particularly like either of his alternatives, but given the choice, sneaking into Rodulf's rooms while he slept seemed like the best option.

He was not born to be a spy, and every moment he spent in the palace increased the risk that Rodulf would see and recognise him. He hoped the changes in clothing, coupled with a beard he was developing to the point that it could be styled in the southern fashion, would make him no more than vaguely familiar if they did bump into one another, but the danger was real and largely unavoidable. He observed from the shadows and made a mental list of the things that would aid him. Rodulf being drunk was one. The deep sleep of an inebriated man was perhaps Aethelman's best chance, although on each of the nights he had followed Rodulf back to his apartment he had been joined by a girl from the kitchens, and it was clear to anyone passing down the corridor outside that they were getting little sleep.

He would draw too much attention if he spent the whole night lurking outside, and likewise if he was constantly walking up and down it. There was only so long he could wait before he made his move, and he knew there would only be one chance. As much as he knew this was the task that had been handed to him, his great test, he prayed to the gods for help and guidance. Despite the great comfort he was living in, he had not been able to shake off the exhaustion that had built during his search over the previous months. He had little appetite for the rich and plentiful food that would once have tantalised him, preferring bread, soup, and water. As loath as he was to admit it, the signals his body was sending him were clear. Time was running out.

✤

## Wulfric

Estranza had been dry, sunny, and hot on every day that Wulfric had spent there. He had grown so used to it that he had come to assume it was like that all the time. It felt odd to see dark grey clouds roll in from the mountains distant on the western horizon, but before long, the day grew dull, and the clouds opened.

It rained heavily, fat drops of water driving straight down from above. The ground, hard after so much sunshine, quickly flooded and the road looked more like a shallow river. They were soaked in moments, and had to slow their pace as parts of the road started to wash away.

'I'm really growing to dislike this country,' Jagovere said, having to raise his voice to be heard over the teeming rain.

'You're not the only one,' Walt said. 'I'm getting too old for this carry-on.'

Wulfric cast him a glance, but could not be sure how old he was. He certainly carried more years than the rest of them, but he still looked to be in his prime. Wulfric hadn't had much to do with him prior to their captivity in Kandamar, but he seemed to have grown increasingly objectionable in the time Wulfric had spent with him.

'There's a town ahead,' Varada said. 'We can stop there until the rain passes. These downpours rarely last more than a few hours.'

It didn't take long to reach the town, which was slightly larger than the one where they had encountered the constable and his men. The inn was clearly marked with a large sign outside, so they wasted no time in stabling their horses and rushing out of the torrential downpour. Wulfric stopped in his tracks as soon as he got inside.

Diego dal Zama and a dozen armed men sat at the tables clustered around the fire. As with the arrival of any group of people at an inn in a small town, everyone looked to the door to scrutinise the strangers. Most immediately returned to their drinks, food, and conversations, but Diego stood and hooked his thumb into his sword belt, a smile spreading across his face.

'Why's that fella staring at us?' Enderlain said.

'He's one of dal Valeriano's men,' Wulfric said.

'Ah. Not the best of news, that, is it?' Enderlain said.

Wulfric had thought Diego would be staring at him. It had been obvious from the moment they met that Diego wanted to fight him, something Wulfric relished equally, but his gaze was fixed on Varada. He said something to the men around him and walked out into the open, away from the table.

'I wonder why he's walking like someone kicked him in the balls,' Jagovere said, referring to Diego's stiff and cautious movement.

'Somebody did,' Varada said with a satisfied smile. 'Hard enough that he still feels it.'

They all looked at her.

She shrugged, and pointed to the faint bruising still on her face.

Enderlain let out a subdued laugh. 'Bit of a coincidence that we'd run into him here.'

'Bad luck?' Jagovere said, but he didn't sound convinced.

'I find that hard to believe,' Wulfric said.

'What now?' Sander said.

'Their numbers will be more of an advantage outside,' Wulfric said. 'Better we do it here.' He drew the rapier he had taken from one of the constables; he had been looking forward to the opportunity to try one in a real fight.

The door opened again, and three more men came in, their oilskin coats dripping with water.

'Looks like they want to do it in here too,' Jagovere said.

The tavern stank of wood smoke, wet cloth and unwashed bodies, but there was nowhere else Wulfric would rather have been. His skin tingled in anticipation. The civilians in the taproom backed away to the bar, but they could get no farther—Wulfric and the others blocked the door, while Diego and his men denied them any escape from the back. They would be unwilling spectators to the fight that was about to take place, and were in as much danger as anyone else there.

Wulfric scanned the men opposite him, looking for the one with the glint in his eye that said he would attack first. It came as no surprise that it was Diego. The crackling of the fire in the taproom's hearth was the only sound as the opponents sized each other up.

Diego drew his rapier and fixed his eyes on Wulfric. 'Shall we?'

Wulfric lifted his rapier and adopted the low, balanced position Jagovere had spent so much time drilling into him in Kandamar. The image of one of the Estranzan court dandies with their feathered hats sprung into his mind, and he felt ridiculous, but that was the way it was done, and he knew there was a reason for it.

The taproom filled with the clash of steel and the roar of battle, as the others hurled themselves at one another. Only Wulfric and Diego remained still. There was something about the cocksure way he had behaved in Torona that had reminded Wulfric of Rodulf, and the memory returned to him, inflaming his temper. Wulfric lunged. Diego moved quickly. He dropped back two paces and easily swatted Wulfric's thrust to the side. He followed up with a quick slash, but Wulfric was able to bring his blade back in time and parry, feeling the jarring strike reverberate all the way up his arm to his elbow.

He countered quickly, not wanting to allow Diego to gain the initiative, but once again the Estranzan parried and Wulfric felt his frustration grow. Without missing a beat, he attacked again, firing in thrust after thrust, stamping his front foot down hard with each one in a fashion that he thought would make Jagovere proud. Diego parried each one and at no point looked troubled by the barrage. Wulfric gritted his teeth in anger, and felt them chatter against one another. No matter what he did, he couldn't get past Diego's blade, and each riposte was getting closer. The rapier felt too alien, and Wulfric wished for a sabre more than anything.

A wave of light-headedness came, but passed as quickly as it arrived. Wulfric realised he was holding Diego's blade with one of his leather-gauntleted hands. It took him a moment to register what he had done, having no memory of grabbing it. He could feel it bite through his glove, but it was a distant sensation rather than pain. Diego reacted quickly, drawing his dagger and swiping at Wulfric in one smooth movement. Wulfric stepped back, still holding the blade, and thrust. Without his rapier to parry, Diego could do nothing but stare at Wulfric with hate in his eyes as Wulfric's rapier pierced his throat. He pulled his sword free, and let go of Diego's blade. Diego toppled over, blood spilling from his throat and mouth. Wulfric stepped back and looked around, but the fight was over. The others had been watching him.

'You almost looked like a gentleman there,' Jagovere said. 'For a moment.'

✹

## Wulfric

As he rode, Wulfric looked at the munitions-grade rapier he had taken from the constable and used to kill Diego. He thought of what Jagovere had said about looking like a gentleman and a measure of self-awareness came to him. Since the battle in Darvaros, he had been struggling to make sense of the new world he found himself in by adopting its ways. The rapier was the physical embodiment of that, and it suddenly made him feel foolish. He hefted it in his hand. It felt good, but would never be part of him the way a well-made sabre was. He looked at the hilt of the sabre tied to his saddle, and threw the rapier into the undergrowth at the side of the road. Surviving among the southerners didn't mean he had to become like them. His attempt to do so had nearly gotten him killed against Diego. His gift had saved him, and he felt shame at the thought that he had not been the better man.

'It's rather odd, don't you think?' Jagovere said, appearing beside Wulfric as they rode.

'What's odd?' Wulfric said, thinking Jagovere was referring to him throwing away the sword.

'That we encountered Diego and his cronies so soon after our meeting with the sheriff and his men.'

'Maybe dal Valeriano sent them both at the same time,' Wulfric said, 'but the constable got to us first.'

'Possibly,' Jagovere said, looking over at Wulfric. 'But we'd accepted that the sheriff had followed us from Torona. Do you still believe that?'

Wulfric shook his head. 'No.'

'Diego would have been with dal Valeriano, which means word has reached him. We've been moving at a good pace. Faster than news could have come from Torona. I think it ever more likely that someone warned him before then. I don't think we were seen in Torona.'

'A Darvarosian?' Wulfric said.

'Unlikely. I don't think they'd want to advertise the fact that they failed in their treaty obligations by allowing us to get back to Estranza. It's someone else.'

Wulfric cast an eye over his shoulder to where Varada was riding. She immediately caught his gaze, but her expression revealed nothing.

'The woman?'

'She's the obvious suspect, I agree. She suggested the northern road. Coin is always king to people of her trade. The same could be said for us, I suppose, but honour is less important when you conduct your trade in the shadows.'

'I'm not killing a woman until I'm certain,' Wulfric said.

'I don't like the idea either,' Jagovere said, 'but if she's selling us out, it has to be done. I'll put it to her when we camp for the night. Her reaction should tell us what we want to know.'

'I'll be ready,' Wulfric said. It was only then that he noticed Jagovere had a small one-handed crossbow sitting on his saddle, primed and ready to fire. Varada might have to wait until that evening for her interview, but Wulfric realised that he had just had his.

# CHAPTER 49

## ADALHAID

'JAKOB, WHAT ARE you doing here?' Adalhaid said as she left Aenlin's room.

'I've been drafted in to help with the Markgraf's daughter,' he said. 'It seems someone mentioned to him that I'm the finest physician in the city.'

He gave her a knowing, and utterly captivating, smile. She had made mention of him to the Markgraf the previous evening, but hadn't realised it would be acted on so quickly.

'I'm to join Doctors Frantz and Oppenburg in the young lady's treatment.'

'There's been no improvement,' Adalhaid said. 'I'm concerned she's making herself ill.'

'It's common enough after great tragedy,' he said. 'But with a monitored approach, it's easily enough treated. It'll simply take a little patience.' His face grew serious. 'You must promise me that you won't do anything foolish. We can handle this. You have my assurance.'

He continued to stare at her, and she realised he wasn't going to let her go until she did.

'I promise,' she said. She was uncomfortable lying, but took solace in the thought that it was a half-truth. So long as Aenlin did not deteriorate dangerously, there would be no need for magical intervention. With luck, the half-truth would soon be a full truth.

'I thought perhaps we could talk later?' he said.

Her heart quickened, but she knew her answer. Petr's death, so sudden and so silly, had driven home, as though the lesson had not already been well enough learned, that life was unpredictable and short. Wulfric could be anywhere. He might even be dead. Men like him lived violent, dangerous, and usually short lives. Aethelman had said he was an even more attractive target because of his gift. He wouldn't want her to throw her life away.

She nodded. 'You know where to find me,' she said, smiling.

❊

## WULFRIC

'Rider coming up behind us fast,' Enderlain shouted.

Wulfric sighed and brought his horse to a stop. He drew his sword, irritated by the delay in getting to where they were headed.

The others got out of his way, knowing by that point that getting between him and a man he had chosen to kill was a bad idea. The rider grew closer, and Wulfric wondered what dal Valeriano hoped to gain by sending one lone man against them. Then the thought occurred that perhaps he would be a truly great opponent, a man on whom a warrior's reputation might be made. He gripped his sword in eager anticipation.

'Make way in the name of the duchess!' the rider shouted when he was within calling distance.

'Duchess?' Enderlain said. 'Did Valeriano have an accident?'

Jagovere laughed. 'Peace, friend,' he shouted. 'What news?'

The rider reined his horse to a halt a safe distance from them. 'Elena dal Torona has been proclaimed Duchess of Torona and has overthrown her half-brother, the usurper dal Valeriano. It is my privilege to bring word of her accession to the provinces. Hinder my task and you will outlaw yourselves.'

'When did this happen?' Jagovere said.

'A few days ago. The morning after her marriage to Lord Carraterro dal Suera, now the Lord Consort.'

'From right-hand man to Lord Consort,' Jagovere said. 'A promotion, I suppose. And where might the former duke be found?'

The messenger shrugged his shoulders. 'I believe he's returned to his fortress in Valeriano. Now, clear the road!'

He let out a loud shout and spurred his horse forward to a gallop, leaving Wulfric and the others in a cloud of dust as they absorbed the new information.

'That paints things a different colour,' Jagovere said.

'I'm sick of this place,' Wulfric said.

'Power and greed,' Jagovere said with a shrug.

'At least it'll make him easier to kill,' Wulfric said. 'If we can get to him in time. There'll be plenty who would like to impress the new duchess with his head. Some of his own men included.'

The sun was dropping below the horizon. Jagovere watched it for a moment before speaking.

'Anyway, we should make camp for the night,' he said, giving Wulfric a knowing look.

Wulfric nodded.

❧

## WULFRIC

Stepping into the realm of intrigues left Wulfric feeling uncomfortable. It went against everything he knew and understood, and considering the stakes, he was worried he would make a mess of things. Jagovere knew better about such things, so Wulfric was content to take his lead. He did his best not to look at Varada, which was difficult at the best of times considering how attractive he found her, but now he felt as though he had to actively concentrate on it.

Conversation at the campfire was stilted, and Wulfric could tell Enderlain knew something was up. Wulfric felt as though his complicity was written all over his face, and had to avoid making eye contact with Enderlain as well. They ate in silence, sitting around the warmth of the fire's flames. Jagovere stared into them as he prodded at the glowing embers with a stick.

'How did you get word to dal Valeriano?' he said, continuing to stare into the fire.

No one said a thing, although Wulfric could see Sander look to Enderlain with a puzzled expression on his face.

'It's the betrayal that irks me the most,' Jagovere said. 'When you take a chance on trusting someone, and they let you down. That's always the worst part.'

He looked up, but did not fix his gaze on anyone in particular. Only the fire's crackle and the chirping of nocturnal insects in the darkness broke the silence. Wulfric wondered how long it would take to draw his sword when it came to it. Varada was fast, and he was not certain he could best her.

'What in hells are you talking about?' Walt said.

Wulfric raised an eyebrow. He knew as well as Jagovere that the first one to speak was most likely the one who had betrayed them.

'Dal Valeriano couldn't have sent men to attack us unless someone told him days ago. The constables might have followed us from the city, but Diego and his men? No. It was too quick.'

'It's the woman, obviously,' Walt said.

Wulfric leaned back into the shadows away from the firelight and drew his sword as quietly as he could. When it came to it, he wanted to be the first man with a weapon ready.

'I thought that at first, admittedly,' Jagovere said.

Varada cast him a filthy look.

Jagovere shrugged. 'I could be forgiven for that, considering the short time she's been with us, but I no longer think that the case. I had considered our Northlander friend also, but discounted him in a conversation earlier. Until this very moment, I did indeed think it was the good lady Varada, but now, Walt, I think it's you.'

'You're out of your mind. I've been with the Company as long as you.'

'Which is what makes your betrayal so much harder to take,' Jagovere said.

Walt was on his feet in the blink of an eye, but Wulfric had been waiting for it, and was younger, and faster. Walt had a sabre tip at his throat by the time his hand reached the hilt of his rapier.

Walt let go of his sword and raised his hands. 'What are you going to do with me?' he said.

Jagovere stood and glared at him from across the fire. 'What was he giving you?'

'Ten crowns for every report on the Company's movements and plans—'

Jagovere could not conceal the disgust on his face. 'You were informing on us *before* we went into Darvaros?'

Walt nodded.

'And now? How much for our lives?'

'I... Three hundred crowns.'

'You were selling us out for three hundred crowns? Surely we're worth more than that. We're your brothers. You, Enderlain, Sander, Conrat, and I. Wulfric too. You'd likely be dead if it weren't for the way he's fought for us.'

Walt shook his head.

Jagovere sighed with frustration. 'And how did you do it? How did you get word to him?'

'By pigeon. From the inn we stopped at on the border. There was someone waiting to meet me at the last tavern to direct us to Diego.'

An agonising silence took hold of the small camp, faces lit only by a meagre fire, Wulfric's sword reflecting its flames.

'What are you going to do with me?' Walt repeated.

'What do you think?' Jagovere said, his voice dripping with anger. He nodded to Wulfric.

'Draw your sword,' Wulfric said to Walt. 'A man should die with a sword in his hand.'

Walt looked to the left and right, but there was no escape. Both Sander and Enderlain stood, and from the looks on their faces it was clear they were ready to step in if Wulfric was not up to the job. Walt took a deep breath.

'You wouldn't let me go? For old times' sake?' he said.

'You'd have led us to our deaths for a handful of coins,' Jagovere said. 'Dying with a sword in your hand's too good for the likes of you.'

Walt gave a wry smile. 'No, I didn't think so.' He looked back to Wulfric and nodded. He took the handle of his rapier and drew it. Wulfric ran him through as soon as the blade was bared.

'Dump his body in the bushes,' Jagovere said. 'He doesn't get a proper burial. Leave him for the wolves.'

❋

## WULFRIC

Valeriano was a small town much like any of the others they had passed through on their journey from Torona. The villagers in the previous settlement they had passed through were delighted to confirm that the Usurper, as dal Valeriano was now being called, had fled to his fortress. More surprisingly, they had heard of the band of ferocious Northlanders who were hunting the former duke down. As flattering as it had been, a melancholy mood had drowned the small group in silence since the confrontation with Walt. That word of their grim mission had preceded them was greeted with both pleasure and consternation. Killing Walt had not allowed them to disappear. Everyone knew who they were, where they were, and what they were planning to do.

They stopped in the town square and looked up to the walled castle sitting atop a hill overlooking the town.

'One last drink before we ride to our deaths?' Jagovere said.

'Cheerful thought,' Wulfric said.

'Ever stormed a castle?'

'What do you think?' Wulfric said.

'I only wish I were able to write the story about it,' Jagovere said. 'Perhaps I should. Then the ending can be however we want it.'

'Won't be the truth then,' Wulfric said.

'Ah, truth is ever the plaything of a writer,' Jagovere said. 'I like to think of it as—'

'Let's get that drink,' Enderlain said. 'I don't plan on attacking a castle sober. The last time I tried, it didn't go well.'

Jagovere shrugged, but didn't try to finish his sentence.

They tethered their horses outside a small tavern and went in. A single drink turned the mood around, far more so than the meagre amount of alcohol warranted. Wulfric had seen it before, when his father and the others had ridden out to battle. The mood was always sombre the night before, but on the day of departure they were always jovial, as if at a feast rather than a farewell. His father had told him that men riding to battle no longer had to fear dying in their beds. If the worst were to happen, they knew they would sup with Jorundyr.

'A second round of your ale, barkeep,' Jagovere shouted, slamming a coin down on the table.

'Best in the county,' the tavern keeper said, as though that was not the claim made by every tavern keeper in every tavern in every county. He started to fill mugs from the tap. 'You those Northern fellas?'

Wulfric looked to Jagovere, who raised his eyebrows.

'What of it?' Jagovere said.

'Reckoned you were. Sure you want another round?'

'Pretty sure,' Enderlain said.

'The Golden Shield arrived this morning,' the barkeep said. 'The du— count's hired them.'

Wulfric could see the colour drain from Jagovere's face.

'Must have cost him a small fortune to lure them away from the king's court at Estravil,' the tavern keeper said. 'Surprised they agreed to work for him, all things considered. Still, I reckon they'll make what you've got planned a mite more difficult. S'not like they don't know you're coming.'

'I'm sure,' Jagovere said.

Wulfric waited until the fresh mugs of ale had arrived before speaking.

'Who're the Golden Shield?'

# CHAPTER 50

## ADALHAID

THERE WERE FEW places a young woman and man could meet in Elzburg without generating rumours of impropriety. Coffee houses were one of them, but the trade-off was that privacy was limited. Coffee was an exotic novelty brought from the far south, and Elzburg had at least a dozen coffee shops dotted around the city, as enthusiasm for the drink was a constant. They were bustling places, packed so tightly with tables and chairs that there was barely enough room to move between them. The air inside was hot, humid, and rich with the smell of freshly brewed coffee, while you could barely hear the person sitting opposite you as your conversation competed with all those surrounding.

Adalhaid waited at a small table by a condensation-frosted window that she had wiped a small clear circle on to peer out of. She wasn't sure if it was the strong coffee or nerves, but there was a slight tremor in her hand. She did her best to still it when she saw Jakob arrive and scan the room for her. She waved and smiled. He walked over and sat.

It wasn't in Adalhaid's nature to make small talk, so she got straight to what she wanted to say. 'There was someone before you,' she said. 'I loved him very much. I *love* him very much.'

She could see the reaction on Jakob's face, so she hurried on.

'I thought he was dead,' she said. 'But I recently found out that he might still live.'

Jakob was clearly nonplussed by the abrupt nature of the conversation. He nodded slowly. 'I understand.'

'No, it's not like that,' she said. 'It came as a shock when I found out, but no one knows where he is. He might even be dead by now. I know it will sound strange, but he thinks I'm dead. He's gone, and I accept that, hard though it is. He has no reason to come back even if he is still alive, and I have no way of ever finding him. I can't waste my life in the hope that one day our paths will cross again. He wouldn't want that, and I certainly don't. What I'm saying is, I'm sorry for the way I behaved. I want to move on. I want to move on with you.'

She reached out and took his hand.

❧

## WULFRIC

'The Golden Shield are Aristonda dal Gascovar's Company. He's the First Son of Estranza, Banneret of the Starry Field, Estranza's most famed and beloved hero,' Jagovere said. 'Tell me, do you think the gods hate me? Hate all of us, perhaps?'

Wulfric frowned and looked to the others, but nobody said anything.

'I saw him once, at the Battle of Borganz,' Enderlain said. 'He was with us that day though, leading a company of a thousand men. By the gods, he was magnificent, a suit of golden armour on a great white steed. Really something to see.'

'A castle defended by Aristonda dal Gascovar,' Jagovere said. 'With dal Valeriano deposed, it would make life easier, I thought. With Diego out of the way as well, I reckoned it would be plain sailing.'

'Maybe you should stop thinking,' Enderlain said.

Sander chuckled. 'It's worked well enough for you, I suppose.'

Jagovere sighed. 'The Graf wouldn't want us to throw away our lives for revenge. We could always wait, come back in a year or two when he thinks he's safe.'

'If he's still alive,' Enderlain said.

They all ruminated on it, until Wulfric broke the silence.

'How many men did dal Gascovar have with him?' Wulfric said to the tavern keeper.

'Five. Six, maybe.'

'Small company,' Wulfric said, surprised.

'Dal Valeriano probably hired them as his personal bodyguard when he became duke,' Jagovere said. 'With dal Gascovar's reputation he can get whatever work he wants, and bodyguarding is a damn sight safer than fighting battles.'

'Not anymore,' Wulfric said. 'Why don't we at least take a look? We've come a long way.'

'Makes sense,' Enderlain said.

Varada remained silent, but Wulfric could tell from the look on her face that she was angry with them. Whatever dal Valeriano had done to her, clearly only his blood would settle the debt. He could understand that, and was eager to finish their business in Estranza so he could settle his.

❊

## AETHELMAN

Aethelman had always held the idea of palaces being places of light, and sophistication and gaiety, where those with great wealth and few impositions on their time would gather in decadence. Elzburg Palace was far removed from that. It bore the trappings that tallied with his expectations, but the mood was as unlike them as could be. It was as though a dark cloud hung over the palace, one that sapped the joy from everything beneath it. It made perfect sense when he discovered the Markgraf's son had recently died, and that his daughter, his only remaining child, was ill.

Many of the courtiers had returned to their estates, unwilling to endure the bleak mood in the palace. Those who remained were preoccupied with the young Lady Aenlin's health, and how they might capitalise on the situation to their own advantage. It was a ruthless place, but so it ever was with centres of power. Aethelman could not help but have a bitter taste in his mouth at the thought.

Rodulf had remained there, and Aethelman saw him frequently, but always from a safe distance. He seemed to have inveigled himself into the Markgraf's inner circle, much to the chagrin of those with a longer presence at court but far less favour. He considered seeking out people at court who might become his confederates, but he had neither the time nor the guile to make the effort worthwhile. Aethelman continued to watch Rodulf, waiting for his opportunity, but always aware that it would be all over if Rodulf recognised him.

He observed that often when dealing with people, Rodulf reached into a pocket in his doublet. It wasn't the fashion, as Aethelman had discovered during his own encounter with a tailor, so it got him thinking. Rodulf had become the very vision of a southern dandy, and Aethelman could only come up with one reason for him to ruin the otherwise perfect lines of his expensively cut suits of clothing. It was so close to his person that Rodulf would certainly notice the Stone's absence from it. While it might be a useful thing to know, unless Rodulf was very distracted, he would realise it had been pick-pocketed within moments, and Aethelman was no longer quick enough to get away in that time.

The writings Aethelman had discovered indicated it would soon start to exact its price, to sap the user's own reservoir of the Fount. Rodulf didn't appear to be showing any signs of that yet. The weakness would have eased Aethelman's efforts, but the consolation was the fact that it meant Rodulf was not using the Stone to anywhere near its full potential.

WULFRIC

'That's a castle?' Wulfric said.

'No,' Jagovere said. 'Not quite a castle. Nice house, though.'

There were parts of dal Valeriano's house that looked old, as though they had been built with defence in mind. Most of it, however, was a statement of wealth and grandeur. The facade was lined with windows, surrounded with ornate cut-stone decoration. There were countless places where an attacker could gain entry, and even a hundred men would struggle to defend it.

'You'd think a fella with political aspirations like dal Valeriano would go for security rather than luxury,' Enderlain said.

'He's a vain fool,' Varada said. 'He'll pay for that.'

'Finally a bit of luck,' Jagovere said. 'The tavern keeper said dal Gascovar only has the Golden Shield with him; the rest of his men have run off. That mansion won't give them much in the way of an advantage.'

'Why don't we burn the place down around him?' Sander said.

'That's not the way a Blood Debt is settled,' Wulfric said. 'We cut the life from him and send him to Jorundyr without a sword in his hand. Ulfyr will torment him and gnaw on his bones for eternity.'

There was a moment of silence while everyone digested the bleak prospect of a Northlander's conception of the afterlife.

'I thought you were Ulfyr?' Sander said, breaking the silence.

Wulfric cast him a filthy look, while Enderlain barked out a laugh.

'Are we just going to sit here looking at it?' Wulfric said. He had hoped the nickname had been forgotten. That seemed not to be the case.

'No,' Jagovere said. 'Time to cause some mischief. Seeing as you're the most terrifying-looking of us, Ulf—'

Wulfric cast his second filthy look in as many minutes.

Jagovere smiled. 'Wulfric, would you like to lead us in?'

Wulfric nodded, the honour he was being afforded placating him. He spurred his horse forward, the others falling in behind him.

They were a hundred paces from the house, having trampled through a fine ornamental garden on their horses to get there, when they were challenged.

'Who goes there?'

Wulfric looked around to Jagovere. 'You're the one who's good with words.'

Jagovere rode forward and joined him.

'We're here to kill Lord dal Valeriano,' Jagovere said genially. 'We have no issue with any other man here, and invite you to quit the property. I give my word that we will not harm any man who chooses to leave.'

A figure appeared at one of the windows and opened it.

'We've been expecting you,' he said. 'I thank you for your kind offer, but I'm afraid I'm contractually obliged to decline. I would extend you the same courtesy, however. If you leave now, I give you my word that you will not be pursued.'

Jagovere continued to smile, but said nothing. The silence persisted a moment longer, until the figure at the window spoke again.

'A shame,' he said. 'We await your arrival.'

❉

## RODULF

'I couldn't bear to be away from you any longer,' Rodulf said as he walked into the kitchen, always the warmest part of the palace with its ovens and open stone fireplaces.

The kitchen girl smiled coquettishly. 'I'm busy,' she said. 'I'm making her ladyship's broth. You'll have to wait.' She stirred the broth one last time, then poured it into a bowl.

'I can think of something that would make the wait more bearable,' he said.

She smiled. 'A pastry?'

'A pastry.'

She turned and walked down the kitchen to where they were cooling. Rodulf took a packet of powder from his pocket and emptied it into the broth, stirring it in until it was invisible. The man he had bought the poison from had told him that only a few grains would kill a large wolf, the vermin Rodulf had claimed needed killing. A spoonful or two of the broth would be more than enough to kill a small girl. Her death would break the Markgraf's spirit utterly. The Stone would yoke him to Rodulf's desire, and then Rodulf would be limited only by his imagination and ambition. He wondered what his father would think, to see Rodulf on the brink of greatness that neither of them could even have dreamed of a few years previously.

She returned with the pastry and looked at him with affection in her eyes as she handed it over. She had probably fallen in love with him, the poor fool. It was every serving girl's dream to fall in love with a lord and be made a lady. It was the stuff of romantic tales—but unfortunately for her, this tale would not have a happy ending. She had proved useful though, and not just for the pastries.

'Will you call on me tonight?' he said.

'Of course, my lord,' she said, mocking a curtsey.

He laughed.

'Now, I best get the broth to her ladyship before it gets cold,' she said.

He watched her go, and wondered if she would get the blame for the poisoning, but he really didn't care.

❀

## AETHELMAN

Although the kitchen girl seemed to be Rodulf's favourite, it appeared to Aethelman that he could not be entirely satisfied with only one bedmate. She was one of a number of women who returned to his apartments with him, courtesans and the more adventurous female courtiers who had identified his rapid rise and were willing to overlook his Northland heritage. He was politic enough not to bother with any of the other women of the palace staff, though. Having two rival interests among the household staff cause a scene would be the last thing a young nobleman trying to establish himself at court needed.

The White Horse was patronised by a number of wealthy merchants, and aristocrats too minor to warrant a house in the city or an apartment at court. That drew with it those of an enterprising nature who saw the opportunity men with disposable income brought. There were often finely dressed women in the inn's lounge, taking tea—usually alone, with no indication they were there to meet anyone specific. While they arrived alone, they rarely departed so. One in particular was so pretty that a plan sprang into Aethelman's mind almost fully formed.

He waited until she had been served tea by one of the waiters with whom she was on first-name terms, then made his move.

'Good afternoon,' he said, as amiably as possible. He had seen the other guests approach these women as though they were items to be bought and sold, and did not want to appear in any way like them. 'I was wondering if you've ever visited the Markgraf's court,' he said.

She regarded him curiously for a moment. 'Many times,' she said, flashing a smile that set even Aethelman's elderly heart racing. 'But why don't we start with a cup of tea?'

'Yes, of course,' he said, sitting in the chair she gestured to. He felt foolish in having allowed himself to be so easily disarmed by her.

'My name's Katya,' she said.

'Aeth— Gustav dal Aetheldorf,' Aethelman said, struggling to compose himself. 'I have a proposition for you.' He frowned at his choice of words.

'Right to business,' she said. 'That's fine by me. What do you have in mind?' She raised a perfectly shaped eyebrow.

'Oh. Nothing like that,' he said, blushing. 'I have a friend at court. The son of a friend, actually. I don't want to go into too much detail, for my friend's sake, you see, but suffice it to say his son has rather... liberal spending habits. When he was last at the family seat, he took something with him, a family heirloom, which my friend fears he intends to sell to cover some of his debts.'

'I see,' Katya said. 'Go on.'

'Well, my friend is at his wit's end, and wrote, asking me to help out of a fear that he won't get here in time himself. My friend's son has an eye for the ladies, and I expect a beautiful young lady such as yourself would provide the perfect distraction while I retrieve the heirloom.'

'You flatter me, my lord.' Her smile broadened. 'But flattery doesn't pay the bills.'

'No, of course not. I was thinking twice your usual rate for whatever time it takes? There won't be any danger, and you won't have to do anything untoward. Simply keep all his attention on you.'

'Three times my usual rate, which comes with my usual guarantee of absolute discretion.' Her smile didn't falter for even a moment. 'I'm sure your *friend* will be so glad of recovering the heirloom that he won't balk at reimbursing you.'

Aethelman could not help but smile at her audacity. 'Agreed,' he said.

# CHAPTER 51

ADALHAID

ADALHAID WALKED TOWARD Aenlin's room for another day of her vigil. Before she had left the night before, it had seemed Aenlin was starting to improve, and Adalhaid hoped that before too long she would be strong enough to get outside for fresh air. It probably had nothing to do with Jakob's arrival, but it coinciding with her improvement certainly made him look good. Her recovery would be a boon to his career which brought Adalhaid additional pleasure.

There were several men standing outside Aenlin's room when it came into view at the far end of a broad, finely decorated corridor. Things being as they were, it was not unusual. Indeed, Adalhaid hoped it might mean they were getting ready to have Aenlin venture out of her room.

Jakob was there, along with the two other doctors, Frantz and Oppenburg.

'Has she gotten out of bed?' Adalhaid said when she grew near.

Jakob looked at her, his face ashen. 'The Lady Aenlin passed during the night,' he said, in a painfully formal way.

'What?' Adalhaid said, the news sending her head into a spin. 'How? She was getting better!'

'Her condition took a turn for the worse during the night,' Oppenburg said, his face betraying his worry. 'Then deteriorated rapidly. All three of us were present through the night. We did everything we could, but there was no saving her. I fear the little girl's heart was broken, and she simply lost the will to live.'

Adalhaid could not believe what she was hearing. Only the previous night she had eaten her first proper meal in days. How could it have happened?

She stumbled back down the hall, distraught.

'Adalhaid!' Strellis jogged down the hall after her. 'Are you all right?'

'How did it happen, Jakob? She was getting better.' She coughed out a sob.

He shrugged and held his hands out. 'Truthfully, I don't know. I thought she was improving, but sometimes this happens. There's just no explanation.'

'I could have saved her,' Adalhaid said, her face twisting with anger. 'You know I could have. Why didn't you come and get me?'

'Magic is wrong,' Jakob said. 'It might seem like a good thing at first, but it's too dangerous. It corrupts. It's too easy to abuse. That's why it's against the law.'

'I've been doing it for weeks,' she said, spitting the words out. 'Weeks and weeks. Every patient I treat. Every one of them has left the clinic better for it. Your opinions on magic are a millennium out of date. Just because it was a bad thing in the past doesn't mean it has to be in the future. You complain about physicians who are unwilling to adopt new techniques? The hypocrisy astounds me.'

Jakob blanched. 'You'd have done magic under the view of two physicians? Two physicians who'd denounce you for witchcraft in a heartbeat?' he said.

'To save a little girl's life? Of course I would. Without hesitation. Why didn't you call me?'

'To save yours,' he said calmly.

Rage boiled within her. She wanted to claw his eyes out. No words would come to her. She hissed and stormed off.

## AETHELMAN

Katya looked even more impressive when she arrived at the palace. Aethelman had not wanted the two of them to be seen together, so he had given her instructions to make her way there alone and take instructions by signal when she arrived. They did not have to wait long for Rodulf to make his appearance. Being seen was an important part of life at court, and it was something Rodulf had mastered. He had identified those beneath him in title, and those beneath him in favour, and greeted them with what would have seemed genuine interest and affection, were it not for the fact that Aethelman knew him too well.

His behaviour came as something of a surprise. Aethelman had expected Rodulf would lord whatever power he had over others, but this behaviour indicated he had quickly developed a political astuteness. It was the behaviour of men who rise to the top, and it was unsettling to see it in Rodulf. He was too avaricious to be allowed to rise far, but that was not Aethelman's problem. It was only the Stone, which no doubt was easing Rodulf's ascent, that he had to concern himself with. That and the beautiful woman he needed to put in Rodulf's path.

Katya was a consummate performer, and seemed to be enjoying the novelty of what Aethelman required of her. He had chosen a likely spot for his theft. It was a corridor used by those in residence in the palace, lined with pillars behind which Aethelman could easily conceal himself. It was not busy, and if Ghyda—goddess of good fortune, and bad—favoured him, he would get the Stone, and have it destroyed before Rodulf noticed it was gone. After that, he did not have a care for what happened to him. He could go to the gods with his head held high.

He gave his signal, and Katya moved into action. She walked across Rodulf's path with the grace and confidence of a woman born to wear a crown, dropping a fine lace handkerchief as she did. Feigning realisation, she stopped and turned with perfect timing to bring herself face to face with Rodulf. It was masterful, and Aethelman had no doubt she would have him eating out of her hand in no time.

'Please, allow me,' Rodulf said, bending to pick up the handkerchief.

It was Aethelman's turn. Surrounded by the thick stone walls of the palace, he could find so very little of the Fount to draw on. Not nearly enough to fade into the ether as he had the day Leondorf was attacked, and his old body no longer contained enough to give him the boost needed. It would have to suffice to give Rodulf the sensation that there was still something there after the Stone was gone, and Aethelman worried even that small piece of magic might be too much for him.

Their flirtatious conversation faded into the background as Aethelman stepped from behind his pillar and focussed on Rodulf's tunic pocket. The shape of the Stone forced the pocket open slightly. Aethelman did his best to magically dull Rodulf's senses, and reached for the Stone.

His heart raced so that he feared it would give up on him. He knew there was only so long Katya could keep Rodulf standing there. He had only one chance, and he had to be quick. He was so focussed on all the other problems, he had forgotten to wear a glove. He felt a burning tingle spread across his hand and engulf his entire body as he grasped the Stone. Coldness followed, and his breath faltered as he pulled it free, terrified that Rodulf would feel the theft.

The Stone came away in his hand, and Aethelman focussed his thoughts on creating a false weight in Rodulf's pocket. He cursed himself for not having thought to find a rock of similar size and weight, but it was too late now. He stepped back behind the pillar, and took a deep breath. Before he knew what he was doing, he realised the Stone was doing his bidding. He wanted to stop it, but his quest was too important. He allowed it to do its work, and took comfort in the knowledge that Rodulf could almost certainly feel the presence of a non-existent Stone in his pocket. Katya knew to bring her act toward its conclusion as soon as Aethelman retreated, but he couldn't stop his heart from racing. The magic he had used to create the illusion in Rodulf's pocket would only last a short time, even with the Stone's help, but it would not deceive him if he put his hand in. Aethelman knew he might have minutes, or only a few seconds.

'Perhaps you could show me to the audience hall, my lord,' Katya said.

'It would be my pleasure,' Rodulf said.

Once they got there, she would give him an excuse and leave. In his best-case scenario, Aethelman reckoned that would be the moment Rodulf discovered the theft. He had brought the knife with him, and only needed a hard surface to rest the Stone on to cut through it. He waited until he heard their conversation and footsteps fade into the distance, and looked about for somewhere he could finish his business once and for all.

## WULFRIC

They dismounted and moved quickly to the cover of the manor house's wall.

'How d'you want to do it?' Enderlain said.

'If I were dal Gascovar, I'd have all my men waiting behind that door with crossbows,' Wulfric said.

'I suppose we should have thought it through before we got here,' Jagovere said. 'Still, too late for that now, and as Wulfric said: The front door is definitely out.'

Wulfric walked to a window and punched the hilt of his sword through it. 'I found another door,' he said, not waiting for the others before clambering through.

His feet sank into a thick rug when they touched the floor. The room was richly decorated with paintings covering the wall and expensive-looking furniture filling it. What was notably absent was any sign of the enemy. He gave the room one more careful look before moving forward to allow the others space to get in.

They fanned out through the room, but there was no sign of dal Gascovar, his men, or his master.

'Do you think they're real?' Enderlain said.

Wulfric looked around. Enderlain's eyes were fixed on one of the room's larger paintings, one of a naked woman with enormous breasts.

'What do you mean *real?*' Wulfric said.

'I've heard of fellas in the city, sorcerers, who make them bigger. There was a girl at the Golden Rose in Brixen. She said—'

'Enderlain, shut up,' Jagovere said.

Wulfric gave the painting another look, then involuntarily glanced over at Varada and then at her chest. If looks could have killed, Wulfric would have dropped dead on the spot. She was holding a long, slender sword with a delicate cup hilt, and he diverted his eyes for fear she might use it.

'Where are they?' Sander said.

Wulfric looked at the two closed doors leading out of the room. 'Waiting for us to walk by so they can stick a blade in our backs,' he said. 'I hate the way southerners fight.'

'Me too,' Enderlain said.

'I think he was including us in that,' Jagovere said.

'Oh. Right.'

Wulfric chose the door that led toward the house's front door. It brought them to a large open hallway with a marble floor. Six men stood waiting for them, swords in hand. There was a central staircase that branched into two at the turn. Dal Valeriano stood there, his face a picture of fear, but it was the man standing a few steps below him who interested Wulfric the most. He was tall and slender, with a few streaks of grey in his otherwise jet-black hair. His moustache and beard were waxed into neat points, and he wore a gilded, engraved breastplate that could only be described as magnificent.

Wulfric felt a tingle across his skin as he looked from man to man. They regarded him silently, bearing all the hallmarks of experienced fighters. He fought to control the shake in his hands as anger welled up inside him. They stood between him and the man he had come so far to see dead, the man who had delayed his return home to avenge Adalhaid, the man who had left them all to die on the Darvarosian plain. His breath quickened and his heart raced as the rage threatened to overcome him. It made him afraid, to feel so close to the brink of losing control, and he fought against it, tried to keep it contained within, but then it occurred to him—*why bother?* He let go of his tenuous hold, and felt it wash over him.

With a roar, Wulfric was in their midst. The first man fell before he had time to react, blood spraying from his throat. Two more were on him by the time he had brought his sword back from its first cut. He parried one and pulled the dagger from his belt to parry the second in one smooth movement. He kicked down on one of his attacker's knees, and the man screamed as it buckled beneath him. Wulfric drove his dagger into the man's eye and slashed at his second opponent.

The sabre felt so much more natural in his hand than the rapier had, like an extension of his arm, and the brutality with which he wielded it caught dal Gascovar's men off guard. *Gentlemen*, Jagovere had told him, *don't fight with kicks, punches, or head-butts.* The thought made him smile. What the gentlemen didn't seem to realise was that Wulfric wasn't fighting, he was killing. As his rage built, it seemed as though everyone around him slowed. All he saw before him were foes to be vanquished, men who would tell Jorundyr of his prowess and warn him of Wulfric's coming. Bared steel and breastplates were barely an inconvenience. He was faster, he was stronger. He heard steel scream against steel. He heard men scream when steel met with flesh. It was glorious and he could feel the eyes of his father, his grandfather, and all those who had gone before him watching from Jorundyr's Hall. They would be proud, and that drove Wulfric to ever greater aggression.

A third man fell, then a fourth. The remaining two hesitated, and glanced back at their captain, who gave a nod. Pride overcame fear, and they too rushed at Wulfric. They came at him in concert, forcing Wulfric to parry attacks in two directions, and out of the corner of his eye he saw dal Gascovar descend the stairs. With both his blades occupied, Wulfric knew that if dal Gascovar was as good as everyone said, he would be at his liberty to run Wulfric through.

He turned his attention to one man, parrying high and allowing his comrade's thrust through. The blade speared through Wulfric's side, but there was no pain. He slashed his sabre deep into the other man's skull, then turned before his attacker could pull his sword free. Wulfric' plunged his dagger into the man's arm, then ran him through with the sabre.

Wulfric stepped back and pulled the rapier out. It had gone clean through the right edge of his abdomen, but the wound closed once the narrow blade was removed. A thin dribble of blood leaked from the wound, and he wondered momentarily if there was anything vital along the blade's path. There would be time to think of that after, though.

He threw the rapier to the side and looked up at dal Gascovar, who had stopped his approach and was at the foot of the stairs. The room that seconds before had been filled with the sound of death was silent. Wulfric was covered with blood, his hair matted with it. Dal Valeriano looked even more terrified than he had before, and was frozen to his spot at the turn of the stairs.

Dal Gascovar held his sword out before him, awaiting Wulfric's attack. Wulfric hurled himself at dal Gascovar, who parried two fast slashes with fluid movements. There was a beauty to it that emphasised the savagery of Wulfric's attack, but Wulfric knew the end result was all that mattered. Dal Gascovar exploded into motion, driving Wulfric back across the chequered marble floor. He was too fast for dal Gascovar, though. He saw the briefest of frowns form on dal Gascovar's brow, and Wulfric attacked again, retaking all the ground he had lost with a series of high and low cuts that flowed into one another.

Dal Gascovar parried frenziedly, until his hand was a moment too slow and Wulfric's sabre parted his cheek. He grimaced and stepped back, raising his hand to the cut. He looked at the blood on his fingers for a moment, then burst into motion again, anger adding weight to his fast, precise attacks. Wulfric parried time and again, and realised he was enjoying the experience. This man was a master, yet he could not find a way through. Then dal Gascovar stopped. Wulfric glared at him and prepared to send another man to his death, another who would serve him in Jorundyr's Hall.

Dal Gascovar stood at ease, then lowered his sword. He kept his eyes firmly fixed on Wulfric.

'What in hells are you doing?' dal Valeriano said.

'My contract requires that I protect you,' dal Gascovar said between heavy breaths, 'not that I die for you. With my men dead, I'm afraid I can no longer do that, my lord. Should you wish to sue me for breach of contract, you know where to find my lawyers.' His eyes still locked on Wulfric, he sheathed his sword and walked toward the door, giving Wulfric a curt nod as he passed.

'Get back here,' dal Valeriano shouted. 'Coward!'

Dal Gascovar walked out the door without so much as a backward glance.

'It seems you have been abandoned, my lord,' Jagovere said, stepping into the hallway. 'I can commiserate with you on that, having experienced it recently myself.'

Wulfric took a step toward dal Valeriano, but Jagovere held out a hand to stop him. He started up the steps, drawing his rapier. 'Do you have a sword, my lord?'

Dal Valeriano shook his head and pressed against the wall behind him. There was nowhere else he could go.

'It's a shame,' Jagovere said, 'but I doubt it would have made any difference.'

'This is murder,' dal Valeriano said. 'Where's your honour?'

'In a small grotto in the Warrens of Darvaros, with my father and a great many men I counted as friends. This isn't murder, my lord. It's justice.'

Jagovere thrust quickly, and dal Valeriano let out a gasp. A twist of Jagovere's wrist, and it was done. Jagovere stood over dal Valeriano's body for a moment before turning.

'Time to go home,' he said.

# CHAPTER 52

AETHELMAN

AETHELMAN HURRIED DOWN the hall toward an alcove he had scouted out earlier. Caught up as he was in his task, he still noticed there was something going on in the palace, a change of mood. Something had happened, but he had neither the time nor the interest to find out what. The Stone was everything. He could not rest until it was destroyed.

He was moving so quickly he did not even see the person he bumped into until after they had contacted. He looked up to see Rodulf staring at him. His heart leapt into his throat, but his mouth had opened and his eyes widened before he realised Rodulf had not recognised him.

'Excuse me, my lord,' he said, turning his face away and moving off as quickly as he could without arousing any more suspicion.

He had only taken a few steps when Rodulf called after him.

'Wait!' he said. 'I know you, don't I?'

Aethelman pretended not to hear him, and kept going. Blood pounded through his ears.

'I said wait! So you bloody well wait!' Rodulf said.

The voice was closer, and followed by a firm hand grabbing his shoulder. Rodulf spun him around and narrowed his one good eye as he looked Aethelman over. The corners of his mouth slowly lifted.

'Aethelman, my old chum. I hardly recognised you in that fancy clobber. Much nicer than those moth-eaten old grey rags. What in hells brings you here?' His eyes widened and his hand went to his pocket.

'You old bastard,' he said, grabbing Aethelman by the scruff of the neck.

Aethelman reached out for the Fount. Rodulf was young and strong, and there was no other way for him to get away. The Stone was in his purse, and his soul screamed in protest as the temptation to draw on it became overwhelming. He had used it once already. To do so a second time might rob him of the will to destroy it. In his mind's eye, he saw the faint tendrils of blue coruscating energy drift through the hall, but they were so weak and far away.

He felt Rodulf tug at his purse, then release Aethelman's scruff and step back.

'Good,' Rodulf said. 'I suppose the girl was in on it. I'll be sure to thank her if I see her again. But what to do with you?' His face lit up with a wicked smile.

'Guards!' he said. 'Guards!'

Men came running toward them, their weapons and armour rattling as they did.

'This man is a sorcerer,' Rodulf said. 'I know him from the Northlands. You'll need to send for an Intelligencier. I saw him outside Aenlin's room last eve. I fear he may have something to do with her sudden death.'

Rodulf took the Stone from his hand. Guards arrived and Aethelman felt firm hands grab him, but what little strength there had been in his old body was gone. He had failed.

❋

## Wulfric

Wulfric breathed deeply when they walked out the front door of dal Valeriano's manor house. The air outside was filled with the scent of the flowers in the garden, a welcome change from the bloody tang of death inside. What was not so welcome was the company of soldiers standing at the end of the path.

'Think you can pull off a repeat of that terrifying bloodlust?' Jagovere said. 'It would certainly come in handy around about now.'

Wulfric drew his sword, but the truth was he was exhausted and it felt like a bar of lead in his hand.

A man in a plumed hat walked forward from the soldiers.

'Is he dead?' the man said.

'Is who dead?' Wulfric said, his voice hoarse.

'Dal Valeriano. Is he dead?'

'He is,' Jagovere said. 'Got a problem with that?'

'Far from it,' the man said. 'I'm Banneret-Captain Peruiz. The Duchess of Torona received word of your plans and sent us to help. I'm sorry we've arrived too late.'

'As am I,' Jagovere said, 'but as you can see, we didn't need any help.'

Peruiz doffed his hat. 'I've been instructed to bring any survivors to an audience with Her Grace.'

'As kind an offer as it is, we'll be returning directly to Ruripathia,' Jagovere said.

'I'm afraid I must insist,' Peruiz said. 'Although I don't think you'll find it any imposition. I expect Her Grace will be extremely grateful.'

'Might be worth seeing *how* grateful,' Enderlain said.

'Very well,' Jagovere said. 'We'll come with you.'

❖

## Rodulf

The Markgraf's office was in almost complete darkness when Rodulf entered. He was nervous. Aethelman's appearance and his attempt to steal the Stone had shaken him. He had become so focussed on his goals that he had become blind to all the dangers around him. He needed to be more observant in future. Nonetheless, it was time to discover if his plan had worked.

'Sit, Rodulf, please,' he said.

'Of course, my lord. I'm so sorry for your loss. So much tragedy in such a short time. The gods can be cruel.'

'I won't be needing you for anything for a time,' the Markgraf said. 'You should feel free to visit home, visit family. Do you have much family in Leondorf?'

'No, my lord. My mother and father are dead.'

'A pity,' the Markgraf said. 'Family is important.' His voice sounded empty; defeated.

'Does this mean your plans are on hold?'

The Markgraf nodded. 'Yes. With Petr and Aenlin gone, there hardly seems any point.'

'I disagree,' Rodulf said. His mouth felt dry, but he clutched the Stone for all he was worth, and forced himself to ignore the sting.

The Markgraf stared at him out of the darkness for a moment. He cleared his throat. 'Really?'

'Absolutely. I think you should continue as you had intended.'

It took the Markgraf what seemed like an age to respond. Rodulf thought his heart would explode as he waited.

'I... I... You're right. I can see that now.'

'I can help you,' Rodulf said. 'I can do far more than carry your messages back and forth.'

'Of course,' the Markgraf said, his voice sounding hollow. 'I've been wasting you. I don't know why I didn't see it sooner.'

'If you make me your lieutenant, I can take on much of your burden in this,' Rodulf said, worried that he might be pushing things too far.

'I would appreciate that greatly,' the Markgraf said. 'Thank you. I'll see to it at once. I'm lucky to have you at my side at a time like this.'

Rodulf smiled, a satisfied calm enveloping him. 'It's both my honour and pleasure to serve, my lord.'

He left the Markgraf's office barely able to contain his excitement. The Markgraf's will was broken. Rodulf had him. He had whatever he wanted. He looked at his red, burned palm and grimaced. He hoped that was all the harm the Stone would do to him, at least until he had achieved everything he wanted.

✻

AETHELMAN

Aethelman looked up through the small barred window on the wooden door to his cell. There was a silhouette blocking out most of the light.

'I came as soon as I heard,' Adalhaid said.

Aethelman tried to smile, but his face was so swollen from the beating the guards had given him it didn't respond. They had told him he was in for far worse when the Intelligenciers arrived. He was going to meet the same terrible fate as his beloved Aesa. It didn't terrify him as much as he had thought it would. Failure was the harshest punishment the world could have meted out. Now, however, he had a glimmer of hope.

He groaned as he lifted himself off the flagstone floor and moved to the door, his joints protesting with every movement.

'They're saying you killed Aenlin with magic,' she said.

'I couldn't even imagine doing so hateful a thing,' he said. 'Please say you believe me.'

She nodded, and he could see tears form in her eyes.

'I can't save you,' she said, the words choked. 'I can't get you out of here. They're sure you're the reason for her death. It was so sudden. When the Intelligenciers come, it will...' Her voice faltered. She held a small, liquid-filled vial to the bars. 'It won't be painless,' she said. 'But it will be fast. It was all I could find in my medicine bag and there wasn't time to look for anything else.' She let out a pained sob.

Aethelman took the vial, and held her hand through the bars. 'Won't you get in trouble? When they find the vial?'

She shook her head. 'You're a sorcerer. This is the type of thing they'd expect from you.'

He smiled and enjoyed the touch of her hand a moment longer. It was home, it was friendship, it was love, it was happiness. It was all the good things in life, and he wished there had been more time to appreciate such things properly. The benefit of hindsight...

'There isn't much more time,' Aethelman said, 'so you must listen carefully. Go to my room at the White Horse. Here is the key.'

He passed the small blackened iron key between the bars of the cell door's small window. Adalhaid took it, and after a moment's consideration, hid it in her bodice and gave him a nod. He returned the gesture, and continued.

'There is an engraved knife and a parchment with instructions on how to use it in the bedside table's drawer. You'll need them for what I'm about to ask you to do, but first I have to apologise. This was my great quest, my great responsibility, and I've failed in it. You're the only person I can ask to take it on, but perhaps the gods smile on me, as I can't think of anyone more capable of doing it.

'Rodulf has an inscribed piece of ore. He keeps it in his pocket. It gives him power. Influence over others and far, far more, but I don't think he's learned even a tiny amount of its full potential yet. You need to take it from him and destroy it with the knife. It will cut through the Stone like warm butter, and send its potential for evil from the world forever. Do you understand?'

'I— Yes, I do,' Adalhaid said.

'I'm so, so sorry for placing this burden on you. I wouldn't unless it was absolutely necessary. Rodulf cannot be allowed keep that Stone. He will eventually realise what it is capable of and when he does, everyone around him will suffer for it.' He frowned for a moment, thinking carefully. Was there anything he was forgetting?

'Oh,' he said. 'Never touch it with your bare skin. It can seduce even the noblest of hearts.'

The sound of approaching footsteps echoed down the narrow corridor outside the cell.

'Scream at me like you blame me for the girl's death,' Aethelman said. 'If the Intelligencier thinks we're friends, his gaze will fall on you also. That can't happen.'

Adalhaid forced a smile, then her face hardened. 'I hope you burn in each of the three hells,' she said, loud enough for anyone in the corridor to hear.

She spat through the window, but the spittle went nowhere near him. He smiled and nodded, and she left. He listened to the footfalls, thinking they were the last friendly sounds he would hear. He opened the vial, drained its bittersweet contents into his mouth, and swallowed hard. It burned his throat and stomach. The room filled with the sound of laughter. Beautiful, familiar laughter. It filled him with joy. There was no pain now. Aesa was waiting for him. She was calling him to her.

❋

## Professor Kengil

Professor Kengil had heard of the Intelligencier headquarters in Ruripathia's capital, Brixen. An old castle with a deep, dark dungeon where sorcerers, spies, and traitors would await their executions. Stories were always told about such places, but one could never know how much truth was in them. Still, if even a seed of it was true, the Intelligenciers were terrifying men to be on the wrong side of. Bringing a false accusation was dealt with as harshly on the accuser as a true one on the accused.

Nonetheless, Kengil was certain she was correct. She had gathered all the information, results, and correspondence about her patient with the mystery illness, but now miraculously cured—her evidence.

Their headquarters in Elzburg was small, and would be called nondescript were it not for the fact that everyone knew who occupied the building. With a deep breath, she walked up the steps and knocked on the door. She was doing the right thing. It was not malice. It was her responsibility. Sorcery was a foul thing.

The door opened, revealing a man in a black doublet and britches; he was every bit as menacing as she had expected. There was a staff, skull, and sword motif embroidered in silver thread on his left breast. He raised an eyebrow but said nothing.

Kengil clutched her evidence to her chest. 'I want to report a sorceress.'

❉

## WULFRIC

Banneret-Captain Peruiz maintained a hard pace, getting them back to Torona as quickly as he could. They were allowed a few hours to rest and clean up, then Peruiz collected them and brought them straight through the palace to the audience hall where Wulfric had spent so many hours of boredom on his previous visit. He spoke to an official and then bade them come forward.

'The men who filled the bounty on the former Count of Valeriano, Your Grace,' the official said.

She was a cold and emotionless-looking woman, with angular, aristocratic features bordering on harsh.

'I understand you came to Estranza on contract to my late brother.'

'Yes, Your Grace,' Jagovere said.

'I thank you for the service you have done me in bringing the Usurper to justice, and also that done for my brother. My seneschal will see that you are paid the bounty and the outstanding amount owed to you for the contract entered into with my brother.'

She fell silent, and the official ushered them away. Wulfric thought it an odd display of gratitude, and a long way to go to be spoken to for only a few seconds, but hoped the payment they were to receive would make the trip worthwhile. Jagovere disappeared with Peruiz through one of the camouflaged doors along the audience hall's back wall.

He returned a few minutes later carrying a small chest in both arms.

'A thousand crowns,' he said smiling.

Enderlain's face lit up, but Wulfric still had no real concept of the value of southern coin.

'Is that a lot?'

'It's not bad at all,' Jagovere said. 'Your share'll be enough to set yourself up with a small farm or tavern if soldiering no longer takes your fancy.'

His smile widened and he stepped to one side to reveal the two men behind him who were carrying a far larger chest between them. 'The ten thousand outstanding on our contract.'

Enderlain whistled through his teeth.

'Now it's really time to go home,' Jagovere said.

❋

## THE MAISTERSPAEKER

Over the years, particularly when he was soldiering, the Maisterspaeker had been in taverns and inns when there were spaekers plying their trade. Some were good, some not so, but he had always made his coming and going as quiet as possible so as not to disturb either the spaeker or those who were listening.

Rodulf and his men had no such compunction. Their departure was accompanied by a symphony of stamping boots, scraping chairs, belches, chatter, and laughter. It was loud enough that the Maisterspaeker stopped and waited until they had pushed their way through the crowd to get to the door, Rodulf at their centre, not deigning to have physical contact with anyone as he passed.

People did their best to get out of the way, but in such a crowded room, one woman fell to the floor and cried out as the group pressed on regardless. The Maisterspaeker was too far away to do anything about it, and surrounded by a press of bodies, could only watch.

'Be careful, there,' a man called, as he too was unceremoniously shoved out of the way.

One of Rodulf's men backhanded him across the face, sending him to the ground also. Nobody else breathed a word. They all stood in silence until Rodulf and his men left and the door closed behind them, without paying for their food or drink. The Maisterspaeker feared his story had put

Rodulf in the mood to have his men inflict some unwarranted punishment on the audience.

'Bastard,' someone muttered, but loud enough to be heard.

A murmur of grumbling followed to support the utterance.

'Wish he'd stay on his own land,' someone said.

'We should complain to the Graf,' said another.

'What good would it do?' said another still.

'Just be grateful he's not your lord,' Conradin said. 'Have a thought for the poor sods on his lands, and think yourselves lucky.'

'Not a popular man?' the Maisterspaeker said.

'No, Maisterspaeker,' Conradin said. 'Far from it. Taxes his tenants into the dirt and shows them the lash when they come up short. He whipped a man to death last harvest. He's scum. Glad I don't have to work for him. Just wish he would keep to his own lands.'

The Maisterspaeker nodded. Their problem would be dealt with before much longer, he thought, although he couldn't make them aware of that. When it was all done, he could return to the tavern and finish the story. He wondered what they would think to discover the man they loathed was the villain of the story? Gradually the murmuring subsided, and the eyes returned to him. The Maisterspaeker took a mouthful of ale and continued, satisfied that he had found Rodulf, a man who needed killing. That could wait, however. First, he had an almost-finished story he needed to tell.

# ABOUT THE AUTHOR

Sign up for Duncan's mailing list and get a free copy of his novella, *The Frontier Lord*. Visit his website to get your copy:

duncanmhamilton.com

Duncan is a writer of fantasy fiction novels and short stories that are set in a world influenced by Renaissance Europe. He has Master's Degrees in History, and Law, and practised as a barrister before writing full time. He is particularly interested in the medieval and renaissance periods, from which he draws inspiration for his stories. He doesn't live anywhere particularly exotic, and when not writing he enjoys cycling, skiing, and windsurfing.

His debut novel, 'The Tattered Banner (Society of the Sword Volume 1)' was placed 8th on Buzzfeed's 12 Greatest Fantasy Books Of The Year, 2013.

Made in the USA
Lexington, KY
28 December 2017